⫸ P9-DEG-830

"The sweeping history of the west has no greater friend than Ms. Bittner. She knows of the people that had to have something extra to survive and she tells their story beautifully."
— *The Paperback Forum*

* * *

ONCE MORE, ADDY

Addy knew she needed to live alone for a while, to acclimate herself to her new home, to gather her thoughts and her emotions . . . maybe someday find the right man, if she even really wanted another man in her life. Cole Parker was not the right man.

"I wish you luck, Cole." She turned away, nervous about the look in his blue eyes, memories . . . hunger. She poured some of the water into a washpan, wishing there were some way to heat it. Before she could wet a rag, a strong arm came around her from behind, pressing her back against a solid chest. Another arm came across her breasts, and she felt a warm breath against her cheek.

"You know we have to do this once more, Addy."

"Cole, please don't. We can't do this again."

"You want to as much as I do and you know it." He kissed her neck. "I hate good-byes. In our case, after knowing each other the way we have—"

"Please let go of me, Cole." The rain came down even harder, and thunder exploded overhead, making her jump. Cole moved his lips around to meet her mouth, turning her almost forcefully, yet part of her wanted to turn. As soon as his warm lips parted her own, she was lost in his embrace, eagerly returning the kiss. Her hands balled into fists, pushed against his shoulders, but to no avail. He was strong, overpowering, deliberate . . . and she wanted him again.

SURRENDER TO THE SPLENDOR OF THE ROMANCES OF F. ROSANNE BITTNER!

CARESS	(3791, $5.99/$6.99)
COMANCHE SUNSET	(3568, $4.99/$5.99)
HEARTS SURRENDER	(2945, $4.50/$5.50)
LAWLESS LOVE	(3877, $4.50/$5.50)
PRAIRIE EMBRACE	(3160, $4.50/$5.50)
RAPTURE'S GOLD	(3879, $4.50/$5.50)
SHAMELESS	(4056, $5.99/$6.99)

Available wherever paperbacks are sold, or order direct from the Publisher. Send cover price plus 50¢ per copy for mailing and handling to Penguin USA, P.O. Box 999, c/o Dept. 17109, Bergenfield, NJ 07621. Residents of New York and Tennessee must include sales tax. DO NOT SEND CASH.

Take me with you,
Though we are strangers.
Still we share heartache,
Loneliness,
A need to love again.

They call you desperado,
An outlaw.
But I see something more.

Take me with you
To a place where we can start anew,
Under western skies.
I will be your woman,
And we will find a new life together.

Don't say we must wait
Until tomorrow.
There may be no tomorrows . . .
There is only today.

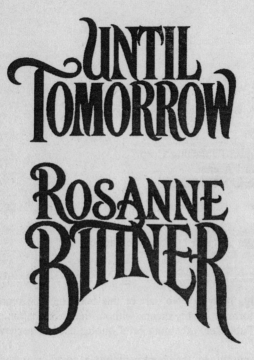

UNTIL TOMORROW

ROSANNE BITTNER

ZEBRA BOOKS
KENSINGTON PUBLISHING CORP.

ZEBRA BOOKS are published by

Kensington Publishing Corp.
850 Third Avenue
New York, NY 10022

Copyright © 1995 by Rosanne Bittner

All rights reserved. No part of this book may be reproduced
in any form or by any means without the prior written consent
of the Publisher, excepting brief quotes used in reviews.

If you purchased this book without a cover, you should be
aware that this book is stolen property. It was reported as "un-
sold and destroyed" to the Publisher and neither the Author
nor the Publisher has received any payment for this "stripped
book."

Zebra and the Z logo Reg. U.S. Pat. & TM Off.

First Printing: September, 1995

Printed in the United States of America

Dedicated to Beth Lieberman, an editor who has been with me through two publishers and many books, and who has taught me to accept criticism with all the good intentions every editor has to make her writer the best she can be. No matter how many books a writer produces, each one is a learning process, and the editor is the teacher. Thank you, Beth.

To my readers . . .

Of all the places I have visited out west, I enjoy the still-preserved old mining towns most, especially those high in the mountains of Colorado. Seeing places like Cripple Creek, Blackhawk and Central City is like stepping into the past, and many of the original buildings still stand today, well preserved by citizens who appreciate the rich history of their towns. The aura of excitement and romance in such places lingers, and that is why I chose Central City as the setting for this story (which at the time was called the City of Central). It lies in the mountains west of Denver, in an area once called the "richest square mile on earth."

Central City is certainly far from a ghost town today. It is alive and growing, its former saloons and businesses now converted to gambling casinos. The quaint buildings, such as the Teller Hotel and the Central City Opera House, as well as surrounding mountains peppered with abandoned mines, give the town a "Wild West" atmosphere that creates visions of America's once-booming gold towns.

Although my characters are fictitious, I hope they come alive for you as they did for me. Certainly people just like them existed in the Old West!

One

Addy waited in line, her heart racing a little faster every time she thought of the reason she was withdrawing her precious savings from the Unionville Bank. Loneliness engulfed her, again trying to destroy her self-confidence. She had to do this, and she told herself that wherever she went, even to a wild gold town in a place too far away to think about, she would surely make new friends, and they would be people who would accept her for who she was, not judge her because of choices her family had made during the war.

She had lived in this same small town in southern Illinois all her life, but she could no longer endure the loss of family to death, the loss of friends to misunderstanding, the insults, the coldness. It could be years before she was allowed to teach here, and she had to get on with her life. It was time to start over. She would take her money and go someplace where she was wanted and needed. When she had answered the ad for a schoolteacher in the city of Central, Colorado, there had been no questions about where her sympathies had lain in the war, no questions about which side her male relatives had taken. They wanted only her age and education and her marital status.

Widow. That was her marital status. Her own family had been torn apart because of the war, a father and husband fighting on the Confederate side, both killed. Her mother was also gone now, dead of a broken heart, she was sure. Her sister

was like a stranger to her, married to a Union man. She had
deserted the rest of the family because she didn't want to be
associated with Confederate sympathizers living in a town
where most hated the southern cause. It was not a firm belief
in the Union cause that had driven Harriet away. She had simply taken the easy way out. It had always been like that with
her sister, and Addy had no respect for her. Harriet had married
a wealthy Union man, and she had abandoned their mother in
her hour of need.

Addy looked down at her own simple yellow calico dress.
Harriet wore only the best and latest fashions now, enjoyed
flaunting her wealth.

"Next?" The teller's voice interrupted Addy's thoughts. She
stepped forward, handing the man her bank book.

"Hello, Mr. Tully. I would like to withdraw all my savings."

"All of it?" Ned Tully peered at her over the top of his wire-
rimmed spectacles, his eyes showing his own lingering irritation
over her father's choice to fight for the Confederacy.

"You say that as though it were thousands," Addy answered.
"I don't believe that withdrawing four hundred dollars is going
to close your doors, Mr. Tully. I am leaving Illinois and I need
the entire savings." Thank goodness the people who had hired
her to come to Central had paid for her transportation. She had
been told by letter that all she had to do was give her name at
the train and stage stations and come to Central on the date
proposed, which was only a couple of weeks away, and everything would be taken care of.

"Leaving Illinois, huh?"

Addy caught the relief in Tully's words, as though a hated
enemy were leaving town. "Yes. I am taking a teaching job in
the city of Central, Colorado."

The man's eyebrows arched as he opened her bank book.
"Colorado! Is it one of those wild gold towns?"

Addy's eyelids closed over her green eyes for a moment in
impatience. "I have no idea how wild it is, Mr. Tully. I only
know that there are families there with children who need teach-

ing. I do have a degree in teaching, you know, and since I can't teach here, I will go someplace else to do it. Please get me my money, will you? And make it in big bills so I don't have a big wad of it to carry around. I will be traveling alone."

Tully shrugged his thin shoulders and squinted at the figures in her savings book. "Stay right there. I'll have to go into the safe for all of it."

He left for a moment, and Addy glanced at an old woman at the next teller's station. It was Sara Webster, who had been a good friend to her mother . . . before the war. Sara glanced at her in return, then quickly looked away, an obvious signal she did not want to speak. Heaven forbid that she be seen talking to a Confederate sympathizer. It was a brand Addy carried, even though her personal sympathies had been for the Union; but her father and husband had both marched off to join the Confederacy, and by then she was home from school to help her ailing mother while her father was gone.

Many of these people had lost sons, brothers, husbands, in the war. It didn't seem to matter to them that she, too, had suffered terrible losses. Mrs. Webster had lost two sons, so she had stopped speaking to Addy and her mother. The old woman's cold shoulder only reaffirmed Addy's decision to leave.

Ned Tully returned with a little canvas bag. "It's all in here," he told Addy. "Would you like to count it?"

"I certainly would," she answered, taking the bag from him. She'd decided that if Ned Tully was going to be rude to her, then she would be rude to him. She dumped out the money, mostly bills, some coins. She quickly counted it and shoved it back into the little bag, along with her cancelled savings book. "Thank you, Mr. Tully. I—"

The outer door suddenly burst open, swinging back and hitting the wall so hard that the glass in the door shattered. One woman screamed, and Addy gasped when she turned to see four men barge into the bank, two waving rifles and also wearing six-guns on their hips; the other two aiming six-guns on everyone inside. All four wore long dusters in spite of the warm weather.

"Nobody move!" one of them shouted. He was a burly, heavy-set man with dark, piercing eyes and a gruff voice. "Hand over your money, jewelry, anything of value!" The man glanced at one of his cohorts, a young man with long, dark, unkempt hair. "Start collecting, Ted!"

Mrs. Webster put a wrinkled hand to her chest in alarm, look-ing ready to faint. The younger man began walking to each cus-tomer, holding his six-gun to their necks and demanding their valuables. Addy grasped her little bag of money tightly and moved it behind her skirt as she slowly stepped away from the teller's window.

One of the men holding a rifle approached Ned Tully's cage, resting the barrel of his rifle on the shelf. He was tall, and it was obvious he was well-built underneath the coat he wore. "Let's have everything in your drawer and in the safe, mister," he said in a deep, steady voice, "and be quick and generous." Tully started to protest when a booming crack shook the bank. Richard Wyman, the teller next to him, was shot by the heavy-set robber when he tried to argue.

Addy's eyes widened in shock as Richard slumped to the floor, and Tully began scrambling to gather everything that was in his drawer. The heavy-set man ordered yet another robber, called Cal, to go in back and see what was in the safe. Cal hurried around back, brushing past her and causing her to stumble side-ways. Her first reaction was to reach out, exposing the little canvas bag that held her money. Her movement caught the eye of the tall man robbing Ned Tully, and he glanced in her direc-tion, noticing the bag.

Addy could not help staring. The man's eyes were an amazing blue, outlined by dark eyebrows and dark lashes. He was a hand-some man, but she could feel only contempt for him, and her heart raced when she realized he had seen the money bag. She wondered why he didn't ask for it. All he did was stare at her for a moment, in that way men had of looking at a woman they thought was pretty. His blue eyes raked her body before he turned back to Tully and reached out to grab a bag of money the man handed him.

"Let's have it, lady." The one called Ted had reached Addy, and he placed his six-gun at her throat. "How much you got in the little bag there, huh?"

Addy suddenly felt like crying, but anger replaced the urge, and she glared right back at the young outlaw. "This is all I have, and some of it is from my parents' savings, from a business they worked hard for and lost because of the war. I have already lost so much. Haven't people suffered enough from the war? Why do men like you have to come and take what little is left?"

The tall man with the blue eyes looked her way again. "Lady, you don't even know the meaning of the word suffer," he told her.

For a quick moment Addy saw a great agony in those blue eyes, but there was no time to contemplate what could have caused him to make such a remark. Ted pushed the barrel of his gun closer against her throat. "Let's have it, woman!"

"Let her be," the blue-eyed man told him threatingly.

Ted looked up at him. "Like hell!" He turned and yanked the bag out of Addy's hand, then stepped back, shoving her own little bag into a bigger bag slung over his shoulder, into which he had put other people's money and valuables.

Everything had happened in less than a minute, and now the man with the blue eyes was asking Ned Tully where Howard Benedict was. Benedict was the owner of the bank, and Addy wondered how the outlaw knew that.

"He . . . he's not here today," Tully answered.

"Too bad," the blue-eyed man answered. "I meant to kill him. You tell him Nick Coleman paid him a visit, and I'll be back to get him someday soon!"

Nick Coleman. So, that was the blue-eyed man's name. Why would he give it out so easily? Why did he hate Howard Benedict so much?

Coleman ordered Tully out from behind his cage. The teller

came to stand beside Addy, and the fat man yelled to Cal, still at the safe in back, telling him to hurry. "The law could show up any minute!" he hollered. He, Ted, and Nick Coleman held their weapons on everyone in the bank lobby, some of whom had crouched to the floor. Coleman kept glancing at Addy, almost as though he knew her. He looked her over with apparent pleasure, yet Addy caught little hints of regret in his eyes, as though by his look he was trying to apologize for Ted taking her money.

Ted hurried to the door, then quickly came inside looking panicked. "The sheriff is coming!" He moved his eyes to the fat man. "This is your fault, Jack! You never should have fired that shot! Now you've killed a man and they'll be after our asses for sure!"

"Shut up, you little bastard!" the fat man answered.

Just then Cal burst into the lobby with a gunny sack full of money. His hat had fallen off, exposing a head of thick, dirty blond hair. "Let's go!"

Nick Coleman swung around and headed for the door. While his back was turned, the fat man, who Addy now knew was called Jack, headed for Addy. Before she realized his intentions, he grabbed her arm and jerked her forward, then wrapped a powerful arm around her throat from behind. "We'll take a hostage!" he growled. "The sheriff won't dare shoot at us with this pretty lady along."

Coleman whirled. "What the hell! Let her go, Jack!"

"Like hell! We need her, and if you're gonna take a hostage, take a pretty woman, I say. They'll be even less likely to shoot at you! Let's go! Ted's got the horses ready by now!"

"Goddammit, let her go!" Coleman demanded.

"You've been a burr in my butt for a while now, Coleman!" Jack growled. "You're either part of this gang, or you ain't!" Suddenly he fired his six-gun before anyone realized he would do such a thing, including Nick, who lurched backward with a bloody hole in his left shoulder. People screamed, including Addy, whose ears rang from the gun being fired so close to her head. Coleman sprawled on the floor, his rifle flying out of his hand, and Jack dragged Addy out the door, telling her he'd blow her brains out if she put up too much of a fuss. By then the sheriff and his deputy were shooting at Ted and Cal, who were ducked behind a wagon. Jack shouted from the bank doorway to hold their fire. "I've got a hostage!" he yelled. "I've already killed two men, and I'll kill this woman if you don't let us ride out of town!"

The firing stopped and Jack moved outside. Addy's heart pounded with fear that bullets would fly again and she would be killed, either by the outlaws or accidentally by the sheriff.

"You won't get far!" Sheriff Page answered. "I'll have a posse after you low-lifes! You hurt that woman and you'll all hang!"

For the moment Addy decided she was wise to cooperate with the robbers. Perhaps she would find a way to escape later, when there were not so many guns pointed in her direction. Jack dragged her to a horse and ordered her to get on, and she realized it must belong to the blue-eyed man inside, who for some strange reason had tried to defend her.

Ted and Cal quickly mounted their own horses, as did Jack. Ted grabbed the reins to Addy's horse and rode off at a hard gallop. Cal and Jack whirled their horses and fired more shots toward where the sheriff and his deputy were hiding behind barrels, then charged after Ted and Addy. Addy heard a few shots being fired at them, felt two bullets whiz by her, much too close for comfort. She ducked down, hanging on to her horse's mane for dear life, and suddenly the four of them were well out of town. She prayed the three men who had taken her hostage would let her go soon, that she had only been taken as a way to get out of town, not for other purposes that she did not even want to think about. That hope dwindled when the three men slowed up for a moment.

"Should we let her go now, Jack?" Ted asked.

They all stopped their horses and looked her over. Jack grinned through yellowed teeth. "Hell no. Look at that pretty red glint to her hair, and look at them pretty green eyes." He raked her hungrily with his gaze. "And the rest of her. Round in the right places . . . and a pretty face to go with it. Let's take her to the cabin. If we high-tail it, any posse the sheriff manages to round up will never find us."

"What happened to Nick?" Cal asked.

Jack sniffed. "That sonofabitch has been contradictin' me too many times lately. He's gonna' cause us to get caught one of these times. So I shot him."

Ted's eyes widened. "You shot Nick? He's our best gun!"

Jack whipped out his own six-gun. "Not any more. You got somethin' else to say about it, kid?"

Ted swallowed. "No, Jack. I just thought . . . well . . . Nick's a good man to have along."

"He's tried to tell me what to do too many times now, so I got rid of him. Now let's get ridin' before the sheriff gets a posse together!" He shoved his gun back into its holster, and the other two looked at each other. Addy could tell they were upset by what Jack had done, but they were not about to argue about it.

They rode off again, and Addy wondered what kind of horror awaited her. Her mind began racing with plans of escape . . . and she wondered why on earth she was upset over the fact that the man called Nick Coleman might be dead. Why on earth should it matter? Perhaps because she felt that if he was along, he would not let the other three men harm her. Now she was at their mercy.

Only minutes ago she had been more at peace than she had been in years. She had managed to rise above the past, to find a way to start a new life and perhaps find happiness again. Now this. How much was a woman expected to suffer? Even if she managed to get away from these men, all her money was gone, and God only knew what might happen to her before she could escape. Perhaps they would just kill her and leave her body someplace where it would never be found.

* * *

Nick could see the flames again, and again he heard the desperate screams. His girl! His precious baby! He had to help her . . . help her! He reached into the flames, and they seared his skin. It was the same dream he'd had a thousand times, and again it made him wake up in a sweat. He gasped, opening his eyes to the smell of medicine, the sight of a sterile-looking room and the sound of men's voices.

"Hang him," someone said.

"Don't know if he's the one that killed Richard," said another.

"Sheriff Page will catch them. Then we'll know."

"What if he doesn't? This one was with them. Whether he killed Richard or not, he deserves to be hanged."

"God only knows what will happen to poor Mrs. Kane. She ain't been the most popular woman in town, what with her pa and husband fightin' for the Confederates, but no woman deserves bein' dragged off by rabble like that."

Mrs. Kane. Was that the name of the woman Jack had taken with him? Nick gritted his teeth and raised up on his right elbow, pain ripping through his left shoulder. More perspiration soaked his face as he looked down at his wound, which apparently had been carelessly bandaged for the moment to help stop the bleeding. From the burning pain there, he realized that no one had yet taken out the bullet. He knew that pain well, could still remember how it had felt in his leg when he was shot in the war.

The war was what had led him to this, had taken Patty from him . . . and now he felt again the agony of being torn between what was right and what was wrong, the desire for peace and happiness in his life, and the desire for total revenge. He and the others in Jack's gang had made a sorry mess of Howard Benedict's bank, and he hoped Jack and the others had gotten off with enough money to cause the bank to fold. Most banks were pretty shaky, what with the uncertainty of things now that the war was over. He would like nothing better than to see Howard Benedict fail, which was why he had agreed to be in on this robbery, had even suggested it to Jack. Trouble was, he had intended to kill Benedict but didn't get the chance. Besides that, a woman had been taken hostage. That was not part of the deal, and he had to try to help her.

He looked around the room, his steely blue eyes taking in every corner, every window, every mode of escape. For some reason the men outside the room had left him alone for a while, probably figuring he was still unconscious. If he could get out of here . . .

Damn that Jack Slater. He had no doubt what the man had in mind for Mrs. Kane. He had to get the hell out of here, find Jack and the woman. Besides, he did not intend to be hanged for a murder he did not commit, and he owed Jack Slater a dose of revenge. He was going to pay for shooting him point blank!

"I'd better remove the bullet pretty quick," came a voice from outside. "He's lost a lot of blood. I was just waiting for that to slow down. I'll try to get some laudanum down his throat, even though he's unconscious. If he comes to while I'm digging into him, you'll hear him holler from here to Missouri."

"Serves him right," someone muttered.

Nick scrambled to think what must have happened. He realized he still wore his pants and boots, so he must have passed out in the bank after he'd been shot and was carried here. He noticed his duster and hat hanging over a chair, and he saw something else that almost made him laugh out loud. His six-gun hung over the duster! The fools outside the room must have taken it for granted he was too badly wounded to regain consciousness, or that even if he did, he wouldn't be able to move. He'd damn well prove them wrong!

He quietly moved to the edge of the bed. He even still wore his shirt, although it had been torn away where his wound was bandaged. He realized his right arm was still in the sleeve, which was good. He didn't have to try to dress himself.

He struggled against pain and hoped he could remain conscious as he walked to the chair where his duster hung, glad for the rug on the floor that muffled his steps. He quickly put on the canvas coat, finding it difficult not to cry out as he managed to move his left arm into the sleeve. He donned his hat and picked up his gunbelt, and just then the door opened. Quickly he grasped the gunbelt with his left hand and pulled out his six-gun with a speed that astounded the man who stood in the doorway looking at him. "Get me a horse," he demanded, his voice gruff from pain.

The man in the doorway frowned, and another stepped up behind him. Nick realized that the rest of the men had left. He had only these two to deal with, and one of them was probably the doctor. He was a balding man who wore spectacles, and who frowned now with what seemed a mixture of disgust and concern.

"Mister, you'll never make it if you try to ride out of here. You have a bullet in your shoulder that's got to come out or you'll die."

Nick swallowed. "It's a better way to go than with a noose around your neck. Besides, I didn't kill that man in the bank. The man who shot me killed him, and I'm going after him. The posse can't find them, but I can, and I intend to find that woman and send her back here."

"You really expect us to believe that, mister?" the second man asked.

The doctor studied Nick's blue eyes. "I think he means it, Brad. I don't believe he really wants to use that gun on us, but I suppose he's used it on plenty of other men. Even so, he seems to want to help Mrs. Kane, and maybe it would be better if we let him go."

"Even if he's telling the truth, he'll die on the way and never be able to get to her."

Nick raised the ivory-handled handgun, cocking it and aiming it at the man called Brad. "Mister, I hate to kill the doc here, but you probably aren't so important. Now get me a damn horse! I'm not staying here, and time is wasting!"

Brad's breathing quickened with uncertainty. "There's one down in the alley, just outside the window to your right. I tied it there myself. It's mine, all saddled, and you'd better remember that if you ride away on it, you'll also be a horse thief, besides a bank robber and possibly a killer."

"You'll get it back somehow." Nick moved toward the window, keeping his eyes on both men.

"I can't believe the sheriff's men left his gun in the same room with him," Brad told the doctor. "It just shows you how inept Page and his deputies are. This is a disgrace!"

"Mister, let me take out that bullet first," the doctor told Nick. "You can't help that woman in your condition."

"There's no time for it, and you'd have to put me out, wasting even more time. Besides, I'd wake up to jail and a hanging." Nick glanced down to see a horse tied in the alley, and he realized the doctor's quarters were on a second floor, but there were fire stairs just outside the window. "If you two are smart, you'll keep quiet until I'm out of town. If I can catch up with the others, I can help Mrs. Kane. Otherwise she'll end up dead . . . or wishing she *was* dead!"

Dizziness swept over him, and he hoped he could get down the stairs without falling. The window was already open because of the warm day, and Nick leaned down and climbed out, then shoved the gun for the moment into the holster he still held in his other hand so that he could use his right hand to cling to the railing of the stairs while he gingerly made his way down. He glanced up at the window and saw no one, but he heard Brad yelling that they couldn't just let him go. "I'll never see Charger again!" the man complained.

"Better never to see that damn horse again than poor Mrs. Kane," the doctor answered.

"Since when does anybody in this town care about a Confederate sympathizer!"

"The war is over, Brad. She's just a woman in a bad situation now. Maybe Nick Coleman can help her."

Nick wondered at the remarks about Mrs. Kane and the war. He untied the horse and gritted his teeth as he climbed into the saddle and managed to throw his right leg over. The horse was not quite as big as the one he usually rode. In fact, he had to bend his legs to keep them in the stirrups, but there was no time for adjustments. He grasped the reins in his right hand and turned the horse, heading for the back side of the buildings, where he would be less noticed. He had already seen when he was mounting up that half the town was still gathered around the entrance to the bank, kitty-corner from the doctor's office. They were so engrossed in the excitement they didn't even notice him. He smiled to himself and lit out, kicking the horse into a fast gallop and realizing why the man named Brad was upset that he might steal the animal. It was a fine horse, strong, one that seemed to enjoy a good run. Charger was a fitting name.

Behind him he could hear Brad screaming at people in the street below. "He's gone! He's escaped! Nick Coleman held a gun on us and stole my horse!" The words faded into the distance as Nick kept riding, and he figured that with the sheriff already out with a posse, there was probably no one left among the civilians in town who would dare to come after him. All he had to do now was avoid riding right into the hands of the posse. He could only hope they would lose the trail of Jack and the others. If it came to a shootout, Jack might kill Mrs. Kane.

Amid pain and panic and the hard ride, Nick found himself thinking how lovely Mrs. Kane was, from what he could remember, with her porcelain skin and reddish hair, both of which reminded him of another woman . . . in another life. The look in those green eyes when Ted took her little money bag had tugged at his heart, and for some reason he had not wanted to rob her. It was Howard Benedict he'd wanted to harm, not a pretty young woman clinging to her last dime. He wondered how much time had passed. Enough for Jack to already have brought harm to her? From the position of the sun, he figured it was around noon. They had robbed the bank at ten o'clock. If he rode hard, he could make it to the cabin without passing out. He just might catch up in time to give Jack what he had coming to him before he raped Mrs. Kane.

"Let it out, Charger!" he ordered the horse. "Let's see how you earned your name!"

The horse stretched its legs and ran like the wind, and Unionville was quickly left behind. In spite of his pain, Nick laughed at the stupidity of a sheriff who would lay an outlaw out in a room and leave the man's gun hanging on a chair not far away. But then maybe that was meant to be, maybe an act of God. Maybe he was supposed to help the woman . . . and maybe it wouldn't have been so important to him if she hadn't looked so much like Bethanne. God, how he had loved her! And how he had loved the little girl she had given him, his sweet little Patty. Forever he would see those flames, feel the heat . . . hear her screams.

Two

Addy wiped at sweat on her forehead with the back of her arm, then slapped at a mosquito. She wondered how she was going to get one wink of sleep tonight. It was bad enough that she was hot, dusty from the hard ride, and would be fending off insects all night; but she would also have to keep one eye open in readiness to defend herself from the three men who watched her as they sat chewing on beef strips and drinking coffee . . . coffee she had been ordered to make for them over a campfire. They had stopped to rest after dark, in a deep ravine where Jack Slater claimed anyone following them would never spot the glowing flames.

"You feel nature callin'," Jack told her, chewing at the same time, "you can go right over there behind that big bush. Just don't think about tryin' to run off. You wouldn't get far in the dark, and we're pretty near the Kentucky border. These woods are so thick you'd never find your way, and at night they're full of bobcats and bears. That's why we lit a fire." He tossed her a piece of rolled-up newspaper. "Use that when you're done."

Addy turned away in revulsion.

Jack smiled. "When the time comes, you remember I'm just this side of the bush. I'll be talkin' to you and expectin' a reply the whole time, so's I can hear your voice."

Cal drank down his coffee. "Why don't you get it over with, Jack, so we can have our turn."

Addy felt sick to her stomach at the realization of the meaning of his remark.

"Not here. We've got to be alert, and besides, there's too many bugs out tonight. At the cabin there's a bed, and she can clean herself up first. We'll have the woman cook us a good meal, count our money and enjoy the whiskey we left there."

Addy felt at least a little relief that she had until sometime tomorrow to find an escape, and she was also glad this bunch of outlaws had not brought whiskey along. If they got themselves drunk tonight, there would be no hope of keeping them away from her.

"You think Nick's really dead? Where'd you hit him?" Ted asked.

"Quit askin' about Nick," Jack answered. "I know you liked the sonofabitch, but I was tired of him arguin' with me about the decisions I make. And yes, I told you before I think he's dead. It all happened so fast, I can't swear to where I hit him, but it seemed to me it was right in the middle of his chest, which means he's already laid out for the townfolk to have a look at before he's buried."

Ted frowned, biting off another piece of beef. "Nick was a good man to have along."

Jack stiffened. "What'd you say, boy?"

Alarm came into Ted's eyes. "You know what I mean. Nick was considered a sharpshooter in the war."

Addy guessed from their southern drawls that all of these men had fought for the South, but she was not about to ask and start an argument over North and South.

"Well, he ain't gonna' be shootin' at nobody no more," Jack answered. "He's strollin' around up in heaven somewhere with that daughter of his he was always talkin' about . . . maybe. Then again, maybe he's roastin' over open flames in hell." He chuckled and Cal grinned, but Ted just pouted. "Think of it this way, boy. There's one less man to share the money with."

"When are we going to count it?"

"It'll keep till we reach the cabin. You boys just get some sleep so we can light out of here bright and early."

Addy wondered at the remark that Nick had had a daughter.

Why had he been living a life like this if he had a little girl somewhere? She remembered Nick Coleman's remark at the bank, that she didn't know the meaning of the word suffer. The look in those blue eyes when he said it told her he was indeed a man who had known personal loss, but he was a worthless outlaw just like these men. Still, she vaguely wished Nick Coleman was with them. Somehow she suspected he would not allow these other three to hurt her, would probably have talked them into letting her go by now.

"You should all just leave me here in the morning," she spoke up. "Having me along will only make the posse that is surely tracking you more determined. You must know you're better off without me."

Jack snickered. "You ain't gettin' out of this that easy, lady. I know a way over some rocks and through a stream that will cause the posse to completely lose our trail by late morning, and the more I look at you, the more I know I want you with me when we reach our cabin in Kentucky." He glanced at her left hand. "Don't worry. It won't be so bad. Hell, you're wearin' a wedding ring, so it ain't like you haven't been with a man. What's two or three more?"

All three men laughed at that remark, and stubborn anger filled Addy's green eyes. She stood up, glaring at them. "Have you no pride or compassion? Pride in a man's honor? Compassion for a widow?" She moved her wedding ring from her left to her right hand. "I have left this ring on my left hand in loving memory of my husband, but its rightful place is on my *right* hand! I am a *widow,* who has also lost both her parents! I was removing what pitiful savings I had left from the bank today so that I could go to Colorado and start a new life! I have suffered enough! I don't need three slovenly, greedy, thieving men who have no honor pawing me against my will! How can you even *call* yourselves men!"

Ted's smile faded, but the other two kept grinning. "Because that's what we are, lady," Jack answered, "and you'll find that out tomorrow in the best way a woman can."

"You're *scum*," Addy sneered, "and *cowards!*" She whirled and stormed behind the bush. All these hours she had forced back the urge simply because she abhorred the thought of having to lift her skirts with these men anywhere around, but now there was no fighting Mother Nature. She quickly squatted, watching in both directions on each side of the bush. "I'm right here, so you don't need to come looking for me!" she shouted, afraid if Jack found her this way he would not be able to control himself.

"Just hurry it up and keep talkin'," came Jack's voice.

Addy used the newspaper the man had given her and quickly yanked up her drawers and pulled down her skirts, hurrying back around to the firelight. She glared at all of them. "None of you will ever be able to speak of pride or call yourselves men if you harm me," see said, her breathing heavy, her green eyes on fire. "If you have any sense at all, you will release me in the morning!"

"You shut your mouth, lady, or I'll shut it for you," Jack warned. He rose, coming to stand closer to her. "You don't want me to do that."

Addy looked right back at him, head held high, but she could see by his dark eyes that he meant every word. This was the kind of man who was not above hitting a woman. She drew in her breath. "You're so brave, using a woman to escape, threatening to brutalize her. How brave will you be, Mr. Slater, if Nick Coleman lives and escapes and comes to find you?" She took pleasure in the hint of fear in his eyes.

"Nick Coleman is dead."

"I have a feeling you're a little worried he isn't."

"If he ain't dead, he's sittin' in jail soon to be hanged. One way or another, he's dead."

"And so are you, Mr. Slater, as soon as the law catches up with you, and they will!"

The stinging blow came with no warning. Addy felt the ground come up to meet her, tasted gravel in her mouth. Before she could regain her senses she felt ropes being tied around her wrists, felt a bandana being stuck into her mouth, another tied tightly around her head to gag her. Someone lifted her and carried her to a bedroll, dropping her onto it and putting a blanket over her.

"Sleep tight, Mrs. Kane. I think that's what you said your name was. Maybe now you'll learn to keep your bitchy mouth shut!"

Addy closed her eyes, fighting not to cry, for that surely was what Jack Slater wanted her to do. The right side of her face throbbed from Slater's big hand slamming into it, and the left side stung from being scraped on stones when she fell. There was nothing to do now but pray—pray that the sheriff's posse would find them before these men did something much worse to her . . . pray that somehow she would escape this mess and be able to put it behind her and go to Colorado as planned. Surely God would help her out of this. Surely He would not let her suffer any more than she already had.

The wind suddenly picked up, and she breathed deeply of the slightly cooler air. It sang through the treetops and cooled her face, and she was glad that at least with the wind there would not be much problem the rest of the night with mosquitoes. With her hands tied she would not be able to brush them away.

Nick swallowed against the pain in his shoulder, not sure he would be able to keep going. A strong urge to give up and go for help engulfed him, but it was overcome by the stronger need to find Jack Slater and give him his due, as well as help the poor woman Jack had taken with him.

He was glad for the strong south wind that had come up during the night, causing enough rustling in the thick woods to keep the posse that was camped east of him from hearing his stirrings. He was tempted to walk right into their camp and let someone dig the bullet out of him, but that would end his quest and probably lead him right back into a noose. If he could just rest tonight and not have to keep going to get ahead of the posse and cut the distance between himself and Jack, things would be a lot easier.

He halted his stolen horse, still grateful it was a strong, fast steed. The animal also needed a rest, but he would not dismount and put out a bedroll. If he did that, he might not wake up until it was far too late to reach Jack and the others in time to help the woman. He was not worried that the posse would find them. He knew the route Jack would take, over a hill of pure rock, along a deep creek, far enough that it would be impossible for the sheriff and his men to track them. Besides, by then they would be out of Missouri. Sheriff Page would have to turn their capture over to Kentucky authorities, and enough time would pass by then that they would never be found deep in the woods where their hideout cabin lay nearly hidden by vines and thick underbrush.

He untied his canteen and swallowed more water, well remembering how thirsty he was in the war when he'd taken a lead ball in his right leg. That same thirst nagged at him now, and it took every ounce of fortitude and determination in his bones to make himself keep going, against the night, against the pain. He recapped the canteen and sat for a few minutes, peering through the trees at the distant camp of lawmen, wanting to laugh out loud at their ineptness, first at leaving his gun in the room with him, then at the fact that he was sitting only a few hundred yards from them now, wounded, riding a stolen horse. He gave Charger a few more minutes to rest, then urged the steed forward at a slow walk, heading around the north side of the lawmen so that the wind would carry neither his horse's odor nor the sound of its hooves rustling through leaves.

With luck the half-hearted posse would not break camp until sunup. By then he would also have made it to the rocky hill and the creek beyond it, surely very close to Jack and the others. Charger balked at having to find its way through a dark forest, and finally Nick had to dismount and lead the animal until he reached the pathway he knew was close by. Now it was just a matter of using the moonlight to keep going into the even-thicker

woods beyond it, where he would be forced to wait until dawn
to keep going or risk having Charger break a leg by stumbling
into an unseen hole, or risk cracking his own head open on a
branch. Whatever the case, he had to get going again as early
as possible, which meant he would take his shuteye right in the
saddle.

He re-mounted with great effort, deciding he'd better not get
off again. He might become too weak to get back on. The night
stretched into forever, the pathway ending after two miles. He
led Charger into a heavy stand of trees, and the sound of all
kinds of night creatures rang in his ears. He hoped nothing would
come along that would spook Charger and cause the animal to
rear up. He might not be able to hang on. Then there was the
possibility he would have to protect the animal by shooting
something, which would bring the posse running. He drank more
water, patting Charger's neck and promising the horse there
would be plenty of water when they reached the creek through
which they would ride early in the morning.

He shook his head. Jack never should have shot that teller,
let alone taken a woman hostage. He knew Jack was a bastard,
but he sure never thought he'd shoot one of his own men besides.
Life sure had turned into a mess! Right and wrong had melted
into nothing. When he thought about the kind of life he used to
lead before the war, he hardly knew himself. Feelings and emotions had left him so that he was just a shell of a man who fed
on hatred and vengeance. Now someone who was supposed to
be his friend had shot him. What the hell kind of a life was this?
There was a time when he had realized at least a little satisfaction
out of raiding and robbing, but now even that didn't satisfy him.
Nothing satisfied him. When he laid with whores, he could only
think of Bethanne, and no wild woman could please him the
way Bethanne had. His only consolation was good whiskey.
Whiskey dulled all senses, physical and emotional. Right now
he could use some to dull the pain in his shoulder.

The only thing that kept him going at the moment was the
thought of freeing that woman Jack had taken and paying Jack

back for shooting him. It haunted him how much Mrs. Kane resembled Bethanne. He couldn't help wondering if it was some kind of message from above, if this whole mess was some way of Bethanne trying to tell him he couldn't live this way anymore. Fact was, there had been many times when he didn't want to live at all, and this was one of them. He would just have to wait until he got rid of Jack and sent Mrs. Kane back home. Maybe by then the bullet in his shoulder would have taken such a toll in blood that he could just lie down and let the life ease out of him . . . end the agony in his heart, which was much worse than the agony in his shoulder.

The wind caused heavily-leafed trees to bend and rustle, casting eerie shadows and making his horse restless. "Take it easy, boy. Don't be whinnying loud or rearing up and dumping me off. I'd never get back on," he mumbled to the horse.

He was well hidden in the dense woods. He had no choice now but to wait a couple of hours until the earliest light allowed him to go on. Then he would head for the rocky hills and the creek, where he would lose the posse. Jack would surely also be holed up tonight, somewhere deeper in these woods. If he could just hang on, it was possible he could reach the cabin only two or three hours after the rest of the men. He just hoped that would be soon enough to help the woman with them.

Addy ached to bathe and change her clothes. The hat she had worn and the purse she had carried at the bank were both long gone. She could feel perspiration on her chest and under her arms, and the skirt of her dress was torn from catching on bushes and underbrush as her horse made its way toward wherever it was Jack and the others were taking her. She did not doubt her face was dirty from her fall into the dirt the night before, and she could feel that it was swollen on the right side. Her hair, earlier neatly tucked into curls at the back of her head, now fell astray, the combs having come loose. There was still a strong south wind, and although it had turned to a hot wind today, it was still better than the still, oppressive air of the day before.

They made their way through some of the most dense forest she had ever experienced, and she despaired that Sheriff Page and his posse would ever find her. They had crossed over rocky hills and ridden through a creek so that their tracks would be lost forever, and she was losing hope of escape. She would have no idea where to go even if she could get away.

By late afternoon they arrived at a sagging log cabin, and Addy's stomach fell at the sight of it. Here was where the men would truly relax, count their money, drink their whiskey . . . and think about what they intended to do with her. There was no hope for her, three men against one woman, yet she continued to contemplate ways of defending herself.

All three men were in good spirits, sure they had lost the posse, relieved to be back home, as they called it. Jack came over to her horse and ordered that she climb down, while Cal carried in their bag of stolen money and Ted began unsaddling the horses to let them graze. Jack put a powerful hand to her back and gave her a shove, ordering her inside. "You're gonna' fix us a nice, big supper," he told her. "We've got meat stored in a smoke house and potatoes inside. That's what we want, beef and potatoes, and a pretty woman to look at while we eat and count our money. Then a little whiskey and—" He grabbed her arm, whirling her around just as she reached the front door. "And then a little dessert." He grinned, and Addy realized how he seemed fat all over, even his cheeks and lips. He moved a hand down to one of her breasts, and she quickly knocked his hand away.

"I'd rather be dead!" she told him.

Jack grasped her around the throat. "Well, maybe I can grant that wish, after I'm through with you," he sneered. He kicked open the door and shoved her inside, where Cal sat at a rough-hewn pine table with money spread out everywhere. Addy stared at it, thinking how hard it had been to save her four hundred dollars. How dare men like this come along and take it from her!

Jack shoved her over to a counter, then reached underneath and plopped a sack of potatoes on it. "Start peelin'," he told her. "I'll get a fire goin' in the cook stove." He put a paring knife in her hand. "And don't get any funny ideas about that knife. There's three of us here. Remember that. Besides, that little thing ain't big enough to do a man much harm."

He left her to get some wood, and Addy glanced down at the knife, wondering if she should just shove it into her own heart and save herself the indignity and horror of what lay ahead. She looked around the cabin, a sorry mess from having been lived in by men who cared little about keeping house. She wondered how they had ended up here. Surely they were simply squatting here, probably had found the cabin abandoned by someone else who had given up trying to survive in these deep woods. She looked up to notice there were two birds' nests tucked along two of the ceiling beams. Cobwebs decorated many other places along the ceiling, and the floor was dirt. The cabin consisted of one main room, with the table and counter, an old iron cook stove and some buckets for water, and one big iron-framed bed in the corner. A curtained doorway told her there was one more room, probably a bedroom with another bed. She shivered to think how dirty the bedclothes must be, felt sick at the thought of Jack taking her in there . . .

She turned to peel the potatoes, deciding to take as long as possible to cook the meal. She had hoped that at least the three outlaws, who reeked of perspiration and who all needed shaves, would try to clean up a little, but Ted came inside after tending the horses, and all three were only interested in counting their money and hollering at her to hurry up and fix a meal. Jack plopped cast-iron pans on the stove for her and got a fire going, and Ted went to a pump outside and brought in some water for boiling potatoes.

From what Addy had observed, Ted was the youngest. He had long, dark hair and a tooth missing at the side of his mouth. His eyes were brown, and she thought how he might be a handsome young man if he would clean himself up . . . and if he were not a part of this gang. He seemed to be a little slow mentally, a young man who followed a man like Jack with no questions. For a little while she had held out the hope that he might help her, but she knew now that he would never go up against a man like Jack. Neither would Cal, who seemed just as eager as Jack to have his turn at her. Cal was pure ugly, with blond hair that stuck out in every direction. He was perhaps forty-five, a man with a very strong southern drawl, who seemed to have gotten a feeling of great importance from robbing a bank.

"Ole' Nick had a good idea taking the Unionville bank," he told Jack. "There must be enough here for maybe a thousand dollars a piece."

"We could have got more if we didn't have to hurry because of that sheriff," Jack grumbled.

Addy thought how that was no one's fault but his own, for shooting Richard Wyman. She placed a couple of smoked beef steaks into the frying pans and began cooking them while the potatoes boiled, hoping that if she did make these men a decent meal, perhaps they would feel some guilt about turning around and hurting her. She used as much time as possible, her whole body aching from her ordeal. She needed to bathe, to rest. She should be hungry, but her situation ruined her appetite, and she only picked at her food while the three men wolfed down the meat and potatoes like hungry bears, mopping up juice from the meat with stale bread that had been left there five days earlier.

Night came too quickly. Addy thought about trying to bolt outside, but she suspected that to suddenly run and then have to put up a fight would only excite these men to the point of making them act on their plans more quickly than they would have otherwise. To try to stab one of them or burn them with hot grease would still leave two more. She decided that perhaps if she was quiet and let them drink to their hearts' content, they would simply pass out and sleep so heavily after such a hard ride, that she could slip out without any of them even realizing it. The problem was, where would she go? She had no idea which direction was the right one.

Already, patting their bellies from a grand meal for which they did not thank her, they were bringing out the whiskey. This was the most dangerous time, men happy from a good meal, money in their pockets, good whiskey at hand . . . She walked to the stove, wondering if there was enough hot water left from the potatoes to throw at all three of them and scald them all. It would be difficult, and she would probably scald herself in the process, although that would be better than being forced to give herself to any one of these men.

She could feel their eyes on her every movement as she cleaned up from supper. The pan of water left on the stove was obviously still hot, since embers from the wood that had heated it still glowed underneath. She walked back to the stove, grasped the pan with hot pads, then heard the click of a gun.

"Don't do it, lady."

She kept hold of the pan, glancing sidelong at Jack. "Do what?"

"Move back, boys." Jack rose, a whiskey bottle in one hand and his gun in the other. He also rose, backing away. "I see what you've got in mind. You can't get all three of us, and you'll only burn yourself in the process. Do you know what it's like to be burned with hot water? Your skin falls off. It's a painful, sorry mess."

Addy stared at the water. Surely there was something . . . something . . . "Please just let me go," she said quietly. "Isn't it bad enough that you have stolen my life's savings and dragged me out here like this? I'll continue to cook for you, if that's what you want. Just don't . . ." She sighed. "Why don't you let me go? I'll just slow you down from whatever you need to do next, and if I return to Unionville, they'll probably stop looking for you."

"We're in Kentucky now, in case you don't know it," Cal spoke up. "That posse doesn't have any jurisdiction here, and they'd never find us anyway."

Addy closed her eyes in resignation. She let go of the pan of water and set down the hot pads. "Go on with whatever you were doing. I am going to wash the dishes." She turned her back, her heart racing when she heard Jack's heavy footsteps. He was behind her then, moving an arm around her waist.

"The dishes can wait, honey."

She stiffened, wiggling out of his grasp. "So can you!"

The man laughed, his eyes raking her body while he slipped his six-gun back into its holster. "I don't think so. I've waited long enough. I don't need whiskey to help me out, not with somethin' as pretty as you."

Addy glanced at Cal and Ted, but she saw no help there, only hungry grins. It was then she did bolt, out of pure desperation and wild instinct. Cal grabbed her before she could reach the door, whirling her and slamming her tight against him. He tried to kiss her while the other two whooped and whistled. Addy's breath came in frightened gasps as she squirmed and kept her face turned away, but Cal began slurping and licking at her neck, then grasped her arms and shoved her toward Jack. She stumbled past him, and Jack started to reach out for her when the door suddenly burst open.

Addy's breath caught in her throat as she grasped the back of a chair to keep her balance. Her eyes widened at the sight of a tall, blue-eyed man standing in the doorway wearing a duster, which he had pulled back on the right side to expose a pearl-handled six-gun he wore on his hip. Jack and his cohorts stared in equal surprise at Nick Coleman.

"What the hell—"

"Your aim was off, Jack," Coleman growled in a deep voice, "and you're a *dead* man!"

Three

"What . . . how the hell did you get away?" Jack's breathing grew heavy, and Addy slipped farther away from him. Coleman looked pale and was perspiring, but he stood steady, his blue eyes cold.

"It doesn't matter how. The point is you shot me and left me for dead, or at least a hanging if I hadn't managed an escape, while you rode off with an innocent woman and planned to enjoy my share of the money!"

Jack stiffened, holding his hand ready beside his gun, squeezing his fingers nervously into a fist. "There's plenty of blood on that duster, Nick. I have a feeling you've still got a bullet in you, and after riding all the way here that way, you don't really think you can take me, do you?"

Addy glanced at Ted and Cal. They, too, had backed away, and both looked scared to death. Addy was just glad that neither of them was wearing his gun. They had already taken them off, and Cal stood there holding a whiskey bottle while Ted looked ready to cry.

"You know I'm mad enough to do it," Nick answered. "You've got a choice! Give Ted and Cal their share of the money and leave your share with me for what you did to me, and all three of you get out of here and leave the woman! Or you can die!"

"The money and the woman are mine," Jack growled. "I meant for you to be dead, you sonofabitch, and I still do!"

Jack went for his gun, and Addy felt as though she was having a strange dream. With lightning speed Nick Coleman's six-gun was out of its holster. Fire spit from its barrel as Nick pumped three bullets into Jack before Jack could even raise his gun. Addy screamed and crouched down as Jack's body lurched backward, landing with a thud on the dirt floor, bloody holes in the middle of his chest. He let out one shuddering groan before his breath hissed through his mouth in death. He lay there with his eyes still open, staring at nothing.

Addy looked up at Nick, who had turned his gun on the other two. "Both of you get your gear together and take your money and get out of here!"

Ted's eyes widened. "Tonight?"

"Tonight! Leave your guns and rifles here. Jack's, too. Throw his body over his horse and take him someplace where you can bury him. Make camp somewhere till dawn, bury Jack and head out. You have enough money to buy guns and whatever else you need once you're away from here. If you're smart, you'll head down through Tennessee and Arkansas into Indian Territory. It's a haven for wanted men."

"Can't we stay together, Nick?" Ted asked. "Hell, it was Jack that shot you, not us."

Nick cocked his six-gun and waved it at them. "The mood I'm in, you're lucky you're alive! You were willing enough to stay with Jack after what he did and divvy up the money three ways instead of four, and you were willing to rape an innocent woman! Taking hostages has never been part of the plan. Be glad you're getting out with your lives!"

The room hung silent for a moment, then Cal threw his whiskey bottle against a wall. Glass shattered, and whiskey spilled down the log wall. "Shit!" he grumbled, looking at Ted. "Get your stuff together! We'll go to Indian Territory, all right, and we'll find some new men, maybe form our own gang! If Coleman wants to stay behind and get caught just to help a damn woman, that's his problem!" He began angrily packing his gear, and Ted followed, although he seemed more hesitant.

Addy watched in wonder, occasionally glancing at Nick Coleman, whose deep blue eyes caught her gaze when he wasn't carefully watching Cal and Ted. She was not quite sure what she read there—apology, anger, pain. Yes, he was in a great deal of pain, and she suspected he was hanging on to consciousness for her sake only.

"Let's see all your guns on the table, and remember that I know you carry an extra in your boot, Cal," Nick said, his voice sounding a little weaker. "I don't intend for you to come storming in here later to kill me."

"Heck, we wouldn't do that, Nick," Ted told him.

"How do I know that? I got shot today by somebody who was supposed to be a good friend. When you run with men like that, you can't trust anybody. Show your guns!"

Cal scowled, reluctantly laying all his weapons on the table. Ted followed, although more willingly. He backed away, swallowing. "How *did* you get away, Nick?"

"It doesn't matter. You just lay Jack's share of the money on the table before you take his body. He owes it to me! You all do!"

Addy rose and moved farther into one corner when Ted came over to rummage through Jack's pockets. Cal took more money out of the man's saddlebag, and they both laid the money on the table. "There's over a thousand there," Cal told Nick. "We took about four all together, probably not enough to hurt Howard Benedict as bad as you wanted. We had to get out too fast."

"Thanks to Jack," Nick answered.

Addy studied him, thinking how strange it was that an outlaw who ran with men like Jack Slater could be so strikingly handsome, even in his sorry condition, dirty and bleeding, needing a shave. She wished she knew the connection between him and Howard Benedict . . . and the story behind his little girl. She suspected that somewhere under that bloody duster and behind those angry eyes lay a man who must once have been decent. Then again, maybe she couldn't trust him at all. Whatever his problem, she did not doubt it had something to do with the war.

She had seen men come home to Unionville totally changed, angry, wounded, disheartened, haunted.

Cal and Ted half dragged and half lifted Jack's hefty body until they got it out the door. Nick followed them to make sure they saddled and mounted their horses and left with Jack. Addy heard them finally ride off, and moments later Nick came back inside, shoving his six-gun into its holster and then closing the door. He used his right arm to lift a thick, solid board that slid into iron bars on either side of the door and across it to create a barrier that would make it almost impossible for anyone to break in. There were only two windows in the cabin, one at the front and one at the side. He turned to Addy.

"Close the shutters on those windows and bolt them with the crossboards laying on the floor under them, like I did the door."

Addy just stared at him a moment, realizing that would protect them from anyone trying to break in, but it also made her a prisoner inside with this tall, strong, forbidding man. Still, he seemed to be growing weaker and paler before her eyes, and, after all, he had kept her from the hands of Jack Slater and two other men who had been about ready to commit a horror against her. She moved on shaky legs to the windows, closing each one, then turned to see Nick staring at her.

"Will you be all right? Your face is bruised and scraped," he told her.

Addy put a hand to her purple cheek. "I'm all right," she answered. "He did it last night."

"Did he do anything else?"

Addy felt a flush come into her cheeks and she dropped her eyes. "No. He was . . . waiting until we got here."

"Did *I* get here in time?"

Addy could not help the tears that formed in her eyes. "Yes." She looked back up at him. "I suppose I should thank you."

His lips twisted in a smirk. "I suppose you should. I'm sorry for what happened. Jack never should have taken you like that. I don't make a habit of running with men who do that."

Addy held her chin a little higher, blinking back the tears.

"You also shouldn't run with men who rob banks and shoot innocent people." She took a deep breath, trying to calm herself against the horror she had known the last two days, wanting to shut out the sight of Jack's bloodied body falling close to her, the sound of his last gasp of life. She could not blame Nick Coleman for killing him. Jack had pulled a gun on him and had meant to try a second time to murder him. Still, Nick had shot him down with such ease and calm deliberateness.

Nick turned and walked over to the iron bed in the corner of the room. He sat down on it, removing his hat and the duster, cringing when he took his left arm out of it. Addy's eyes widened at the sight of his shirt torn away from his left shoulder, a crude bandage around what was apparently a still-bleeding wound. "Do you still have a bullet in you?" she asked.

Nick sighed deeply and laid back on the bed, still wearing his gun and boots. "Doesn't matter," he answered. "I'm probably dying, and that's okay with me. You can leave in the morning. Take the black horse I rode in on. It belongs to a man back in Unionville. I said he'd get it back. Head away from the sun and you'll eventually get out of these woods. After that it's open country for a ways. You'll probably find a farmhouse or something. If I die by morning, take that money with you and give back what there is."

Addy frowned. He truly seemed not to care if he died. Still, these woods were so dense and confusing . . . and Cal and Ted might be out there somewhere. "You . . . you can't die. I need you to help me get out of here. I don't know my way."

Nick put his right hand to his forehead, and it was then Addy noticed a long scar across his forehead at the hairline. "You'll make it. I have a feeling you're a strong, smart woman." He looked at her, studying her face. "You look a lot like someone I once knew."

Addy cautiously stepped closer. "Your wife?"

He closed his eyes. "There's another bed in that extra room. Go in there and get some sleep."

Addy came even closer, feeling a little sorry for his condition, and his mental state . . . his desire to die. "I don't know a thing about taking out bullets, but it's obvious that in your case it needs to be done soon if you're going to live."

"I told you I don't want to live. Don't worry about it."

She leaned closer. "I will not go to bed and sleep while a man who just saved my honor and probably my life lies here and dies alone. Please let me try to help you. Those men left some whiskey here. You could drink some to kill the pain, and I could pour some in the wound and try to find the bullet. I . . . I'm not sure how."

Nick did not answer. His hand dropped away, and at first Addy thought maybe he had already died. She carefully reached out, felt for a pulse and realized he still had one. His face, normally tanned dark from the sun, was now a sickening gray. How could she stand and watch someone die when there might be something she could do to help him? Besides, she needed this man to show her how to get out of here.

She cautiously reached over and pulled his six-gun from its holster, carrying it gingerly by its pearl handle as though it was something abhorrent. She laid it on the table. She walked to the counter and picked up another bottle of whiskey and the paring knife she had used earlier to peel potatoes. She walked back to where Nick lay, apparently unconscious, and she leaned down to cut away the gauze around his shoulder. It was stuck to the wound, and she poured a little whiskey on it to moisten it and at the same time cleanse it. Nick jumped when she did so and she backed away, but he still did not seem fully conscious.

She peeled away the gauze, then hurriedly searched around the cabin for more. Finding none, she quickly pulled up the hem of her dress and ripped away several yards of her ruffled slip, thinking what a torn, dirty mess her yellow dress was by now. She laid the torn pieces of slip on a small table beside the bed and stared at the wound. How could she just let this man lay there and die? Yet she had no idea how to take a bullet out of someone.

She tapped lightly at his face. "Nick. Nick Coleman, wake up. I want you to drink some whiskey."

He opened his eyes and looked up at her, but it was a blank stare. Addy hoped he was in enough of a stupor to not be fully aware of what was happening.

"Drink this whiskey," she repeated. "It will ease the pain." She held the whiskey bottle to his lips and tipped it. "Drink!" she demanded.

Nick gulped and coughed and seemed to wake up a little more. He grabbed the bottle from her then and seemed angry. He drank it down then the way a man would who was accustomed to drinking heavily. For a moment Addy wondered if she had done the wrong thing. Maybe a drunk Nick Coleman was a far different man from the one who had just rescued her.

"Glad to oblige," he mumbled between gulps. "Might as well . . . go out of this life . . . with a good slug of whiskey."

Addy waited until he drank nearly half the bottle, and by then he passed out again, dropping the bottle on the bed. She quickly grabbed it before too much could spill, then watched him awhile. He breathed deeply. She called his name several times but got no response. She poured a little whiskey into his wound, and he hardly moved, although he groaned softly.

"Here goes," she whispered. She laid the paring knife on the wound and poured whiskey over that, too, then crinkled her nose and gritted her teeth in fear and sick dread as she forced herself to be quick and cut a deep slit across the bloody hole made by Jack Slater's gun. A louder groan emitted from Nick's throat, and Addy knew she had to work fast. She poured whiskey over her left hand, and with all her courage she reached into the wound, shuddering at the feel of soft, bloody flesh. She felt something that didn't seem right and pulled it out to discover it was a piece of the checkered shirt Nick wore. It had been forced into the wound by the bullet. "Dear God," she murmured.

She doused the wound once again with whiskey and Nick groaned louder. Quickly she reached inside again and felt around, going all the way to the base of her fingers before feeling an object that seemed as though it could be the bullet. With great difficulty she used two fingers to grasp it, but her fingers were slippery with blood, and it was difficult to hold on. She managed to get it nearly to the surface before losing it, and Nick seemed to be waking up. With all her resolve she reached into the wound again, this time getting a better hold on the object, and she yanked it out, nearly shouting with excitement when she saw that it was indeed the bullet.

She set it on the table beside the bed and poured whiskey over the wound once more, praying she had done the right thing. There was no time to go get clean water, so she wiped her fingers on her dress and began wrapping the wound.

"What . . . are you . . . doing?" Nick asked.

"I've taken out the bullet. I just hope I can wrap this tight enough to stop the bleeding."

". . . told you . . . not to . . ."

"I am not going to sit here and watch you die, although that might still happen. And why on earth would you *want* to die?"

"Long . . . story."

Addy yanked away more of his torn shirt and worked as swiftly as she could, reaching under him and wrapping the pieces of slip around the wound, feeling ready to pass out herself. Although she would never forget the day she learned her husband had been killed in the war, and the last four years had been nothing but struggle, none of that was as trying as what she had been through the last two days. She felt frightened, sore, tired, defeated, at a loss over what she would do if Nick Coleman died.

She tore away the rest of his shirt and pulled it off his other arm, frowning in surprise at finding burn scars on that arm. So many scars. It seemed that at every turn she discovered more about this man that made him a mystery. She unbuckled his gunbelt, pulled it away, hung it over the end of the bed. Then she grasped a boot and tugged at it, pulling off first one, then the other, then his socks. She pulled a blanket over him, not knowing what else she could do now but wait. She was bone weary herself, and after watching Nick for a few minutes and

deciding there was nothing more she could do for him, she decided to go to sleep in the spare room.

She glanced at the table where all the guns lay. What if Cal
or Ted tried to come back, found a way to get in? She walked
over and picked up one of the guns, then headed for the extra
bed. She did not care to sleep in a bed where probably Jack or
the other two had slept, realizing the blankets could not possibly
be very clean, but she had no choice for now. Perhaps in the
morning she could do a little cleaning, find more food and make
Nick Coleman a breakfast. Maybe with rest and food he would
get stronger and be able to take her out of here.

She sighed as she sat down on the bed. How ironic that she
was now going to have to depend on the blue-eyed outlaw who
had robbed a bank and had wanted to kill Howard Benedict. She
had even saved the man's life. Had she been a fool to do that?

She had no choice but to wait and find out. For now she was
too tired to think, too tired to care how clean or dirty the bedclothes might be. She lay down, slipping the six-gun under her
pillow. She could not help a few tears as she relaxed. "God help
me," she groaned. "I just want to get to Colorado." Sleep finally
came to relieve her of her agony.

Nick awoke to the smell of frying bacon. He frowned, started
to rise, but pain shot not only through his shoulder but also his
head, the familiar pain of too much whiskey. How could something that made a man feel so good make him feel so lousy a
few hours later? He lay back down, trying to think, remember.
He'd shot Jack, hadn't he? How he had reached the cabin, he
couldn't even be sure, and he only vaguely remembered chasing
Ted and Cal out, making them leave their guns behind. The last
memory he had was of passing out on this bed . . . and Mrs.
Kane . . . yes, the woman had said something about taking out
the bullet.

He opened his eyes, saw a woman with reddish brown hair
standing at the stove. He remembered that hair had once been

tucked into tidy curls. Now it hung in long, tangled waves down her back nearly to her waist. He remembered the yellow calico dress, but now it was torn and dirty, and there was blood on the skirt. He turned his head to look down at his shoulder. It was heavily bandaged with some kind of material. Had she managed to take out the bullet? It didn't burn so badly now, although it hurt like hell to try to move it.

He was a little disappointed that he wasn't dead. He never seemed to be able to quite accomplish that goal. For now he was alive and dearly needed to relieve himself. He gritted his teeth and raised up on his right elbow, realizing then that his shirt was gone. Mrs. Kane had surely seen the scars on his arm, and the damn woman would probably want to know how he got them. That was something he didn't like talking about. Mrs. Kane caught his movement and glanced in his direction.

"Well, Nick Coleman, you *are* still alive."

"Thanks to you, I suppose," he grunted. He managed to swing his feet over the side of the bed. "I've got to get outside and answer Mother Nature's call." He used the end of the bed to pull himself up.

"Do you need help?" Addy asked.

"No," Nick grumped. He stumbled to the door and managed to take out the board that barricaded it, then went out.

Addy turned the bacon, which she had found in the smoke house that morning, not yet sure if she should be relieved that Nick Coleman had lived. By the time he came back inside, the bacon was done. "Sit down at the table if you like. You can have some bacon and bread, although the bread is awfully stale. If we have to stay here long, I'll bake some fresh bread for you, and I intend to air out all the bedclothes. There isn't a tub around here big enough to wash them in. As for yourself, I can heat some water and you can bathe and shave if you like. I would like to clean up myself, if you will allow me some privacy."

Nick grunted as he sat down at the table. "Do what you like." He noticed the guns and money were no longer on the table, and he looked around the room.

"The guns are all stacked in the corner there," Addy told him. "I stuck all the money under your mattress. I wasn't sure what else to do with it. As far as I know, no one tried to come back last night. I managed to take the bullet out of your shoulder, although it certainly was not a professional job. Are you in a lot of pain?"

Nick rubbed at the top of his shoulder. "Enough. How in hell did you get the bullet out?"

Addy shrugged, bringing the bacon over to the table on a tin plate. "I just cut it open a little more and dug it out with my fingers. I made you swallow plenty of whiskey first, which seemed easy enough for you."

Nick caught the sarcasm in the words. "Some men reach the point where it goes down like water." He watched her slice some bread, noticing how slender and pretty her hands were. It still almost hurt to look at her, that red hair and those green eyes, that slender little shape. She sure did look like Bethanne. She sat down near him and buttered the bread, then handed it to him.

"When I find everything I need, Mr. Coleman, I'll be able to cook better meals. This morning I am just too worn out to care."

Nick picked up a piece of bacon. "Call me Nick, and you don't need to do anything if you don't want. Soon as I feel better I'll get you out of here, maybe even today."

Addy glanced at him, allowing herself to study his build. Nick Coleman was a big man, with muscled shoulders and arms, a body that equalled his face in handsomeness. Cleaned up and shaved, she realized he would look even more handsome, and she felt guilty for even thinking such a thing about a thief and probably a murderer. "I don't think you'll be going anywhere today. You had better rest a couple of days and build your strength." She rose. "I'll pour you some coffee."

Having a woman make him breakfast brought back painful memories for Nick, of days when he was a family man with a wife cooking for him, her belly heavy with his child. They had lived in a nice little house. He'd had a very decent farm back then. He was happy. It had been a long time since he'd known that kind of happiness, and now this Mrs. Kane had brought back a tiny hint of those good memories. "I expect your husband will be plenty worried," he spoke up.

Addy brought two cups of coffee to the table. "My husband has been dead for four years," she answered, taking a chair again. "Killed in the war."

Their eyes met. "I'm sorry."

Addy was surprised to realize he really meant it.

"The war did a lot of things to a lot of people," she answered. "I suspect you are one of them."

Nick looked away, picking up another piece of bacon. "What side did your husband fight on?"

Addy wasn't sure what his reaction would be. "Confederate," she replied. "He and my father both. You were a Confederate, too, weren't you?"

Nick swallowed the bacon. "My reasons were personal, not political."

Addy leaned back in her chair. "Did they have something to do with Howard Benedict?"

A sneer came over his face. "A lot. Benedict led some civilian raids into Kentucky and Tennessee during the war."

Addy detected the growing anger and hatred in the words. "Against your family? Did he hurt your little girl?"

His blue eyes looked at her in blazing affrontery. "You're pretty nosey for hardly knowing me. Just forget about it. Go heat some water like you wanted to do and take it in the spare room there and clean up. I won't bother you. I'm just sorry you don't have a clean dress to put on."

It was obvious he wanted to change the subject. Addy sighed and rose, picking up a wash pan from the counter and taking a kettle of heated water from the stove. "I hope I can trust you."

Nick snickered. "You should know you can by now. Besides, I'm in no shape to go wrestling around with anyone, man or woman."

She carried the pan and water to the curtained doorway, then turned to face him. "When I'm through, I'll come out here and help you wash up. I can shave you if you wish."

Nick shook his head. "I can do it myself."

"Whatever you like." Addy hesitated again. "It might help to talk about it, Nick."

"About what?"

Addy wondered where she was getting her courage, and why she cared. "About the war . . . what happened to you, your family."

"How do you even know I had a family?"

"I heard Jack and the others talking about your little girl. Where is she, Nick?"

He dropped a piece of bacon and rose. "She's *dead!* And you're a goddamn nosey woman! Considering the circumstances, the only thing you should care about is me getting you back to Unionville!"

Addy stiffened. "Fine. But tell me, why did you defend me in the bank, and later come here to help me? You risked being captured again, risked being killed by Jack or the other two. You could have been well on your way to Indian Territory, where you say it's safer for outlaws."

He sighed in seeming disgust. "I told you. I don't go in for taking captives, especially women. Besides, I had a score to settle with Jack."

Addy nodded. "You looked at me so strangely in the bank, as though you knew me. I don't recall ever having seen you anyplace before."

Nick grabbed his cup and swallowed some coffee. "Forget about it. By the way, what's your first name?"

"Adrianne Rawlins Kane. They call me Addy for short." Addy turned and went into the extra room, pulling the curtains shut. She set the pan and water on a bare, dusty table and sat down on the bed. There was a lot she wanted to know about Nick Coleman, but she realized none of it mattered. He was an outlaw, the kind of man some would call a desperado, and she was stuck with him for the time being.

She got up and poured the water into the wash pan, then wet a rag she'd found on a shelf along with some towels in the spare room, relieved to discover they were clean and unused. She wrung out the washrag and walked to a faded, yellowed mirror that hung over a dilapidated chest of drawers. She looked at herself in the mirror, shivered at the bruised woman who stared back at her, then pressed the hot moist rag against the scratches on her other cheek, gingerly washing away as much dirt as possible without bringing herself too much pain. She caught a movement behind her then and turned to see Nick Coleman standing at the curtains. His bare feet against the dirt floor had made no sound. "You said you would leave me alone," she told him, startled and alarmed.

"I did and I will." His blue eyes moved over her again. "I'm sorry for my temper. I didn't used to be this way, and I just wanted you to know that. I used to be a normal, decent man with a family. And if you have to know, it's my dead wife you resemble." He looked around the room. "I'll have you out of here soon as I can. Thanks for digging the bullet out of me. You're a brave woman, Addy Kane."

He left, and Addy looked back into the mirror. So, she looked like his wife. She could not help feeling some pity for him. The war had probably somehow done all of this to him, something so terrible that last night he had wanted to die . . .

Four

Nick looked into the self-standing mirror he had placed on the table beside the bed and carefully shaved his face, taking occasional glances at Addy. She was some woman. After washing herself and pulling her hair into a neat bun, she had begun pulling blankets off the beds and taking them outside to hang them over a clothesline and beat them. Now they hung there to soak up some fresh air while she walked around inside washing off tables and chairs. Whenever he returned to his shaving, he felt her looking at him now and again, probably curious to know how he really looked under all the dirt and the beard.

He didn't consider himself vain, but he damn well knew women thought him handsome. At one time all he had cared about was that Bethanne thought so, but she was long dead, and over the last four years since his little girl's death had left him alone, he had quickly discovered how easy it was for a handsome man to find an easy woman. There had even been a few more virtuous ones, like Addy, who told him with their eyes they might be interested, women in homes where his troops would stop for help and food in the war. Still, he hadn't been much interested in either kind of woman, except to get rid of built-up needs with a whore now and then. None satisfied him like Bethanne had.

Now here was this woman who looked so much like her. And she had grit. He liked that. He also liked this little taste of living a normal life again, with a woman cooking and cleaning. Did she have any thoughts for him besides revulsion for the fact that he was an outlaw? Any concern for him other than the fact that he could lead her out of the forest? Her eyes met his. God, they were pretty eyes, green as fern.

"How on earth did you and those men end up here?" she asked. "It's obvious a family lived here once. Poor, no doubt, but carousing men don't go putting up clotheslines."

Nick finished a last strike of his razor and took up a hot, wet rag from a washpan nearby to wipe off the soap. "We found it this way—abandoned. I have no idea why anyone would settle and build a cabin this deep in the woods. Maybe they figured it was free land and they could clear it. Maybe the woman died and the man just gave up, or the other way around. I don't know. Just don't go thinking we killed the occupants or chased them out. You can see by its dilapidated state that no one has really taken care of it for a long time. We were only going to use it ourselves for a few more days before heading into Indian Territory."

Addy walked to she door. "Is that where you'll go when we leave?"

"Most likely."

Addy did not like the feelings she had from looking at Nick Coleman. Now that he was shaved, his hair washed . . . he had a firm, square chin, high cheekbones, deep-set eyes so blue they were stunning. Dark lashes and brows outlined them, and his hair was also black. It hung in thick waves to his shoulders . . . broad shoulders. Dark hairs were scattered across his chest, growing thicker down over his flat belly. His lips were full, and the one time she had seen him actually smile, it had been a very handsome smile, with white, even teeth. The scar across his forehead did not seem to distract from his looks in the least. In fact, it almost helped his looks, made him seem more rugged.

She looked away, chastising herself for liking the way he looked. He was a man no woman of decent reputation should care about in any way, and she had probably been wrong to take out that bullet. "I am going to sweep off the porch," she told him.

"Why bother? We'll probably leave here tomorrow."

"I don't know. I see things that need doing, and I do them."

"You should get some more rest."

"I will when I'm done."

Nick watched her go outside, and he wondered with a secret grin if she was just keeping herself busy because she had discovered she was attracted to him and didn't know how to handle it. She kept herself busy for nearly another hour, then stood at the table and kneaded some bread dough she had mixed earlier.

"It's a miracle I found that old tin of yeast on the shelf. Some woman must have left it. I wasn't sure it was any good, but this dough is rising just fine. Even if we leave tomorrow, we can take the fresh bread with us. When you leave me off near town, you can take it with you when you go. After what you did for me, I have to say I hope you don't get caught." She met his eyes again. "How *did* you escape?"

Nick grinned again, and Addy felt a little flutter deep in her stomach she had not felt in years.

"Your sheriff is not very professional. They left me at the doctor's office thinking I was unconscious, and hung my gun over a chair. When I came to, what men were there were in another room talking. I managed to get up and get to my gun before they knew I was awake. One of the men had a fancy horse tied in the alley below. Name's Charger. I'll let you ride back on him and he can have his horse back. One thing I'm not is a horse thief."

Addy's eyebrows arched mockingly. "Oh, how good of you."

Nick actually laughed lightly, and Addy found herself beginning to like him. "Tell me, Nick, where did you get that scar across your forehead?"

Nick put a hand to the scar, and he lost his smile. "Raiders. Came to my farm in Kentucky. Burned my house. Shot me. They were led by Howard Benedict."

Addy stopped kneading the dough, surprised he had told her so much for once, more surprised that Howard Benedict, the fancy-suited man who ran the Unionville Bank, would have done such a thing. "How do you know it was Mr. Benedict?"

Nick turned and picked up a clean shirt he'd taken out of his gear. Now that the whiskey had worn off a little and the sun was up, Addy thought he seemed to be in slightly better spirits.

"I heard one of the raiders mention his name and where they were from. I went to Unionville and asked around. Everybody knew who Howard Benedict was. When I heard he owned a bank, I knew that one day I would get my revenge. I planned on killing Benedict."

Nick winced as he put his arm into the left sleeve of the shirt, and Addy was relieved to see that there were no new bloodstains on the material she had wrapped around the wound. It appeared to be about the same as last night.

"Those men killed my little girl," he added, his voice dropping from remorse. "They set my house on fire. They were just civilian rabble, following the coattails of Union troops that had attacked Forts Donelson and Henry, using the war as an excuse to plunder and steal. My own parents had been dead a long time, my wife dead five years . . . died in childbirth. My grandparents were helping me raise Patty." He turned and picked up the bottle of whiskey that still sat on the table nearby, and it struck Addy that only a man who was a heavy drinker could down something like that in the morning . . . or a man so consumed by grief that he needed it to soothe his soul. He sat down on the bed. "They shot my grandfather dead. I was out tilling a field, couldn't get there in time. When I did, the house was engulfed in flames. My grandmother and my little girl died in the fire." He sat with his elbows on his knees, his shirt still open, the whiskey bottle hanging in his hand. "The worst part was my little girl was screaming for me to help her. I tried to get in . . ." He shook his head. "It was impossible." His voice broke on the last words, and he drank down another gulp of whiskey. "I'll never forget her screams . . . or stop dreaming about it."

Addy understood now where he had gotten the burn scars on his right arm. She understood a lot of things . . . a man consumed with revenge and hopelessness, a man who felt he had nothing left to live for. "I'm so sorry, Nick. I didn't mean for my question to bring up such pain."

Nick raised his eyes to meet hers. He studied her bruised face, saw in her eyes true sympathy. Why did he find it so easy to talk to this woman he hardly knew? "It was four years ago. I buried what was left of my little girl and I buried my feelings and anything good about me along with her. I abandoned the farm and joined the Confederate army just to kill Union men. I took a bullet in my right leg, spent some time in a prison camp. That's where I met Jack and the others. All of us had reasons to continue the war after it was over, except that Jack was just plain mean. I didn't care. I *wanted* to find someone mean, someone to match the meanness I felt in my own heart. After I leave you off I'll go find some more men just like him. If I get lucky I'll get shot down by some lawman somewhere and end the misery." He set the whiskey bottle back on the table, and Addy left the bread dough to rise again.

"Is that what you really want? Seems to me somewhere inside of you is a man longing for the life he used to have."

Nick shook his head, then turned and laid back on the bare mattress. Addy had taken away all the blankets. "I can never live like that again."

Addy picked up a potato and began peeling it. "I don't believe that."

"Believe it. I don't even know why I told you any of it."

"It needed telling. I know the feeling of being alone, Nick. I have no one now myself. My husband was killed in the war. I was living in Michigan then, going to school to become a teacher. We met there, but Tom was from Virginia and left to put on a gray uniform as soon as war became inevitable. When I finished school I came to Unionville to be with my mother. My father believed in states' rights, and he had also gone off to fight for the Confederacy. Because of that, and the fact that my own husband was a southerner, people in Unionville treated me and my mother rudely. Old friends turned their backs on us and I couldn't get a teaching job. I worked at whatever menial labor

I could find to keep us going. My father was Phillip Rawlins. He owned a dry goods store, but people stopped coming, and Mother finally had to close the doors. In August of '63 I received word that my husband was dead. Not long after that we heard my father had also been killed. My mother just went downhill after that and was dead herself a few months later."

She began slicing some potatoes into a pan, working vigorously to keep from breaking down. "I decided I had to get out of Unionville, start my life over someplace new. I'm twenty-five years old and totally alone and without friends. I answered an ad for a teacher in Central, Colorado, and they hired me. I was withdrawing what little savings I had in the bank in order to leave for Colorado when you and your men came in and . . . well, you know the rest. As soon as I get back and fully recover, I will be leaving for Colorado."

Nick sighed. "From what I know, Central is a mining town. I've never been west, but I've heard the mining towns can be pretty wild. Might not be a good place for a woman alone."

Addy picked up another potato to slice it. "I'll survive. At least I'll be able to teach, and I'll be away from places that have only bad memories." She glanced at Nick, seeing an understanding look in his blue eyes. "You see? I fully understand how you feel." She looked back at the potatoes. "Except that I have never lost a child. Tom and I never had children. We were only married a short time before he went off to war. I do have an older sister in St. Louis, but she turned her back on my parents when my father joined the Confederacy. She married a Union man who is quite wealthy. They have two children. We are nothing alike, and I have no desire to live near her. I need to go far away and start my life over. That might be a good idea for you . . . to get completely out of this area. Your face is probably on wanted posters by now, since you announced your name so blatantly in the bank."

"I wanted Howard Benedict to know who was looking to kill him."

Addy set her knife aside and faced him. "Killing isn't the

answer any more and you know it. If you stop the robbing and killing now, maybe I can find some way to get the law to stop looking for you, tell them you died or something. You would have a chance to get away from here, start over."

"You'd do that?"

"Maybe. You'd have to promise to stop going around robbing banks and hurting innocent people."

Nick sat up and began buttoning his shirt. "I can't make promises like that yet." The whiskey worked on his emotions. Addy Kane looked even prettier now, and he couldn't get over how easy it was to talk to her. What were these strange feelings the woman stirred in him, old longings he had not felt in years. Talking about Patty had stirred the pain again, and he was surprised he'd been able to talk about it.

Addy closed her eyes and sighed in exasperation. "What was your wife's name?" she asked.

Nick laid back down and turned to his right side. "Bethanne," he answered. "Don't finish that lunch yet. I'm not hungry."

Addy looked over at him, her heart aching for the man. She had brought back memories he really had not wanted to think about. She felt a strong urge to walk over and put her arms around him and tell him everything was all right, but that could be a dangerous move with such a man.

After a few minutes he appeared to fall asleep. The weather had cooled considerably, and Addy walked outside and retrieved one of the blankets. She brought it in and carefully covered him. He pulled it over his shoulders.

"Thanks," he muttered.

Addy blinked back tears. "You're welcome," she whispered.

Nick slept and Addy baked bread. It was three o'clock when Nick began to stir and toss. He flailed his right arm and began mumbling, and Addy moved closer, realizing he was speaking Patty's name in an agonizing groan. She could imagine how horrible it must have been for this man to listen to his little girl screaming for her daddy to help her, but not be able to get to her. It was no wonder he was so full of hatred, no wonder he was not concerned over his own death, but rather seemed to welcome it. He had lost his own parents, watched his wife die, lost his grandparents and a child to the ugly brutality that comes with a civil war.

She stood staring at him, watching him thrash and groan. He called Patty's name again, then suddenly woke with a gasp. He sat straight up and stared at Addy for a moment, as though he didn't even recognize her. "Bethanne!" he whispered, reaching out his hand.

Addy stepped back. "It's me, Addy. You were dreaming and you aren't fully awake."

Nick blinked, looked around the room. "Jesus," he muttered. "I had the damn nightmare again. The flames, the heat . . . Patty screaming for me." He rubbed at his eyes. "I'm sorry."

Addy turned away. "You had better eat something." Why did her heart ache so for him, this near stranger? "I've baked some bread. I'll cook some potatoes and pork."

Nick thought how he wouldn't mind just staying here a while, days, weeks, letting Addy Kane clean the cabin and make his meals. He thought how she just might make a damn good wife, quiet, understanding, educated, pretty, and she could even cook. But then he was beyond the point of ever falling in love and marrying again, and what decent woman would want him now? Such thoughts were nonsense. It was just suddenly seeing her when he awoke, still dazed, her looking so much like Bethanne. He felt embarrassed and got up and went out to check on the horses, needing to shake away the cobwebs of the dream.

Addy looked up when he came back inside nearly a half hour later. His tall, broad frame seemed to fill the cabin. He sat down and ate voraciously, warning her she had better take a nap in addition to getting a good night's sleep. Addy could see he did not want to discuss the dream.

"We'll leave early in the morning, no time for more than

coffee and bread," he said. "I can have you close to town by late tomorrow night. Then I'll be on my way."

For some reason Addy realized she might miss him a little. "How is your shoulder?"

He drank down some coffee. "Still hurts like hell, but you must have done a decent job. I'm feeling good otherwise. I'll bet a doctor would have laughed at how you got that bullet out."

Addy smiled. "I didn't know how else to do it."

Nick leaned back in his chair. "I'm giving back your share of the money, but I'm keeping the rest. It's the least Howard Benedict owes me. When you get to town you can tell the others that I came here and Jack killed me. If the law finds Jack's grave out there somewhere, they'll just think it's mine. You can tell them they did you no real harm, and they finally let you go because you were slowing them down. Make sure they're convinced you weren't raped. People tend to treat a woman different after a thing like that, even though she's entirely innocent." He rubbed at the back of his neck. "Tell them you think they headed for Indian Territory. They let you go on the horse I stole so the owner wouldn't keep searching for it. That should end the search, and I can get the hell out of this territory. You don't need to tell anybody that you got your share of the money back. They'd wonder why. As far as the bank is concerned, it was stolen. If they want to make up for it, take it. You deserve the extra."

"After what you told me about Howard Benedict, I am inclined to agree with you." She watched his eyes. "Does this mean you've decided not to kill the man? Are you going to stop your outlaw ways?"

He smiled rather bitterly. "I won't go back to Unionville and I won't kill Benedict. That's as far as I go with promises. Will you keep yours to convince them I'm dead?"

She nodded cautiously. "If you're being honest with me."

"I'm a lot of things, but I'm no liar." Nick walked over to his saddlebags and took a thin cigar from his gear. He took it to the iron stove and lifted one of the burner lids, bending down and lighting it by the lingering fire inside. "I hope you find a good life in Colorado," he told her, straightening and taking a deep drag on the smoke.

"And I hope you find a way to change your life, Nick, a way to get over the past. You're too young and too good inside to die with a noose around your neck."

He studied her soiled dress, still feeling sorry she had nothing to change into. "I'm thirty, but these last four years have made me feel much older."

He walked outside to smoke, and he stayed outside most of the afternoon. Addy felt time slipping away, wondered why she wished she could stop it for a little while. Later Nick came inside with a gunny sack in his hand. "Some of the smoked meat," he said. "I'll need it." He set the meat near his saddlebags and walked over to the stash of guns, taking up his pearl-handled six-gun and whirling the chamber, adding bullets. Then he opened a rifle and peered down the barrel. "Most of these need cleaning, but I don't feel like it tonight." He laid his own gun plus one other and two rifles near the meat. "Soon as we eat a little more, we'll get some sleep. You strong enough to travel?"

"Yes." Addy wondered if she would be safe sleeping in the same cabin with this man now that he was much better. Still, he had been respectful of her all day. Part of her still feared him, yet part of her did not.

"You should take one of those guns for yourself, not that you'd need it for protection with me along, but you might want one along on your trip west."

"I am not in the habit of carrying guns."

"Just a suggestion. Maybe you should buy yourself a small pistol when you get back to town—something that would fit in a purse."

"I'll think about it." She went to the door. "I'll bring in the blankets. You might want to roll up a couple extras for your gear. I'll take that nap you suggested after they're folded." She went outside, feeling strangely sad, and as though she was living in an unreal world, far removed from anything she had ever known. She brought in the blankets, still feeling sorry for Nick and his nightmares . . . a screaming little girl calling for her daddy. What a horror!

She folded and rolled a couple of blankets for his gear, then went into the other room to lie down and try to sleep. The afternoon passed into evening, and they ate again. Nick grew quiet, and Addy wondered if he was thinking the same thing she was . . . that for some reason she didn't want to leave him. He laid down to sleep and told her to do the same.

"We have no choice but to get moving in the morning. The law will find this cabin sooner or later," he told her.

Addy felt an odd sense of disappointment. When she first came to this cabin, she could imagine nothing more wonderful than escaping and getting back to Unionville. Now there was a small part of her that did not want to leave, and she had no idea why, except that it would mean leaving Nick Coleman, who seemed so alone. Now that she knew he was a man once loved, and capable of loving in return, a family man who had loved and lost a wife and a little girl, he had become more human. No man should turn to murder and theft in his grief and need for revenge, but who was to say how any one person would react to such things? She had heard and read many stories of other men so changed by the war that they did the same.

She went into the tiny bedroom and lay down, but it was not easy to sleep. She had her own conscience to deal with now. If Nick kept his promise and got her back to town, should she lie the way he asked her to and tell the law he was dead? Or should she do what was surely the honorable thing . . . tell the truth and let him be caught?

Sun shone through a forest mist when Addy awoke. She was not sure of the time, but she could hear noises in the outer room. She sat up and poured water from a small bucket into a wash bowl and rinsed her face and toweled it dry, then quickly brushed her hair and twisted it into a bun. Taking a quick look at herself in the stained mirror, she saw a hollow-eyed, haggard-looking woman wearing a torn, filthy, bloodstained dress. She turned and peered through the curtains then to see Nick packing his saddlebags. He glanced her way.

"I was about to come and rouse you," he told her.

"I fell asleep late, and now I have apparently overslept."

"We've got to get going. I have your money here. I believe you said four hundred dollars, so I'm giving you five. You deserve the extra hundred for what you've been through. More than that, actually, but I'll need the rest to head into Indian Territory, maybe go even farther."

Addy walked closer, realizing this man could have used his strength to do whatever he wanted with her last night, but he had left her alone. "Farther?"

He shrugged. "Maybe do the same as you—get a new start somewhere. I don't know. I'm torn between wanting to die, wanting to kill and wanting to find the life I had once with Bethanne." He turned with the money. "Here." His gaze moved over her body. "You don't want anyone in town to know that you got this back. They'll figure men like Jack would never do that, so you'd have to explain, and you can't explain it if I'm supposed to be dead. You'd better hide this somewhere under that dress, in your camisole or . . . wherever."

Addy reddened, more from surprise at the way his remark stirred womanly emotions than the fact he had alluded to her underwear. She walked closer and took the money, feeling a strange tingle when his fingers touched her own. She realized it was the first time they had touched at all in any familiar way. The only other time she had touched him was to dig her fingers into his flesh to search for a bullet. "I . . . don't feel right taking the extra hundred. Doesn't that make me a thief, too?"

He flashed a handsome grin. "I guess so. But I'd say the town of Unionville owes it to you, wouldn't you?"

She could not help a smile of her own. "Yes." She took the money and went into the bedroom, unbuttoning the front of her dress and spreading the bills evenly inside her camisole. She glanced at the curtain to be sure Nick Coleman hadn't decided to take a peek, then chastised herself for worrying he would do such a thing. She walked back to the wash pan and picked up a small box of baking soda she had found the night before on a shelf, using some to rub on her teeth to clean them, then dipped a tin cup into the bucket of water and rinsed her mouth, spitting into the already-used water in the wash pan. "Would you like some baking soda for your mouth?" she asked Nick.

"Sure."

She walked out and handed it to him.

"Put some bread in this and we'll leave," he said, handing out a small cloth sack. "No time to cook breakfast. The horses are already saddled and my gear is packed. We'll eat bread and drink water on the way."

He picked up his saddlebags and walked out to the pump with the baking soda, and Addy felt strangely panicky at being so rushed. She had planned on taking her time, making him breakfast. Again, she wondered why such a thing should matter. She picked up two loaves of bread and shoved them into the sack, thinking what a strange experience she had had here over the last three days, being so terrified, seeing murder and blood, digging a bullet out of a man with her bare fingers, learning to understand and accept a man who anyone else would consider worthy of nothing more than a hanging. She glanced around the cabin, wondering how she could be a little nostalgic over the memories she had here.

She turned and went out, and Nick was already on his horse, a big, dark gray gelding that seemed just right for a man his size. He wore his duster again, and he looked every bit the dangerous outlaw he was supposed to be. How odd that she felt perfectly safe with him. "Are you sure you can travel?"

"I'll be all right."

"You'd better buy yourself a new coat. The tear and blood-stains on that one are a giveaway."

He nodded. "I will. Just a little chilly this morning. You'd better put a blanket around your shoulders. I left one on Charger's rump there. Do you ride all right?"

"Yes, I can ride."

"You remember what to tell the law?"

She nodded. "You're dead."

Their eyes held, both realizing that once he took her back he truly would be dead to her, to this part of the country. They would go their separate ways and never see each other again.

Nick was also feeling odd emotions over things he had experienced the last three days. He had come here to help this woman, but he had not expected to end up with these strange feelings of attachment, or that it would almost hurt to let her go and never see her again. "You're a strong, brave woman, Addy Kane. Thanks for digging the bullet out of me. You figured I was dying, and you could have let me just lay there."

Addy nodded. "I could have, but I needed someone to lead me out of these woods."

He grinned. "That's the only reason you helped me?"

Addy smiled wryly. "Of course it is."

Nick knew better. She was a decent, Christian woman who couldn't let any man, even an outlaw, just lay there and die before her eyes without trying to help him. "Let's go," he told her.

Addy turned and climbed up onto Charger.

"I shortened the stirrups," Nick told her. "Are they all right?"

"Almost a little too short, but they'll do."

Nick nodded and turned his horse. "Follow me, Addy Kane. You'll be back home by late tonight or early morning." *Late tonight, if I can swing it,* he thought. *I'm not sure I want to spend another night trying to sleep with you so close by.* Damn if she didn't look like Bethanne. Damn if she didn't have his total respect. And damn if she didn't stir memories of another life, family, love . . . He headed out. It was too late for him now, and Addy Kane had her own plans. They sure as hell did not include running off with an outlaw. She was headed for Colorado and a new life, and she damn well deserved that.

Five

"She's back, Sheriff Page, and she's got my horse with her!" Brad Barlow barged into the sheriff's office with the words. "She's out here! Mrs. Kane! Her dress is all torn and dirty, but her face . . . well, she said she washed in a stream on her way. The outlaws led her in the right direction and then—"

Sheriff Page sat up on his cot, rubbing at his eyes. "What the hell?"

"Mrs. Kane. She just rode in, Sheriff!"

Page looked at Brad, noticing it was barely light outside. "What time is it?"

"Only about six o'clock. I was just opening the livery when Mrs. Kane rode by headed for your office. I followed along, took hold of my horse for her. She looks ready to fall off it."

Page stood up and ran a hand through his gray, thinning hair, then tucked his shirt into his pants and pulled the suspenders up over his shoulders. His pot belly hung out between the suspenders as he walked over to grab his hat, leaving his gun hanging on a hook. "I'll talk to her myself." He moved to the door, embarrassed he would not have a chance to wash his face before facing Mrs. Kane and the few people who happened to be up at dawn to see her ride into town. As he walked outside, a man was helping Addy dismount, and everyone had questions for her, but she answered none of them.

Addy well knew what many of the men and the one woman around her were thinking—that she had been raped. But she ignored them as she faced the sheriff. "I wasn't sure if you would even be here," she told him. "Apparently you gave up searching for me."

The sheriff removed his hat. "I'm sorry, Mrs. Kane. We lost the trail."

Addy nodded. "Can we go inside?"

"Yes, Ma'am." Page stepped aside and let Addy go ahead of him, telling Brad and the one woman in the crowd, Hilda Temple, the owner of a hat store, to come in with him as witnesses to what Addy had to say.

Addy walked inside, taking a chair near Page's desk, wondering what these people would think of her if they knew the real reason for the look of sorrow on her face. It wasn't so much for what she had been through. It was over the fact that she and Nick Coleman had parted ways only an hour ago. They had shared a twenty-four hour ride together, and she had admired his skills in the wilds, enjoyed watching his broad-shouldered frame on the big horse he rode. He had been protective and respectful, and through the dark night they had spent together she had not feared wild animals . . . nor had she feared Nick Coleman, who slept in his own bedroll only a few feet away from her. It had been obvious he was accustomed to sleeping under the stars, that he was a man who could find his way around any kind of country and could guard himself against any intruder, man or beast, as well as make a camp anywhere and fend for himself.

"Anything we can get you, Mrs. Kane?" Page asked.

"No. I just want to get home and rest. I have to get my things ready for my trip. The house is already sold, you know. I'm supposed to be out in five more days."

"You sure you're up to traveling that far now?" Brad asked her. He took a chair near her, and Sheriff Page sat down at his desk, scratching at the shadow of a beard. Hilda Temple remained standing behind Addy, and Addy thought how silly it was to have her here. If she *had* been raped and needed a woman's comfort, Hilda would certainly not be the one she would pick. The woman had totally turned her back on Addy's mother and Addy all through the war.

"I'll be all right. I have even more reason to leave, Mr. Barlow," Addy answered. "After the strain of the last few days, I just need to get away and start a new life." She turned her gaze from Barlow and met the sheriff's eyes. "I was not abused, if that is what you are thinking."

Page frowned. "There's a bruise on your face, and some bad scrapes."

Addy sighed. "Jack Slater hit me and knocked me to the ground because I refused to cook for him when they made camp," she lied. "On the journey to their hideout, they were in too much of a hurry to harm me otherwise." She felt her face flushing redder. "When we reached their cabin, all they wanted was eat and drink and count their money. Then the one they shot and left behind . . . he showed up for revenge. He told Jack to let me go and . . . there was a gunfight. Jack shot him again and he . . . died." Yes, Nick Coleman truly was dead to her now. "Jack made the other two take him out and bury him. I have no idea how far they took him. They were gone a long time. I could never even find that cabin for you, let alone a grave in those deep woods. I think . . . I think we were somewhere in western Kentucky, since Unionville is so close to the border, and we headed in that direction."

Page nodded. "We figured as much, but we lost the trail when it led to some rocky hills and a deep stream. We were worried maybe you were killed. That big one, his name's Nick Coleman, he managed to get to his gun and escape, stole Brad's horse. How'd you happen to come back on it? Doesn't seem to me men like that would let a good horse like Charger go, or that they'd see that you got back here all right."

Addy looked at her lap, always finding it difficult to lie. "They apparently decided they could make a better run for it if they returned me and Mr. Barlow's horse. They didn't want kidnapping and horse stealing added to the list of things they're wanted for. They were also afraid Nick Coleman had been followed. They just wanted to get out fast and get rid of anything that might slow them down."

Page frowned, rubbing his chin. "They're already wanted for bank robbery and murder. I'd say that's plenty."

"I suppose." Addy closed her eyes and sighed. "Who knows how such minds work? I only came here first to return the stolen horse and to tell you what happened. I was used like a slave, cooking mostly, washing their clothes and blankets, helping them prepare for a long journey into Indian Territory. Jack Slater was slightly hurt in the shootout with Nick Coleman. I had to dress his wounds. That's how I got the blood on my dress. They had to wait until Jack could travel, which is another reason why I was kept those extra couple of days. You should know they kept all the money. When Jack was ready to travel they put me on Charger and brought me close enough to town for me to find the rest of the way alone. They all headed south into Tennessee, said they were going into Indian Territory to lay low for a while. I . . . considered trying to escape several times before that, but we were so deep in a dense forest that I had no idea which way to go. They would have caught me, and I was afraid that would only aggravate them into perhaps killing me . . . or doing something worse than death, so I cooperated."

Page studied her a moment, and Addy prayed her lies sounded valid. "You sure you aren't hiding the fact that those men did more to you than you say? You don't have to be afraid to tell us, Mrs. Kane. It just adds to the things those sorry bastards are wanted for."

Addy shook her head. "No. I swear. They didn't . . . abuse me that way. All I know now is that they're on their way south with the stolen money, and that the one called Nick Coleman is dead."

"Serves him right," Brad grumbled.

"Can I do anything for you, dear?" Hilda asked, moving to stand beside Addy's chair.

Addy looked up at her, tempted to give her a sneer. *Where were you when my mother and I really needed you?* she thought.

Now her mother was buried, partly from a broken heart because of people like Hilda. "No, thank you," she answered.

"Well, at least one of them is out of the way," Page spoke up. "We can take down the wanted posters for Nick Coleman, although one has to give him a little credit for trying to get them to release you. When he left here he did say that was one thing he was going to do, besides kill Jack Slater. Too bad he didn't accomplish both."

"Yes," Addy answered, staring at her lap. *God be with you, Nick Coleman.* At least there would be no wanted posters on him. Perhaps if he just kept going west, maybe someplace like Texas, he could be free. Still, there was no one to care about him. If he kept his attitude of not worrying whether he lived or died, kept running with thieves and pros—why on earth did it upset her to imagine him with prostitutes? She must stop this! "I would like to go now," she said, looking up at Sheriff Page. "I need a hot bath and some sleep."

"Of course, but I need the names of the other two men, if you know them."

Addy rose. "One was Cal Arden. The other one was called Ted, but I don't know his last name. He was the youngest one. I don't think he's as bad as the others. He seemed upset that Jack Slater had shot Nick Coleman during the robbery."

Brad Barlow folded his arms in disgust. "But not upset that Slater had shot an innocent teller."

"I've contacted Paducah and Mount Vernon," Page said. "The three that got away are pretty well known, and we have pictures of them. I'd like you to stick around, Mrs. Kane, till a rider can get here from Paducah. I want you to look at the pictures and make sure they're the same men. I guess nobody's got a picture of Nick Coleman, but if he had lived, it would have been easy to describe him, big as he was, with that dark hair and that scar along his hairline, blue eyes. After he was shot we all got a good look at that one, but I guess that doesn't matter now."

"No, it doesn't," Addy answered, relieved that no one would be searching for Nick. Maybe she was wrong to lie this way and let the man go free, yet she could not bring herself to tell the truth. "Are you going to go after the ones who got away?" Page rose and stretched, and Addy thought what a lazy excuse for a sheriff he was. This time she was glad. She didn't want Cal and Ted to be found. They would tell the truth—that it was Jack Slater who was dead, not Nick Coleman.

Page rested his hands on his hips. "I don't think so. Men like that, they know their territory. In the deep woods and mountains of Tennessee, where they're most likely headed, it's pretty hard to do any tracking, but I'll alert the authorities in Kentucky, Tennessee, Arkansas. I doubt they'll have any luck. I think Mr. Benedict's money is just plain gone. He's pretty upset."

Good, Addy thought. She stood up, the trauma of the last five days beginning to catch up with her now. She felt suddenly weak and deathly tired. "I'll look at the pictures when they arrive," she told Page. "I just want to go home now."

Page studied her, thinking what a pretty woman she was, soft-spoken, reputable. He liked her all right himself, thought it was about time the townspeople put the war behind them and quit condemning people for what their relatives did in the war. But then it didn't matter much now. Addy Kane was headed west. "What about the money you lost?" he asked her. "How will you be able to get to Colorado?"

It irritated Addy to think that the whole town knew what she had planned to do. Obviously they all had been gossiping about her, gossip most likely fueled by women like Hilda Temple and old Sara Webster. She struggled not to look guilty as she thought about the money she had hidden on her person right now. "I'll manage," she told him. "My transportation there is paid. Maybe once I get there they can give me an advance on my teaching salary."

"Oh, but you must have a little money to take along, for food and such," Hilda spoke up. "I'll see about taking up a collection for you."

Addy turned and met the woman's eyes, amazed at the offer, feeling sick that now, after her mother had gone to her grave with a broken heart, this woman would finally offer to help. *Where were you when I was scrubbing floors for a living because I couldn't get any other kind of work in this town?* "Fine," she answered aloud. "That would be . . . very generous of you." Yes, she would take every cent this woman could raise for her. This town owed it to her, and Addy felt like laughing, knowing that under her clothes was some of *their* money, as well as all the money she had lost in the robbery . . . and all thanks to an outlaw she had led them to believe was dead. Nick Coleman had made it possible for her to get a little revenge of her own against this town . . . and the last laugh.

She moved past Mrs. Temple and went outside, where people still waited, whispering and staring. She walked on shaky legs toward the little frame house at the north end of town where her mother and father had lived since she was born twenty-five years ago, a house where many cherished memories from childhood remained. She had left it at seventeen to go to Hope College in Michigan, where she had met Tom Kane, married, lost him to war. The war had brought so much death and injury, not just to the men who had fought in it, but to those left behind. It frightened her to go someplace new and far away, but even if these people started being kinder to her because of her ordeal, the damage was already done. She could not stay.

People peppered her with questions, and a reporter for the town paper ran up to her, repeating those questions. Addy refused to answer, telling the reporter she would talk to him after she had rested. She really did not care about feeding their sick curiosity, but talking to the newspaper was just one more way of making sure everyone thought Nick Coleman was dead.

She struggled to her house, turning and asking everyone to please leave, telling the reporter she would come and see him when she was rested. She went inside and closed the door, locking it and leaning against it for a moment to gather her thoughts. She moved to a window and peered through lace curtains to see people gradually leaving, exchanging theories on what might have happened to her. She moved to a side window then, watch

ing the wooded hills to the east. Nick was out there somewhere . . . alone.

Nick broke camp, tired of the sleepless nights he'd had since
leaving Addy Kane near Unionville. He wondered why that one
night they'd camped outside, it had been harder to stay away
from her than when they were alone in the cabin. Maybe it was
because he knew it was the last night they would spend together,
that the next day they would say good-bye for good. Part of him
had wondered if maybe trying to get closer to her, maybe one
little kiss, might have changed both their minds about parting.
He could have offered to take her with him.

Hell no! A beautiful, educated woman like that wouldn't go
running off with an outlaw into Indian Territory! She was a
decent woman, like Bethanne. Women like that married men of
good reputation with good jobs. They lived in nice houses, stable
homes, where they raised their children. They lived the kind of
life he used to live with Bethanne, the kind of life he could
probably never live again. Besides, neither of them was truly
healed from the war. They would go on with their lives in very
different ways, each finding his and her own way of forgetting.
He had chosen the wrong way, and now he was stuck with it.

He poured leftover coffee onto the few hot coals from the fire
he'd made the night before, then kicked some dirt over it. He
packed his gear, angrily stuffing things into his saddle bags and
rolling up his blankets, wishing he could get Addy Kane off his
mind. That first time he looked at her in the bank . . . it seemed
he felt fate pulling at him, felt some strange connection to the
woman. The only explanation was that she looked so much like
Bethanne, but damned if she wasn't easy to talk to. He'd never
told anyone the whole story about Patty before, the burns on his
arm. The only thing a few men he'd run with knew was that his
wife and little girl were dead. Jack and the others had only known
that somehow Howard Benedict had been responsible, but he'd
never told them the details.

He'd never told anyone . . . except Addy. Something about her made him feel better inside, and for the first time in years he realized what he missed in life. He missed having someone give a damn about him . . . and God, he missed the way Bethanne had loved him, how good it felt to wrap himself around her at night. And he missed his precious Patty, her bright smile, her little kisses, the way she used to proudly make cookies for him, with her grandma's help.

"I ought to hate her," he grumbled, speaking of Addy. It was her fault all these memories had been awakened in him, her fault he had allowed himself to experience feelings again, to want to hold someone lovingly. It was her fault it suddenly hurt to realize there was not one person on this earth who cared about him, probably not even Addy Kane.

He saddled his horse, tightened the cinch, then tied on his gear. "What do you think, Shadow?" he said to the animal as he mounted up. "Should we really head into Indian Territory?" He thought about the crumbling little cabin where he'd spent two nights with Addy, how just her presence had made it seem almost like home. He touched the little burlap bag that held the bread she had baked for him. What was it about fresh-baked bread that gave a man a good feeling? He remembered when Bethanne used to bake. There was something about warm bread from the oven that seemed to represent the warmth from a woman's heart.

"This is ridiculous," he grumbled. He took a moment to pull out his six-gun to make sure it was fully loaded, then headed Shadow south. He figured he'd better stay clear of homes and towns for a while. Once he turned west he'd come upon the Mississippi. After he crossed that he could head straight into Indian Territory . . . or he could board a riverboat and head upstream to St. Louis, then west to Independence and hop a train across Kansas into Colorado. If Addy thought that was a good place to start over, then maybe it could be for him, too. He would just have to be careful and hope no one recognized him. By now, if Addy did her job right, everyone thought Nick Coleman was dead; and if he got far enough away, he'd be a free man. He could get out of the hellish life he was living now . . . maybe. Then again, he knew the real reason he thought about heading farther west. Addy was going there, too.

"The hell with it," he said, adjusting his leather hat. He rubbed at his sore shoulder, grinning at the vision of Addy digging her fingers into him to try to find a bullet. "It's Indian Territory," he told Shadow. "Let's go."

Man and horse continued their way through the dense forest toward the Tennessee border.

Addy disembarked the *River Queen* to greet her sister on the dock at St. Louis. They embraced, but Addy could feel the lingering distance between them. Harriet had written a few times, had said she would gladly help Addy and their mother financially when their mother was still alive; but because their father had fought for the Confederacy, Harriet's husband, Gary Burns, who was from Illinois had refused to help. Gary was a pompous ass as far as Addy was concerned, a man born into money, who went into the Union Army as an officer only because his father could pull strings. He knew nothing of struggle, and in Addy's opinion, he knew nothing about how to truly love anything but money. She could not imagine what Harriet saw in him besides riches, and because she had let the man keep her from helping her own family, Addy had lost respect for her sister.

"I'm so glad you stopped to see us before going on to Colorado," Harriet told her. "I got your wire three days ago. Gary said it was all right to come and meet you, bring the children. I have our carriage, too. What hotel are you staying at?"

The words hurt deeply. Apparently Gary did not intend for Addy to stay at their home tonight. "I still need to get a room." She stepped back, looking Harriet over. Her sister had their father's ash blond hair, but she and Addy both shared their mother's green eyes. Harriet, of course, wore an elegant dress, a deep blue silk day gown with a matching hat and parasol. She had put on a little weight, but then she also had two children now, two little girls, five and seven, who presently sat in the carriage arguing about something, scratching at each other like the spoiled brats that they were.

"I'll take you to one of the better hotels," Harriet answered. "When do you leave St. Louis?"

Addy followed her sister to the fancy open carriage, which was pulled by a fine black horse. The driver followed them with Addy's luggage, and two baggage men from the steamboat carried a small trunk she had also brought along. They loaded everything onto a baggage rack at the back of the carriage, and the driver climbed into his seat.

"Tomorrow," Addy answered her sister. She climbed into the carriage and waited for Harriet to softly scold her daughters and pull them apart. She plopped one in a seat beside Addy, telling her to say hello to "Aunt Addy". The child just stared ahead, lips pressed together in anger over her fight with her sister.

Harriet took the opposite seat, facing Addy, and keeping the other child beside her. "Will I ever see you again, Addy?"

Addy wondered if it truly mattered to her. How different Harriet was from the little girl she used to play with when they were all a happy family back in Unionville. How could people's lives change so drastically? Look what the war had done to Nick, once a family man, now— She sighed deeply, again chastising herself for allowing her thoughts to constantly turn to a desperado she would never see again.

"Probably not," she answered. "There is nothing left here for me to come back to, Harriet. Your husband wants nothing to do with me, which means he prefers *you* have nothing to do with me. It's all still a sorry mess, and I hope to make life easier for you by leaving. I just thought the Christian thing to do was to come and see my sister before I go. Perhaps you can take supper with me tonight at the hotel."

Harriet nodded. "Yes. I'm sorry, Addy, but I have to abide by my husband. I do have a wonderful life here, you know. Gary and his father own many businesses here in St. Louis. We have a beautiful home, almost a mansion. He won't mind if we go there first so you can see it. He's not home today anyway. We'll take tea there. Then my driver can take you to a hotel and I'll come later for supper."

You've changed so much, Addy thought. She didn't know this sister of hers anymore. All the time she and their mother struggled in Unionville, all the time their mother was dying, there was no word from Harriet. She had only come for their mother's funeral, and she had not brought the children. Their mother had seen her granddaughters only when they were babies. "That will be fine," she answered.

"You're late," Harriet told her. "You were supposed to come a week ago."

"I got held up—literally," Addy answered. "There was a bank robbery. They took me as a hostage."

"What!"

Now Addy had the full attention of not only her sister but also the two girls, who gawked at her in near awe. "I'll tell you all about it when we get to the house. I have some extra newspaper articles about it. I'll give you one to keep."

Harriet looked her over. "Are you all right? Did they—"

"I'm fine. They didn't do me any real harm."

"That looks like a faint bruise on your face, and the way your hat ribbon is tied—" She looked closer. "There are scratches on your other cheek!"

"I'll explain. I really am fine, Harriet. Actually it's been close to two weeks since the day of the robbery. I was returned five days later and I had to rest the next four or five days before getting on the *River Queen* to come here." She wondered what Harriet would think if she told her she had grown rather close to one of the outlaws, and had saved his life.

"That's amazing! You're such a strong woman, Addy. I could never have survived what you have these last few years, let alone being taken off by outlaws! You must tell us all about it."

Addy studied her sister's chubby face, thinking how, in spite of the woman's wealth, she must surely be bored to death. Addy was certain to experience something different and exciting in the next few weeks—traveling alone to a wild mining town.

From then on she answered endless questions, explaining her entire adventure. She put up with a tour of the "mansion," listened to her sister chatter about her wealth, found a hotel room, listened to the night sounds of St. Louis, wondering if she would ever see such a civilized place again. In the morning Harriet's driver brought the family carriage to pick her up and take her back to the docks to board the *Missouri Lady,* which would take her across Missouri to Independence. This time only Harriet came, and when the driver took Addy's luggage on board the riverboat, Addy turned to Harriet, both of them realizing they would not likely see each other again.

"Life is strange, Harriet," Addy said. "We were so happy once."

Harriet nodded. "I have to abide by my husband," she repeated, "and I truly am happy, Addy. I always wanted to be a rich lady."

Addy felt a lump in her throat. "I remember. Father was once moderately wealthy, you know."

Harriet stiffened. "He threw it all away when he joined the Confederacy and he destroyed his family. And *you* had to go and marry a *southern* man on top of it!"

Addy felt a stabbing pain at remembering how it felt to learn Tom was dead. She had never even known where he was buried. Such a short marriage it had been. It all seemed almost unreal now. "I don't want to talk about the war, Harriet. The war is over, and now you can relax in your own life. I'm going to Colorado and you don't have to worry about any of it now. You've chosen the life you want, and I have chosen mine."

Harriet blinked back tears. "You should marry again, Addy."

A gust of wind blew a piece of Addy's auburn hair across her lips. She grabbed her wide-brimmed hat and re-tied the loosening band that was secured under her chin. "Marriage is the last thing on my mind right now. I'll be teaching—something I love—the reason I went all the way to Michigan to school. That's all I care about right now."

Harriet folded her arms, the feathers in her fancy yellow hat rippling in the breeze. "You always were the independent one. I prefer to let a man take care of me."

"Oh, yes, I know. But I prefer to know how to take care of myself if the need arises, and that is certainly my situation now. Oh, I don't mind the thought of falling in love again, but I'm not ready for that right now." Why did the comment make her think of Nick Coleman? "I'd better get on board, Harriet." *I've done my duty coming to see you before I go, for what it was worth.* She felt suddenly and terribly alone. She wanted to grab her sister and cry, but she could see the feelings were not mutual. "Good-bye, Harriet."

"Bye, Addy. Good luck. Write me."

Addy nodded. "I will."

A steam whistle blew loud and long twice, signalling passengers to quickly board. The carriage driver and another man came and got Addy's trunk, and the two sisters just stared at each other a moment longer before Addy turned and walked to the boat. The driver disembarked, tipping his hat to her, and Addy walked the broad plank onto the boat, feeling an overwhelming urge to go to her knees and weep. How many drastic changes in her life could one woman endure without breaking down? The strangest part about this sudden depression was not just her estrangement from her sister, all she'd been through the last few years in Unionville, losing her parents, her husband, all her money . . . it was the finality of it all.

She really was going to do this. She really was going to Colorado and a new life, with no one left who cared about Addy Kane. And for some reason, it still hurt to imagine Nick Coleman also out there alone, trying to bring some kind of order to his life. So many people left alone by the war, trying to start over.

She turned to wave to Harriet, but she was already gone.

Six

Addy studied the information that had been sent to her by the citizens of Central who had hired her. They had sent her a copy of their newspaper, the *Register.* She read about the doings of the more prominent citizens, such as Grant Breckenridge, a metallurgist and manager for Chadwick Mines, based in Chicago. A widower of several years, with a son attending law school, Mr. Breckenridge was also apparently the biggest shareholder in one of the mines at Central. From various articles she read, it was apparently Breckenridge's money that backed many of the efforts at "civilizing" the city of Central such as plans for a Methodist church and a new school. Addy did not doubt that it was Breckenridge's money that was paying her fare.

She smiled at the realization that the *Register* was not just a newspaper but a good place to read the latest gossip. She was becoming anxious to see what Central really was like. She imagined it was quite wild, and worried she was getting herself into something she might regret. As she sat on a bench on the deck of the *Missouri Lady,* she carefully scanned each newspaper, alarmed to read that in 1859 there were still only six women in Central! Apparently, as it became more evident just how rich the gold finds were, the population had boomed, for now there were approximately fifteen thousand permanent residents, still mostly men, but enough women and children to warrant a school.

Still, things continued to be quite untamed. Some of the newspaper articles were complaints from citizens asking that "bawdy houses" be closed, specifically naming a place called the "Hurdy Gurdy," which was located across the street from the newspaper office on Eureka Street. It was called a "dance house," and was declared by the paper to be a public nuisance. Another house of "ill fame," the Hard Luck saloon, was also mentioned. Addy shivered at the thought of any woman selling her body.

There were other articles about gunfights, fist fights, the need for more law and order. Two men had recently been shot during a drunken brawl at a tavern. The same problems apparently presented themselves to Black Hawk, a mining town situated just two miles from Central. Addy found the newspapers so interesting that she read them for a third time, wanting to familiarize herself as thoroughly as possible with life in the strange new land where she was headed. According to one article, the area where the cities of Central and Black Hawk were situated was called "The Richest Square Mile on Earth." Perhaps it was. It certainly had attracted a wild assortment of people, and now with the war over, more would surely go there.

She folded the last newspaper and shoved it into a canvas bag, then rose and walked to the rear of the steamboat, watching the paddle wheel turn lazily, the water splashing rhythmically, almost musically. So far from home. The *Missouri Lady* would reach Independence soon. After a night's stay there she would board a train, the Kansas Pacific, which would take her to a town called Abilene, where, according to the letter from the Education Committee of Central, she must be wary of "cow punchers" who sometimes arrived there in great numbers and usually drank heavily. From Abilene she would ride a stagecoach to Denver and into the mountains through a canyon called Clear Creek Canyon. The letter from the Education Committee had warned her not to be alarmed by the sometimes "harrowing" journey. She was assured that the stage drivers were experienced and reliable. "We hope to some day build a better road and perhaps even a railroad from Denver to our town," the letter had read.

Addy took a deep breath. What was she getting herself into, going to a lawless town where "soiled doves" abounded, as well as gunfights, a place so remotely high in the mountains that it was still difficult to get there by any way but pack mules? She would know no one when she arrived, but there would probably be plenty of women anxious to make friends, since decent women were few in number.

She retrieved her canvas bag and walked up some steps to her cabin, glad that at least those who had sent for her had provided her with very nice accommodations. Even so, traveling alone was not easy. People stared at her often, both men and women. It was unusual to see a woman traveling alone, and she knew she had to be careful. She was an easy target, although after what she had been through in the bank robbery, she supposed nothing much more exciting or fearful could happen to her. Still, she'd had Nick come to her rescue. Where was he now? What path in life would he choose . . . and why did she find it so difficult to stop thinking about him? Their parting had left an ache in her heart, which was made worse by the way she had left her sister, the way Harriet had just pulled away without even a last wave.

Life was so empty, but maybe it wouldn't be that way once she reached Central. She closed her cabin door and locked it, hoping that the Education Committee of Central would be pleased with her once they met her. She would be their first female teacher, something people in many areas still did not accept. If they did not want her to teach after all, she was not sure what she would do, where she would go.

"The seat is wiped off, Ma'am." A Negro train conductor nodded to Addy as she climbed into a passenger car of the Kansas Pacific train that would carry her half way across Kansas. She looked around the car, noticing that nearly everywhere things were stained dark from soot.

"Thank you," she told the conductor, making her way to the

other end of the train. Her baggage had already been loaded, and she was growing weary of travel, yet there was so much ahead of her. The farther she traveled from home, in spite of the bad memories there, the more doubtful she became that she was doing the right thing, although her dream had always been to teach. It was just that her destination was so remote . . . and she was so alone.

Now she realized how foolish she had been to wear yellow today. It was going to be hot, so she had picked her coolest dress, a light weight cotton with short sleeves and a skirt that was only slightly full. It needed only one slip instead of several, and the scoop neckline was cooler than a high collar. She wore a matching yellow bonnet with a wide front brim that kept the sun off her face, as she had been warned by those who had written her that the farther west she went, the more precautions she must take against the sun. The problem was the train was filthy. The windows were open because of the heat, but that only let in more soot from the engine's smokestack.

She sat down carefully on a seat the conductor had promised was clean, deciding to sit against the front wall of the coach with a view of the rest of the train car. She hoped that would help protect her from wind and soot, which were both bound to blow in through the window once they got moving.

The train whistle blew three short toots, and her heart tightened when the conductor shouted "All aboard!" Another step in her journey. The trip by steamboat was over, and it had been lonely, as she had kept to her cabin most of the time because she was traveling by herself. Now there was no place to hide. A few passengers were already seated, and more climbed on. Two men who were apparently traveling together spotted her, and they both grinned, one of them pointing at her.

Addy's heart fell when they approached, obviously deciding to plop down next to her. They both needed a shave and, she suspected, a bath, yet they wore suits, and on one of them, a short, chubby young man, the suit was far too tight. The other man was older, tall and lanky, and his suit was too big in the shoulders, the pants too short. Both apparently felt their clothes made them look respectable and maybe even handsome, and Addy would have laughed if not for the fact that they came to sit beside her, one right next to her, the other in the seat facing her. He was the fat one. "Howdy, ma'am. You travelin' alone?"

Addy felt sick to her stomach. This would be a long train ride. Would these two stick by her side the entire way? They reeked of perspiration, the strong kind that comes from bodies never washed, even before the heat. "I believe that is my business," she answered. "I would like you to choose another seat, please. I do not wish to sit with strangers."

The skinny one beside her nudged her arm. "Well, now, we don't have to *be* strangers, if that's your problem. Where are you headed? We'll jes' kind of watch over you, if you like." His eyes dropped to her chest, and Addy suspected they thought she might be one of those dance hall girls she'd read about, headed west to get rich off men.

"I *don't* like." Addy faced the skinny one, growing angry. "Please sit someplace else. There are several other seats left elsewhere."

The man grinned, showing two teeth missing in front. "We're goin' to Denver, maybe find us some jobs there . . . maybe go on up into one of them gold towns and get rich. You like rich men, do you? Maybe you're one of them war widows who's lonely and goin' off to start a new life."

Addy wanted to cry. This trip was strenuous enough, and she didn't need to put up with this. She started to speak up when the words caught in her throat at the sight of a tall, broad-shouldered man who entered the car at the last minute. Addy just stared, unable to believe her eyes. Nick!

He walked the length of the car, looking for an empty seat. The search led him to her end of the car, and it was only then that he noticed her. Their gaze held for several seconds, both of them feeling a rush of excitement, astonishment, pleasure. "Addy!" he exclaimed.

Addy swallowed, surprised at how her heart rushed at the

sight of him. "Nick, I . . ." She took advantage of the situation. "These men are upsetting me. I prefer that they sit somewhere else, but they insist on sitting here."

Nick quickly caught the hint in her eyes. He glanced at the men, both of whom had lost their smiles at the sight of the big man standing there with a gun on his hip. "I suggest you move," Nick told them. "This woman is a good friend of mine, and I don't like it when someone upsets her."

The two men looked at each other, then the skinny one stood up. "Sure, Mister." He glanced down at Nick's gun. "Ain't there a law against carryin' weapons in Kansas?"

"Not in Abilene, and that's where I'm headed. In the meantime, mind your own business."

Addy smiled inwardly at the sureness of Nick's composure and the sudden nervousness of the two men. She could not help noticing how wonderful Nick looked, wearing clean denim pants that fit his hips fetchingly, a clean red checkered shirt. His hair had been nicely cut, and his handsome face was clean-shaven. She moved her eyes then to the two men Nick was ordering to leave, and she felt guilty for this feeling of joy at seeing Nick Coleman on the same train she was taking.

The skinny man glanced at his partner. "Let's sit someplace else. He moved to another seat farther back, and the heavy-set man followed, glancing at Nick and smiling nervously.

Nick moved his gaze to Addy, and they just stared at each other a moment. "This is a surprise," Nick finally spoke up.

"More for me than you! I thought you were well on your way to Indian Territory. Sit down, Nick."

The train whistle blew again, and the car lurched as the steam engine got underway. Nick took the seat across from Addy, sighing deeply and resting his elbows on his knees. "Obviously I, uh, changed my mind. I guess that little bit you said to me about starting over got me to thinking, and I figured maybe this place called Central was the place to do it. There must be a lot of jobs in a fast-growing town like that." He smiled softly. "And I also figured at least there would be one person there that I know. I felt a little bit obligated to kind of look out for her once I'm there. I just didn't expect to land on the same train on the way. I figured you were way ahead of me."

Addy felt a flush come into her face at the thought that he cared enough to be thinking of her. "It took me a few days to recover in Unionville. Then I visited my sister in St. Louis before leaving. Did you take a riverboat to this point?"

Nick nodded. "Landed just this morning. I decided I'd better not hang around Missouri more than five minutes, considering the reasons I'm leaving in the first place. I got a ticket on the first train headed west."

Addy glanced around at the other passengers, none of whom seemed to be giving Nick any special notice. "You took a chance, Nick."

He shrugged. "Probably. But then I'm dead, remember?"

She watched his blue eyes and nodded. "Yes. That's what I told the authorities."

He leaned a little closer. "Well, since Nick Coleman is dead, I figured I'd better get rid of the name, too. My name is now Cole Parker. Remember that."

Addy nodded. "Cole Parker," she repeated quietly. She shook her head. "This is all so strange. I never dreamed I'd look up and see you standing there like that. I worried and wondered about you, Nick . . . I mean, Cole. How is your shoulder?"

He rotated his left arm. "Pretty good, thanks to a certain excellent nurse."

Addy made a face at the memory. "A terribly amateur job. It's a wonder you can use that arm at all."

Again their gaze held, both of them experiencing feelings of joy and wonder, and both of them fighting stronger feelings, thinking it was impossible to feel this way. She was a proper lady, headed to a school teaching job; he was a desperado. No matter how straight he went now, he would always have once been an outlaw. Addy fought a ridiculous urge to hug him, for the loneliness of the journey had set deeply in her soul. To see even one person she knew, even though he was a bank robber and had killed a man in front of her eyes, brought great relief. Now the trip would not be so lonely. Nick would be with her the whole way. She reminded herself then that she must not call him Nick. His name was Cole . . . Cole. "I'm glad you changed your mind, Cole. It's time for a lot of people to put the past behind them."

He nodded. "It's not always very easy, especially when it comes to visit you in the night."

She saw the agony in his blue eyes. "I know. Maybe with time, and by starting a new life in a new land, the dreams will go away."

He looked down at his hands. "Maybe. You know, you're the only one I ever told all the details to about what happened." He met her eyes again. "I don't know why. You're just easy to talk to, I guess." He leaned back in his seat. "I don't know. This whole thing has been kind of strange and ironic, hasn't it?"

"Sometimes fate leads us into strange situations," Addy answered. "I have to admit I'm glad it led you to this train. I was not looking forward to making this entire journey alone. There are apparently places farther west where it isn't wise for a woman to be caught on her own. I have some newspaper articles about Central, by the way." She reached over and picked up the canvas bag where she carried the papers and took one out. "You can read about this place we're going to." She handed it over, but Nick took it hesitantly.

"I, uh, I don't read very good. My father took me out of school at a young age to help on the farm. I kept that farm going for a lot of years, even after my folks died."

"Read what you can. Maybe I can read some of the articles to you if and when we reach someplace quiet." She frowned. "Your parents must have been young when they died."

The passenger car rattled and clacked, rocking back and forth as the train developed speed. Prairieland passed by quickly, and a hot wind and sooty smoke began filtering in through the windows. People began wiping their faces with handkerchiefs, and Nick squinted. "They died a year apart from each other. My father just collapsed. Heart attack, the doctor figured. My mother died from congested lungs. Her parents were already dead, but both my father's parents were alive. They had come over here from Ireland. My grandfather and father were both big and dark-haired like me. Those are the grandparents I was living with when the Union rabble attacked our farm. My grandparents were good people. Losing them along with my little girl just made the hatred inside me burn that much hotter." He adjusted his hat. "What about your folks, your husband? I'm not so sure you gave me the full details."

Addy felt the old hurt. "I told you most of it. I met my husband in college. He had just graduated." She looked down and toyed with a piece of lace on her dress. "We were married just a short time before he went off to war. It seems like such a long, long time ago now."

"How was the visit with your sister?"

Addy smiled sadly. "Not much of a visit at all. Her wealthy Union man refused to let me stay at their house. When our mother was alive, he wouldn't let Harriet have anything to do with her. The only time I saw her during those years was when she came down for Mother's funeral." She shook her head. "I hardly know Harriet any more. She's very cold and distant."

The train whistle blew again, and Nick looked out the window to see a herd of cattle not far away. "That's too bad. We both have a lot in common, I guess, losing all our family, leaving home and memories behind."

Addy's eyes teared. "Yes. I was very happy once. You were, too."

Nick nodded, and again Addy reminded herself she must think of him as Cole. He pulled a thin cigar from his shirt pocket. "Do you mind?"

Addy looked down and brushed at the soot on her dress which only smeared. "Why should I? This whole car is filling up with dust and soot."

Cole lit the smoke and took several puffs as he watched the passing scenery out the window. Addy studied the clean lines of his face, a straight nose, full lips, high cheekbones. He wore a new wide-brimmed hat, and she smiled inwardly when she realized it was probably purchased with money from Howard Benedict's bank.

"We'll probably see some buffalo farther on." Cole turned to look at her, and she was embarrassed that he had caught her staring at him. "Probably some Indians once we take the stage-coach."

"Indians! I never thought of that."

He nodded thoughtfully. "They're a little restless right now, I hear. During the war they did a lot of raiding. The army didn't have enough men to fill their forts out west and protect things. I expect the coach line knows the safest route to take, so I wouldn't worry too much. Besides, I imagine there will be more people going west again now that the war is over."

Their eyes held on the words. *Now that the war is over.* That war still raged in some peoples' hearts. Bitter, bitter memories. A scarred forehead and an arm covered with burn scars, a little girl buried on a farm somewhere in Kentucky, a dead husband buried in an unknown grave.

"I never asked you where your sympathy really lies," Cole said. "Your husband and father fought for the Confederacy. How about you?"

Addy thought a moment. "I would have to say the Union. I never thought it was right to try to divide the United States."

Cole slowly nodded. "Neither did I. I only chose the Confederacy because of what happened to my family at the hands of raiders who called themselves Union sympathizers."

Addy was startled to feel sudden desire move through her when she looked deeply into Cole Parker's eyes. It was a sweeping pull at her insides that she had not felt in years. She reminded herself that in spite of his good looks, this man had lived the life of an outlaw, running with men like Jack Slater, hating, robbing, killing. He also apparently liked his whiskey, used it to bury bad memories. He was a very unsettled man, who might turn to someone for all the wrong reasons, the kind of man a woman had to be wary of. His eyes moved to glance at her breasts, and just the look made her tingle all over. It was not difficult to judge his thoughts, considering the fact that part of his attraction to her was because she looked like his first wife.

To have to be close to Cole Parker for the several-hundred-mile journey ahead could stir feelings better left buried. He was too undependable, and she was on her way to teach school. Such a position brought with it special rules. Female school teachers were expected to be proper ladies who, if they were even allowed to associate with men, must choose only the most respectable kind. She reminded herself that she had been through too much to allow any special feelings for any man right now. She didn't know her own heart, and loneliness sometimes caused a person to make unwise decisions.

She folded her hands primly over her lap. "I'm glad you happened to get on this train," she told him, glancing at his gun. "At least I know I'll be safe. How did you learn to draw a gun so fast, like the night you shot Jack?"

He shrugged. "When you decide to live by the gun, you figure you'd better know how to use it well. I was already a good shot with a rifle—did a lot of hunting back home, was a sharpshooter in the army. It just came kind of naturally, I guess." He leaned back in his seat, his knees nearly touching her own because of his long legs. "Mind if I put my feet up on the seat next to you?"

"No. I don't mind."

He moved his booted feet onto the seat, then tipped his hat forward a little over his eyes to relax, still puffing on the thin cigar. Addy, too, put her head back to try to rest, but she could not shake the pleasant feeling deep inside at being close to this man again, the relief she felt to have him along, the worry she felt over how awkward that closeness might become before this journey was over.

Seven

The train rumbled over open country, wide, flat land with few trees. Addy and Cole, both accustomed to hilly, forested country, were amazed at how the land began to flatten out, until in some places it seemed a man could see forever. Here and there they passed a farm, most of them rather sad looking, omens of a harsh life in a harsh land.

The train stopped a few times, and people had only minutes to clamor off and find the train station privies, leaving even less time to grab some food at eateries set up along the way. Meals were usually nothing more than a piece of meat and a stale biscuit, the prices outrageous. With every passing mile Addy wondered more and more if she had made the right choice. It seemed that every little town they passed was more primitive than the last, dustier, lonelier. More than once the engineer stopped the train to allow cattle to meander over the tracks, hundreds, sometimes thousands of them herded along by whistling, shouting "cowpunchers," the conductor called them. They looked wild and unkempt, but Addy could see by Cole's eyes that he was wondering what such work might be like. He would fit right in with men like that, and Addy half expected him to leave the train and go join them at times, but he remained sitting near her, apparently determined to go all the way to Central.

It took three days to reach Abilene, and each day grew hotter than the last. Cole grew strangely quiet, and Addy suspected it was for the same reason she also spoke little. Perhaps it was not wise to allow themselves to get too close. They were, after all, as different as night and day. Not only that, neither of them was emotionally ready to get too close. If not for the bank robbery, they would never have known each other at all; and after that first·strange meeting at the bank in Unionville, counting the days at the cabin and the time spent on this train, they had known each other a grand total of six days.

Six days. Why then, Addy wondered, did she feel this odd closeness to the man? Perhaps it was just a matter of fear and loneliness. She found herself hoping Cole Parker would stick to his decision to go all the way to Colorado. There they could go their separate ways, each finding his and her own answers to what their futures held for them. She could already feel the friendly acceptance of the committee in Central who had hired her, and it felt good to be going off to a respectable job for which she would be well paid. Apparently in gold towns money was no object. She would be given free room and board, and was being paid nearly twice what a school teacher would make in the East.

"We's approachin' Abilene," the conductor announced. "End of the line for the Kansas Pacific, folks, but one day these tracks will go all the way to Denver."

Addy looked at Cole, who sat two seats down from her but facing her. He had decided not to sit next to her all the time, afraid of what people might think, since she was traveling alone. Addy suspected it was partly because he wanted to remain removed emotionally, and she was grateful. She wanted the same.

The steam whistle let off several loud blasts as the train rattled and chugged into Abilene, which did not look much different from other dusty towns through which they had passed, except that it seemed a little bigger. As in the other towns, the streets were mere dirt, with piles of horse manure scattered here and there. Addy curled her nose at the smell, not just of horses, but large pens of cattle. She could see them from her window now, hundreds of them, maybe thousands. The intense heat of the day only accentuated the odor of what she figured had to be tons of manure, and she hoped that it was not going to be like this all the way to Central. At least the city was in the mountains. There would be no cattle there, and she had read they had even bricked some of their streets.

The train finally came to a halt, and Addy rose, feeling filthy, embarrassed at how she must look. She dabbed at the perspiration on her face with a handkerchief, noticing the hanky looked dirty when she took it away. She had taken every opportunity to wash the soot from her face at every stop, yet it covered her again, and she supposed she was only smearing it when she tried to wipe at the sweat.

"I must look a mess," she told Cole when she reached his seat.

He stood up behind her and followed her out of the car. "No worse than anybody else," he answered. "Looks to me like it's no better out there in the streets than it is inside. There's nothing but dirt everyplace you go in these parts."

They disembarked the train car, and Cole pushed back his hat a little. "You need some help getting your things to a hotel and all?" He looked around. "If there's a decent place for a woman to stay in this town."

"Perhaps you could find someone with a wagon who might haul my trunks and baggage for me. I'll be fine on my own after that."

Cole caught the meaning in the words. Don't get too close. It wouldn't look right, a man showing her to a hotel room. There were more reasons not to get too close, and he damn well knew it. It had been hell traveling with her these last three days, having to watch her, that face that was pretty even with soot smudged on it, those green eyes. She seemed so alone, and he wanted to hold her, wanted to relieve his own loneliness. "I'll unload my horse and gear and then find somebody for you. Just stay here on the station platform beside your baggage."

He left, and Addy watched him walk to a car toward the rear of the train. Men like Cole Parker fit out here. He was unaffected by all the dirt and the lawless atmosphere. She figured he was probably growing excited about going to a new place, totally confident in his ability to take care of himself. Men like Cole could go anyplace in the world and have nothing to fear.

Only three other women were on the train, and two of them were apparently traveling with husbands. Perhaps they were all related, as they disembarked together, and the two women stood talking while the men began seeing to their baggage. Addy wondered if they were all going farther west like herself. The third woman exited the train, and Addy thought she dressed rather brazenly, wearing dresses cut much too low, although the dresses themselves were well made, with matching hats and parasols. She had traveled here from Independence with a heavy-set man who always wore a suit and hat, but the woman wore no wedding ring. She and the man with her exchanged words, and the man nodded and headed for the baggage car. The woman, who Addy guessed was about her same age, strolled toward her. She had a confident, rather hard look to her, and she looked Addy over as she approached. "Hello."

Addy nodded. "Hello."

The woman looked down at Addy's hands. "I can't help wondering. You're apparently a widow, since you wear a wedding ring on your right hand."

"Yes," Addy answered. "Why do you ask?"

The woman shrugged. "I just wondered if maybe you're here for the same reason I am. You're very pretty. We could open our own place together."

Addy frowned. "Our own place? Doing what?"

The woman snickered. "I guess maybe I was wrong."

"I don't understand. I'm headed for the city of Central, Colorado, to teach school. What business are you in that you thought I could join?"

The woman opened her parasol to protect her face from the sun. "You're apparently well educated in book learning, ma'am, but not so much in the ways of the world." She leaned a little closer. "I'll tell you one thing. I'll make a whole lot more money than any schoolteacher can make. Any time you want to join me, I'll be here in Abilene. Any town that's full of lonely men wanting some excitement after seeing nothing but the rear ends of cattle for weeks at a time is the place for women like me." She smiled then. "Name's Darla Simms." She looked around. "How about that big, handsome guy who's been sitting with you part of the way out here? He mean anything to you?"

Addy thought a moment, and realized what this woman was trying to tell her. She was a prostitute, come to Abilene to sell herself to men! "I . . . Cole is just a friend." Why did she feel this ridiculous jealousy over this woman's interest in Cole? "I really don't even know him all that well."

Darla snickered. "The way you look at each other sometimes, one has to wonder. Is he going on to Central, too?"

Addy looked away, wishing this woman would leave. She really did not care to be seen consorting with a prostitute, especially in a town full of men. "I'm not sure, and it really isn't my business."

Darla's eyebrows arched. "Nor mine, you're saying. But then what isn't one person's business might be important to another. Sorry if I offended you, Mrs. . . . what's your name?"

Addy stepped a little farther away. "Addy Kane."

"Well, have a good trip, Addy Kane. How long before you hop a coach to Denver?"

"A couple of days, I believe."

"Through Indian country. No thanks. I'll stay here in Abilene. Sorry if I've made you uncomfortable. Good luck in Colorado." The woman left, and Addy watched her, noticing then that Cole was walking toward her, leading his horse. Before he could reach her, Darla Simms sauntered his way, stopping him. Addy could not hear what was being said, except that Darla pointed to a building not far down the street. She seemed to be indicating a place called the Roundup Saloon. Addy struggled with burning aggravation to think the woman would come up to her and suggest she might be here as a prostitute, then turn around and offer herself to Cole right in front of her.

Cole looked toward the saloon and grinned. Whatever was said, Darla laughed and flirtingly pressed her hand against Cole's chest, then waved as she strolled away. Cole watched after her for a moment, then came toward Addy, who struggled with feelings of anger, feelings she knew she had no right experiencing. Cole Parker was a man free to do whatever he pleased. He had probably consorted with plenty of prostitutes, and she already knew he liked his whiskey. He was a man with any man's desires. Of course he would be interested in women like Darla, certainly interested in the best place to go for a drink later this evening. She had no right caring what the man did with his spare time.

"Hold my horse and I'll get your baggage," he told her as he approached. "Just take the reins. When did you say the stagecoach leaves for Denver?"

Addy forced back her unwarranted jealousy and anger, hoping it did not show in her eyes. "According to the schedule they sent me, if I got here by June eighteenth, the coach for Denver would leave on the twentieth. They don't head there every day. Some go south to Texas and New Mexico, some to Indian Territory."

His eyebrows arched, and he looked to the south. Would he still change his mind and head for outlaw country?

"Others go north to Nebraska. At any rate, as soon as I get settled I'll check at the stage station. If you're going on to Central, you'd better check also."

Cole sighed, turning and looking toward the Roundup Saloon. Addy could hear the tinkle of piano music coming from more than one direction, the distant laughter of men and women. Wagons and horses moved busily back and forth, stirring up dust that carried with it the smell of manure. "I don't know for certain what I'll do from here. I'm not so sure about going on to Central. I might just stay right here in Abilene and see what's up. But I'll check anyway."

Addy felt her heart fall a little. Not go on? He was letting her finish this harrowing trip alone? But then why shouldn't he? What obligation did he have to her from here on, or ever had? He had boarded the same train out of Independence by accident, not because he intended to travel with her and watch over her.

She had no right expecting him to continue to Central at exactly the same time as she, yet she had counted on him doing so. Being near him made her feel safe, protected. She reminded herself this man had been a loner for years, that he had no idea what he wanted to do with his life now. He had said he'd go to Central, keep an eye out for her, but men like Cole could not be depended upon.

"Fine," she answered. "If you will just find someone who can take my things to a hotel or rooming house, you can go off on your own and do as you please."

Cole caught the irritation in her voice. Inwardly he knew she had expected him to stay with her all the way, but it was just too hard. For too many reasons they couldn't make any more of this friendship than there already was, and it was best she went on to Central City alone and he did something else. He hated the idea of allowing her to travel through Indian country without protection, but then the stagecoaches surely wouldn't be running at all if there was that much danger. "I'm sorry if I've upset you," he told her.

Addy put on a show of unconcern. "Not at all. We both know this has been a strange friendship from the very beginning. Neither of us has an obligation to the other, and considering how this all started, we shouldn't even be speaking to each other. I appreciate your getting rid of those men when I first boarded at Independence, and I enjoyed the conversations we've had on the way here." Why did she feel even more alone than when she first left Unionville? It angered her to feel this terrible, unnecessary disappointment. "I just hope you find whatever you're looking for, Cole, and that it will be something honorable, perhaps working for a cattle rancher or something, anything but going back to running with men like Jack Slater."

He grasped her wrist gently, putting his horse's reins in her hand, which he held for a moment. "I hope you find what you're looking for, too, Addy. Hang on to Shadow. I'll get your things."

He turned and left, and Addy felt a ridiculous urge to cry. She blinked back the tears and swallowed, taking a deep breath to gather her composure. From then on she managed to remain aloof to her feelings as Cole brought her baggage, then went back to get her trunk and carried it on his shoulder over to where she stood. He hailed down a man driving an empty wagon past the depot, and when the man saw the pretty woman who needed help, he gladly offered to take her things to a building that simply read HOTEL across the front. Addy looked back at Cole, who waved, then walked with Shadow toward the Roundup.

It was early evening when Addy awoke from a deep sleep. The hot, monotonous train ride to Abilene had worn her out, but then she was sure part of that weariness was her own nerves, the trying times of the past three weeks piled on top of her mixed emotions over Cole Parker, who to her would always be Nick Coleman.

She sighed and sat up. Her tiny hotel room felt hot and stuffy. She walked over to open a window wider, and the sounds of a town that awoke at night hit her ears: the laughter of men and women having a good time; lively piano music coming from taverns; now and then a woman's good-natured scream; men riding up and down the streets, shouting at each other, sometimes in jesture, sometimes in challenge.

Cole was out there somewhere, a man who fit right in with the wild night life of a cattle town. He was probably drinking whiskey, gambling . . . or maybe he was with Darla. The thought pierced her heart like a sword, but for the life of her she could not imagine why. She had no reason to have any feelings for the man or to care who he was with. She was only disappointed that he had left her so suddenly and changed his mind about continuing on.

She turned away from the window and walked over to a wash stand, stripping off all her clothes and pouring some fresh water from a pitcher into the bowl. She washed all over, and it felt good to get the soot off her face. She wished she could wash her hair, but at least she had worn it wrapped on top of her head and covered with hats. It wasn't very dirty, except that she had perspired from the heat. Perhaps she could find a bath house in the morning and pay some woman to wash it for her before she began the next stage of her journey by coach across the plains of Colorado. She did not doubt that there would be little opportunity to wash again until she reached Denver.

Everything out here was so different from anything she had known before—rugged, dusty towns with no churches, no law, thick smells that stung a person's nose, women like Darla Simms strolling about casually, men walking around with guns strapped to their hips. She pulled on clean underwear, then her slips and a clean dress. She had meant to check at the stage station before going to sleep, but the moment she had sat down on the bed it had been too tempting to close her eyes just for a moment. That moment had turned into hours. She wanted to be sure she did not miss the next stage to Denver, so she donned a hat, put a handkerchief and a little money into a handbag and left, needing no outer garment. It was much too warm for that.

She took a deep breath for courage, considering how wild the street had become, and she left her room, going down a narrow staircase, every step creaking. The steps led to a wider landing in the lobby, then a few more steps to the door. "You going out, ma'am?" the man at the front desk asked her.

"Just to the stage station. I'll be right back."

"You be careful now. It's no place for a proper lady out there at night."

"I'll be careful." Addy went out, glad the station was only about a half block away on the other side of the street. She hurried across the street, and two men who rode by on horseback whistled, asking her at which saloon she was employed. Addy ignored them, practically running to the station. There was a light on inside and an old man standing behind a desk, so she went inside, relieved to know someone was still around. The old man's eyes lit up when she entered.

"Well now, ma'am, what can I do for the pretty lady? You're a traveler, I take it, not one of the gals from the saloons."

Addy was already getting tired of being taken for a prostitute. Apparently decent women were a rarity in this town. She envied the other two ladies who had gotten off the train earlier and were staying at the same hotel as she. At least they were with their husbands. She straightened, reminding herself she had been taking care of herself for some time now and could damn well keep doing it. Maybe she would buy herself a small handgun before she left Abilene.

"No, I do not work in a saloon, sir. I happen to be a schoolteacher headed for Colorado. I was just checking to see if the stage headed there will still be leaving day after tomorrow."

The man adjusted a pair of spectacles and picked up a clip board to study a schedule. He shook his head. "Nope. Leaves tomorrow afternoon."

"Tomorrow! But the schedule I was sent—"

"Schedules get changed, ma'am. You plan to be on the stage?"

"Well, I, I had hoped to have one more day to rest. I'm sure it is not a very comfortable journey."

The man grinned, shaking his head. "Sure ain't. I used to drive it. I'm lucky to still be alive." He chuckled. "Well, I'll put you down. You're lucky you came and told me. That makes us full up. If somebody else had come here before you, you'd have to ride up top with the baggage or wait for the next stage."

Addy breathed a sigh of relief. "Well, I'm glad for that much. How serious is the danger of Indians?"

The man shrugged. "That's always a danger. Fact of life. I need your name."

Addy spelled it out for him, "Adrianne Rawlins Kane. Could you tell me, did someone by the name of Cole Parker sign up earlier today to go along?"

The man studied the roster. "Nope. I don't see that name."

Addy's heart fell. If Cole hadn't signed up to go along by now, there wouldn't be room for him, which would be all the remaining push he would need to stay on here in Abilene. "Thank you," she answered. "What time should I be here?"

"Two o'clock. If you need help with baggage, I've got men who'll come and carry it for you."

"Yes. I have a trunk someone will have to carry. It's not large, but too awkward for me to bring. I'm at the hotel across the street, Room 6."

"I'll send them over about one-thirty."

"Fine." Addy turned to leave, and a tall, broad figure filled the doorway. "Cole." She struggled not to look excited. "You're too late for the stage. It's leaving tomorrow instead of the next day and it's filled." He looked wonderful, clean clothes, bathed and shaved. He wore a black, wide-brimmed hat, black pants that fit his hips snugly, a white shirt with a black string tie. He had the ever-present gun on his hip, and his blue eyes studied her intently.

"I didn't come here for that. I went to the hotel to talk to you. The man at the desk said you had come here."

Addy stepped closer. "You must have found a bathhouse."

Cole grinned and nodded. "A man has to wash off the dust once in a while."

Addy caught the light scent of whiskey on his breath. Had he been with the woman called Darla? Was that why he had bathed? Maybe Darla had bathed him herself. She looked away to hide her jealousy. "I have to go back to my room. This town is no place for decent women at night. What did you want?"

Cole glanced at the old man, who was peering at them over his spectacles. He took hold of Addy's arm and led her outside. "For one thing, you shouldn't be walking around these streets at night. For another, you must be hungry. I thought I'd take you to a respectable eatery for supper, maybe a little wine, kind of a good-bye dinner, you might say."

Why did the words hurt? "I thought we already said our good-byes."

"Maybe so, but you have to eat, and you can't be wandering around this town alone. I got to thinking about it and was worried about you."

Addy shook her head. "Considering how we first met, that's quite funny."

Cole chuckled. "I suppose. What do you say? Can I buy your supper with Benedict money?"

The remark made her grin. "Yes. That would be nice."

Cole took her arm. "Just down here on the right. Someone told me this place up here called Swanson's Eatery has good steaks. Lord knows there shouldn't be a shortage of beef in this town." They reached a dark alley, and Cole stopped, gently pushing her into the shadows. "Addy, I'm sorry if I've disappointed you. I just think it's best this way."

Why did he look even more handsome in the moonlight? She shook away the thought. And he was right. It *was* best this way, a last meal, a good-bye, each one going their separate way. "I know."

Their eyes held in the soft light, and for a moment Addy thought he was going to try to kiss her. She prepared herself to ward him off, but then he just sighed. "Let's go eat. I'll walk you back to your hotel afterwards."

Addy jumped when two men shot their guns into the air in drunken celebration about something. Cole put a hand to her waist reassuringly, and she shivered at the familiar touch. "I suppose you fit right in here in Abilene," she commented.

"I suppose. I spent most of the afternoon playing cards, after visiting the bath house." Cole led her into the eatery, which was small but quite pleasant for such an unruly town. Cole bought her the best meal in the house, along with red wine, which Addy at first refused but then decided would relax her for a good night's sleep, which she would need before beginning her journey tomorrow.

Their conversation was sparse, both of them enjoying the best food they had had in days. The wine was so relaxing that Addy drank more than she should. It felt wonderful to forget all her troubles and loneliness . . . forget for a little while that after tonight she would never see Cole Parker again. Cole paid for the meals and took her arm, leading her outside and across the

street, pulling her out of the way of a drunken cowhand on a
runaway horse.

Why did she feel so tired? Addy was sure all the pressures
of the last several weeks had come to consume her in a fit of
weakness that made her lean on Cole. The wine. She should not
have drunk so much of it. Everything seemed so unreal. What
was Addy Kane doing in a town like Abilene, Kansas, getting
ready to board a stagecoach to a remote mining town in the
Rocky Mountains? How could someone's life have changed so
drastically? It seemed only yesterday she was a young college
student in Michigan, then a new young wife . . . then suddenly
a widow caught up in the painful emotions of a civil war . . . a
woman caught in a bank robbery . . . a hostage! How strange
life had been these last few years, months, weeks.

Who was Addy Kane? She hardly knew her now. The sensible
Addy Kane would not be hanging on the arm of an outlaw who'd
been drinking and gambling. She would not let him help her up
to a hotel room this way . . . or let him inside. She heard the
door close. Too much wine! Too much wine! Someone turned
up an oil lamp, just enough to shed soft light in the room.

"Addy," she heard Cole say softly. "I don't want to leave you
tonight."

She felt her breasts pressed against a hard chest, felt strong
hands pressing at her lower back. She looked up into a handsome
face. "Then don't leave," she heard someone answer.

The handsome face leaned closer, and full lips touched her
mouth, parting her own lips in a searching, intimate kiss that
set her insides on fire.

Eight

Deep, so deep Addy fell under a strange spell she could not fight. She felt she could almost hear voices shouting at her to stop, but there was no stopping this. A deep hunger from long-neglected needs raged deep inside of her, and it took only one kiss to awaken that hunger, which was made more painful by a desperate loneliness that made her reach out to this forbidden man.

This was Nick Coleman, alias Cole Parker, an outlaw, a man who would be wanted in Illinois and Missouri, if they knew he was alive, a man who drank too much whiskey and consorted with thieves, murderers and whores. Perhaps he only wanted her because he'd drunk too much whiskey, or he simply had gone too long without a woman, or just because she looked like the wife he'd lost to death . . . and because he was himself reaching out in aching loneliness. Surely they needed each other for all the wrong reasons.

So why didn't she stop him? Why didn't she push him away? Tomorrow they would part ways and probably never see each other again; but he kissed her as no other man had ever kissed her, including her own husband. She and Tom had been so young, so new at the art of making love. But Cole Parker knew all the right moves, and for years she had longed to be a woman again.

Yes, Cole Parker was his name now. He was a new man, changed. She wanted to believe that. His kisses were sweet, hot, soft, searching. He made her want to open her mouth in return, to taste his lips, his tongue. She had never kissed this way before. She felt herself being carried to her bed. It was hot, so hot, but it didn't matter. Cole lay beside her, running a big, strong hand over her belly, her breasts, setting her on fire and turning up the heat even more.

"I need you, Addy," he groaned. "Please let me be inside you."

He did not say "I love you." Why didn't she care? She couldn't even say the words back to him, yet her own need was the same. "And I *need* you inside of me," she whispered.

Could she possibly have said such a thing to a man she'd known such a short time, a man with his reputation? She felt her clothes coming off, and she ached to be naked, touched, invaded. She tore anxiously at Cole's shirt. He sat up and removed it, his boots, gunbelt, pants, longjohns. Addy sucked in her breath at the sight of him, his shaft swollen with need. He was a damn fine-looking man, slim hips, flat stomach, broad chest with just enough hair to accent his virility without being offensive.

He came closer. There was the scar at his left shoulder where she'd taken a bullet out of him. She hardly noticed the burn scars on his right arm. They did little to detract from the hard masculinity of the man, the handsome face, square jaw, full lips, the blue eyes that melted all her defenses, the dark, wavy hair, little pieces of it now dangling around his face and forehead, hiding another scar there . . . a scar from the war . . . from the day his whole life was changed forever.

She hadn't even bothered to notice the scar on his leg from that same war. How could she be so brazen? Those blue eyes were raking her naked body. Now his big hands were touching her at the knees, running along her thighs, gently pulling her legs apart. "God, you're beautiful, Addy," he said softly. He moved between her legs, ran his hands up her ribs, massaged her breasts, toyed with her nipples until she groaned. He leaned down then, taking one breast into his mouth hungrily, pulling at it until she felt insane with the need of him.

She gasped then when suddenly his hot shaft slid deep inside of her, filling her to glorious ecstasy, satisfying a hunger long neglected. She arched up to him in total abandon, and in only moments she felt an almost agonizing climax that made her dig her fingers into his muscled arms and cry out his name. "Cole! Oh, Cole, don't stop!"

He came closer, moving his hands under her bottom and grasping it as he moved rhythmically, surging deep, groaning her name in return as he kissed and licked at her neck, her mouth, then stretching out flat so that her face came only to his shoulders. She groaned, licking at his salty skin, surprised she wanted to do these things. She had never been so wanton with Tom.

Finally he raised up, grasping her hips and pulling her to him as he rammed into her almost violently before finally his own release came. He held himself there for several seconds, then remained inside of her as he came closer again, resting his elbows on either side of her. "Stay right there," he told her softly, before kissing her wildly again.

There it came. She felt him swelling inside of her again. He would continue the sweet, rhythmic fulfillment, and she didn't even mind. She ran her hands over his shoulders, to his face, touched his lips. She opened her eyes, looked straight into his. Wrong, so wrong. They both knew it, but their bodies would not obey the mind's common sense.

The night swirled with lovemaking, touches, kisses. With Tom there had only been kisses and intercourse. With Cole Parker it was kisses so deep that a woman couldn't think, more kisses along her body, her breasts, her thighs, secret places her own first husband had not touched this way. And the way he had of using his hands, so gentle for such a big man, exploring, touching that magical spot in light, circular motions that made her ache for more.

Addy remembered getting up a couple of times to wash, but

it had all been like a dream, and she had climbed right back into bed with Cole, neither of them aware of the heat from the outside air, only the heat from their own bodies. The dark of night settled upon them, and sometime during the night they fell asleep holding each other, each of them needing to be held, longing for just one night not to have to sleep alone.

Dawn snuck up on them, and before Addy could come to her senses, Cole was gently rubbing the insides of her thighs, his mouth covering her own, then moving to her neck, her shoulder, her breasts, savoring, groaning her name. "You're the most beautiful woman I've ever met," he told her, "even prettier than Bethanne."

A little voice told her he was only pretending she was someone else . . . another voice warned her that perhaps he said those same words to every woman, even the whores. "Cole," she started to protest. She didn't finish the sentence. A thrilling shiver moved through her when his blue eyes raked her nakedness in the morning light, and when she realized few men could match Cole Parker in bed. He knew every right touch, and before she realized what was happening, he surged inside of her again, filling her deep and hard, again awakening long-buried needs and wiping away all protest. She raised her hips to meet him, and she clung to his powerful forearms. For several more minutes they enjoyed the pleasures of being one, coming together in sweet passion, savoring the ecstasy of having long-felt needs satisfied.

Addy could not understand what had happened to her. She had taken this man with wild desire and wanton abandon, as hungry and wicked as any prostitute, she supposed. This was so wrong! He had not even said he loved her, and although somewhere deep inside she knew she was herself falling in love, she could not bring herself to say the words; not just because Cole had not said them, but also because she could not believe it was proper to love such a man.

So, what was she doing in bed with him? With one last thrust he pushed deep, groaned when he found his release. A brighter morning light and the sound of a waking town in the street below brought Addy back to reality, and as soon as Cole moved off of her she turned on her side, feeling sick with guilt and shame. She pulled a blanket over her nakedness and lay there trying to gather her thoughts, and when Cole moved beside her and put an arm around her, she asked him to take it away.

"You planned this, didn't you? You knew if I drank all that wine I'd be vulnerable." She covered her face and groaned. "My God, what have I done?"

Cole rolled onto his back and sighed deeply. "I didn't plan anything. I just wanted to take you for a nice meal before we parted ways. I didn't know wine made you so tipsy."

"I seldom drink."

Cole rubbed at his eyes. "All I did was help you to your room. I didn't want you to get in any trouble out in the streets, and when we reached the stairs you didn't seem too steady on your feet. When I got you into the room . . ." He turned and touched her shoulder, but she jerked it away. "I didn't mean to take advantage of anything, Addy. We both had a need, and that's all right."

"No, it isn't!" Addy sat up, keeping her back to him, vividly remembering all the things she had allowed him to do last night, brazenly allowing him to explore private places even Tom had not invaded so intimately. "I have never behaved so shamefully, let alone with a man I still hardly know. You don't even know what you want to do with yourself now, and I don't suppose you can even say that you love me."

Cole thought about the words, wanted to say them for her sake. He suspected love was what he truly felt for Addy Kane . . . or did he just want her to be Bethanne? He knew Addy needed to hear him tell her he loved her, in order to feel better about what they had done last night and this morning; yet he could not bring himself to say it. He had no right loving her, was not worthy of someone like Addy Kane, not anymore, nor was he sure his emotional wounds were healed enough to make such a commitment.

"Just as I thought," Addy said, wrapping a blanket around herself as she rose.

"Addy—"

"You used me, took advantage of my own loneliness, the wine . . ."

"And you didn't take advantage of me?"

Addy blushed, realizing her own desires had been great. She remembered now. He had said he needed to be inside of her, and she had answered that she needed him in return. "I've never drunk that much wine before. I wasn't myself. I hope you don't think I've ever done this with anyone else since Tom died. I haven't. And if I didn't feel so out of touch with my true feelings, confused and lost by this trip, last night would never have happened."

Cole felt his own heart fall a little. He had half hoped to hear her say she loved him, even though he couldn't reply the same . . . not yet . . . or could he? "Addy, I didn't just use you for my pleasure. I was lonely. I wanted to hold someone and be held in return. I think you wanted the same."

Addy's thoughts raced with the shame of it. Had she really been that lost and lonely? "I always thought I was much stronger than that. I am disappointed in myself, ashamed of myself. And no matter what you say, I can't believe you didn't plan all of this. You had already been drinking, maybe even plotting with that—that Darla—how you could get me into bed." She let out a little gasp, whirling to face him. "Dear God! You didn't—you hadn't already slept with her, had you?"

Cole shook his head, his own anger rising. "Hell no! The woman wanted to do business with me, but I left to find you. I *told* you, all I wanted was to come and see you, take you to eat someplace. I didn't plan any of this, Addy. You have to believe that. It just . . . happened. I don't know how to explain it."

"I do! You had a need, and if it hadn't been me, it would have been Darla Simms! I was nothing more than a prostitute to you, and I—" Her eyes teared, and she turned away again, covering her face with one hand while she held up the blanket with the other. "I *feel* like a prostitute! In my whole life I never would have dreamed I could do such a thing, and with an *outlaw!* Do you know what the rules are for school teachers? They're supposed to be the epitome of proper morals. They're supposed to conduct themselves—"

"Who the hell in Colorado is going to know what happened between us?" Cole interrupted. "Who the hell in this town even knows, or cares? Do you think I'm going to run to your damn education committee, or whoever, and tell them I slept with you? Hell, I'm not even going there!" He threw back his covers and walked to the washpan to clean himself.

Addy turned to say something, saw his nakedness and turned away again. After last night, why was it suddenly embarrassing for her to look at him? "What . . . what are you doing?"

"I'm getting dressed so I can get out of here!" he answered angrily.

Addy heard him moving around, the sound of him pulling on clothes. *I want you to stay,* a little voice inside longed to shout. *I want you to hold me once more, tell me you love me. I want to at least still be friends.* She had insulted him when she said she couldn't believe she'd done such a thing with an outlaw. Yes, he had been one, but for reasons anyone could understand. Yet she had said it as though he were something repulsive, and perhaps the way she had said it would only drive him right back into that life at a time when he might have been helped out of it. The man was lonely, confused. Perhaps it might even have helped to tell him she loved him. But then how could she say that yet? Such things took time, and they had had no time at all. Now he was leaving. After today she wouldn't see him again, yet she had spent a night more intimate than she ever could have dreamed, a night of ecstasy, exotic fulfillment, pure pleasure unlike anything she had ever experienced. She wanted to feel that way again, and she already knew only Cole Parker would give her that pleasure. But he was not the kind of man a woman considered spending the rest of her life with.

She heard his footsteps behind her. "You believe what you want," came his deep voice. "I don't need you to tell me I'm not good enough for you, that we're not right for each other. I already know it. But damn it, last night was pretty damn great. I didn't use you or trick you, Addy. You have to believe that. I just plain wanted you, for *you*. No prostitute could have made me feel the same. We share a special kind of friendship because of what we went through back at that cabin, and we both understand each other more than anybody else could. Consider what happened last night a kind of special good-bye."

There it was again, that word good-bye. Why was it men were capable of sharing something so special and considered it nothing more important than a good-bye kiss? It was so easy for them to stay uninvolved, to unite with someone physically but not emotionally. She drew in her breath, refusing to allow her own emotions to take over. She was on her way to start a whole new life. She could not let her own confusion and loneliness cause her to sell herself short here in Abilene, to go falling all over a man who was wanted in some states, who drank too much, who whored with nameless women, and who was still essentially an outlaw.

"Fine," she answered. "Good-bye, then. Thank you for coming this far with me, wanting to . . . take me to eat last night. I hope you find work here in Abilene, discover what you want to do with yourself, maybe settle. Perhaps you'll be able to start a ranch of your own, something like that."

Cole wanted to grab her, shake her . . . wanted to make love to her again. "Yeah, maybe." He turned and walked to the door. "Don't feel ashamed about last night, Addy. Not that the opinion of a man like me matters, but I don't think any different about you. In my book you're still a fine lady, and I hope you find whatever it is you're looking for in Colorado. I'll always think highly of you, and I damn well won't soon forget a woman who reached inside me and pulled a bullet out with her bare fingers . . . or who made me feel like I felt last night."

Before Addy could reply he was out the door. She turned just in time to see it close, and she felt sick inside. Last night had only added to her confusion and loneliness, not helped it. She walked to a window to see him step out into the street. He headed for the Roundup. "I suppose you need your breakfast drink," she murmured.

It infuriated Addy that she had to fight tears through everything she did the rest of the day, and she hated Cole Parker for giving her this problem. Her insides still ached pleasurably from a night of heated, almost painful lovemaking by a man who had more to offer than most women could handle. Still, she was not sure she could call it lovemaking. Sinful. Yes, it certainly could and should be called that. A shameful attempt at satisfying base desires. Apparently it was nothing more than that, two casual friends who each needed satisfaction. At least that was how Cole looked at it. It didn't matter that he said he thought no less of her. It was something *she* had to live with, something she never dreamed she could do, and it only left her more torn emotionally, wondering who Addy Kane really was. When she remembered Nick Coleman storming into the bank back in Unionville, sporting a rifle threateningly, to think she had spent the night with that same man was astounding . . . and unforgivable.

She stood in front of the stage station now, waiting for departure, feeling totally unprepared for this next part of her journey . . . into dangerous Indian country. There would be no Cole Parker along to protect her in case the stage was attacked by Indians or bandits. She watched a man load her trunk and other bags onto the top of the coach, arranging them amid boxes and mail bags. "Your bags will be tied on securely soon as I get everybody's up here," the man called down to her.

Addy nodded, turning to see the two couples approaching who had disembarked from the train the day before. One of them, a tall, skinny, dark-haired woman of perhaps forty, smiled and put out her hand.

"Hello. My name is Rebecca Bean. You were on the same train as me and my husband when it stopped here yesterday. This is my husband, George." The woman's husband, a balding man who wore a lightweight suit, nodded to Addy, but he had too many bags in his hands and under his arms to offer a handshake.

Addy grasped Rebecca's hand. "Hello. Yes, I do remember you. I am Addy Kane. I'm widowed."

"Oh, I'm sorry. The war?"

Addy nodded.

"We lost a son. We have another living in Denver, so we're going there to be with him, since he's our only remaining child."

Addy squeezed her hand. "I'm terribly sorry. I have no children, but I can imagine what a sad experience that must have been for you." She turned to watch the baggage man again. Mr. Bean was throwing bags up to him. "I just hope we all make it as far as Denver without Indian trouble," she told Rebecca Bean.

"Oh, yes!" Rebecca put a hand to her flat chest. "I hear sometimes there is no trouble at all. I suppose we simply must take our chances."

Addy nodded, then moved her eyes to the second couple, who had walked up beside Rebecca after dropping their luggage near the coach. They were younger, perhaps not much older than Addy herself. The woman was quite pretty, blond hair, brown eyes, her dress a simple calico. The man wore denim pants and a light cotton shirt. They were obviously not wealthy, but they looked very happy, and Addy suspected they had not been married long. The man tipped his hat to her, and his wife smiled eagerly. Addy suspected she was happy that two more women would be on the coach. She detected a nervous fear about her, probably the same fear they all felt going into a strange new land.

"Addy Kane," Addy offered again, putting her hand out to the younger woman.

"Hello! I'm Jeanette Booth," she said with a strong southern accent. "This is my husband, Sylvester. Most just call him Buster. Where are you going, Miss Kane?"

"It's Mrs. I'm widowed."

Jeanette's smile faded. "Oh, I'm sorry."

"That's all right. I'm going to the city of Central, in Colorado, to teach." She turned to the Beans and introduced them to Jeanette and Sylvester.

"My husband and I are going to Denver," Jeanette told them. "Buster hopes to find work there, or maybe he'll even go into the hills and find gold!"

"Well, I wish you luck," Addy told her.

Buster a bashful-looking, sandy-haired young man, grinned and shook Addy's hand, and then the older George Bean joined them, introducing himself to everyone. Addy sensed the nervous tension among all of them, none of whom had ever been farther west than the Mississippi. Buster's parents had died in Georgia when their farmhouse was shelled. It had been located right in the middle of a battle between Union troops and Confederates. The farm they had run had been taken over by tax collectors, and Buster was on his way to Colorado to get away from bad memories and start a new life.

So many lives affected by the war. They all shared something in common, just as she and Cole did. But Cole was not here.

The stage driver, a cranky, gray-haired man who was not very tall, came out of the station, adjusting a soiled, wide-brimmed hat. "All get aboard!" he told them, before turning to spit out tobacco juice. "We'd best get started if we're to make it to the first station stop tonight. How many we got?"

"Five." The man Addy had spoken to at the desk last night came out with him. "Did have seven, but a man and woman who was gonna' go on from here changed their minds, decided to stay in Abilene. They figured business was good enough here, I guess, for what they do." He grinned. "The man's a professional gambler, and the woman is a professional . . . well, uh, let's just say she's a professional."

The driver guffawed, and Addy felt a burning rage in her heart again at the thought of Cole staying here and probably bedding Darla Simms, who she was sure was the woman to whom the clerk was referring. Apparently Darla and her male companion had been planning on going even farther west.

"Hell, I can't take seven anyway, Jake. You know that," the driver told the clerk.

"Well, I only had six to begin with. This single lady here . . ." He nodded toward Addy. "I didn't have her down till she come in for a ticket. I had a suspicion the other couple might cancel, so I booked her."

"Well, it's a good thing. I like a full load." The driver scanned his passengers, noticing the men wore no guns. "You men carry guns hidden on you? You got rifles along?"

"Well, no, sir," Buster answered. "Do we need them?"

The driver rolled his eyes. "Never mind." He turned to the man tying baggage on top of the coach. "You ready, Ken?" The man shouted back that he was, and the driver faced his passengers again. "I'm Orum Brown. I've drove this route for months now, know it well, but there's always danger of Indians. It helps to have passengers who know how to use a gun, but we'll make do. Ken Wilson up there, he'll be ridin' what we call shotgun, keepin' watch, shootin' at whatever needs shootin' at, that kind of thing."

The man spit again, and Addy crinkled her nose. She thought how much better she'd feel if Cole was along. There certainly were few men any better than he with a gun. She looked around, half hoping to see him coming to join them, yet glad he was nowhere in sight. Having him along would only complicate her emotional state. He was the last man in the world she should take an interest in, in spite of last night, and if this was good-bye, then all the better. Still, it hurt. She boarded the coach with the two couples, sitting beside Mrs. Bean and facing Jeanette and Buster. She grabbed hold of a strap for support, already realizing that this part of the journey would be even more uncomfortable than the swaying, sooty train. Being stuffed into the leather-seated coach with four other people and only tiny windows for air was not going to be pleasant.

The driver and "shotgun" climbed aboard, and she heard a whistle and a shout. The coach began to roll, and in only moments it began to rock and sway, its big, wooden wheels stirring up dust that rolled into the window so that Addy had to roll down a leather shade to help keep it out. She did not notice someone standing in front of the Roundup Saloon, watching the coach leave.

Cole Parker puffed on a thin cigar and held up a shot of whiskey. "Bye, Addy," he said. He took the cigar from his mouth and downed the whiskey.

Nine

"This is as close to unbearable as anything I have ever done," Rebecca Bean lamented. She wiped at her brow with a handkerchief. "I am afraid I must unbutton the top few buttons of my dress. I hope no one will think I am being too brazen."

Addy also wiped at the perspiration with her own handkerchief, rubbing it around the back of her neck. "I have already done so, Mrs. Bean. No one is going to think anything of it." She wondered when the nausea would ever leave her. She wasn't sure if it was from the intense heat and the stuffiness inside the coach, or if it was from the rocking and swaying motion as the stage barrelled from one station to the next. According to Orum Brown, the point was to get to Denver as fast as humanly possible, as well as keep the coach at a rapid pace in order to discourage Indians from trying to chase it. Because of the wear on the horses, teams were changed at each station.

She took down one of two canteens that hung on either side of the coach, uncorking it and using it to wet her handkerchief. The canteens were there primarily for passengers to drink from when necessary, as the dust that rolled in was choking, and the heat caused loss of body fluids. She handed the canteen over to the Booths. "Do you need any water?"

Jeanette rested her head against the side of the coach, eyes closed. She did not seem to even hear, but Buster took the canteen. "Thanks." His own shirt was unbuttoned half-way down, and George Bean had removed his suit jacket.

Addy wiped her face and neck with the wet handkerchief,

feeling at least a little relief. She could not imagine how the horses could keep such a fast pace in the heat, and she felt sorry for the animals. "Mr. Brown claims we're about half way to Denver," she spoke up. "We can be grateful for that much. At least we haven't been bothered by Indians or outlaws."

"No wonder!" George Bean answered. "Who would be crazy enough to bother in this heat?"

They all laughed lightly, needing something to smile about. From earlier conversations, Addy could tell all four of her fellow passengers were as unsure as she was that what they were doing was right, casting off into an unknown land to start new lives, although they all had valid reasons for leaving their pasts behind. She could not help wondering about Cole, what he was doing now, if he thought about her. She was confused over the right and wrong of what she had done.

These past years had certainly changed her from the Addy who had existed before the war. She couldn't find that Addy, and she didn't know this one. Sometimes she felt removed from her body, as though perhaps she was living in some other woman's body, some other woman's mind, a woman who was nothing like the pre-war Addy Kane.

A gunshot interrupted her thoughts then. It was distant, but unmistakable.

"What was that!" Jeanette Booth asked, opening her eyes and sitting up straighter.

Rebecca grasped her husband's hand. "It sounded like a gunshot."

"Yes, it did," Addy answered. How surprised all of them would be if they knew just how familiar she was with that sound, except that she had heard gunfire only a few feet from her ears. She could remember vividly Jack Slater shooting down that innocent bank clerk, and then Nick; could still see Nick's own smoking gun after shooting Jack dead. She had decided to tell no one about her ordeal back in Illinois. They would only ask more questions than she wanted to answer, and now that Nick was considered dead, she did not want to have to describe him

UNTIL TOMORROW   117

to anyone. He had saved her from rape, and had probably saved
her life. He deserved to be free, if only he would use that freedom
to change his way of life, which she doubted now that he would.
She had in turn saved his life, so they were even, weren't they?
They had had one night of sinful passion, loss of common sense.
Now it was done.

She clung to the hand strap then when the coach seemed to
lurch forward at an even faster pace. The driver was shouting,
"Hah! Hah! Get up there!"

"My God, someone must be chasing us!" Jeanette exclaimed,
her voice high with fear. Buster moved to the window at his side
and stuck his head out.

"There's too much dust! I can't tell!" he shouted.

"Keep your heads inside!"

Addy recognized Ken Wilson's voice.

"Indians!" he added. "We're gonna' try to make it to the next
station!"

"Oh, dear God," Rebecca Bean groaned.

Addy closed her eyes, wondering what else could possibly
happen to one person on her way west. Indians! If she did happen
to reach Central, what other atrocities were going to happen to
her in that wild gold town? At the moment it was quite possible
she would never get there.

Now she could hear the Indians, whooping and yipping. They
were getting closer! How many were there? Would they all be
scalped? The women taken as hostages and raped, made slaves
in some Indian village? "Do either one of you men know how
to use a handgun?" she asked. "I have one in my purse."

"I can," George Bean replied. "I was in the war."

Addy quickly opened her bag and took out a small pistol.
"The man who sold it to me said it wasn't any good unless a
man is quite close, but it might help. There's no sense using it
from this distance, but it might come in handy."

George took it from her. "I don't know," he said, shaking his
head. "It's probably pretty useless in this situation. I hope Ken
Wilson knows what he's doing up there."

They could hear gunfire now from up top the coach.

"I doubt a man can hit anything when he's sitting on top of a coach that's swaying and bouncing as bad as this one," Buster spoke up.

All five of them clung to the hand straps, hanging on for dear life as the coach bounced and jolted and careened at a maddening pace. Addy feared it would tip over.

"Next station's not too far ahead!" Wilson shouted down. "Hang on to your hats!"

His own rifle fired several more times, but the sound of approaching Indians did not fade. Apparently they were not giving up. Addy closed her eyes and began praying. The coach hit something that sent them all flying right up out of their seats, and Jeanette screamed. Addy hit her right cheek against a wooden garment hook at the side of the coach, but she kept silent, more concerned about her life now than a bruised cheek. For the moment she wished with all her heart that Cole was here. He would know what to do, and he was a crack shot. She considered telling George Bean that if the Indians got to them to please shoot her and the other women before he let the savages take them captive. She had heard so many conflicting stories about the Plains Indians. At times she had felt sorry for how they were treated, all the land they were losing. After all, they had been on the plains for centuries. But she had also heard stories of atrocities that now terrified her.

"Almost there!" Wilson shouted down. Suddenly he cried out, and Addy gasped when a body fell off her side of the coach.

"Oh, no!" she shouted. "He's been shot!" She could not help sticking her head out to see Wilson go tumbling off in the distance, his rifle flying through the air. "Oh, the poor man!" she bemoaned. Her eyes widened then when she saw arrows stuck in the coach. She pulled back inside and looked at the others. "I wonder if our driver is still up there. Maybe this coach is running wild!"

Terror engulfed all of them until they heard Orum Brown

whistle at the team. "Station just ahead!" he yelled. "Get ready to make a beeline for the door! Don't waste no time for nothin'!"

Addy reached over and grasped Rebecca's hand. Rebecca in turn grasped her husband's hand, and he reached across and took hold of Jeanette's, until all five passengers had formed a circle of hands. "Dear God, save us," Addy prayed. She screamed then when the coach again bounced wildly and she fell forward onto the floor of the coach. The others helped her up, and then Addy, Rebecca and George all flew forward into Jeanette's and Buster's laps when the coach suddenly came to a scraping halt, dust flying.

"Out! Out! Make a run for it!" Orum shouted.

Addy quickly gained her balance and opened the door closest to her, while George opened the other side. All five passengers clamored out and headed for the station, which was nothing more than a sod building, built partially into the side of a small hill. There was only the one door and one window. They all ran, and Addy could feel arrows whizzing past her.

"Buster!" Jeanette suddenly screamed. "Buster! Buster!"

Addy turned to see young Sylvester Booth lying face down with an arrow in his back. She started to go to them, but George Bean grabbed her arm. "Get inside! You can't help him now!" The driver in turn grabbed a screaming Jeanette and dragged her into the station, slamming shut the door just as arrows sailed into it. He bolted it with a heavy wooden bar, then quickly closed the shutters to the window.

Jeanette kept screaming her husband's name and ran to peek out of a hole in the shutters. "No! No!" she screamed even louder. "They're scalping him! They're scalping my husband!"

George pulled her away from the window, and the woman swooned to the floor. Addy went to her side, pulling her into her arms. "I know how it feels," she told her, rocking the woman as she wept against her shoulder.

"We're doomed," Rebecca said, sitting down on the dirt floor beside Addy.

The sod structure was hot and stuffy, made worse by having to close the door and window. It was also very dark, and it took a few seconds for Addy's eyes to adjust enough to see who was who. Now the driver was at the window, peering through the same hole Jeanette had used. "They're unhitchin' the horses, herding the spares out of the corral," he said. "That's probably all they want. Maybe they'll leave us alone after that." He hesitated. "Damn," he muttered then. "They've already killed Jed Corey, the station master. He's hung up on a fence post out there. Looks like he was tortured."

"Oh, no, no," Jeanette wept.

Rebecca covered her face with her hands.

"What are we going to do?" Addy asked the driver.

The man sighed. "I can get a few with my rifle, but not all of them. Right now it would only incite them to find a way in here and murder all of us. I'm gonna' wait for now, see if they're happy enough with the horses. I'm just afraid that now that they've seen women run in here, the horses won't be enough for them. They like to use women to get the army and the government to give them what they want. If they get horses, guns, land, they give prisoners back. Women prisoners are the best. They know white men will do anything to get women back from Indian men."

"Shoot us first!" Rebecca wept.

"Well, ma'am, I just might have to do that," Orum answered. "Let's wait and see." He looked back out the window. "They're ridin' off with all the horses," he said then. "Let's hope they don't come back."

Addy sat rocking Jeanette. "And if they don't, what do we do then? We have no way of getting out of here. We don't have enough food and water with us to try walking to the next station."

"One thing at a time," Orum answered. "Another stage will be along within a couple of days, headin' east."

"My husband! If the Indians are riding off, somebody has to bury him while they're gone," Jeanette moaned.

Orum sighed and looked at George. "You game?"

"Certainly. We can't let him lie there in the sun and let the buzzards—"

Jeanette cried harder.

Orum opened the door carefully and peered outside. "I'll see if I can find a shovel in the horse shed." He kept his rifle steady as he walked farther out, turning and looking up the hill to make sure there were no Indians waiting stealthily above them. Addy left Jeanette to Rebecca and walked to the doorway.

"I'd like to help," she told George. "I can say some words over his grave."

George nodded and they both waited. It seemed so strangely silent now, after all the yelling and war whoops, shooting and screaming. Addy thought what a strange land this was. It could be so deadly silent, or filled with gunfire and war cries, or with the plunking pianos and general noise of its wild towns. Orum returned with a shovel, and for the next three hours the women waited for the two men to dig a hole big enough for a body. The ground was hard as a rock, and by the time they finished both men were bathed in sweat and looked ready to pass out. Addy felt sick over the thought of Ken Wilson lying farther back, dead, probably scalped. There was no way to go back and bury him.

Finally the men were able to put Buster Booth's young body into its grave. They covered it, not wanting his wife to see how awful he looked covered in blood from the arrow as well as having part of his scalp ripped off. They called for Jeanette and the other women then, and Rebecca and Addy helped Jeanette outside, holding on to her while Addy managed to quote some scripture from memory and then said a prayer. Orum ordered them back inside then, and he and George began covering the grave with rocks so that animals could not dig into it.

The women sat down inside at a coarse, home-made table, with chairs made of logs. Addy thought what a poor excuse for a rest stop this place was. There was no place to bathe, no privacy, no sleeping quarters and apparently no food of any substance. There was only one privy that she had seen, a sagging structure near the horse shed. Apparently this stop was here strictly for changing horses and riding on, but all of them were hot and dirty and miserable, as well as hungry and thirsty.

Orum and George came back inside, leaving the door open for air, deciding there was no sense closing it until absolutely necessary. He told them to be careful not to drink their water supply too fast, as Orum had checked the well and found it almost dry.

"There's a river about a mile from here," he told them, "but it's too dangerous to try to make it there now. Them Indians could come back any time. Maybe after dark I can sneak down there and get us extra water. That barrel over there has some beef in it, stored in lard to keep it from spoilin'." He walked over to a wooden bread box on a shelf. "Ole Jed, he was pretty good at bakin' bread, if you can believe it. He baked it in little pans right on top of the pot-belly stove over there. Maybe—" He opened the box. "Here's part of a loaf. We'll eat on this for now, just to get somethin' in our stomachs."

"I can't eat," Jeanette said. She had stopped crying, and she sat in a dark corner, just looking at her lap.

Orum set the bread on the table, looking at the others. "Everybody take a little."

They reluctantly gathered around the table, all with dejected faces. "Your stage line got us into this," Rebecca grumbled, her thin face looking more shriveled with worry. "Surely you knew this could happen."

Old Orum ran a hand over his eyes, getting nervous for another chew of tobacco, but George Bean had asked him not to chew inside in front of the women. "Of course this could happen," he answered. "But there hasn't been trouble for a while. The Cheyenne have been causin' more trouble up in Nebraska, not around here. We thought it was safe. This time of year they're usually farther north. Now that the Army is buildin' back up out here, I reckon' somethin' happened to get them lathered again."

"We're all going to die," Jeanette lamented, "and I don't care now. At least I'll be with Buster."

"You must not talk that way, Jeanette," Rebecca told her.

'And you're welcome to come stay with me and my husband in Denver if we do get out of this, at least until you know what you want to do; unless, of course, you choose to go back home."

Jeanette sniffed and shook her head. "I've got nothing to go back to. Family's gone. Farm's gone. We were going to be so happy, going to a place like Denver, maybe finding gold or at least a decent job." She wiped at her cheeks with the palms of her hands. "I don't care now. I'm just tired of fighting. First there was the Civil War, now the Indians. Why can't people just leave each other alone?"

Addy broke off a small piece of bread. "I'm sure the Indians feel the same way when you think about it." She sighed, thinking about all her own calamities. "This country does seem to be in a mess, doesn't it?" She looked at Jeanette. "I've lost a father and mother, as well as a husband, Jeanette, and Mrs. Bean has lost a son. We understand your grief, and all I can say is that time will take care of it."

Jeanette shook with a sob. "But it hurts so now! I can't believe time will make it any better."

Addy could not find the right words to help her for the moment, well remembering there was nothing anyone could say to make the hurt any better when she lost her family and her husband. She held her bread in her hand and walked outside, breathing deeply to shake away the ache of her own losses. She wondered if her auburn hair was now gray from dust. She looked down at her dress, a lightweight cotton calico that was once a bright green and was now dull and soiled. She sighed, realizing it didn't much matter. She was probably going to die soon anyway, and there was absolutely no one left who cared, certainly no family, and not even Cole. She decided she would get her pistol back from Mr. Bean so that she could shoot herself when the time came, rather than hope there was someone left alive to do it for her.

She felt her hair falling out of place, and she removed the combs to shake it out, brushing dust from it with her hands. She pulled back each side and replaced the combs, leaving it hanging long in the back. She took a handkerchief from where she had tucked it into the bodice of her dress and walked over to a bucket of water that sat on the sagging porch of the little sod station. She tipped the bucket and poured a little water on the handkerchief, then used it to again wash over her face and neck. She poured more water on it and then laid it across the back of her neck under her dress, breathing deeply at the cooling relief.

It was then she heard them, the thundering sound of several horses approaching. "Dear Lord," she whispered. She watched the horizon, half hoping that by some miracle perhaps a troop of Army men was approaching. But even before she could see clearly who the riders were, she heard their war whoops. She turned and ran back inside. "They're coming back!" She quickly closed and bolted the door.

"Get Ned's rifle down from the wall there," Orum told George Bean. "And grab some boxes of ammunition off them shelves just below it! Can you shoot?"

"Pretty decent. I was in the war."

Addy noticed he seemed very proud every time he made the remark about being in the war. She was glad no one had asked which side her husband and father had chosen in that war, but right now was no time to worry about such things.

Orum opened the window shutters. "There's only room for one man to shoot from here," he told George. "You just keep the rifles loaded for me."

"I want my pistol, Mr. Bean," Addy told him. "I'll use it for Rebecca, Jeanette and me if necessary."

George hesitated, looking lovingly at his wife. "We had to come out here, Rebecca, to see our only remaining son. We did the right thing."

Rebecca nodded, and George handed the pistol to Addy. She turned to the other two women. "We'll make it through this. I'm making it to Colorado somehow, and these Indians aren't going to stop me." She said the words not just to give them hope, but to give hope to herself, but it didn't work. The Indians bore down on the little station, hooves pounding, voices yipping, guns shooting, arrows thudding into the door. The earth all around and above them shook from thundering horses, and dirt began to sift into their hair. The women put their heads down and covered them with their arms, while Orum Brown began firing.

"Got one!" he shouted once. "Got another one!" came another excited yell, but Addy knew that his hits were too few to make a dent in the number of Indians that were now bent on killing all of them.

"How many do you think there are?" George asked him.

"Not sure. Times like this, it seems like there's a lot more than there really is. It's a small party. They've probably split up to spread themselves around and cause trouble for others—ranchers and the like." The words were shouted above the hollering and rumbling. More dirt sifted down, then began to fall in bigger chunks.

"My God, they're bent on pounding in the top of this station and smothering us under the dirt. They're riding over the top of us!" George said.

"They just want us to think that," Orum answered, "so's we'll run out. Then they'll kill us and grab the women." He fired a few more shots. "There's another, and another—" He drew back from the window and looked at George. "Wait a minute! A couple went down that I didn't even shoot at!"

Both men squeezed together to look out. "Look at that!" George exclaimed. "Three more!"

Addy noticed that the thundering above them had stopped.

"They're gatherin' in the distance," Orum commented. "They seem confused. Hell, they've stopped whoopin' and shootin', but . . . listen!"

All three women gathered behind the men, straining to hear. Gunshots came from another direction! With every shot, another Indian went down. Two. Three. Four. A couple seconds pause between shots. Five. Six.

"Ain't that the damnedest thing!" Orum almost whispered.

"Must be the Army," George added. "But the way the shots are coming, it seems like just one man doing the shooting."

Seven. Eight. One Indian after another cried out and fell from his horse. The others began turning their horses in confusion, looking in the direction of the gunshots, fear beginning to show in the way they rode back and forth in disarray. Nine. Ten.

"Jesus! Over half of them is down," Orum said. "Whoever that is, he's a crack shot with a rifle, but he's takin' a chance. Them Indians could take after him."

"Not when he's that good of a shot."

Addy wondered . . . no, it couldn't be. The shots continued to echo through the hills until what was left of the war party turned and rode off in what seemed sheer terror.

"I don't believe it," Orum commented.

"They're gone!" George exclaimed.

Orum jumped up and went to the door, unbolting it and stepping outside. Dead Indians lay strewn everywhere, from the few close by whom Orum had shot, to the many in the distance shot by their mysterious savior. The stage driver walked farther out, followed by the others. The women stepped cautiously around the bodies. A few seemed to still be alive, and they groaned. Addy started to kneel down to one.

"Leave them be!" Orum warned. "We'll get the hell away from here and the rest of them will come for the bodies, dead or alive. They'll want to give the dead ones an Indian burial, and they'll do what they can for the ones still alive. It's their custom. Besides, I don't think more than a couple of them is alive anyway."

Addy forced herself to look away, again struck by what a wild, violent land this was, with sets of rules that would never be tolerated in the East. She stepped farther away, again realizing that the air hung strangely silent for all the noise and gunfire that had penetrated it only moments before. Now they all spoke in near whispers as they watched the hills, waiting. Finally a lone rider made himself known riding down a hill to their right, a big man on a powerful-looking gray horse. He wore a duster, and he wielded a rifle in his right hand. Addy stepped away from the rest of them, astonished when she realized who it was.

"Cole!" she said softly.

Ten

Addy could not help feeling a great sense of relief at the sight of Cole Parker approaching, in spite of knowing she'd be better off if she never saw him again. She felt her cheeks growing hotter, not from the weather, but from the realization of what she had shared with this man a few nights ago, a sinful secret she must keep buried forever. How had he come to be here at such a crucial time? Had he been following them all along? Watching over her after all?

"You know that man?" Orum Brown asked her.

"Yes. I met him on the train through Kansas. He stayed behind in Abilene. I had no idea—"

Cole rode closer. "You people all right?"

"We lost our shotgun and this woman's husband," Orum answered, indicating Jeanette. "He's buried, but I'm afraid we had to leave poor Ken to the buzzards, and there wasn't time to bury Jed Corey, the station master. He's strung up on the fence out there. We ought to get him buried, too."

Cole looked around, then shoved his rifle into its boot that was attached to his saddle. "I found your shotgun, dragged his body to some rocks and covered him with more rocks to keep the buzzards away," he answered as he dismounted. "That's all I had time to do. I figured I'd better ride hard to catch up. From the tracks I saw and all the shooting I heard, I knew you people were in trouble." He glanced at Addy.

What was that she saw in his eyes? Worry? Relief? Was he concerned about only her, and so had followed just for that? Did he love her? No, they must not talk about love. Neither of them was ready for that. Maybe he had only decided to come because he thought he could get her into bed again . . . and maybe he could. There he stood in all his handsome stature, a hero to the rest of these people who didn't know about his past.

"Mister, we don't know who you are, but thank God you came when you did. I've never seen anybody shoot like that!" George Bean put in. His shirt was soaked with perspiration, and he wiped at the glistening sweat on his balding head.

Cole finally moved his gaze from Addy. "Name's Cole Parker. I had planned on taking this stage in the first place, then changed my mind. A little later I changed it again."

"Well, you must have rode awful damn hard to catch up like that," Orum put in. He held out his hand. "Orum Brown. I'm the stage driver."

Cole took his hand, but he looked at Addy again. "Yeah, I rode pretty hard to catch up." He looked back at Orum. "Damn near killed my horse getting here." He looked around again. "Looks like it didn't do me much good. Apparently there are no horses to take us on from here."

"George Bean," George said, stepping up and putting out his hand also. "That there is my wife, Rebecca, and the young lady who lost her husband is Jeanette Booth. The other lady—"

"He knows Mrs. Kane," Orum interrupted him. "Remember?"

"Oh! Yes," George answered, letting go of Cole's hand. He looked from Cole to Addy, then arched his eyebrows as though he'd gained sudden knowledge. "I see."

Addy bristled at what the man was probably thinking, that Cole Parker had ridden a mad dash out here because he was chasing the woman he loved. How little they all knew about the true situation between her and Cole, how they met, that Cole was much too dangerous a man for a proper lady to become involved with.

"The Indians took our horses," Orum told Cole. "All we can do is wait for another stage to come by."

Cole pushed back his hat, scanning all of them. "Well, you all look pretty hot and tired and hungry. Why don't I ride on ahead to the next station and see about bringing back some horses so you can get started sooner." He looked around at the dead Indians. "Trouble is, the Cheyenne, or whoever did this, will be back for these bodies." He looked at Orum. "Maybe I should stay here and you could ride ahead instead, use my horse. That way I'll be here to use my rifle on any Indians who try to make trouble. It's probably no more than a day's ride to the next station, is it?"

"Yes, sir, just about that," Orum answered. "I can make it back here by early mornin', day after tomorrow, maybe even by tomorrow night, and we can all be on our way."

Cole nodded "Just don't ride Shadow here too hard. He's pretty worn out."

"I'll leave him at the next station and let him rest and eat till we get there. I can come back on one of the stage line horses. Then yours will be fresh for goin' on with us when we get up to that point. We'll tie him to the back of the coach."

"I just hope you make it," George put in. "What if you're attacked by Indians on the way?"

Orum removed his hat and ran a hand through his stringy, gray hair. "Well, then, I guess you folks will have to wait for the next coach."

"It's a brave thing you're doing, Mr. Brown," Rebecca told him.

Orum shook his head. "Well, now, I'd say it's a toss up over who's braver—me, or you folk for stayin' behind here. Them Indians could come back with an even bigger force. And our sharpshooter here," he nodded to Cole, "he's pretty brave, too. There could have been more of them out there in the hills to come after him. Let's just hope they don't come back here with so many braves that he can't keep up with 'em."

Cole grinned. "I'll risk the challenge." He looked around at all the dead bodies. "It's too bad things like this have to happen. The farther west I go, the more problems I see with settling this land out here. I'm sure these poor Indians think they're in the right."

"Poor Indians!" Jeanette sneered. "They're savages! They scalped my husband!"

Cole looked at her. "Most of the time, ma'am, men have a reason for killing." He glanced at Addy, then back to Jeanette. "When a man thinks he's defending something that belongs to him, he does what he has to do, just like I did what I had to do when I saw all of you being attacked. No matter what they did, it doesn't feel real good having to kill so many of them, and a few of them are still alive, so we'd all better get inside. You can bet their friends will be back for them. We'll have to wait till tomorrow to bury the station keeper."

Orum climbed up on Cole's horse, and the stirrups had to be shortened for the man. He bade them all farewell and headed west, and Addy said a silent prayer for his safety. Cole herded the rest of them inside, but they left the door open. Cole sat in a wood chair on the little porch and watched the surrounding hills for signs of returning Indians. Addy stood at the doorway, watching him open his rifle and blow out the barrel. "This thing still needs cleaning, but there isn't time," he said, more to himself than anyone else. He turned and looked up at her. "You all right?"

Addy nodded. "Except for being so hot that I feel like I can't breathe, and I feel dirty as a pig."

His eyes moved over her, and she felt a tingle inside she would rather not feel. Again she was consumed with shame and embarrassment, still confused over what he truly thought of her now. An easy woman? No different from someone like Darla? Back at the hotel he said he had not lost his respect for her, but could she believe that? It irked her to realize this man knew every inch of her. He had touched, tasted and invaded every private place, and that gave him a strange power over her she would rather he did not have. "Why did you come, Cole?"

He turned back around, taking a cloth from a pocket of his duster and using it to wipe off his rifle. "Seemed like the right thing to do, not just to watch out for you, but because the farther I get from Illinois and Missouri—" He hesitated, looking past her inside the cabin as though afraid someone had heard him. "You know what I mean. The farther I go, the easier it will be to maybe start over."

She folded her arms, stepping closer and talking softly. "And which life will you start over? I am sure the west is full of outlaws."

He grinned and shook his head. "Well, then, that gives me a lot of options, doesn't it?" he quipped.

Addy wanted to hit him for constantly confusing her emotions. Now he was being sarcastic, probably still angry for the way she had talked to him that morning after . . . One minute she felt she could almost love him, the next she hated him. One minute she thought there was some goodness left in him, the next he seemed as wild and worthless as the day she met him in the bank. One minute she felt sorry for him because of his little girl, the next she wanted to scream at him that turning to outlaw ways was not the answer. He drank and whored and gambled and robbed, yet he had saved her life twice now, and he had taken her on a journey into womanhood she would not soon forget.

Damn him! Why hadn't he simply gone to Indian Territory in the first place, or stayed in Abilene? Twice she had primed herself to simply forget about Nick Coleman, then Cole Parker. Now here he was again, disturbing her heart and her ability to think straight. "Aren't you too warm in that duster?"

He clicked the rifle shut and began loading cartridges into it, taking them from a pocket of the long duster. "Some. I'll take it off in a minute. I like wearing it when I ride. Keeps the trail dust from dirtying up my clothes. When you have to pretty much stay in the same shirt and pants for days at a time, it helps to wear something to keep them from getting any dirtier than necessary. If you rode the open trail as much as I do—"

He stopped short, sitting up straighter, his blue eyes squinting as he watched the horizon. "Here they come. Get inside."

Addy obeyed, and Cole followed. He closed and bolted the door. "They're coming for their dead and wounded. I hope that's the only thing they're after."

"Oh, no!" Jeanette crouched into a corner, and Rebecca and Addy both moved against the wall.

"Let's hope coming for their wounded keeps them occupied enough to let old Orum get to the next station," George told Cole.

Cole moved to the window and leveled his rifle through it. "Let's hope," he answered. "Keep that rifle over there loaded and ready. I'll do the shooting.

George grinned. "I certainly won't argue with you there." He stood beside Cole, the extra rifle in hand. "How'd you get so good with a gun, Mister?"

Cole did not take his eyes from the approaching Indians. "I don't know. I used to hunt pretty often. Had a family to feed and not a lot of money. I just seemed to have a knack for shooting straight. Nobody ever went hungry."

George laughed nervously. "You were in the war, I'll bet. The army must have loved getting somebody like you. You seem to have a touch of southern accent. Which side did you fight on?"

Cole didn't answer right away. "Some things are better left alone," he finally said. "The war's over."

"Some of us would like to forget it so easy," George answered. "But me and Rebecca, we lost a son. He fought for the Union. We're headed for Denver to be with our only other son. He lives there."

Cole sighed. "Well, Mister, be glad you've *got* a second child. I only had one, and she was five years old when she was killed by Union raiders."

George reddened and swallowed. "Oh. I'm sorry. I shouldn't have brought up the subject."

"I guess not," Cole said. "The point is we're always going to be running into people from both sides, and a lot of men will try to keep the hatred going for a long time to come. It would be easy for you to think you should hate me, and the same goes for me; but right now there are about twenty more Indians out there who hate both of us and don't give a damn whose side we were on. They've got a whole different reason for hating."

Rebecca moved closer to Addy, clenching a handkerchief in her fist, her eyes wide with fear. "Can your friend take on twenty Indians?" she said in a near whisper.

"I . . . don't know him that well," Addy answered, realizing it was the truth, even though she had slept with him. Rebecca Bean would probably faint if she knew that. "He just happened to take the same train with me out of Independence. I only know his name and that he has a reputation as a sharpshooter."

Cole took a moment to look back at her with a frown, and Addy glared right back at him, warning him he'd better not let on she knew him any better than that. He looked back out the window. "So far they're coming in slow, probably not sure if we're still here or if the one who shot so many of them is still around." He spoke very softly. "What worries me is that if they could go back and get so many more that fast, where'd they come from? Is there a whole village not far away, maybe even more warriors? If so, they'll be out for blood."

Cautiously the warriors came closer. Some pulled travois behind their horses, and others dismounted and began loading bodies onto the travois. They leaned close and talked to the few who were still alive. They worked until every last body was retrieved, looking around defensively as they did so. Everyone waited tensely, and finally Cole seemed to relax a little. He turned from the window. "They're leaving, but that doesn't mean they won't be back."

George wiped more sweat from his brow. "Dear God, we've got a long night ahead of us, don't we?"

Cole glanced at Addy. "Yeah."

Everyone tried to rest, but it was nearly impossible in the stuffy sod dugout. Because of the darkness, they could not leave the door open, for fear the Indians would come back in the night.

Addy and Cole could not talk about anything that needed discussing, as quarters were too close, and they did not dare let the others know just how intimately they knew each other. They spoke in near whispers, ate pieces of bread and drank water sparingly. Jeanette Booth sat in a corner the entire night sobbing quietly, and nothing Addy or Rebecca had to say could console her, until Addy told her that Cole Parker lost both a wife and a child. The others looked at Cole sympathetically, but Addy could see that the comment had brought new pain to his heart.

Jeanette finally fell asleep, and night stretched into dawn. There was still no sign of returning Indians. "Maybe they're just happy to have the horses," Cole said. He cautiously opened the door, and the fresh air that rushed inside gave relief to all. Cole walked out and looked around. "Anybody that needs to use the privy can go ahead," he announced.

They all rushed out at the same time, even Jeanette, but Addy lagged behind. "I'm glad you came along," she told him after they were gone. "We all are."

Cole rubbed at tired eyes. "We aren't out of the woods yet, and I'm so tired now I'm not sure I could shoot straight if I had to."

"Well, Orum Brown should show up by tonight or tomorrow early, if he made it. If he didn't, I guess we have to stick it out here a couple more days. I just hope the Indians haven't raided the next station. That would mean no one can help us. Maybe the next regular stage won't even make it."

Cole looked at her, realizing she had more to say, wanted to say something much more personal. She was dirty and tired. He wanted to hold her, but couldn't let the others see him do it. Besides, she had her defenses up. She probably didn't *want* to be held, not by him anyway. The other night had been a big mistake, and she was still angry—angry that he couldn't say he loved her. What she didn't understand was the only reason he couldn't say it was that he was afraid to love that way again. A man could only bear to lose so much.

"We'll worry about that when we have to," he answered.

Addy walked off the porch, her back to him. "I'm sorry for some of my insults, Cole. It's just that you don't seem ready—"

"You're right. I'm not ready. I'm sorry if I hurt you. It just . . . happened."

She did not turn around. "I need to hear you tell me again that you don't think less of me."

Cole took a thin cigar from inside his shirt pocket. "I only think less of myself," he answered. "Go use the damn privy. I'll go find a bush or something." He walked off the porch, lighting the cigar on his way. "And don't make any fires," he called after her. "If those Indians are still camped out there somewhere, they might see the smoke and decide to come back after all."

Addy watched him go, studied his slim hips, the big steps he took with his long legs, and she wondered if and when reality would return to her mind and heart. She wasn't sure that anything she was doing was right, and she still ached inside almost to tears at old memories, a life that could never be again. That was why she must not succumb to any feelings for Cole Parker. She had no way of knowing if those feelings were real, no way of knowing if the man would ever amount to a hill of beans, if he would be able to stop drinking, able to lead a lawful life. In fact, the law could catch up with him and take him away from her. She could not bear another loss, and she suspected he was thinking the same.

She walked back inside, found one more loaf of bread in the bread box and two cans of beans. She frowned at the thought of such fare for breakfast, and she longed for a strong cup of coffee; but Cole had said no fires, and that made sense. It was possible that the Indians who had come the day before thought they were gone, or had just decided they had their own great "warrior." They did, in the form of Cole Parker.

She opened the beans, then left to use the privy herself, returning to find Rebecca divvying up their pitiful breakfast of beans and bread. The little group ate as best they could, and even Jeanette ate a little. Addy realized they owed their appetites to the presence of Cole Parker and his expertise with the rifle he kept by his side at all times.

The wait began, everyone quiet and edgy, praying Orum Brown made it through. Cole sat on the porch and smoked, and Jeanette sat in a corner speaking to no one. Rebecca and George sat on a cot holding hands, and Addy walked out to the stagecoach to climb up to the top, where she managed to open a carpetbag of hers and take out a book. She walked back to the sod house and sat down on the porch steps to read Charles Dickens's *Oliver Twist*. She felt Cole's eyes on her, knew they still had much to talk about if he was going to be along the rest of this trip, but they couldn't talk about it here. She rose to go inside, and suddenly Cole jumped to his feet, literally pushing her through the door. "They're coming back!" he said, closing and bolting the door after himself.

"Oh, dear God!" Rebecca groaned.

Already they could hear the whooping and yipping and thundering hooves.

"They must want revenge," George said, hurrying over to the window beside Cole. "How many are there?"

Cole leveled his Springfield rifle. "More than before. I'm not sure how many."

Addy felt sick. She picked up her purse from where it lay on the cot and she opened it to take out her small pistol, wondering what use it could be other than to shoot herself. What an odd way for her life to end, Addy Kane, twenty-five years old, a schoolteacher from a town in the East with bricked streets; dying out here in western Kansas by an Indian's knife or arrow, after having spent a night of unbridled passion with a near stranger. How strange were the turns life took.

Jeanette just cringed farther into the corner, and minutes later Cole started firing, as rapidly as possible for a man to take aim and hit his target each time. "Damn!" he muttered. After several rounds he handed the rifle to George, who then handed him the loaded rifle kept at the station and began reloading Cole's.

"There are too many this time," Cole said. The urgency in his voice filled the women with terror. "I'm doing the best I can."

He handed the older rifle back to George and took his again, and by then they could hear horses thundering around the sod dugout. Cole had to duck aside when arrows began singing through the window. Quickly he closed the wooden shutters, turning to the others. "I'll do all I can," he said, looking at Addy.

They all looked at each other then in terror, and Addy clung tightly to her pistol. Dirt began to fall from the ceiling, and there came a pounding at the door. Rebecca screamed when the head of a hatchet cut partially through the wood, and Cole faced the door and fired. A hole splintered into the wood, and they heard someone outside cry out. More dirt fell then in bigger chunks, and it was obvious the Indians were chopping through the roof. Cole fired again, this time upward. There came a muffled cry, but more dirt fell, and a hole appeared in the rooftop. A warrior jumped inside, and the women screamed and jumped back. Cole shot the warrior, but then the rifle was out of bullets. Another warrior jumped in. Addy held out her pistol and fired, hitting him in the neck. He turned to stare at her in surprise, and Cole pulled his six-gun and put a second shot in the warrior. Addy watched the man fall, surprised she had actually shot him herself.

Another jumped inside, and again Cole shot. Then two more. George tried to fire at the intruders, but the older rifle jammed. Addy shot one of them in the chest, and Cole shot the other. His six-gun was empty then, and there was no time to reload, as yet another Indian jumped through the hole, tomahawk raised. Cole grabbed the older rifle from George and swung hard, bashing the Indian in the side of the head. He sprawled on the dirt floor with a grunt and by then the door was beginning to split. Cole grabbed his own rifle again, which a nervous George had not had time to fully load. He fired at the door, then whirled to aim at the hole in the ceiling again, but no one was there.

They all waited, and it took a few minutes to realize the sound of galloping horses and the screams of warriors had suddenly diminished. They heard gunfire somewhere in the distance, and Cole straightened, listening. "Someone's out there chasing them off," he said. He cautiously opened one of the shutters, which was full of arrows and wouldn't open all the way. Still he could see out enough to get his answer. "I'll be damned. It's the Army."

"The Army!" George pushed open the other shutter. "Thank God! Orum must have run into those troops somewhere along the way!"

Everyone began to breathe easier, and Cole turned to face them. "Everybody all right?" His eyes were on Addy, who still stood staring at one of the Indians she had shot, her pistol still in her hand. She felt numb.

"We're all fine, thanks to you, Cole," George told him. "If not for your fast action—and, by God, Mrs. Kane there! She got a couple of them with her pistol! You two make quite a pair!"

Addy raised her eyes to look at Cole, who only turned away to open the door. Six Indians lay dead inside. Cole stepped over three of them to walk out and greet a troop of soldiers who approached the station to see if anyone was left alive. Addy's only thought was how hard it must be for him to face men in blue uniforms.

Eleven

Soldiers dragged the bodies of dead Indians to a far hill. This time there were none still alive, as Cole had shot most of them at close range. Addy watched the two she had shot carried away on an ambulance cot. She still felt rather stunned that she had managed to do such a thing. Some of the soldiers had tipped their hat to her when they learned what had happened, calling her a brave woman; but she felt more the coward. It had been pure terror that had made her pull the trigger.

Cole paced nervously while the captain of the troops explained they would stay around the station until Orum Brown got back with a team of horses. They had run into Orum while on patrol late the day before, and they had ridden to the station as fast as possible. Addy knew Cole did not like being around blue-coated soldiers yet, even though these had saved their lives. To Cole they were still Union army.

Addy sat down on the porch steps, and moments later Cole came to stand near her. "Good shot," he told her.

She rubbed her hands nervously. "I don't like the feeling. I never want to have to do that again."

Cole sighed. "It never feels good, no matter how many times you have to do it, unless it's for revenge."

Addy looked up at him and saw him scanning the soldiers. "They aren't the enemy any longer, Cole. They're just regular army now, and they saved our lives. Orum should be here by late this afternoon and we can get out of here, with soldier escort, no less." She rubbed at her temples. "Thank God. I hope there is some way to bathe at the next station."

"You'll be in Denver in three or four more days. I hear it's getting pretty big. I'm sure there will be places there to bathe, maybe find a decent hotel and rest up before going on to Central City. George Bean said he heard from his son that it's a wild ride into the mountains, a dangerous road through a steep canyon, so you'd better catch up on your sleep before you go the rest of the way."

"Have you changed your mind again about going?"

He removed his hat and ran a hand through his thick, dark hair. "No. But I'll be going up on horseback. Sounds a lot safer than taking a coach on such a narrow road. I probably won't even go up at the same time. I'll take in the sights and job opportunities in Denver first. As soon as we reach the next station, I'm going on to Denver alone on horseback. These soldiers say they're supposed to go to a fort near there themselves, and I can't abide going that far with men wearing Union uniforms, even though they did save our lives. Besides, you would rather I stayed out of your life, and I don't doubt that's best. The sooner we go our separate ways again, the better."

Addy frowned, feeling sad but also angry. "I thought we had settled that when you left my room back in Abilene. Yet you caught up with my coach, and now we have to go through this all over again."

"I only came out here because I was worried about you traveling through Indian country. Now you'll have army escort most of the way to Denver. You'll be safe." He looked down at her. "We've shared some damn wild times together, haven't we?"

Addy felt her cheeks growing hot. "We certainly have." Yes, he was right. It was best he stay out of her life for once and for all.

Their gaze held for several silent seconds. "I'm glad you're all right," he told her then.

She nodded. "I'm glad you are, too." She turned away. "I'd

better go talk to Jeanette, see if there is anything more I can do for her."

Cole watched her walk inside. *You're some woman, Addy Kane,* he thought. He would not soon forget the sight of her holding out her pistol and shooting a wild Indian dead. *I guess you're more suited to this land than you realize.*

Orum finally arrived, leading a fresh team of horses. Everyone cheered his arrival, and no one wanted to wait until morning to leave. They wanted to go as far as they could tonight, not wanting to spend one more minute at the partially destroyed stage depot that held so much terror and so many bad memories. They would camp out on the trail if they couldn't reach the next station in time.

Cole helped Orum hitch the team, and everyone boarded the stage. Cole climbed onto the seat beside Orum to ride shotgun. Addy took a last look at the place where she had learned even more about herself, her strengths and weaknesses . . . the place where they all might have died a horrible death if not for Cole holding the Indians off until the army arrived.

Again she had been through something that made her feel removed from the Addy Kane she used to know. Orum snapped a small whip and whistled, and the four horses lurched into a gentle run, followed by the soldiers.

The next station was just across the Colorado border, a much finer stop than the sod dugout they had left behind. The log building was large enough to accommodate several cots and a large table, where lunch was offered to everyone. They had traveled into the night, made camp and reached the station the next day just as a storm began moving in from the west.

Besides the main building there was a storage shed, a horse barn and a blacksmith. It was decided to set up the storage shed as a place of privacy where each passenger could wash and change. Never had the well outside been so busy, everyone eager for fresh buckets of water to take to the shed, and all in a hurry to get cleaned up before the rain would begin to pour.

By the time it was Addy's turn at the well, it began to sprinkle. The windmill that pumped the water creaked and groaned as it whirled in a wind that was getting stronger. She hurriedly dipped the bucket into the water and turned to see Cole standing behind her. "Need help?" he asked.

Why was he so handsome even when he was dirty and needed a shave? It was those eyes that disturbed a woman. "I'm fine. I thought you were going on alone from here." They practically had to shout because of the rising wind.

"I am. It's just a little late to start now, especially in a storm, and I need to clean up and eat. I just hope we can find a decent meal at this place."

"Anything would be better than bread and beans." She ducked against harder rain. "You're staying tonight, then?"

Cole took the bucket from her. "Come on! You'd better get yourself cleaned up so you can get inside the main station." He ran with her to the shed, and they both pushed through the door. Addy had already set her carpetbag inside so that she would have clean clothes to change into.

"I guess the men will have to find places to sleep tonight," Cole said, setting down the bucket, "maybe in the coach or in the shed. There are only five cots inside, and we have three women plus the driver and the station master. That leaves me and George and the blacksmith. The soldiers have already pitched tents, but I'm not about to sleep with someone in a blue uniform."

He grinned and turned to go, but when he opened the door a loud clap of thunder made Addy jump, and Cole ducked back inside because of rain that had almost instantly begun pouring down in sheets. "Damn!" he muttered. "I'll get soaked just getting to the main cabin."

Addy began taking combs out of her hair. "Stay here, then. Maybe it will stop in a few minutes. I can wait." She shook her hair out and looked at him, realizing then how ironic it was that she thought she couldn't wash and change in front of him. After all, he had seen all there was to see.

It grew very dark inside the shed because of the black clouds overhead, and thunder and lightening crashed around them. Addy had never liked storms, and she felt a great urge to run to Cole and let him hold her, but she warned herself that would be a bad idea . . . wouldn't it? What was this ache that suddenly crushed at her insides? After tonight he would be gone again, and surely this time would truly be the end of it, as it should be. He said he would come to Central, but he probably wouldn't, and even if he did, she planned to have a new life there. She needed to live alone for a while, to acclimate herself to her new home, to gather her thoughts and her emotions . . . maybe someday find the right man, if she even really wanted another man in her life. Cole Parker was not the right man.

"I wish you luck, Cole." She turned away, nervous about the look in his blue eyes, the memories . . . the hunger. She poured some of the bucket water into a washpan, wishing there were some way to heat the water. Before she could wet a rag, a strong arm came around her from behind, pressing her back against a solid chest. Another arm came across her breasts, and she felt a warm breath against her cheek.

"You know we have to do this once more, Addy."

"Cole, please don't. We can't do this again."

"You want to as much as I do and you know it." He kissed her neck. "I hate good-byes. In our case, after knowing each other the way we have—"

"Please let go of me, Cole." The rain came down even harder, and thunder exploded overhead, making her jump again. Cole moved his lips around to meet her mouth, turning her almost forcefully, yet part of her wanted to turn. As soon as his warm lips parted her own, she was lost in his embrace, eagerly returning the kiss. Her hands balled into fists, pushed against his shoulders, but to no avail. He was strong, overpowering, deliberate . . . and she wanted him again. They kissed eagerly, hungrily, acting on repressed needs. Ever since he rode up to the last station she had wanted him again.

He finally left her mouth but kept a strong arm around her waist and kept her pressed close as he searched the small room, spotting a blanket. He never once let go of her as he grabbed it and tossed it onto the floor with his other hand.

"Cole, we can't. Someone might come."

"Not in this rain, but we can't take too long or it would look bad for you." He pushed her to the floor, his big frame hovering over her as he met her mouth again, groaning with the want of her. A strong hand moved over her breasts, pulled at the front of her dress, popping open buttons. He reached inside her camisole, grasping a full breast and freeing it. His lips trailed down her neck then, her chest, until he came to a firm nipple. He kissed it, trailed his tongue in a circle around it.

"Dear God, Cole," she whispered. "We just can't do this."

He quieted her with another kiss. "Yes, we can," he answered softly between more kisses. "We have to."

He pushed her dress to her waist. Why was she letting him do this? He pulled her bloomers down to her ankles, over her high-button shoes. He tossed them aside. He unbuttoned his own pants, his gun still laced to his thigh. He leaned down again. "Just once more, Addy."

She felt his gun pressing against the inside of her left thigh, and something else that was hard pressed against private places, except that it was soft as velvet, and it was hot. In the next second it was inside of her, thrusting deep, in rhythmic movements that removed her from all reality. She found herself arching up to meet the thrusts, wanting all of him. He worked in circular motions that sent her into a realm of ecstasy where all she had known meant nothing. She felt a wonderful need rising inside of her until a rippling climax ravished her insides, making her cry out with the want of him.

They continued that way for several more minutes, heated, rhythmic, eager thrusts, her head coming up off the floor, flung back, her free breast aching to be tasted again. She felt his seed spill into her, but he did not let up. He kept up the movement until his shaft grew large again. He pulled her dress and camisole away from her other breast and leaned down to kiss and pull at it, and again he rammed into her over and over, filling her almost painfully, until his life surged inside of her again.

They both lay there spent, and finally Cole raised up with a deep sigh and turned away. He picked up a wash rag and dampened it, washing himself and quickly buttoning his pants. "I'll wash better when it's my turn in here. I'd better get over to the cabin. I'll tell them I had stayed here because I'd carried in your water and it was raining too hard to leave." He re-tucked his shirt while Addy pulled her dress down over her legs and closed it in the front. "No one will suspect anything. Sounds like the rain has let up a little. I should be able to run over there now."

Addy looked up at him. "What have we done? I don't understand this."

He studied her green eyes. "We've done what two adults need to do. Maybe it's love, maybe it isn't. It will take time for us to know. There *is* something special between us, Addy, but neither one of us is ready to face it. I still think you're the damnedest woman I ever met . . . and the prettiest." He turned and opened the door, ducking out into the rain, which was not so heavy now.

Addy, still on fire, but also ashamed, sat staring at the door. Her emotions whirled inside almost painfully. She could hardly believe what she had just done, yet she had not been able to stop it. She could only pray his seed would not take hold in her belly. She put a shaky hand to her hair, and then the tears came, tears of guilt, tears of confusion, tears of loneliness. She angrily wiped them away and got up to wash and change. She folded the blanket and put it back in place, looking around to be sure there would be no evidence of what happened left for anyone else to find. She brushed her hair and rolled it into combs to give her the look of the prim widow. What a lie that was, yet she would not have done such things with any other man. Why Cole then? Why an outlaw? A man who liked to drink, with no job and no plans for his own future?

She rolled her dirty clothes into a ball and stuffed them angrily into her carpetbag, then opened the door to see that the rain had stopped completely. She stormed to the main cabin, stopping to breathe deeply and compose herself before going inside. She wished she had just one person she could turn to for advice, but there was no one. She had to wrestle with the right and wrong of her feelings for Cole Parker all by herself; and how could she not wonder if he had just used her again? He seemed so sincere about his respect for her, but still there had been no words of love.

She stepped inside and was welcomed by everyone. No one seemed to think anything of Cole Parker having been caught in the shed with her, or at least no comments were made. All were seated at a long table set with biscuits and gravy, a plate of meat and one of potatoes. Addy took her place, keeping her eyes averted from Cole, who then rose.

"I'm finished," he announced, "and anxious for my turn at cleaning up." He left, and Addy breathed a little easier. The food was surprisingly good, and she joined the others in the best feast they had had in days. The women helped the station master, Billy Ward, clean up the table, and Addy was glad for something to keep her busy so she would not have to think about Cole and their second liaison.

When things were finished she went to the door, stepping out into a late-afternoon sun. The air smelled of wet earth, and it was cooler since the rain. She noticed the shed door was open now, and she wondered what had happened to Cole. She and the others had taken nearly an hour to eat and talk and clean up. He should have come back by now.

She walked off the porch, realizing she really should talk to Cole again. They couldn't leave things as they were. Perhaps it was time to admit to the truth, that they must be in love. Somehow they had to sort out their feelings. She walked to the shed and peeked inside, but no one was there. She looked around, saw him nowhere. She glanced over at the corral where his horse had been when they first arrived. It was gone.

Her heart pounded harder, and she walked over to a man called Skeeter, who tended the teams of horses kept ready for the stagecoaches. "Hello," she called out. "You're the one called Skeeter, aren't you? I believe Orum Brown told us that when we first arrived."

"Yes, ma'am." Skeeter was short and stout, looked part Mexican. "What can I do for you?"

"I'm looking for Cole Parker. He's the tall, dark man who rode shotgun for us—"

"Oh, sure, I know all about Mr. Parker. I was standing there, you know, when all of you first came in with the soldiers. And Orum, he had told me all about what Mr. Parker did when he first came across you folks, killing all those Indians and all. It's Mr. Parker's horse Orum rode in on. I guess Mr. Parker figured the horse was rested enough to go on his way after all."

Addy put a hand to her stomach. "What? He's . . . he's gone?"

"Yes, ma'am." Skeeter pushed his hat back a little. "Lit out of here just a few minutes ago. Said he could gain some miles yet before dark and he was anxious to be on his way."

Addy fought a sudden urge to cry. Cole! Surely this time she truly would never see him again. So much left unsaid! How could he be so cruel? But then in ways she had been cruel to him, too. "Thank you," she said quietly, turning away. She walked back to the shed, went inside and closed the door. Had she only dreamed what had happened there no more than two hours ago? She looked around, touched a washpan that was still wet, spotted a straight razor lying beside it. He had forgotten it.

She picked up the razor and folded the blade into the handle, and clinging to it tightly sat down on a crate and wept.

Twelve

Addy relished the feel of hot water in a real tub. The hotel she had chosen in Denver was the closest thing to luxury she had known since leaving St. Louis, and she wondered if perhaps she should stay right here and not go on into the mountains. Denver was a fast-growing city built on gold discoveries in places like Central, but people had told her that Central also was growing fast, and that it was in competition with Denver. People in Central had already hired her, paid her way west. She couldn't let them down now. Besides, she was curious. The mountains were breathtaking to see, even from this distance, although the desk clerk and some of the maids had verified that the road to Central was very dangerous.

She wondered with some trepidation if she would end up virtually trapped away from the rest of the world up in those mountains. She had never seen anything like the rocky peaks west of Denver, so high that even in August some of them still had snow on them. This was truly wild and beautiful country, and it left her feeling still more lost. Could this land really be part of the United States? It seemed like some foreign country, the terrain nothing like the land back East, wide-open plains and prairie land that stretched far beyond what the eye could see, lonely land where the wind blew almost constantly, flat land that led to swelling hills . . . hills that led to magnificent purple mountains that held precious metals in their bowels, luring men who dared to try extracting that metal . . . men who lived a lawless life in a lawless land.

She put her head back and closed her eyes. She had splurged and paid a maid to fill the copper tub in her room with hot water. This was so much nicer than a public bath, private, quiet. Here she could think about those lawless men, about Cole Parker. Her chest hurt every time she thought about him riding off without a word, after making love to her. How would she ever know how he really felt, if he had just used her after all? He was a man of mystery. Just when she thought she understood him, wondered if perhaps she loved him and he might change his life for her, off he would go again, leaving her wondering if she would ever see him again.

How could she understand what she had done if he wasn't there to talk to? She put a hand to her belly, feeling another cramp, thanking God she was having her time of month. Cole's seed had not taken hold in her, and she felt very lucky that it hadn't. She blamed Cole for the worry she'd suffered these last few days on the way to Denver. How could he just leave like that? What if she *had* gotten pregnant? What would she have done? It would have been Cole's fault she was left with no one to turn to. She might not have minded giving the man a new family, if that was what he wanted. But she almost hated him for riding off like that, giving no thought to the possibility he could have left her in a humiliating, embarrassing situation.

"No, Cole Parker, you don't want a family," she said softly, her eyes still closed. "You want a woman, someone warm beside you, but you don't want to commit your heart to loving her. You want to recapture the past through me. But you don't want the present. You don't want Addy Kane. You want Bethanne Coleman." The trouble was, Addy herself was not looking for another Tom Kane. She had lain with Cole Parker because she needed a man to hold her again, to make her feel like a woman again . . . and it was Cole she had wanted, not some ghost.

She sat up and began vigorously washing, glad to be able to finally get rid of all the dirt and grime of the journey here. She told herself it was useless wondering where Cole was now, if he would go on up to Central City after all, or stay here in Denver, or maybe head south into Texas or New Mexico. How could anyone tell what a man like that would do? He was a man who could not make up his mind as to what he wanted, a man torn by the past, confused about the future, probably sorry for his outlaw ways, yet could probably return to that life without much prompting. He drank too much, and . . .

"Stop it, Addy!" she grumbled. "You have to forget him!" Yes, she could do that, since she no longer had to worry he'd made her pregnant. She had been a fool—a stupid, lonely woman who'd gone too long without a man. She had let that virile build and those blue eyes get to her. She had allowed herself to feel sorry for the man, to sympathize with his loneliness. She had actually used her body to help comfort him, and she felt like an idiot, wondering how a Christian woman with a college education, a woman who had always lived by high standards and strict morals, could have done such a thing. It was obvious to her now that Cole had wanted only her body and now he was done with her. If she *could* see him again, she would slap him in the face and tell him what a bastard he was!

She finished washing, then dried off and powdered herself, luxuriating in the feeling of being clean. She pulled on a robe. In the morning she would go down to a special room set up in the hotel where maids washed women's hair for them. Oh, how good it would feel to have clean hair! She had sent all her dirty clothes down to be laundered for her, and she hoped she could find such services up in Central. She walked to a window and peeked through the lace curtains. The rooms here were small but clean, and her room was on the west side. From her window she could see the Rocky Mountains on the horizon, lying in wait for her, beckoning her.

She breathed deeply against tears of hurt. She had to forget about Cole. He was just a part of her life that was over now. She had done a stupid thing, allowing her emotions to run away with her like that. Now she had to think about what lay ahead for her. In just a couple of days she would reach her new home up in those mountains, start a new life, meet new people. The ugliness of the war was behind her, Unionville was behind her, her sister's cruel coldness was behind her. Her eyes misted at memories of her father and mother, memories of Tom and how happy they'd been those few short weeks they'd had together before Tom left, never to return. Now she had another memory that hurt, but this one could have been avoided.

She walked over to the bed, crawling between clean, flannel sheets and blankets, sinking into a feather mattress. Her mind raced with thoughts of what she had been through to get this far. Addy Kane, a Christian woman who had never known violence, ripped away and threatened by outlaws, digging a bullet out of one of those outlaws, shooting Indians, sleeping with a wanted man! She supposed she shouldn't tell the people who had hired her about the outlaws, about killing an Indian . . . certainly not about having an affair with a wanted man she hardly knew!

All that had happened left her utterly exhausted. "Please just stay out of my life now and let me forget you," she muttered, thinking about Cole. There was more to a relationship than the man being meltingly handsome and knowing exactly how to touch a woman, more to it than the fact that he had happened to save her life more than once. A man had to be ready to give his heart, had to be settled, have a job, leave the past behind him. Cole wasn't ready for any of those things.

She fell into an exhausted sleep.

Cole leaned close to his campfire and lit the end of a small stick, then held it to the tip of a thin cigar. He puffed on it and threw the stick into the fire, staring at the flames for a moment while he smoked quietly. Shadow stood hobbled and grazing not far away, and in the distance he could see hundreds of lantern lights in the darkness. Denver lay in the wide, flat land northwest of where he'd made camp. He had already been there, had bathed and shaved, even drank and gambled some. He liked Denver, might even stay; but for now he would camp away from the city, give Addy time to get there and leave again. He didn't want to run into her.

She probably hated him now, and it was best that way. Trouble was, what if he'd got her pregnant? He picked up a small rock and threw it, disgusted with himself. "You're a damn fool, Nick Coleman!" he growled, using his rightful name. It was best for Addy if he stayed out of her life, but now he had no choice but to go on up to Central. It shouldn't be difficult to find her there. All he had to do was find the school. The only honorable thing for him to do was make sure he hadn't left her in a bad situation.

If he had, they'd have to marry, and what a damn awkward marriage that would be, neither of them even sure they loved the other, neither of them ready to commit to something like that. He didn't have any right loving the woman just because she looked like Bethanne. For God's sake, there had to be more to it than that! And what the hell was he going to do for money? In a town like Central, he supposed it would be easy to get it the way he'd been getting it for some time now—just rob a bank or a gold shipment. What was he thinking? He sure as hell couldn't earn it that way if he was married to a proper woman who was carrying his child!

He stood up, keeping the cigar between his teeth as he watched the city in the distance. She was probably there by now. God only knew what was going through her mind. How badly had he hurt her by just riding off the way he had? But he couldn't stay and have to look at her, wanting her again, knowing it was all wrong. He couldn't bear the hurt in her own eyes, or the hatred.

He walked over and petted Shadow's neck. "I'll go up there, see her, make sure she's all right," he said aloud to the horse. "If I see any hope, I'll find work, get myself settled . . . or maybe I'll just leave. There are probably a lot of men up there more worthy of an Addy Kane than I am—preachers, bankers, store owners—settled men who have a lot more to offer than bad dreams and an outlaw past."

Damn! He could just ride away from it all right now if he

wasn't worried he'd left her pregnant. That would be the wisest thing to do, but he didn't have any choice.

"Hello there!"

Shadow whinnied, and Cole swung around to see three men step into the light of his campfire. He'd been around bad seed long enough to know by a man's eyes if he could be trusted. These men looked hard, packed a lot of weapons. And where were their horses? There could be no reason for leaving them behind but wanting to sneak up to his camp on foot. "What do you want?" he asked.

The tallest one, who sported a beard, stepped in front of the other two. "Oh, we were just headed for Denver, saw your campfire." His hand rested casually on a six-gun at his hip. "We thought maybe you were headed back down from the mountains . . . maybe one of them prospectors that's sold his claim to the richer mineowners, and maybe you're packin' a good amount of money, headed for Denver to put it in the bank? There's a lot of gamblin' and whorein' to be done in Denver. A man needs money for them things and we're a little low, Mister. You understand what I'm tellin' you?"

Cole kept the cigar clenched in his teeth as he spoke. "I'm no prospector, and all I understand is you're a bunch of thieves who go around at night preying on people. You'd be best to get the hell away from my camp." He slowly reached up with his left hand and took the cigar from his mouth, tossing it aside.

The man facing him chuckled. "Well now, you see, we want to give you a fair chance. There's three of us, and we've made ourselves visible to you."

Cole glanced at the other two, one young and clean shaven, the other perhaps old enough to be his father, grizzly and dirty. The man in front could be a relative, a friend . . . didn't matter much.

"Now, you just hand over any money you've got," the man continued, "and your weapons and your horse, and we'll leave you by your fire here. You can even have your food and water. Deal?"

Cole's upper lip moved into a sneer. "No. I'll make a deal with you though. All three of you leave now, and I'll let you live."

One of those in the background chuckled.

"Hey, Mister, we don't want to kill you if it ain't necessary," their leader told Cole.

"Same goes for me," Cole answered.

They all stood silent for a few seconds, no sound but the night wind, and very distant, indistinguishable voices coming from the city in the distance. The three men eyed Cole carefully, and Cole could see a hint of doubt and fear in their eyes.

"I remind you there's three of us, Mister," their leader repeated.

"One man who's damn good with a gun can take three men any time," Cole answered. "Now, which one of you wants to be first?"

Again the air hung silent.

"This is bullshit!" one of the others finally grumped. He went for his gun, and instantly Cole's was out and fired. Everything happened in only a second. The first man went down. The leader drew his gun at almost the same time, but Cole got off three shots, putting the last two bullets in the man in front. He cocked his six-gun again, aiming it at the third man, who had not drawn his gun. The man simply stood transfixed, gun hand ready but frozen in an arch outside his holster. His eyes bugged out in fear, and Cole stepped a little closer.

"You take your friends here and go find a place to bury them. But first you drop your weapon, and you take theirs and place them beside it. Then you leave all your rifles and any other weapons right here with me as well. You can come back in the morning and get them. I won't be here."

The man swallowed. "Who . . . who the hell are you?"

"You don't need to know. Now do as I say!"

"Y . . . yes, sir." It was the youngest man. He walked off into the darkness to get their horses, then returned and scrambled to lay all their weapons beside Cole's campfire. Cole helped him load the two dead men onto their horses. The younger man mounted up and picked up the reins to the two horses. "What if somebody catches me burying them?" he asked. "How do I explain it?"

"I don't give a damn. Tell them you were ambushed in the dark and didn't see who did it—maybe it was Indians or somebody who was drunk. Just leave me out of it."

"Why? You could go to the authorities yourself and tell them the truth."

Cole nodded. "I could. Let's just say I'm giving you a break. If I tell them the truth you'll go to jail. Is that what you want?"

The young man shook his head. "Why do you care?"

Cole nodded toward the jacket the young man wore. "You're wearing a Confederate jacket. You fight for the South?"

The boy's eyes lit up a little brighter. "I did."

"And you lost everything back home and came here hoping to start over."

The boy frowned. "How'd you know that?"

"I know the look. Now get going."

The young man shrugged. "Sure. Thanks, mister." He turned and rode off. Cole looked down at his gun, wondering when he would be allowed to quit this life, not even sure anymore where it had all started. He only knew it had to end somewhere. And for now, he didn't want the attention of a shooting. He listened and watched for a few minutes to be sure the young man had truly left, then began saddling Shadow.

"Sorry about this, boy, but as soon as dawn cracks we're getting out of here." He finished loading most of his gear onto the animal, then sat back down on his bedroll, piling up an extra blanket for a pillow, since he wouldn't have his saddle to lean on while he slept. He stared at the campfire a while longer, too worked up now to sleep, and he wondered if this was how it was going to be forever. Stay a few days here, run, have it out with someone, gamble, drink, run again, stay a few days there, wanting to settle but not knowing how to live that way any more. He picked up a small flask of whiskey that lay beside his bedroll and uncorked it, taking a swallow. He licked his lips and corked it again, telling himself this was all the more reason he couldn't settle with a woman like Addy.

Addy's eyes widened when she looked out the window of the stagecoach that carried her and other passengers up Clear Creek Canyon. Jeanette Booth had chosen to stay in Denver with the Beans, and Addy again felt totally alone. She had met and made friends with people on this long journey, even almost fell in love, and now they were all gone from her life. She actually missed the people with whom she had shared so much danger. Fighting for each other's lives drew total strangers very close. She'd heard that sometimes on the trail west, women widowed by the elements or Indians sometimes married total strangers just to have a man take care of their family. She was beginning to understand how that could happen.

Now she would have to start over again, making completely new friends in Central, but first she had to make it there alive. What she saw out the window led her to wonder if she might never get there. This road was not nearly so dusty as the roads out on the plains, and that was because it was almost pure rock, a ledge cut out of the side of a canyon wall! If they were to meet someone coming down from above, how would they even be able to pass? She stuck her head out to gawk at canyon walls hundreds of feet high, where here and there a scraggly shrub grew out of pure rock. Up top were pine trees, and everywhere huge boulders hung out from nothing, looking as though they would surely drop at any moment, tumbling down to crush the coach and all its passengers. Another few hundred feet below she could see a creek flowing, and it looked yellow. She wondered if that meant it flowed with gold dust.

"Don't be worried, ma'am," a young man told her. He rode in the coach with her, along with a painted, buxom woman who was undoubtedly headed for Black Hawk or Central to sell herself to men. Addy had tried to be casually friendly with the

woman so as not to insult her, but the woman, who called herself
Sassy Dillon, had such a wicked mouth it was difficult. Besides
that, Sassy was rude, looking her over as though she was a sorry
prude to be laughed at.

A prim little schoolteacher, huh? the woman had said when
they first met as the stage left Denver. *You sure ain't the kind
the men up at Central City need.* She had laughed a bawdy laugh,
her big breasts jiggling. She wore a rather prim dress for a
woman of such wild mannerisms. Addy suspected she dressed
much differently when in Central. Her yellow hair was twisted
up under a feathered hat, and she wore far too much powder and
color on her face. The young man riding beside her, whose name
was Benny Reed, seemed to already know her, and as they talked
with each other, it was obvious both had been to Central several
times and knew it well, just as they were familiar with this hair-
raising ride to get there. Apparently both had had business in
Denver, but Addy was not about to ask what it was. She decided
it would not be wise to get too friendly with these strangers,
especially a woman like Sassy. She would not want to be seen
warmly addressing the woman when she got off the coach, for
fear it would look bad to anyone who might be there to greet
her.

"They make this trip just about every day," Benny continued,
trying to calm Addy's fears. "They almost never have any accidents."

Addy pulled back inside and looked at him. "Almost?" She
put a hand to her chest. "I've never seen such country. I can
hardly believe people made it all the way up here and built a
whole city!"

"Aw, heck, lady, where there's gold, men will find a way to
get to it," Sassy told her. "You'd be surprised. Central is practically as big as Denver, and it's growing every day. Someday
we'll have fancy hotels, churches, even an opera house. Hell,
they're even talking about building a new school. That should
make you happy. And thank God there's plenty of saloons! You're
in the wrong trade, honey. If you want to make real money, you

ought to do what I do!" The woman guffawed, and Addy felt herself blushing, wondering what Sassy would think if she knew the things she had done with Cole Parker. Was she really any different from the woman who sat across from her?

She shook away the thought. Of course she was! She had wanted more than anything to be able to love Cole, to hear him say he loved her, to make some meaning out of their liaisons besides lustful desire. The coach bounced over a rock, and she grabbed the hand strap, her heart taking a leap along with the coach. She looked at Benny, wanting to change the subject from Sassy's joking about prostitution. "You're familiar with Central, then?"

"Sure am. Worked in the mines there for a while. Left with a couple of friends, but they, uh, they got shot. Now I've decided to go back."

Addy's eyebrows arched. "Shot? How did it happen?"

Benny frowned and thought for a moment. "Well, you promise not to tell?" He looked at Sassy. "You, too, Sassy?"

The woman rubbed his thigh. "Honey, you know you can trust me. I don't much care what a man does with his life, long as he pays me good when he's in my room."

She laughed again, and Addy felt almost sick at the sound, not sure how much longer she could bear having to ride in the same coach with the woman. Benny looked back at Addy.

"Lady, I got mixed up with some men I didn't know were bad, you know? We headed down to Denver, and low and behold they started robbin' people. I went along with it because I was afraid of them. Then the other night, we come upon this man camped in the hills just southeast of Denver. He was a big guy, tall, broad. From what I could tell by the campfire light, he was pretty good lookin'. I think he had blue eyes, and them eyes, they had a way of starin' right through a man. I mean, I could tell right off he wasn't a man to mess with, but the men with me, they thought that with three against one, there wasn't no problem."

Addy put a hand to her chest. A big man with blue eyes that

could look right through you? Cole? Was he somewhere near after all? No, that couldn't be. "What happened?" she asked.

"Well, Gary, the guy who told us what to do, he stepped up and faced the man, told him to hand over his weapons and any money he had. The man up and says no! He says we'd better be the ones to hand over our weapons and go away and leave him alone, or we'd die. Ken, the other man with us, he just laughed and drew on the guy." He shook his head. "I've never seen anybody draw so fast. That man had his six-gun out and fired at both Ken and Gary before either one of them could shoot back. Me, I just watched. I didn't draw, and he didn't shoot me. He made me give up all our weapons and load Gary and Ken onto their horses—said as I should lie about how it happened and say that I never saw who did the shooting. I guess he didn't want the attention for some reason."

Didn't want the attention. That sounded like Cole. Why did her heart rush at the thought that he could be coming here after all? She should hate him. She *did* hate him!

"I turned in the bodies at Denver, told the authorities there somebody ambushed us, maybe Indians. I went back to that camp and all our guns was still there, but the man was gone— who knows where? Strangest thing I ever saw."

"Well, if he was so good lookin', I hope he comes to Central," Sassy spoke up.

Addy felt an unwarranted jealousy at the words, but also anger. Yes, this was the only kind of woman men like Cole Parker should lay with, women who didn't care that he didn't love them, who needed nothing more than sexual pleasure.

Addy turned and gawked out the window again, and the coach swept past a boulder on her side that stuck out so far she thought the coach would hit it. The driver shouted and whistled, the coach rocked and bounced. A few minutes later it pulled onto a ledge, and they waited as another coach went by in the opposite direction. "We'll rest the horses a minute!" the driver shouted.

Addy moved to look out the other side again, feeling almost sick to her stomach when she saw how high they were. "Dear

Lord," she whispered. The only sound was a droning wind coming down the canyon, combined with the distant sound of water roaring below. "What is that yellow stuff?" she asked then, noticing a pile of yellow-looking dirt outside what appeared to be a mine entrance on the side of a mountain across the canyon.

Benny leaned over to look out. "Oh, that's tailings from a mine, the junk that's left over after sorting out the ore. Some of it gets in the creek water, makes it run yellow. People farther below complain that it's souring the water and making it no good. Probably right, but when it comes to gold, men don't much care about what gets spoiled trying to get to it."

Addy jumped when she heard a rumbling explosion. "What's that!"

Benny just grinned. "Dynamite in one of the mines. That's how they loosen up the rock to find the ore. We're gettin' close to Black Hawk now. You'll have to learn to live with the explosions. They go on all day long up here. It's just a fact of life. One good thing, though—eventually you won't have to take a coach up this road to go between here and Denver. They're talkin' about buildin' a railroad."

"In these mountains? It doesn't seem possible."

"How many times do we have to tell you, lady?" Sassy put in. *"Anything* is possible when it comes to gold and men getting to it. You'll like Central. It's a wild, exciting town."

Addy rolled her eyes. "I am not exactly looking for wild and exciting," she answered. "I have been through enough the last few years for all the wild and exciting I want, especially the last few weeks. The trip here was as wild and exciting as I want."

"Well, the excitement ain't over yet," Sassy told her. "Hang on to your hat, honey."

Addy absently did just that, putting a hand to her hat as the driver got the coach underway again. They headed up an even steeper grade, and Addy could hear more explosions. She closed her eyes and clung to the hand strap as the coach climbed higher, at such a steep grade that she was afraid something would break loose and they would go crashing backward downhill. Finally they balanced out and began heading downhill.

"Almost there!" Benny told her.

Addy looked out, and sprawling ahead of them was what she knew must be Black Hawk, as she had learned they first had to go through that gold town before reaching Central City. The town did not seem to have any specific layout. It was simply a mass of brick and wooden buildings, and everywhere in the hills the land was dug away in ugly layers, piles of tailings everywhere, mine entrances, smokestacks.

So, finally she was here. Whether or not she had made the right decision, there was no going back. The city of Central was just a mile below Black Hawk. Mrs. Addy Kane had arrived.

Thirteen

Addy had never known so much noise and confusion. As soon as they disembarked the stagecoach, Sassy grabbed a couple of bags and sauntered away, quickly surrounded by a herd of men, many of whom seemed to already know her. Addy had learned during the last of their journey that Sassy owned a saloon in town called Hard Luck, and she remembered reading about it in the *Register* as one of the places Central's citizens wanted to close.

Addy could hear the woman cackling all the way up the street. Benny Reed quickly disappeared without bothering to offer Addy any help, and Addy stood on the boardwalk waiting for her bags and her trunk to be unloaded.

The city of Central was a mass of businesses, some of the streets still dirt, now muddy from a rain the night before. People swarmed everywhere, mostly men; horses and wagons lined the street in front of businesses, and farther up in the hills that rose steeply all around the town Addy could see homes in some areas, mostly mines in others. When coming through Black Hawk she had been amazed to see some mining going on right along the main street, huge holes dug, ore cars rumbling right alongside the horses and wagons in the street. Every minute or two she heard another explosion in the surrounding mountains, and smokestacks from processing mills belched black smoke, the residue from the coal used to run steam engines inside the mills. Up and down the street she could hear piano music and laughter, and once in a while gunfire.

So, this was "the richest square mile on earth." Addy wondered how many of the men packing the streets had ever truly seen riches from looking for gold. From things she had read, most men who struck gold did not have the money to mine it properly and ended up selling out to wealthier men, who in turn increased their own fortunes while paying nominal amounts for the original claims.

Benny's words of *wild* and *exciting* hardly described this town, but in spite of all the busy commotion, Addy felt even more lonely and lost. "Can you tell me where a place called Miss Ada's Rooming House is located?" she asked the driver, who stood watching another man unload the rest of her baggage.

"Miss Ada's?" The man shoved back his hat and pointed uphill. "Way on up there where you see all them nicer houses. I ain't sure the street, but once you get up in there, somebody can tell you. You won't find a room, though. This town is in bad need of more roomin' houses and hotels. What they have is packed full all the time."

"Someone is supposed to have reserved a room there for me," Addy answered. "A Mrs. Hester Collingswood."

The man's eyebrows arched. "Mrs. Collingswood? She's a rich lady—lives up there where I just showed you. Her husband owns a pharmacy and a bank here in town. If she's holdin' a room, then I reckon you're set. You need somebody to take you up there?"

"Yes. Please."

The man nodded, walking into the street and hailing down another man who happened to be driving by with a buckboard. "You willin' to take a pretty gal up in the fancy area, Mister?"

The man driving the wagon grinned. "Pretty? Will I see her in one of the crib houses later on?"

Addy rolled her eyes in disgust. Was that all men in these parts thought about?

"Heck no. She's a new schoolteacher, widow woman come here from Illinois to teach. You gonna help her or not?"

The man rubbed his chin. "I guess so. Where's she goin'?"

"Up to Miss Ada's Roomin' House."

The man with the wagon pulled over, and the coach driver and his helper began loading Addy's things into the back of the wagon. Addy stepped forward, addressing the stranger who would give her a lift. He was a middle-aged man, tall and lanky and looked as though he needed a bath. He wore soiled cotton pants, and only longjohns for a shirt. His boots looked well worn, as did his hat. "Hello," she said. "My name is Mrs. Addy Kane, and I appreciate your helping me." She pulled a shawl she had taken from one of her bags around her shoulders, surprised at how chilly it was high in the mountains this time of year. All the way here she had sweltered in the summer heat, and for the moment the only advantage she could find for being in this rowdy, unorganized town was that it was cooler here than in the broad, flat plains to the east. She wondered how the wagon driver could stand to wear only a shirt and no jacket.

"Sam Stark," the man answered. "I make deliveries for different stores around town. Wife and I live up the other way." He pointed in the opposite direction from where the boardinghouse was located. "Got four kids. Glad to see another schoolteacher come to town. Won't be long before we'll need a lot more."

Addy could not help feelings of disgust. This man was married and had children, yet he'd wanted to know if she was a prostitute. She forced back an immediate dislike for him, grateful that at least he acknowledged a need for her presence, which meant maybe there were a lot of other parents who would be grateful for her presence and would want to make friends with her. "Thank you," she answered, beginning to wonder how anyone was supposed to find anything in this town. The only directions anyone seemed to be able to give were "way on up there" or "up the other way." She supposed she would simply have to do some exploring on her own and learn her way around, if it was safe for a woman to be out and about alone here.

"Your things is all loaded," the stagecoach driver told her. "Climb on up there with the man."

Addy lifted her skirt slightly with one hand, taking hold of the man's hand for support as she stepped up into the wagon seat. She stayed on the far edge so as not to be seen sitting too close to Sam Stark. "Thank you for finding someone to take me," she told the stagecoach driver, "and thank you for getting us here safely. I don't believe I want to travel the road here again any time soon."

The man laughed, and Sam joined in the laughter. "You get used to it," Sam told her, snapping the reins to get his two large draft horses going.

"A young man on the stagecoach told me that," she answered, "but I don't quite believe it." She clung to the side and back of the wagon seat as the wagon bounced and clattered over ruts in the road, splashing mud onto its wooden wheels.

"Illinois, huh?"

"Yes," Addy answered. "Unionville." Had she really lived there once? "I lost my husband and family because of the war, and came out here to start over."

"Sorry to hear that, but you'll learn to like it here in Central. Up here the war don't count, who fought for who. Folks have to rely on each other to get by. It's a whole other world up here in the Rockies. Most people who come here never go back."

"I can see why!" Addy answered. "No one wants to go back down that road!"

Sam laughed and headed the wagon up a steep road that led away from the main part of town. Addy took in the sights, jumped slightly at the sound of another explosion. "Do you know where Miss Ada's is?"

"I make deliveries, remember? I know every house and business in Central. Miss Ada's is one of the nicer boarding houses, and believe me, there ain't a lot of nice ones. The hotels is worse. Most of them are log buildings with dirt floors, blankets to divide the rooms—no place for proper ladies to stay. Things is gettin' better, though. There's talk of building better hotels and such. If you're a church goer, there's been a Methodist church organized, St. James, I think they call it. Right now they hold services in peoples' homes, lots of times at Aunt Clare Brown's house. She's a Negro slave woman who bought her freedom and came out here to look for gold. Anyways, I guess they're tryin' to raise money to build a church. Mrs. Collingswood can tell you about all that. There's a Presbyterian church up at Black Hawk."

Addy looked around in wonder as Sam's horses huffed and puffed their way up the steep incline. She wondered if anyone could go anyplace in these parts without having to climb to get there. "Where is the school?" she asked.

"Well, right now there ain't one. School's held at Lawrence Hall, but folks is raisin' money to build a real school building. You ain't the first school teacher hired, you now. Central is a lot bigger than you think. We've got about a hundred and forty kids goin' to school now and not enough teachers. That's why they advertised back East. I'll bet they're payin' you good. Most teachers ain't willin' to come to remote places like this."

I can understand why, Addy felt like saying. "I'm being paid quite well," she answered, thrilled at the offer she had been made of $45.00 per month. "I knew it wouldn't be easy, but I just needed to go someplace completely new to get away from bad memories."

"Well, ma'am, you'd be surprised how many folks up here came for that very reason. Everybody in Central and Black Hawk is from someplace else. I'll bet every state and every territory is represented in this town. I'll tell you, too, that if the teachin' job don't work out, there's all kinds of work for women up here, and not just in the brothels. Fact is, Central's prominent citizens and the local newspaper are tryin' to roust out the town's, uh, soiled doves, so to speak. But I think the miners would put up a big fuss over that."

The man laughed, and Addy stared straight ahead, her cheeks growing hot with embarrassment that he would speak so casually of such women in front of her. Apparently, prostitution was such a common way of life out here that no one thought anything about discussing it openly.

"Anyway, heck, women are needed for workin' in dining rooms, as chambermaids, laundresses, housework for the richer families up in the hills, cooks, clerks . . . some even work in the mines! You can make two to three dollars a day workin' in the mines, but most of that work is just too hard for a woman. Laundresses and maids and such make sometimes thirty dollars a month."

"Oh, I prefer to teach, Mr. Stark." Addy looked back. Most of the city was spread out below, and she could not help wondering if Cole Parker was down there somewhere. Maybe he had not come at all. She hoped he had not. She had left one life behind her at Unionville, another phase of it on the trip here. All of that was over now.

After a good fifteen minutes of climbing Sam drew his wagon to a halt in front of a neat frame house. A sign in front read simply "Ada's". "Here you are, Mrs. Kane," Sam told her. "You've had quite a journey, haven't you?"

Addy felt a catch in her heart. She turned and looked to the east . . . her parents, her sister, Tom . . . Cole. Finally she had made it to her new home, her new life. "Yes," she answered. "I'm very tired."

"Well, I'll carry in your things for you." Sam climbed down and Addy blinked back tears, telling herself she must not do any more crying. It was all done now. She was here, and that was that.

Cole puffed on a cigarette as he looked at his cards, then eyed the men around the table where he sat. The only one challenging him was an older man who had drawn two cards then raised Cole on the next round of betting. Cole had drawn three queens and had also taken only two cards, but neither one improved his hand. Still, three queens was damn good for five-card draw. He matched his opponent's raise and threw down his cards. The other man scowled.

"How many times do you draw three jacks in this game and lose?" he grumbled. He threw down his own cards and rose, putting on his hat. He rested a hand on a six-gun at his side. "Mister, you wouldn't be cheatin' me now, would you? Ain't a man in Central who'd put up with that."

Cole pulled the money toward him. "I wouldn't put up with it either," he answered. "You'd better sit back down and play, or leave. Just don't think about drawing on me because if you do, you'll never play another game of cards." He shoved the money into a leather drawstring bag he'd brought along for that very reason.

"We don't even know your name, mister," his challenger answered. "You say you've only been here four days, don't have a job yet."

Cole sighed with disgust, taking the cigarette from his mouth and setting it in an ashtray beside him. "And I suppose every man in this town *does* have a job?"

A few other men laughed.

"Let it go, George," one of them spoke up. "The man beat you fair and square. Let's get on with the game."

George, who had drunk far too much already that night, stood a little straighter, holding his chin high. "All of you know how fast I am—so fast that nobody around here will go up against me anymore—fast enough that I don't take bullshit from any man."

"You'd better take it from that one," another voice entered. "I've already seen him in action, and it ain't pretty."

Cole frowned, glancing sideways to see a young, blond-haired man watching them. He didn't recognize him at first, but then he remembered—the man he'd let live after shooting his two cohorts who had threatened him back near Denver.

"How do you know?" George asked.

" 'Cause I was right there," the young man answered. "He out-drew two men at once, and now they're dead."

Cole kept his eyes on George, realizing that in his drunken condition, he was unpredictable. He slowly rose. "Look, mister, I don't want any trouble. I beat you at cards. So what? What man here hasn't had his good nights and his bad ones at the card table? Just get the hell out of here."

George shook his head. "I ain't been beat yet with the gun, and I don't aim to start now."

Instinct told Cole it was time. He saw the split second decision, and in a flash his own gun was drawn and cocked. George's was not yet out of the holster. Gasps could be heard throughout the room, and George stood there gawking at Cole's gun. "Unloose your gunbelt and get going," he warned. "I'm sure the bartender here will keep it for you until tomorrow."

George swallowed, slowly unbuckling his gunbelt. "Who the hell are you?" he asked.

"What difference does it make to anybody here?"

George laid his gunbelt on the table. "I'll see you again, mister."

Cole nodded. "You probably will. Maybe you'll be sober then."

A few men laughed, and George scowled, turning and walking away.

"Sit down and we'll play some more, mister," one of the others told Cole.

Cole looked over at the young man he'd let go free back in Denver. "Maybe later," he answered. He picked up a glass of whiskey and swallowed what was left of it, then took up his cigarette and took a last drag before putting it out, all the while staring at the young man who had warned George not to draw on him. He stood at the bar with a buxom blond woman who wore a dress that fit too tightly over her breasts. She smiled at him, looking him over as though he were a delicious piece of cake. Cole tried to guess her age . . . twenty but looking older because of too much paint and a hard life? Or was she actually at least thirty? Maybe forty? Who could tell with women like that? He picked up his leather bag of money and walked over to the two, while a few others continued to stare at him and talk quietly about how fast he was. Everyone else returned to their drinking and gaming.

"What the hell brings you to Central City?" Cole asked the young man.

The youth grinned. "Money, women, drink, maybe a job. I've lived up here off and on for a while now." He put his arm around the woman. "Sorry about what happened back by Denver, mister, but the men I was with, I just couldn't stop them. I didn't know they were like that till I ran off with them. I didn't want to rob you."

Cole nodded slowly, watching his eyes. "I knew that. That's why I let you go."

"And because of the Confederate uniform," he added with a grin. He still wore the tattered jacket.

"That, too," Cole told him.

"Names Benny Reed," Benny told him. "Apparently you don't care for people to know your name, so I won't ask."

"Well, well!" the painted woman spoke up. "Is this the man you told us about in the stagecoach on the way up here, about how fast a draw he was?"

"Sure is!" Benny answered with a grin. "Small world, ain't it?"

The woman gave Benny a look that told him to leave her alone with the handsome newcomer. Benny nodded to Cole. "See you around, mister. I live above the Wildcat Saloon if you ever want to find me. I can tell you how to get a job in the mines, if you want one. They pay real good."

"I'll think about it. I don't really intend to stay that long," Cole answered.

Benny shrugged and left, and the painted woman beside him eyed Cole hungrily, looking him over carefully, obvious appreciation in her eyes. Cole couldn't decide if she was pretty or ugly, twenty or forty. She was a little plump, and her hair looked stiff.

"Well, I'll be." She put a hand against Cole's chest. "Buy you a drink, mister? I'm Sassy Dillon, owner of this saloon. I just got back from Denver. I keep most of my money there. It's safer than at any bank in this town or Black Hawk. I'm sure you can see why. There's not much law around here. We've got a sheriff, but he can't keep up with so many unruly men."

Cole eyed the patrons of the Hard Luck Saloon, some in fancy suits, others looking as though they'd need to beg for their next nickel. Silk vests, torn pants, top hats, floppy, soiled leather hats. The room was blue with smoke and reeked of whiskey and un-bathed bodies. Painted women hung around the tables, asking if the men would buy them drinks, a ploy to get more business for the owner.

"I can see why you take your money to Denver," he answered the woman, turning his eyes to meet hers. She had quickly removed the jacket-like top of her dress, brazenly exposing a low-cut neckline underneath. Cole glanced down at her bosom, thinking how some men might be tempted; but there was only one woman's bosom he longed to touch and taste again. Trouble was, he just couldn't let that happen. Even if Addy was here in Central, his purpose was only to make sure she wasn't pregnant. That was his only reason for coming here. After he'd talked to her, he would leave. He had no doubt she would want it that way.

"How about that drink, mister?" Sassy asked. She put a hand against his chest. "Damned if you aren't the best lookin' thing that ever walked into my place. You ready to give out your name yet?"

Cole pulled his thoughts away from Addy and looked back down at Sassy, breaking into a grin. "Cole Parker. And I'll take another shot of whiskey."

Sassy ordered the drink, her hormones running full speed at the sight of Cole Parker. Tall, broad, flat stomach, handsome face, square jaw, a smile that would melt a statue, and eyes that made her ache. She wanted to run her hands through his wavy, black hair, taste those full lips, feel this one ramming himself inside her. She hadn't planned this life. Circumstances had led her to this, and she had learned to enjoy men. Besides, she'd made damn good money sleeping with them, especially in the gold towns. Now she owned her own saloon, and she planned to eventually own more businesses as her body aged and made it impossible to sell her charms. "Here you go," she told Cole. "So, how long have you been here?"

Cole slugged down the whiskey. "Just a few days. I'm staying at a hotel that has no right being called one, but at least it's shelter, and they serve food there at reasonable prices."

Sassy laughed. "In towns like this a man or woman can put up any kind of business and do good. Most folks think we should be more civilized. They're building another church, talking about building a regular schoolhouse. I'd just as soon it stayed this way. Before you know it, women like me will be outlawed. We'll be replaced by the prim and proper ladies of society, like the ones who live up in the hills, the wives of the businessmen and mine owners." She chuckled, handing him yet another shot of whiskey. "You should have seen the woman me and Benny rode up here with in the stagecoach. Pretty as a picture, but so stiff and prim I almost felt sorry for her. Said she was comin' here to teach school."

Cole slowly lowered his now-empty glass. "That so?"

Sassy nodded. "Mrs. Addy Kane, she called herself. A war widow." She shook her head. "Sometimes I feel sorry for women like that. I'll bet the poor thing hasn't had a man in years, and even when she did have one, she probably didn't know how to enjoy it." She put a hand to Cole's waist. "Now I'll bet *you* know how to give a woman a good time."

Cole felt an old ache reawakened. So, Addy had made it to Central. All he had to do was find where she was staying. He'd ask her if everything was all right and then he'd leave. Trouble was, his heart beat faster just hearing her name. He looked down at Sassy. "I've had a few women enjoy my company," he answered.

Sassy laughed. "I'll bet you have! I'd like to be one of them. You ain't married or anything like that, are you?"

His smile faded, memories of Bethanne and little Patty returning. "Not anymore," he answered.

"Oh, I struck a nerve! I'm sorry, Cole."

He sighed, thinking how maybe if he got a few things out of his system it would be easier when he saw Addy again, easier not to want her, easier to go away. "Aren't you tired from your trip?" he asked Sassy.

"Not too tired for the likes of you."

She smiled through painted lips, and Cole convinced himself that this was the only kind of woman he was worthy of from now on. He had already thrown his life away. He never should have let himself care even a little for the likes of Addy Kane. "You clean?"

Sassy laughed. "You bet! And if you're worried, I've got those things some men like to use for protection. I get myself checked out by a doctor every couple of weeks. Hell, the prostitutes in places like this keep the doctors busier than anybody else!"

Cole shook his head and grinned. "Why don't you show me your room, then?"

Sassy's eyes lit up with pleasure. "Just follow me."

The woman turned and picked up a bottle of whiskey from the bar, then took up one of her bags. "Take my other bag, will you?" she asked Cole. She proceeded up a flight of stairs, and Cole picked up the other bag and followed.

"Got any idea where that schoolteacher is staying?" he asked Sassy.

The woman turned on the stairway, frowning. "No. Why would you ask that?"

He shrugged. "Just wondered where women like that keep themselves in a town like this."

Sassy studied his eyes. "You know her, don't you? I know men, Mr. Cole Parker, and I thought I saw something funny in those blue eyes when I first mentioned that woman's name. Now you're asking where she's staying." She knit her eyebrows in wonder. "Now how would a gun-slinging, shiftless man like you know a proper lady like that?"

Cole leaned forward and kissed her cheek. "None of your business. It's you I'll be sleeping with tonight."

"Mmm-hmm." She shrugged. "Well, when it comes to ones like you, I take them any way I can get them." She went on up the stairs and Cole followed her into a large room with red curtains and a brass bed. He kicked the door closed and took the whiskey from her, taking a long drink.

Fourteen

Addy smoothed the skirt of her dress as she disembarked the carriage that had been sent for her. She tugged at the matching jacket, upset that some of her dresses had been ruined on the long journey to Central. At least she had saved this one, one of her best summer dresses, a light blue cotton with dark blue trim that was sewn into a gentle swirl design around the skirt. The jacket was the same blue, edged at the short waist and at the cuffs and around the lapel and collar with the trim, the buttons also dark blue. Her hat was a small blue bonnet with little up-turned edges, perched at an angle on top of her auburn hair, which she had twisted into a roll at the back of her head.

Mrs. Hester Collingswood had sent a messenger to Miss Ada's boarding house to see if the new teacher had yet arrived, and upon learning she had, the messenger returned to tell her to take one day to rest from her long journey, and that the following day someone would come for her to take her to see Mrs. Collingswood. A carriage had indeed been sent. Addy was to breakfast with Mrs. Collingswood at her home.

It seemed silly to be so nervous, yet she was. After all, she had come so far, and she had no one and no place to return to if this job did not work out. She was here now and had to make the best of it. It would be nice to meet new people, make new friends. Apparently, in spite of the wild town Central was, those who ran the city were trying to civilize it and make it respectable. They were bringing in more teachers and treating her with such courtesy and dignity. Miss Ada's was indeed a fine boarding-

house, amazingly clean for all the dirt streets and belching processing mills that surrounded what was apparently the only truly
lovely spot in the area. These couple of hillside streets where
the homes were located were quite elegant, the lawns neatly
manicured.

Her room at Miss Ada's was small but comfortable, with an
adjoining room that held a wash table, mirror, bathtub and a
chamber pot that a maid would empty twice a day. Her bed linen
would be changed every two days. Clean lace curtains hung at
her window, and a bright, braided rug decorated the hardwood
floor.

Everyone who stayed at Miss Ada's was someone of respect
and prominence, visiting businessmen and their wives, a male
schoolteacher, a woman who privately tutored the children of
one of the wealthier families. The house was white, with roses
all around it that were already in bloom. Miss Ada herself was
an old maid of perhaps forty-five, Addy guessed, who had come
here to live with a brother who had discovered gold in the nearby
mountains, then sold his claim for a considerable amount of
money just before taking sick. Miss Ada had nursed the man
until his death and had inherited his money, which she used to
realize a dream of her own, to own a boarding house. What more
lucrative place for such an enterprise than a thriving town like
Central, but the woman claimed she stayed only because she
had fallen in love with living high in the mountains.

Addy breathed deeply, realizing that at least up here away
from town the air smelled sweet and clean, full of the scent of
pine. Already she was beginning to understand how someone
could fall in love with this country. But it was lonely, too, in
spite of the thousands of people who now swarmed the mountainsides looking for gold or helping extract it from deep in the
earth. The loneliness came from being so removed from the rest
of the world, and from the mere fact that half the people here
had come to get away from the horrors of war, from bad memories.

She thanked the driver of the carriage, who said he had instructions from Mrs. Collingswood to wait for her. She approached a white picket fence and opened a small gate that led past manicured lawns and flower gardens, up a stony walk to a lovely home painted pale green with darker green trim. White shutters decorated the windows, and the front door was white with oval-shaped frosted glass in the center. She picked up the door knocker and rapped it, and moments later a woman wearing a white cap and apron answered the door with a smile. "You are Mrs. Kane?"

Addy nodded. "Yes. I believe Mrs. Collingswood is expecting me."

"Yes, she is, come inside. I will show you to the dining room."

Addy followed the woman down a hallway decorated with plants. The polished wood floor was made more lovely by a miriad of oriental rugs. They passed what Addy guessed to be the parlor, and at a swift glance she saw rose-colored velvet davenports and a matching love seat, as well as a white marble fireplace. Another room held a wall of books and a large desk— Mr. Collingswood's study, she presumed. They reached a bright room with a huge dining table in the center. The light came from French doors that faced the rising sun, and a large chandelier hung over the table. Plants abounded, and the floor was covered with a velvet rug. A huge picture of a garden scene hung on the wall.

"Mrs. Kane is here, Mrs. Collingswood," the maid spoke up.

"Thank you, Jenny." An elderly woman with graying blond hair rose from where she had been seated at the end of the table. She smiled, her face revealing a woman who had been beautiful in her youth and was still beautiful in gracious manner. She wore a soft green day dress, her many slips rustling as she walked over to greet Addy. "Finally you have arrived," she said. "You're a few days late, Mrs. Kane. Do tell me what problems you had getting here. It was such a long journey."

The woman put out her hand and Addy took it, shaking it lightly, thinking how bony the hand was, although the skin was soft. "Yes, it was, Mrs. Collingswood. It would take all day to tell you everything that happened to me on the way here." Should she tell it all? Perhaps she would leave out being abducted by outlaws. The woman would wonder if she'd been raped, and perhaps that would put a stain on her reputation. If only Mrs. Collingswood knew the stain she really did carry. She must put all that behind her. What else could she do? There was no need for anyone ever to know, and this woman would put her out of her house if she knew the truth.

"Well, come sit down, and tell me most of it. We have plenty of time," Mrs. Collingswood told her. "Jenny will serve us a nice breakfast. Would you prefer tea or coffee?"

"Tea would be nice." Addy took a chair around the corner from where Mrs. Collingswood sat back down at the head of the table.

"Now, first, do call me Hester. May I call you Adrianne?"

"Addy is fine. That is how I have always been addressed."

The woman studied her intently with discerning gray eyes. "And you studied at Hope College in Michigan, according to your resume."

"Yes, ma'am . . . I mean, Hester. I received a teaching degree. That is where I met my husband, but we were married only a few weeks before he went off to war . . . never to return."

Hester frowned. "How sad. I'm sorry, Addy. And there has been no man in your life since?"

Addy thought it a very nosey question, but she supposed it seemed important to those who had hired her. Her heart rushed at the memories. Oh, yes, there had been a man, one who had made her feel alive and on fire, one who had made it impossible for her to be a proper lady, a man whose touch . . . "No one," she answered, hoping her eyes showed the same sincerity with which she spoke the words. "It's been four years. My father was also killed in the war, and my mother died not long after. I have a sister in St. Louis, but she's married and has children and her own life to live. I . . . needed to get away from the past and hoped to start a new life here in Central."

Hester breathed deeply with a satisfied smile. "And indeed

you shall. I will introduce you to many of Central's finest, including available men who are respectable enough for a woman of your education and station to see. We do, however, expect discretion and proper etiquette from our first female schoolteacher. We have six male teachers already, and we felt that a female was necessary. There are times when the young girls at the school might have questions or needs that they are afraid to discuss with a male teacher."

Addy nodded. "I see. I do appreciate the offer and look forward to my first teaching job."

Jenny brought in a tray holding a pot of tea, cups, cream and sugar, and warm biscuits. "I'll bring your eggs and ham in a few minutes," she told Hester. She poured tea for both women and left again.

"So, back to my original question. We have so much to discuss about your job and what is expected of you," Hester said, picking up the cream and pouring a little into her tea, then handing the creamer to Addy. "But first do tell me about your trip here. My own husband and I came here from Chicago. Stuart owned many businesses there. Now our two sons run them. My husband always wanted to come West, and once our sons were grown and able to take over things back home, he decided to live his dream before he dies. He's a pharmacist, and because of the wealth he gained in Chicago, he was also able to open a bank here in Central. We have been here four years. I'll certainly never forget my own trip here. It was entirely by wagon, but what a parade it was!"

The woman leaned back her head for a moment in memory. "Stuart hired several wagons and drivers to bring all our finest things. Luckily we had no major problems, but it was a hard journey for people our age. Stuart made up for the hardship by hiring builders when we reached Denver, as well as buying most of the material that would be necessary for building me a fine home once we got here. I probably don't need to tell you what a frightening trip it was, coming up here through Clear Creek Canyon with all those wagons and supplies!"

Addy laughed lightly. "I can't imagine such a venture." She realized Mrs. Collingswood would much rather talk about herself than hear Addy's own story, and she sipped her tea while the woman rattled on.

"Well, here we are, and I am so pleased with my home. Isn't it amazing what a man can do when he sets his mind to it? A few years ago there was nothing up here but wilderness and mountain lions and grizzlies. Now the mountains rumble from dynamite, we have a whole city, and Black Hawk is not far away. The mountainsides are peppered with mines, and men like Stuart are able to bring in all the finest materials to make life here as close to living back East as possible. I cried when we first came here, sure it would be impossible to live a civilized life." She folded her hands in her lap and looked at Addy again. "Again I have taken us off the pathway of our conversation. Did you have problems getting here?"

Addy set down her cup. "If you call being attacked by Indians and trapped in a sod station house trouble, then yes, I certainly did have trouble." She decided not to tell the woman that she had killed an Indian herself. When it came to being rescued by Cole, she simply said that a man came along who was able to kill several of the Indians and hold them off until finally the army came to their rescue. Hester gasped and exclaimed over the story, listened intently when Addy told her about the hot, hectic stagecoach ride, the wild cattle town of Abilene.

"After breakfast we will take the carriage to town," Hester told her. "I will show you the safest places to go, where to shop. We'll go past Lawrence Hall, where you will be teaching. Do you know how to drive a horse and buggy?"

"Yes," Addy answered.

"Stuart will leave a small carriage and a fine strong horse stabled at Miss Ada's. She has a stable boy who will hitch the horse and carriage for you each morning to drive to the school, use for going to town, whatever your needs. We will take care of the cost of feed and care of the horse, and, of course, your board at Miss Ada's will also be paid for by the city council as part of your pay. School won't start for several weeks yet, so you have plenty of time to relax and make friends and get to know your way around."

Addy shook her head in surprise, already feeling obligated to these people. "Hester, that's so generous. Surely I should pay my own board."

"Nonsense!" Hester turned to greet Jenny, who set a plate of eggs and ham in front of her, another in front of Addy. "The better citizens of Central are always glad to welcome someone of elegance and breeding. Slowly but surely we will rid this town of its riffraff, and all that will be left will be the businessmen, mine owners, and the miners and their families. For now this town is too full of drifters, shiftless men without jobs, men who are still coming here hoping to find gold . . . and then, of course, there are the painted ladies of the night. We will soon be rid of them, too."

Addy thought about Sassy Dillon, and how the woman would cackle over Hester's pompous attitude.

"The only thing we ask of you, Addy, is that you stay away from the riff-raff, even the miners. Those with families are civilized enough, but the single ones—" She rolled her eyes. "No single man is to be trusted. And when he is as rough and flamboyant as those men who work the mines, it is even worse. They are simply a necessary evil in order for our city to survive. But at least there are several single men in Central City who are quite proper for a young widowed schoolteacher to be seen with. You are quite beautiful, you know. They will be scrambling for your hand, but it is best that you're not seen alone in public. If you should start seeing someone, to which you have every right, it's best that you are always with another couple or a chaperone."

Addy wasn't sure what to say. It was obvious that Hester Collingswood was a busybody, whether intentionally or unintentionally. She was beginning to wonder if this woman and her cohorts intended to direct every move she made. It seemed ridiculous, considering the fact that she was a twenty-five-year-old woman who had already been married once. If this woman knew what she had done in Abilene . . .

"This evening we are having a reception for you at Lawrence Hall at six p.m. What you are wearing now will be just fine for the reception. My husband and I will come and get you and take you with us. You aren't too tired for it, are you?"

Addy's mind began to race with confusion at all the things Hester was throwing at her at once—asking all kinds of questions, telling her how to behave, what to wear, whom to see. "No, I don't mind. I'll be ready a little before six."

"Oh, that's fine. All the other schoolteachers will be there. We'll have a delightful time. Let's eat our breakfast now, and I'll show you around town a little today, some more tomorrow. Have you met John Withers? He's our only single male schoolteacher. The rest are married. Mr. Withers stays at Miss Ada's. We will ask him to room somewhere else, as it just doesn't seem proper that both of you live at the same rooming house."

Addy told herself to be patient with this woman's mothering attitude. "Yes, I've met Mr. Withers," she answered, wanting to laugh. John Withers was an older man with a bald head and gray mutton chops and beard. His stomach was huge, and he scowled most of the time. She had met him at the dinner table at Miss Ada's last night, and she thought how ridiculous it was that anyone would think she would have an interest in the man, who spoke little and held no attraction for a woman. To think they should not room in the same house was ridiculous.

Hester carried on about Central, the people Addy would meet tonight, her family. They finished eating, and Hester told her several things about the school, how many children would be attending, what hours and grades she would teach. She talked about churches to be built, the best shops, showed where to "powder" herself in preparation for their trip into town. They would be escorted by the buggy driver, who would wait for them outside of each store. "We must be careful, you know. It seems there is a saloon between every place of business. In a city like this, it is difficult for any woman to keep her husband in line and away from the gambling tables. It seems to be a weakness of most men, even the more prominent ones. And a woman must never go to town after dark. By then many of the more shiftless have had too much to drink. If you start taking the paper, you'll read about all the things that go on. Just the other night there was a near shooting at the Hard Luck saloon." Hester rose. "Some man who apparently values himself by his quickness with a gun challenged some stranger over a misunderstanding involving a card game. Apparently the stranger drew his gun and had it aimed before the other man could even get his gun out of its holster. Everyone is still talking about it, but they aren't sure of the stranger's name. The paper described him as quite tall and good looking, and it's been suggested that perhaps he'd be a good man to hire as a sheriff's deputy. We certainly need more law here, and men who know how to handle themselves, but then we know so little about him." She led Addy to a room off the kitchen where there was a wash basin, a mirror and a chamber pot. "Freshen up, dear, and we'll go to town."

She closed the door, and Addy stood staring after the woman, rather astounded at the way she had of subtly ordering people around, only with a soft voice and gracious manner. She turned and looked in the mirror . . . *A tall man, good looking, fast with a gun,* she thought. Could it be? "Please don't let it be," she whispered. "Not now. Not ever again."

Cole groaned. He could feel the heat of the flames, heard his little girl screaming "Daddy! Daddy!" He kicked open a door, but roaring heat and flames greeted him, driving him back. He ran around the house, frantically searching for a place to enter, but like a monster from hell, every entrance was blocked by flames. He screamed Patty's name over and over. In his mind he saw himself running from window to window, always going back to Patty's bedroom window, finally reaching inside in spite of the flames, screaming for her to take his hand; but by then her own screaming had stopped, and the searing heat forced Cole to withdraw his arm, his shirtsleeve smouldering. Tears streamed down his face, mixed with blood from the wound across his forehead.

"Patty," he moaned. He felt a jolt then, heard a voice.

"Hey! mister! You all right? I'm tryin' to get some sleep next door, and these blankets ain't no good at keepin' out sound. Wake up! You're drivin' me crazy with all that yellin'."

Cole opened his eyes, took a moment to remember where he was. The man before him looked a little blurry. "What's wrong?"

"You must have been havin' a bad dream, mister. Maybe if you sit up for a few minutes you can shake it off and let other people get some sleep."

Cole rubbed at his eyes and slowly sat up. His head pounded. He'd drunk too much whiskey again last night. He stretched and breathed deeply, noticed the room was light. "What time is it?"

The man who had wakened him scowled. "About ten o'clock, I think. Too late for me to try to go back to sleep."

Cole squinted at the man, who stood there in wrinkled clothes looking upset. "Sorry. I won't be staying here much longer anyway. I have to see someone and then I'll probably leave Central."

The man scratched his head. "Don't matter none to me about your personal plans, mister. Just let a man get his sleep."

The man turned and left, and Cole looked around the little square space divided off by blankets that was supposed to be his room. The floor was dirt and the cot was uncomfortable for a man his size. Sassy Dillon's bed was a hell of a lot softer, but one night with her was enough for him. The only thing he had accomplished since coming here was drink, gamble and sleep with a notorious prostitute who asked too many questions. Last night he'd slept here in this excuse of a rooming house, intending today to try to find Addy, make sure she was all right and get the hell out of this place and leave her alone.

He took a deep breath and shook his head in an effort to clear away the recurring dream that always left him feeling depressed when he awoke. He rose, running a hand through his hair, wishing he had not drunk so much last night—something he wished all too often the last few years. He looked down at himself to see he'd fallen asleep with his clothes, gun and boots on. He rummaged through his gear and pulled out a razor and a change of clothes, put on a denim jacket and his hat and left to find a bath house, stopping on the way out to gulp down some black coffee offered him by the boarding house cook.

The bright morning sun gave him a headache, and he pulled his hat down lower over his eyes as he headed across the street to a building that sported a sign saying simply "Bath And Shave." He emerged looking and feeling at least a little more human. He headed up the street to a laundry and dropped off his dirty clothes with two women, one older and frail, the other, he guessed, weighing perhaps two hundred fifty pounds, and with a mean scowl on her face that would make even a man think twice about wanting to tangle with her.

He left, looking for a place to eat a decent breakfast. He needed some food in his stomach. He tried to quell the anxiety he felt over finding Addy again, arguing with himself that he really must get out of here once he found out she was all right. Somehow he had allowed himself to think that he needed her. He sure as hell did miss her, but they had proven to each other too many times that theirs was a lost relationship that could never work; his craving for whiskey in order to live with bad memories would always cause problems. Addy Kane was too much a lady to live with that. She deserved better.

God, he hated this life . . . wandering, lonely, so unsure what the hell he wanted now, except for a woman he couldn't have. He'd spent that first night with Sassy, slept half the next day and gambled the rest of it, putting off the inevitable—finding Addy. He could not avoid that any longer. She was his reason for being here, and he had to finish what he'd come for. He walked into a small building with a sign that said Food on the front and the smell of bacon wafting through the front door. He ignored the other patrons as he sat down and ordered eggs, ham, biscuits and coffee.

He ate quickly and left, going to the livery where he'd left

Shadow. He saddled the animal and headed north of town to find a place called Lawrence Hall. That was where a man he'd questioned told him school was held. He had not asked Sassy about the school or where a female teacher might board herself. Sassy had already guessed he somehow knew Mrs. Addy Kane, and he had refused to give her any details or ask anything else about Addy.

He looked up at a mountainside covered with buildings and homes. Central was much bigger than he'd figured it would be. It was a bright, sunny morning, and the day promised to be warm and beautiful. Explosions rumbled now and then in the surrounding hills, and if not for having to be near Addy, he figured maybe he could have stayed, tried his hand in the mines, where a man could supposedly make good money.

"Better off stealing a gold shipment," he grumbled. He guided Shadow up past two streets, preparing to turn the horse to the right and head for the brick building he supposed was Lawrence Hall; but a carriage coming down another street to his left caught his eye. Two women sat behind the driver in a separate seat. It was a fine-looking carriage, pulled by a gray spotted horse that trotted rhythmically, its long mane dancing. The women were already close enough that he thought one looked familiar . . .

Addy! He saw her eyes widen, saw her stiffen, look confused. The woman beside her was chatting away, pointing out various homes, hardly noticed him sitting there until the carriage drew closer. Addy stared speechless, and the woman with her glanced up at him, nodding politely. Cole tipped his hat slightly and nodded in return, immediately moving his eyes to Addy again. He saw so many things in those green eyes—surprise, apology, anger. She looked away as the carriage turned toward town. He watched after it. Addy looked back once, and he could hear the woman with her say something about being careful not to take a second look at strangers in this town. ". . . just another drifter," he heard.

So much for finding Addy at Lawrence Hall. His heart

pounded harder than he'd like at the sight of her. She was the most beautiful he had ever seen her, probably all gussied up like that to impress those who had hired her. He wished he could tell for sure by those eyes that she was all right, that he hadn't gotten her pregnant; but the fact remained he still had to ask her. If not for that he'd get the hell out of town right now.

It was apparent that his best bet to find her and get her off alone for a minute was at school. He headed for Lawrence Hall to make sure he had the right place. As he approached the building he saw several women coming in and out, one carrying a punch bowl inside. "May I help you?" one of them asked when he halted Shadow to watch.

"I, uh, I just wondered if this is the school."

"Yes. Do you have children you would like to send?"

Cole felt the pain of bittersweet memories. "No. I'm just exploring Central."

The gray-haired woman smiled. "Well, school doesn't start for several weeks anyway. We use this building for many social events in the summer. We've just hired our first female teacher, a Mrs. Kane, and we're having a reception here for her tonight. We're trying hard to provide a good education for our children here in Central. In the near future we'll be building a real school and won't have to use Lawrence Hall any longer."

Cole nodded. "Thanks for the information."

He turned his horse and headed away. Tonight. Maybe he'd come back here tonight and find a way to pull Addy aside and talk to her . . . or maybe he'd follow her home, find out where she lived. That would be even better. Apparently she didn't want the woman she was with to know she was acquainted with a "drifter" like him. She hadn't uttered a word of acknowledgement when the buggy passed by. If that was the way she wanted it, he'd leave it that way . . . a few words, a last good-bye.

A few streets below him Addy sat listening to Hester Collingswood point out town sights, but she could not concentrate on what she was seeing, nor could she still her heart, which rushed with a mixture of love and hate. Cole! She couldn't call out to him for fear of having to explain to Mrs. Collingswood how she knew him, not sure what the woman would think of her being too friendly with a near stranger she'd "met" on the trip here. So, he *had* come. Why? The man never failed to keep her totally confused. He had ridden away without a word that day after they'd made love in the shed at the stage station. Now here he was in Central. Had he been riding around up in the hills trying to find her?

"My, that was a big, rather dangerous-looking man we passed up there, wasn't he?" Hester said. "Did you see he was wearing a gun? I'll be glad when this town can weed out the drifters and outlaws who come through here. I hope that man we saw wasn't up there thinking to rob someone. I thought for a moment he might pull his gun on *us!*"

Addy did not reply. She looked back again, but they were too far away to see where Cole had gone.

Fifteen

Addy greeted a line of well-wishers whom she quickly learned were part of Central's esteemed "elite." Hester did the honors, keeping Addy at her side as people welcomed her, all of them important businessmen who made decisions about town policy and who'd had a hand in hiring her as their first female schoolteacher.

She had dressed demurely, as she supposed these people would expect her to dress. Hester had told her the blue dress was fine, but she had chosen another instead. Her velvet skirt and matching short jacket were a soft gold color, with dark brown trim around the cuffs and lapel. She had braided her hair and twisted it around the sides of her head, then donned a dark brown velvet hat. She'd wanted to look elegant but respectably plain, not too much color on her cheeks and lips, not too fancy a dress or any jewelry, more the way she would dress for teaching.

Her wardrobe was limited, as there had never been enough money to buy the most expensive clothes, and she'd had to give away some of what she did have before she left Illinois. Her trunk and bags could hold only so much. What she had brought was a few day dresses, four evening dresses; she had saved the most room for several dresses and skirts that she thought best suited for teaching, and for the coats she knew she would need in a mountain town. She hoped to find a good seamstress here in Central, as she preferred to have her clothes made for her. She decided she should ask Hester if she knew anyone who could help her, since she'd lost two of her day dresses to wear and tear on the trip.

"Mr. Dresden Howard and his wife Susan," Hester introduced. "Mr. Howard owns a livery and a dry goods store. His two children will be attending school."

Howard, sporting a fine silk suit, smiled pleasantly. Addy guessed him to be in his thirties, a pleasant-looking man, his wife quite pretty.

Next came Ethel and Lee Brown, an older couple, Brown tall and skinny, his wife short and heavy and rather grim-faced. She looked Addy over as though she was deciding whether she was worthy of the position she had been given, but her husband smiled affably and shook her hand.

"Mr. Brown is in real estate," Hester explained.

"We have a fifteen-year-old daughter," Mrs. Brown told Addy with an arrogant pose. "I expect any woman who will be teaching her to be someone of respect and honor, someone who will set a good example."

Addy forced a smile. "Well, I certainly hope to fill all your expectations, Mrs. Brown."

The woman took her husband's arm. "We will see." She frowned at her husband, who obviously found Addy pleasant to look at. "Come along, Lee. I want some punch." She pulled her husband away, saying loud enough for Addy to hear, "She's too young and pretty. That spells trouble. A school teacher ought to be older and more experienced. She had better set a good example for the young girls."

It was obvious the woman wanted Addy to hear her, and Hester looked embarrassed. "I'm sorry, Addy. Mrs. Brown tends to be rather critical of strangers, especially a female schoolteacher. She was against the idea."

"I can see that," Addy answered, holding her temper. After her experiences in Unionville, she was accustomed to such rudeness, but she had hoped things would be different here. She was determined to prove herself to these people and win their friendship, so she turned to Hester and smiled. "Don't be concerned.

I understand the doubts some people might have. I will do my best to make all of you glad that you hired me."

Hester patted her arm. "I'm sure you will."

Addy couldn't help wondering about Cole. Was he going to try to see her? What did he want from her? She could not risk losing this job just for being seen with him. If he was no more ready to settle down and make her a respectable wife than he had been before now, she had to keep this job, for she would be supporting herself for some time to come.

She wondered how some of these women she was meeting could bear to just stay home and live off their husbands. She had never wanted life to be like that. Her mother had always worked hard beside her father, and Addy wanted to do the same. She never wanted to be totally dependent on any man, but then if and when she did marry again, she was not going to marry a man who drank too much and had no plans for his future.

"Mr. H. M. Teller," Hester introduced, "one of Central's most prominent citizens. Mr. Teller is a lawyer, and he has done much to help our city grow. He is currently working with other businessmen to raise money to build one of the finest hotels in Colorado, right here in Central!"

Teller wore a well-fitted wool suit with a silk tie around the high collar of his shirt. He was a good-looking man with slightly receded hair and a graying beard. His countenance was of a well-educated man who was highly intelligent. He took Addy's hand briefly, smiling and nodding to her. "A hotel fit for kings," he added to Hester's remark with a light laugh. "Pleased to meet you, Mrs. Kane."

"Thank you."

"Mr. Teller is already thinking about running for the Senate when Colorado becomes a state, which we hope will not take too many more years," Hester added. "And he and several of the other businessmen are discussing building railroads into the mountains."

"That seems like an impossible task," Addy told Teller," but then I am already seeing what men of vision can do. The fact that a city of this size even exists so high in the mountains is quite astounding to someone like me who has never seen such places before."

Teller's eyes twinkled with pride. "And you will learn to love it here, I am sure," he told her. He turned to a handsome man beside him, who was wearing a gray silk suit and ruffled shirt. The man held a top hat in one hand, and his dark eyes scanned Addy appreciatively. His dark brown hair was slicked back into a fine cut, showing a touch of gray at the temples, and he sported a neat mustache. He smiled pleasantly, but there was something about him Addy did not quite like. There was a tiny hint of ruthlessness deep in his eyes, yet he was quite dashing.

"Grant Breckenridge," the man spoke up, moving in after Teller and putting out his hand. "I manage several of the mines in the surrounding hills. I'm very glad to meet you, Mrs. Kane, and even happier to discover what a gracious beauty our new teacher is."

Addy felt herself blushing as she took the man's hand. "Mr. Breckenridge! I'm so glad to meet you, since you were one of those who signed the letter telling me I had been hired. And I've read a great deal about you in the *Register.*"

Hester bubbled with pleasure at the meeting. "Mr. Breckenridge is another of our finest citizens," she told Addy, "as important to the city of Central as Mr. Teller. After all, where would we be without the gold mines!" She laughed nervously, and Breckenridge joined her, shaking his head as though somewhat embarrassed. Addy suspected he was only pretending the embarrassment. She saw a glitter of pompous pride in his eyes as he bowed slightly.

"May I say you are the loveliest creature to ever grace our fine city?" he said.

Addy wanted to feel flattered, but there was something about the man that made it difficult to fully accept the compliment, as she guessed this was someone who often used flattery for ulterior motives. "Thank you," she answered.

"I would be glad to show you around some of the mines if

you would ever be interested in learning how things operate, seeing a real gold mine." Breckenridge looked at Hester. "That would be acceptable, wouldn't it, Mrs. Collingswood? I mean, if Mrs. Kane were to oblige me? You or one of the other ladies could certainly come along as an escort."

Hester blushed and put a hand to her chest. "Oh, Mr. Breckenridge, you know in your case that wouldn't be necessary! There would be nothing wrong with Mrs. Kane being seen with someone as respected as you are."

Addy bristled at being treated like Hester's daughter rather than the independent woman that she was—certainly independent enough to make up her own mind who she would and would not see. It was being taken for granted that she would jump at the chance to see Grant Breckenridge socially.

"Then I hope you will remember my offer," Grant said to her.

"I will consider it," she answered. She hoped her job did not depend on how well she cooperated with the man. She saw the flicker of disappointment in his eyes, even a hint of effrontery at the fact that she had not fully accepted his offer.

"Good," he said, still squeezing her hand. "Can I get you some punch?"

"Yes, that would be nice."

Breckenridge left her and walked over to a table where cake and punch were being served. "It is obvious Grant Breckenridge is already very interested in you, Addy," Hester told her then. "Did you see his eyes light up when he saw you? Oh, you lucky lady! Please excuse me for suggesting you would be interested in another man yet, but it *has* been four years since your husband's death, and you *are* still so young and beautiful. Mr. Breckenridge is a widower, such a lonely man. He has a grown son in Chicago attending law school. He's very proud of the boy, and the way he talks about him, it is apparent they are quite close. Mr. Breckenridge would be a wonderful catch for any woman, and he is quite wealthy."

Addy felt a headache coming on. She wanted to shout at

Hester that she did not come here to have people dictate her social life, but she told herself perhaps there would not be so much intrusion into her life once she was settled in and began teaching.

"I am sure he is quite the gentleman," she answered, "but I am really not interested in seeing a man, Hester, certainly not so soon after arriving here. I am still getting used to my new home, so to speak. I have many things to think about."

"Oh, of course, dear, but don't let someone like Grant Breckenridge slip away if he is interested—and he most certainly is, as I knew he would be!"

There was no time for a reply. Addy was introduced to the six male schoolteachers. She already knew John Withers, the bald, heavy-set single teacher who would now move from Miss Ada's boarding house just because Addy lived there.

Next came Herbert Welsh, then Oscar Sage, Ermine Barenger, Lyle Penny, Alfred Rhodes, along with their wives, some with children. They were all amiable, except Alfred Rhodes, who frowned on women teaching and was sure Addy would not be firm enough with the children. "It is my belief that a woman's place is at home," he commented, "and that teaching and discipline are a man's job."

"I graduated with high marks from a fine college, Mr. Rhodes," Addy assured him. "And being a widow with no other family, I must support myself. I am happy to be able to do that and at the same time be doing something that I love."

The man questioned her reason for coming all the way to Central to teach, and again Addy bristled at being put on the spot. By then Grant Breckenridge had returned with her punch, and he stood waiting as eagerly for her reply as did everyone else.

Addy was not sure how any of these people had been affected by the war, but she decided she might as well tell her story and let those who might be upset by the choices her family had made have their say. If it cost her her job, then she would simply have to go to Denver and look there.

"My husband was from Virginia and fought for the South," she answered. "I had met and married him in college. After he left for the war and I graduated, I went home to Unionville to be with my mother. Unionville citizens were adamantly for the Northern position, and in my own heart I, too, believed the Union should be preserved. Many sons and husbands of Unionville citizens also went off to war, all fighting for the Union; but my father decided to join the Confederate cause because he believed in States' rights. Because of that, my mother's support of his decision, and the fact that my own husband was a southerner, my mother and I were branded as the enemy. We lost many old friends. People boycotted my father's place of business until finally my mother and I couldn't keep it going. My own sister also deserted the family for a time. Her husband was an officer in the Union army."

She folded her arms, gaining more courage. "It was all very hard on my mother. I later learned my husband, Tom, was killed, and then we found out my father had also been killed. My mother died only a few months later." She scanned her listeners. "Because of all the bad memories, I wished to get out of Unionville, even though that is where I was born and grew up. Out of respect for my husband's memory, I couldn't bring myself to declare that my sympathies lay with the Union, but no matter which side anyone took, it was an awful war; one, I feel, that could have been avoided." She sighed. "But it happened, and like many others I lost everything. I decided that I needed a fresh start. I saw the ad for a teacher here, so I answered it, and here I am."

Grant handed her a cup of punch. "Mr. Rhodes and Mr. Barrenger both fought for the Union," he told her, turning and nodding to the two men. "I stayed in Chicago to run my businesses, but I did supply medical necessities to the Union army. I suppose most of us here are pro-Union, but there are a few Confederate sympathizers. There isn't a day goes by that there isn't a fight in town over the war, but . . ." He turned and smiled at the others. "We must learn to put the war behind us, mustn't we? The time has come to move forward, especially with our fair city. Mrs.

Kane has done well to choose our town to come to, and Central has done well welcoming such a lovely young woman into its fold."

Everyone seemed to relax a little. "Yes, welcome to the city of Central," Lyle Penny's wife spoke up.

"We have a women's circle that meets every Sunday afternoon," Oscar Sage's wife told her. "You must join us. The next meeting is at my house. It's near Hester's home."

"I'll be glad to join you." Addy drank some punch, feeling suddenly lonely again in spite of having met so many new people. Apparently one had to "earn" his or her place among the elite here, and she felt like an outsider, even though Grant Breckenridge took her arm and led her around to meet even more people. He explained that a new school would be built soon.

"You'll see nothing but growth here," he told her. "My own son is going to come here to practice law after he's graduated."

Addy finished her punch, wondering if any of these people ever thought about anything besides improving their city.

Grant looked down at her with brown eyes that sparkled with humor, and with admiration for what he was looking at. "Let me come for you tomorrow, will you? I can drive you up into the hills to see some of the mines."

Addy was not sure how to feel about the man's attention. It was flattering to have such a prominent man be interested in her, but she still could not feel comfortable with him, and her heart had suffered too much to allow any interest in return. Besides, Cole was somewhere in Central. She was still very confused about her own feelings toward him, except that this would be a bad time to be seen with any stranger. If Cole was the one involved in the near shoot-out in town that Hester had told her about, then he was still frequenting saloons and was still inviting trouble. To these people he would be considered a drifter.

"Yes, I'd like to see a gold mine," she answered Grant truthfully, deciding the only way she was going to begin to feel comfortable in this new place was to cooperate with the others; attend their meetings; get to know all of them better; go for a ride with

Grant Breckenridge, if that was what he wanted, and learn about mining operations.

"Wonderful!" he replied. "I'll be by around noon. Can I get you more punch? Would you like to share some cake?"

She handed him her empty glass. "Yes," she answered with a smile, "but I'd like to step outside for a moment for some fresh air. Do you mind?"

"Not at all. I'll go have Mrs. Welsh cut you a piece of cake."

He left her, and Addy walked through the door and outside, needing to be away from all of them, especially the rather stuffy women. She breathed in pine-scented air, thinking how beautiful it was here in spite of the mines and the noise. Higher mountains loomed in the background, colorful, snow-capped. This truly was God's country, and maybe once she got to know everyone better, she would feel more at home. This loneliness would leave her. It would also help when she could actually begin teaching and keep herself busy, meet all the children. Then there would not be so much time to think about the past, about Tom, her loneliness . . . Cole.

"Addy?"

She jumped at the voice, which came from the bushes to her left. A man stepped into the dim light of a lantern that hung at the corner of the brick building. He wore a duster and a wide-brimmed hat. It was Cole. She looked back toward the front doors.

"Don't worry. I won't let you be seen with me. Apparently you don't want to be."

Addy detected the hurt and anger in the words. "It isn't what you think." Cole! Why did this man keep coming back into her life?

"I know. You're a proper lady, a respectable widow who can't be seen with the likes of me if you want to keep this job . . . and this job means everything to you."

"Cole, you caught me off guard this morning. I was completely shocked when I saw you right there in the middle of the road. I—"

He held up his hand, stepped closer and grasped her arm, pulling her into the shadows. "When you go home tonight, I'll follow. Go on in, then come back out later. Give whatever explanation you want to the landlady. We have to talk."

Addy remembered the hurt of him riding away without a word after having his way with her in the shed. "Yes, we certainly do!" she answered, feeling like hitting him.

He squeezed her arm. "Do what I said, then." He turned and left, and Addy felt stunned. Sometimes it seemed she was only watching her life take place in front of her, she was not really participating in it.

Grant called for her from the front door then, and she walked back up the steps to go inside. "Come have your cake," he told her. He put a hand to her waist, and another explosion rumbled in the distant hills as he led her back inside.

Cole watched, feeling a silent rage at the handsome, apparently wealthy older man smiling at Addy, putting his hand on her that way. So, Addy was meeting Central's elite now. She was where she belonged.

Addy looked into the shadows as Hester and Stuart Collingswood talked about what a pleasant evening it had been. They had picked Addy up to take her to the reception, and now were dropping her off in front of Miss Ada's. Addy wondered if Cole was already close by, watching.

"Oh, things went so well," Hester told her. "You will come to our women's circle day after tomorrow at the Sage house, won't you, Addy? I'll pick you up again and show you where they live."

"Yes," Addy answered, bringing her thoughts back to where they belonged. "I would enjoy that."

"And if you like to embroider or knit, bring that along." Hester sat opposite Addy in a two-seater carriage. She reached over and grasped Addy's hands. "And you can tell all of us about your outing with Grant Breckenridge! Everyone will want to know how it went, and what you think of Grant!"

The woman giggled like a schoolgirl, and Addy smiled grudgingly. She had only accepted Grant's offer because she wasn't quite sure how to turn him down, afraid she would offend one of those most responsible for her coming here. Besides, it would be interesting to see a gold mine and stamp mill. If she was going to live here, she might as well learn everything about what pumped life into Central and get a first-hand look at what it was that brought men to places like this from thousands of miles away.

"I'm sure I'll enjoy the outing," she answered Hester, wishing she and the other women would not take it for granted she would be interested in Grant Breckenridge romantically. "Mr. Breckenridge seems to be a fine man. And thank you for the very nice welcome," she added. "I've enjoyed meeting everyone, although I'll never remember all the names."

"Oh, these things take time, but I'm sure you'll adjust quickly."

Stuart Collingswood, a hefty man with white hair and mustache, stepped down from the carriage, offering his hand to Addy. She obliged, all the while feeling Cole Parker's eyes on her from somewhere. "You're a lovely addition to our city," Collingswood told her as he helped her step down. "If you need anything, you just let me or Hester know."

Addy smiled. She liked Stuart Collingswood. He had kind blue eyes and seemed a genuinely nice man. He walked with her to the door and Addy thanked him and went inside. She waited a moment for the carriage to leave, then walked down the hallway to her room. She removed her gloves and laid them aside, seriously considering not going back out to talk to Cole. He was still a dangerous man . . . dangerous to her heart, her best interests.

She walked to a window and looked out, left her room again and quietly stepped down the hallway. She looked into the dining room, saw a lantern lit in the kitchen beyond it. Ada was standing at a counter peeling potatoes, apparently unaware Addy had returned. She hurried to the door then and stepped outside, closing the door quietly and walking off the porch. She moved out of the light of oil lamps that hung on the front porch. "Cole?" she called softly.

A horse whinnied nearby. "Over here," Cole spoke up to her left.

Addy turned, walked toward the voice, then gasped when he suddenly stepped out from a thick shrub. He grasped her arms and drew her farther away. "Quite a party they had for you."

She suddenly felt a little sorry for him for the mere fact that she was suddenly getting celebrity attention from Central's elite, while Cole Parker had to hide in the shadows and couldn't even let himself be seen with her. She well understood what a lonely man he was, but she reminded herself that feeling sorry for a man was no excuse for letting him have his way with her. "Yes. Most of them are actually quite boring, but they did pay my way here, and they have given me a home and a job and have been very gracious." She caught the scent of whiskey on his breath, and she pulled away from him. "What do you want, Cole?" He sighed, but she could not see his eyes. Was he angry? Insulted? Or perhaps he thought that if he got her off alone again . . .

"I wasn't even going to come to Central," he answered. "But I got to thinking."

"About what a cruel and thoughtless thing it was to just ride off like that back at the stage station, after what you'd done to me in the shed?"

Cole felt stunned and angry. "Why don't you let me finish what I had to say?"

"Because I've heard it all," Addy answered. "You're lonely. I'm lonely. We became good friends. None of those reasons is good enough for allowing ourselves to . . ." She turned away. "I can imagine what you think of me. The first time was one thing, but to let it happen again . . . You half forced me the second time, Cole, then just rode away. I could almost hear you laughing at me! Now I have this guilt to live with, facing people like those tonight, people who think I'm a prim, proper lady, people who—"

He grabbed her arms and turned her to face him. "You still *are* prim and proper! You know goddamn well I'd never think less of you for any of it, and you also know I never *forced* you to do a damn thing! We *wanted* each other, *needed* each other, but we're not right for each other. That's not the end of the world, Addy. It doesn't even mean we don't *love* each other."

She yanked herself away. "Don't talk about love. It's a little late for that. We both know we didn't know our own minds. I *still* don't! I'm just getting oriented, Cole, meeting people, trying to think about my teaching, trying to . . . forget about you, because I know it's the wisest thing to do."

Cole let out a snicker of disgust. "Yes, let's make sure we do what's right and proper, Mrs. Kane! That's why I'm here, to do what's right. I rode off because I thought *that* was the right thing to do! I had complicated your life enough, without being able to say I was ready to settle, or to say that I loved you, or to be able to give up the kind of life I've been leading. I couldn't promise I could find decent work, or that I could quit drinking."

"That's obvious! I can smell it on your breath! And where have you been staying while you're here? I suppose with some fancy painted woman in town!"

The air hung silent for a moment. "That bother you?"

Addy bristled. It was not supposed to bother her. This man did not belong to her and never could. "No! It only makes me understand that you are not the kind of man a decent woman considers caring about. In fact, you're the kind of man who destroys decent women and makes them ashamed of what they've done."

They both talked heatedly but in a near whisper for fear someone would hear.

"Damn you!" Cole growled. "Why don't you let me finish what I came here to say."

"Then say it and go! *Go!* You keep riding out of my life, Cole, telling me each time that it's ended, that you'll never see me again. I'm left alone to try to figure out what happened to me, who I am, what I should do. Each time you go I feel more lost and lonely and confused than before. And just when I begin to adjust and think I can go on with my life, save some of my dignity, you show up again, and I never quite know why. I hope you don't think that you can just get me off in the dark and have a good time with me in the grass. In spite of what I've allowed to happen between us, I'm not that kind, Cole, and you know it!"

"Of *course* I know it!" He grasped her arms again. "How many times do I have to tell you that you're no less honorable and good in my eyes than the day I saw you in the bank at Unionville? And let's not forget who saved you from Jack Slater's bed! And for God's sake, woman, *you* saved *my* life! There are some special things between us that we'll never forget, and there's nothing wrong with that."

Addy closed her eyes, hating him, loving him. "Finish it, Cole. You said you just wanted to explain why you needed to see me again."

He squeezed her arms gently before letting go of her. "Like I said, I got to thinking . . . about what we did, and the fact that we . . . you know. We weren't very careful. I started worrying I'd left you in a bad way. You could have gotten out here and discovered you were carrying."

Addy almost groaned at the words, words that only reminded her how brazen and careless and lustful she had been. She turned away and rubbed at her forehead. "I'm all right," she answered quietly. "You didn't . . . leave me in a bad way, as you put it." She heard him emit a deep sigh of relief. She wondered if he was relieved for her sake, or for his own. "I guess I should be grateful you bothered."

"Addy, it's not a bother when it's for you. I would have done the right thing by you."

But not because you really would have loved me, she thought.

I love you, Addy, were his thoughts at the same moment. Why couldn't he tell her? But then why *should* he? She didn't know her own heart, except to feel they weren't right for each other. And what did he have to offer? Nothing. He couldn't even trust these feelings of love, because the real Cole Parker was Nick Coleman, and he had lost the real Nick Coleman somewhere years ago—the Nick Coleman who farmed, tried to raise a little girl without her mother.

"I'll always care about you, Addy. I hope you find some man who'll be the kind of husband you deserve."

Addy turned to face him in the moonlight, so handsome and virile, so lonely. "Thank you for coming to make sure . . ." She had to look away. "What will you do now?"

Cole rubbed at his neck. "I don't know. I'm not even sure I'll leave Central, but we'll be moving in two very different circles, Addy, so don't worry about running into me. Even if you did, I wouldn't acknowledge that I know you. It was obvious when you passed me in that buggy this morning that you didn't want that woman you were with to realize you knew me."

"Cole—"

"That's okay. I understand." He put a hand on her shoulder. "I hope you find a good life here, Addy."

She turned to him. "And I hope you find love and happiness again, Cole, wherever you go. Please try to stay away from what you left back there. You were a good man once, still are in most ways. You've got to stop letting the memories destroy you. Just ask yourself, would Bethanne and Patty be proud of me if they saw me now? Are they watching me from somewhere, crying over what I've become? If you can't pull yourself out of the saloons and away from the whiskey and stay away from the outlaw life for yourself, then do it for *them,* Cole, in respect for their memory."

He only looked at her a moment, then leaned down and kissed her cheek. Addy felt the heat begin to stir deep inside again, but she forced herself not to let her mouth turn to meet his own.

"Bye, Addy," he said. He turned and walked away, and she heard the squeak of leather as he mounted Shadow. He rode close to her then, looking big and dangerous on that horse, every bit the Nick Coleman she had first met.

"Good-bye, Nick," she answered, suddenly only able to call him by his real name. He turned his horse. "Nick," she called out. He halted Shadow, and she ran up to him, reaching up. He grasped her arm and hoisted her up in front of him. She flung her arms around him, and they kissed, a long, hot, hungry, painful kiss of a true good-bye, for this surely was the right thing to do, each go his and her separate ways . . . yet there would always be this sweet thing they had shared, something that simply had to be in order for each of them to survive and want to go on with life.

The kiss lasted several long seconds, tongues exploring, hearts pounding, until finally Addy tore herself away. "Go now," she whispered.

His hand moved over her breasts as she slid off the horse, and Addy kept her back to him when he rode off. Finally, she put trembling fingers to her lips, closed her eyes and wept. This simply had to be the end of it.

Sixteen

Ethel Brown held her chin proudly as she marched into Hester Collingswood's parlor, her heavy frame billowing through the double doors and causing the floorboards to creak wherever she stepped. "I wanted a moment with you, Hester. I know you're busy today, but we should talk before the women's group meeting tomorrow." She faced Hester authoritatively, judging her to be much too trusting a woman. *"Before* Addy Kane has a chance to charm you even more, and to equally charm the rest of our group."

Hester frowned. "Whatever do you mean, Ethel?"

Hester's maid carried in a tray of tea and crackers, which Hester had already requested when it was announced Ethel had come visiting. Ethel waited until the tea was poured and Jenny was out of the room before continuing. "I mean that there is more to Mrs. Kane than meets the eye, as far as I am concerned. I am not so sure she is to be trusted."

Hester frowned in surprise. "Do sit down, Ethel."

The woman obliged, hardly able to fit between the coffee table and love seat that Hester offered. "We must discuss this," she reiterated, reaching over and pouring some milk into her tea. Hester joined her, remembering that last night at the reception, Ethel seemed a bit ruffled at the way her husband reacted when he set eyes on Addy. Hester supposed Addy was one of the prettiest women in Central, and Ethel Brown very well knew it. She had obviously decided that someone so young and pretty might only cause problems. "What are your concerns, Ethel?"

Ethel sipped some of the tea, then leaned closer, lowering her voice. "Think about it, Hester. What do we *really* know about this woman? We only know what she has told us. Has any one of us talked to anyone back in Illinois who knew her? For all we know, she might have never been married, might not be a widow at all. Perhaps she was a soiled woman back there and came here to get away from a bad reputation. Who's to say? Nowadays anyone can use the war as an excuse to run off and start life new someplace else."

Hester smiled softly and shook her head. "What difference does her past make, Ethel, if she is a good teacher and if she conducts herself properly while she's here?"

"Oh, Hester!" Ethel spoke the words scoldingly as she set her cup aside. "This woman will be teaching our children. Your sons are grown, but my daughter is fifteen and still impressionable. I intend to look a little deeper into the reputation of a woman who will be teaching her. Not only that, but it just doesn't look good for such an attractive young woman to be working with six men!"

"Ethel, I have spoken with Mrs. Kane quite a bit. Yesterday we had breakfast and shopped together. She seems quite sincere, intelligent and worthy. Why don't we just let her teach and see how things go?"

Ethel's plump cheeks turned pinker with indignation. "It isn't just her questionable past, Hester. I happen to agree with Mr. Rhodes that women should not teach at all. Teaching is a job for *men*. They can be firmer, can better control young people. I'm a woman, too, but it is my opinion that a female simply cannot learn and retain all that she should to be a good teacher. I know that Mrs. Kane went to Hope College in Michigan, which, I might add, is much too independent a thing for a young lady to do—going away alone to school like that. Be that as it may, a woman simply does not have the mental ability to learn as men do. How she managed to graduate from such a good college is beyond me. And there again, we have only her word.

Maybe she did not graduate at all. Maybe she never even attended!"

"Oh, Ethel, don't be ridiculous," Hester grumbled. "Anyone can see after talking to her only a little while that she is well educated and most certainly a fine lady."

Ethel sniffed. "I have my doubts, and I'll tell you why." Her dark eyes narrowed in that way the woman had of preparing to spring juicy gossip on someone. She folded her plump hands in her lap and held Hester's full attention. "My suspicions about her reputation were only verified by a visit I got this morning from John Withers, the male teacher who is also living at Miss Ada's." Her eyes lit up with delight at being able to tell the story. "He tells me that last night, after you and your husband left Addy Kane off at the boardinghouse, she came inside and went to her room. He knows it was her because he was already home and his room is beside hers. He heard her go inside her own room, and then she walked out again! He opened his door slightly and looked out and saw her go outside alone. He supposed she wanted another breath of fresh air for some reason, so he closed his door and did not think much else about it until he was sure he heard voices somewhere in the darkness outside his window." She straightened, smiling victoriously.

"Voices? Was one of them Addy's?"

"He couldn't be sure, because he could not hear what exactly was being said, but one of them was definitely a woman. Who *else* would it have been that time of night? The point is, she walked outside alone. Mr. Withers heard two voices, and the *other* voice was a *man's*! Who in the world would she have been talking to in the dark late at night like that? A few minutes later Mr. Withers heard a horse whinny and trot off, and he was sure that soon after that he heard a woman *crying!* Now don't tell me you don't find that very mysterious and questionable."

Hester looked away, sipping more of her tea, trying to digest everything she had been told. "As far as I know, Mrs. Kane knows absolutely no one else in town. She seemed so lost and lonely when I first met her, and I'm certain she's never been to

Central before. She did agree to meet with Grant Breckenridge today to visit one of his mines, but she just met him last night. They certainly would not have made plans to meet alone in the dark later. Mr. Breckenridge is too much the gentleman for that. And there would be no reason whatsoever for Mrs. Kane to be crying about anything to do with a man she just met."

Ethel snorted with indignation. "I'm not suggesting it was Grant Breckenridge. I am suggesting that she knows some man intimately, that she came here to run away from him and that he followed her here! If she really is a widow as she claims, then she is lonely. Something that young and pretty won't want to go for long without a man in her life. Who knows what has been going on, or why she might want to stay away from this man? All we know is that she met a man alone in the dark last night and was heard crying after he left." She rose, folding her arms. "I'm telling you, Hester, something is not quite right, and I intend to find out what it is."

"How do you intend to do that?" Hester stood up, facing the woman.

Ethel's eyes showed her determination and confidence. "I am going to write to the sheriff of Unionville, Illinois, ask him if he can refer me to people who knew the woman, tell me what he himself knows about her—if it's true she went to college, was widowed; and tell me if he has any idea if she was romantically involved with anyone in Unionville. Perhaps he can shed some light on the truth about Mrs. Addy Kane!"

Hester put a hand to her chin and walked over to look out a window. "I don't know, Ethel. There is something about Addy that I like very much. I don't think she has lied to us or done anything wrong."

"I hope that you are right, but I have said all along that you people on the educational committee should have done a better job of investigating this woman before hiring her, rather than simply take her word on everything. Alfred Rhodes is the only one who voted against the hiring, but everyone else just blindly accepted the woman's credentials as truth. I know that we all

want to show that Central is a forward-thinking town, willing
to give a female teacher a chance, but we can still at least mak
sure the woman involved is truly as educated and reputable a
she claims."

Hester sighed with irritation. Ethel Brown seemed to tak
innate pleasure in sticking her nose into other people's lives. "
can't say that you're wrong, Ethel, but why have you come t
me about it?"

Ethel placed her hands on her hips authoritatively. "Becaus
I feel Mrs. Kane has already won your complete confidence.
came to warn you not to be too intimate with the woman, an
not to encourage the ladies of our circle to be too receptive a
first. What if she turns out to be some soiled dove who's bee
cast out from some other town? Just think how embarrassin
that would be for all of us, welcoming her into our homes, in
troducing her to our husbands, allowing her to teach our chil
dren! We must be very careful, Hester—friendly, but not too
intimate. It will probably be a good six weeks before I get a
answer from someone in Unionville, and in the meantime, w
must all be skeptical and watchful. I will tell Miss Ada to kee
an eye open for the woman's comings and goings at night."

Hester knew there was no use arguing with a determined Ethe
Brown. "Fine. I will keep it all in mind."

"I also want all of us to meet early at Jessica Sage's hous
tomorrow so that I can discuss this with all of them before Mr
Kane arrives."

Hester rubbed at her eyes. "I don't like being unkind to peo
ple, Ethel."

"Oh, I didn't mean that you or any of us should be. I onl
want them to be aware that we could be associating with som
one with a less than reputable background, that we must refrai
from getting too close just yet. I do hope Mr. Breckenridge isn
risking his heart and his own honor by wanting to be seen wit
the woman so soon. What if he takes an intimate interest in he
and then discovers she's . . . well, you know. It would be har
on him, embarrassing."

"Yes, I suppose."

"Well!" Ethel smiled with near glee at having such wonderful gossip to share with everyone. "One o'clock tomorrow then at Jessica's? Mrs. Kane won't come until two. I'll get messages to everyone to come earlier, and I'll go and tell Jessica."

Hester nodded. "Personally, I hope that you're wrong, Ethel. I like Addy."

Ethel bent over and picked up her tea, gulping down the rest of it quickly, as it had already cooled. She took several crackers into her plump hand then. "We shall see. Do you mind if I take a few of these crackers along with me? I was to meet Jessica for lunch and am running late, and I am so hungry."

Hester thought how Addy Kane was much more a lady than Ethel Brown when it came to appearance and manners. "Take all you want."

The woman smiled, picking up her handbag with her free hand. "I'll see you tomorrow then. Thank you for listening, Hester."

Hester smiled grudgingly. "Certainly. She showed Ethel to the door, watched her walk to her waiting carriage, watched the carriage sink down noticeably as soon as the woman climbed inside. The carriage moved off, and Hester walked out onto the porch. From where her house stood, she could see down all across Central. She could also see the rooftop of Miss Ada's rooming house two streets below. Had Addy Kane left yet with Grant Breckenridge? Would anything come of their meeting?

"Who on earth did you see last night, Addy? What is going on?" She wondered if she should simply flat-out ask the woman; but then Addy would surely be terribly hurt that she was being gossiped about when she was so lonely and trying to make new friends. And what would come of all that hurt if they found out after all that Addy was just as honorable and educated as she claimed she was? If she let Addy know their suspicions, then they would be even more embarrassed and feel more like fools when they had to face her than if they never said a word.

"Are we fools to trust and believe you, Addy; or are we fools

to go sticking our noses into your personal life?" She felt sorr
that someone had made Addy cry. "But *who* in this town coul
possibly upset her that way?" she mused. Much as she like
Addy and hoped none of Ethel's suspicions were true, she coul
not help being just as curious as Ethel was, though not in
mean-spirited way. It would be interesting to see what kind c
reply the woman received from Unionville.

Addy looked out across both Central and Blackhawk, able 1
see everything from the high, hairpin road over which Gra
Breckenridge had brought her to show her one of his mines.
both thrilled and frightened her to be so high. The road wa
rocky and treacherous, with no barriers to stop them from tun
bling to their deaths hundreds of feet below should the carriag
go off the edge; yet this same road was traveled by much larg
freight wagons carrying supplies up and gold down.

In spite of her loneliness and the ache still in her heart ov
seeing Cole the night before, she was certain of one thing. Sh
was beginning to love this area. The surrounding mountains we
beautiful, and a person was so high she felt closer to God. Th
was an exciting place to be, meeting new people, living in
town that was growing every day, where the surrounding hil
were full of gold, an enticement that brought men and wome
from thousands of miles away with dreams of getting rich. I
spite of some resentment toward those who felt they could ru
her life, at least here she did not have to put up with the hurt c
being scorned by those she once called friend.

"That mine opening you see just ahead is the Chicago lod
I call the mine the Chicago because that's where I'm from an
where my employer is based," Grant told her. "Chadwick Mir
ing Company. I'm out here managing their mines and workin
with crews developing new mines. I judge the value of the o
discovered and the company allows me to name the mines my
self. I'm also a troubleshooter . . . deal with the miners ov
wages and so forth, kind of an overall manager. I caught anoth

Chadwick employee, a metallurgist like myself, trying to stake a claim for himself once rather than for the company, and I corrected the situation. The man was fired and has had a hateful grudge against me ever since, but I was only doing my job."

Addy thought the words were spoken rather piously. "Is he still in Central?"

"Oh, yes. Works in one of the other mines now, not a Chadwick mine, of course." He pulled up to the mine entrance, and Addy listened to him carry on about mining. It was obvious he was trying to impress her, but she had decided she had better learn all she could about the industry that supported this town, so she listened well. She did not consider this venture with Grant as a prelude toward being interested in the man romantically, as Hester hoped. She had only agreed to this because she wanted to learn about mining gold, who owned which mines and so forth, since that was practically all anyone in this town talked about; and she wanted and needed to make more friends. If nothing more, she supposed Grant could become that much, and he seemed quite the gentleman, although there was an air of arrogance and even a little hint of ruthlessness about him that still bothered her. She supposed she only had to get to know him better, and, after all, no one seemed to object that she be seen with him. He was apparently respectable enough for a single woman in her position to see socially. And who better to teach her about mining?

"A lode mine is one where the ore deposits are enclosed within other rock," he was saying, "usually gneiss or what we call conglomerate rocks. Another Chadwick mine, the Jackpot, has open veins that are incredibly rich and run for miles into the mountain. That's the easiest way to mine, when it's right there for the taking with a few whacks of a pick."

"It must be exciting to see something like that," she answered, "let alone actually own it."

Grant looked at her, his gaze dropping to her full breasts, then back to her face. "It is. I happen to be seventy-five percent owner of another Chadwick mine, the Jamesway. That's the one the employee I told you about tried to steal. I call it the Jamesway after my son, James. I told you the other night he'll be coming here to practice law. He'll graduate soon from law school in Chicago. James is the light of my life, and we're very close. I'll be so glad to see him again."

Addy was confused over what to think of the man. When he talked about his son, a softer look came into his eyes. But other than that, there was a hardness about him that disturbed her. She wondered how he had managed to own such a large percentage of the Jamesway, the very mine he'd caught another employee trying to claim for himself. "How old is James?" she asked.

"He's twenty-one. His mother died ten years ago."

"I'm sorry."

Grant halted the carriage and looked at her. "It's been many years now. I'm forty-three, if you're wondering." His gaze moved over her as though he were assessing her figure, and it struck Addy that that was what made her uncomfortable around him. She told herself it really made no difference. He was nearly old enough to be her father, and she had no personal interest in the man.

She turned away, not caring for the way he looked at her. "What is the name of the employee who got fired over the Jamesway?" she asked.

"Ed Foley. He tries to threaten me in various ways once in a while, tries to start trouble, but don't worry. He's harmless."

I wasn't worried, Addy thought. The arrogant man already thought she cared enough about him to be concerned.

"I'll take you up to the Jamesway now," he told her. "What people don't realize is how expensive it is to get the gold out of these mountains once it's been discovered, and to process it correctly in order for it to truly be worth anything. Most prospectors can't afford to do that, so once they find the gold, companies like mine pay them for their claims and then bring in the right equipment to mine them profitably."

Addy suspected companies like Grant's paid prospectors far less than they deserved for their claims. Then they moved in and made a fortune on them, while the poor prospector was left to go through all the hard work of picking away at the earth or panning more streams to find yet another claim. But that seemed to be the way of life out here, and she could tell by the arrogant glitter in Grant's dark eyes that he enjoyed taking advantage of men too foolish to realize how much more they could be getting for their claims.

There it was again, that ruthless glint in his eyes. Grant Breckenridge was a rich man who took great pleasure in making a fortune from a raw deal he'd given another man, and he held no regrets or guilt about it. She couldn't help wondering if he'd told her the whole truth about Ed Foley. Still, he was being quite gracious and friendly today, and she supposed that what he did in the way of business decisions was not her affair. Maybe the best way to forget Cole was to force herself to look to another man, even though she wasn't ready for any new relationships. Perhaps, if Grant was interested in seeing more of her, she should accept any other invitations he might propose. It could help her forget a relationship that only brought pain and heartache.

"A lot of gold in Colorado is found by placer mining," Grant continued, obviously quite proud to be able to explain these things to her. "Gold is washed down from the mountains into ravines, gulches and such, lies in the beds of streams, mostly in places where two streams wash together. Men pan for the gold, dig a shallow pan into the stream bed, swirl the water, dump off the debris. They keep doing that until all that's left in the bottom of the pan is particles of gold. Gold is heavy and sinks to the bottom, so as you pour off the dirt and debris, only the gold is left. It's a pretty slow way of collecting gold, but some men are content with what little bit they find that way. I prefer mining the big stuff, owning half a mountain."

The words were spoken with pompous pride. Addy did not doubt that a good portion of the women in town *would* be impressed by the man's money, but wealth had never been something she required in a man.

"In some places where there are deep streams, mine owners

can speed up the panning for gold by using steam engines to operate a hydraulic system, pumping high volumes of water at the side of a mountain to wash away the dirt and rock by force. The debris is forced into sluicing flumes."

"Sluicing flumes?"

Grant smiled. "Oh, that's just another form of placer mining. A flume is a contraption normally set up along streams. As the water flows downhill it's run through flumes. Some are up to a mile long. Debris from the bottom of the stream is shoveled into the flume. Mercury is deliberately put into the bottom of the flumes because mercury attracts gold. The heavy particles of gold sink to the bottom to amalgamate with the mercury, and the rest of the debris just keeps flowing on, leaving nothing in the bottom of the sluice but the amalgam. That is collected and run through a processing method to separate the gold from the mercury. All of that is called placer or gulch mining. When the gold is in lodes, embedded deeply in rock so you can't see it, getting to that gold is called practical mining."

Addy shook her head. "I never knew it could all be so complicated. Back East people think you can just come out here with a pick and collect pure gold into bags and walk off rich."

Grant laughed. "Yes, many are surprised at how hard it really is. Down in the deeper mines, the gold is drilled out of the rock, sometimes blasted out with dynamite, then dumped into carts that are pushed to hoists. It's lifted then with steel cable. The hoists are run either by steam, or sometimes pulled by horses. That noisy building below is a stamp mill, where the gold is separated by a complicated series of steps, using chemicals. You probably saw piles of debris, mostly a yellow color, when you were coming up here. You can see several down there around the stamp mill."

"Yes. Another passenger in the stagecoach told me they were called tailings, leftovers from extracting gold, debris that's dumped."

"That's right."

The ground shook with an explosion somewhere deep inside

the nearby mine. Addy jumped at the noise and vibration which was very close. "It must be very dangerous down there," she told Grant.

"Sure it is, but most of those men know what they're doing. Those who set the dynamite obviously *have* to know what they're doing. The real dangers come when shafts have to be sunk deeper and deeper. Good ventilation becomes a problem, and sometimes they begin to fill up with water that has to be pumped out. We sink air shafts for fresher air that helps blow out gasses and smoke and blasting dust. Some mining is done by tunneling horizontally instead of going deeper. The tunnels have to be shored up with timber to help prevent collapse. There are lots of injuries, broken bones from falling rock, broken scaffolds. Once in a while a man falls down a shaft to his death. Explosions, of course, are a big cause of death and injury, and sometimes there are cave-ins. It's all part of the job."

Addy wondered if the man had any true concern for those who risked their lives to dig his precious gold. Was it all part of the job? "Do they make much money?"

"Depends on their particular job. The average is $3.50 a day. Not much for the risks they take, but the country is full of men desperate for jobs now."

And full of men like you to take advantage of them, Addy thought. Another shaking rumble came from below the earth. "How many mines does your company own?" she asked, hoping he would not think she was trying to gauge his wealth.

"Four. The Chicago and the Jackpot, one a lode mine, the other open veins. The Hannah is a sluice mining operation, and the Jamesway is another lode mine, although as I said, they own only one-quarter of that one. I'd take you through the stamp mill down there, but as you can tell from the noise it's awfully loud, and they're full of men shouting, sometimes not too careful about their words. It's really no place for a lady."

His eyes moved over her again, this time with a little more respect in his gaze. Addy felt a tiny hint of attraction, as any woman would to a handsome, successful man. But she realized it was nowhere near the kind of attraction she'd had for Cole.

She looked away, angry that she had again allowed herself to think about Cole. "How long has it been since you've seen James?" she asked.

"Oh, about eighteen months. I've been here since sixty-four and I've been back to Chicago only twice. I love it here in Colorado, and I intend to stay and make Central my home."

"How did your wife die?" she asked, looking back at him. "Or perhaps I shouldn't ask."

"It's all right. It's natural to ask. The doctors didn't know for sure what it was. She just seemed to waste away, got worse over the months, until she was thin and weak and in constant pain. They think it was a disease they call cancer. They don't know much about it and couldn't do anything for her."

"I'm sorry." It didn't seem to Addy as though the man showed true grief, but then, it had been ten years. Still, when Cole spoke about his own dead wife, who had died nine years ago, she still could see the love and sorrow in his eyes, and she could not help respecting him for that.

"Well, it was a long time ago," Grant answered, looking her over again. "And people have to get on with their lives. I'm sure you understand that, considering the reasons you gave for coming here, and the fact that you lost a husband yourself." He rested his elbows on his knees. "I know we've just met, Addy, but I have to tell you I was instantly struck not by just your beauty, but your intelligence and your courage. I'd like to see more of you socially. I'd like to take you to dinner tomorrow evening. Central still lacks a truly refined, elegant eating establishment, but there is one that will do for a lady. I'm sure that in no time at all we'll have some better restaurants, and I *know* for a fact that we'll have a really fine hotel in a couple more years. There is even talk of an opera house. At any rate, there are only a few choices when it comes to a man properly courting a woman. Perhaps you would like to join me as a guest when I have my annual picnic for the miners in late August."

Addy told herself it only made sense to give a man like Grant Breckenridge a chance, no matter what her first instinctive feelings were toward him. After all, this man was part of the reason she had been able to come here to start over, the reason she could finally teach.

"I can't think that far ahead, Grant. My biggest concern is just to prove I am a good teacher and can do my job. I have a feeling several of your friends think a female is not the best choice. I won't make you regret hiring me. And yes, dinner tomorrow evening is fine."

He flashed a handsome smile. "Good," he answered. "Well, I'll take you on over to the Jackpot. It's mostly horizontal mining and not too deep, so you should be able to go inside. Would you like to see a real vein of gold?"

Addy smiled. "Who wouldn't?"

Grant laughed lightly, sure he was impressing this woman with his wealth and knowledge. Addy Kane was beautiful and young, and he wanted her. Once she saw real gold, realized what a catch he was, surely she would give consideration to his attention, in spite of the fact that he was so much older than she. He'd had plenty of affairs back in Chicago, both before and after his wife died, with women who were impressed with his wealth and status. Surely Addy Kane was no different. Marriage was something he wasn't sure he ever wanted again. He liked women too much. But Addy didn't need to know that, and here in Central there was a scarcity of women, especially young, pretty, available ones like Addy. Perhaps, if he saw her enough, led her to believe there was a future with him, he could at least get this one into his bed and not have to sneak around to get satisfaction from the whores in town. Besides, if women like Ethel Brown had their way, Central would be rid of its prostitutes. Then what would he do? If things went well with Addy Kane, maybe he'd *have* to marry her, just to have a woman in his bed at night. That wasn't such a bad prospect. She had a lot of good years in her yet. She would certainly make a beautiful and proper wife for a man like himself.

Seventeen

Addy watched the smiles and smiled in return, but she could feel a definite chill in Jessica Sage's parlor, where the wealthy women of Central gathered for their "circle" meeting. She had met most of them two nights ago at her reception, the wives of the male schoolteachers, the wives of Central's most prominent businessmen; and she was introduced to a few additional women new to her acquaintance. She met Esther Jonesboro, wife of Dr. Creighton Jonesboro, one of only two doctors in town. The other was Doctor Jonathan Brooks, and his wife, Roslyn, was also at the meeting. Elizabeth Howley, a recently-widowed seamstress with her own business in town, was also present; and there was Marianne Conrad, wife of Clarance Conrad, who owned several businesses, including a men's clothing store.

Many of these women had school-age children, whom Addy would be teaching. She wanted to believe that was the reason these women were scrutinizing her so closely today, but she could not help wondering if there wasn't more to it than that. Some of them seemed to be literally studying her, and it felt as if she was answering the same questions over and over about where she was from and why she had come to Central.

"And there has been no man in your life since you were widowed?" Ethel Brown asked. The question came with a teasing smile, but Addy saw the hint of warning behind the woman's puffy eyes. She already knew Ethel did not like her one whit, remembered the remark she had made to her husband the night of the reception. She could just see all these women fainting dead away if she told them the truth about Cole.

"No," she answered. "I was too busy helping my mother try to keep the family business going. When it folded, I worked two different jobs just to make ends meet. When I learned of my father's death, and then later after my mother died, I just didn't have the heart to take an interest in anything but figuring out how to go on."

She noticed looks of true sympathy on some of their faces, and several looked at Ethel with frowns of scorn, as though they were upset with something she might have said earlier. Had the woman been saying things about her behind her back? Why did there have to be people like Ethel Brown, nosey biddies who enjoyed tearing other people down?

Jane Rhodes, a waif of a woman with ash blond hair and blue eyes that seemed too big for her bony face, set a cup of tea on a table beside her. "Well, if you haven't been around men much these past years, won't it be difficult to have to teach alongside six men? I'm sure they'll be watching everything you do. Wouldn't it be easier to do something truly feminine, like being a housekeeper, maybe working for Beth in her seamstress work?"

Addy knew the woman's husband was completely against a woman teaching. She suspected he had given his wife instructions to try to discourage her. She looked around at the sea of faces, some pleasant, some not so pleasant; thin, heavy, gray-haired, many younger . . . all watching her carefully, gauging her every word.

"Being female doesn't mean I can't do what I want as far as an occupation," she answered. "It will be very gratifying to teach. It is something I always wanted to do. I am not concerned with what the other teachers think. I can only do my best, and I assure you, I am very capable. The very fact that I have no one to be concerned about but myself is beneficial. I can devote all my time and attention to your children."

They seemed pleased with her answer. Hester gave her a re-

assuring smile, but many of them kept looking back at Ethel
Brown, as though they needed her permission to be friendly.
Something was definitely amiss, and Addy resented not being
asked about whatever it was directly, not being allowed to defend
herself because she had no idea what it was that bothered them.

"It does seem strange that a woman so young and lovely as
yourself has had no suitors and no male attention in all these
years," Ethel said, again trying to dig something out of her about
men.

Addy met her eyes squarely. "I have had invitations. I simply
did not accept them. I would much rather talk about your fine
city, Mrs. Brown."

"Yes, let's get to the real reason for this meeting besides meeting our new school teacher," Hester spoke up, glad for the
chance to change the subject for Addy's sake. She rose, looking
around at everyone, an array of elegant day dresses, hats and
gloves. "We have discussed this many times, and the *Register*
has written articles calling for the banishment of prostitution.
We have even discussed parading in front of Sassy Dillon's Hard
Luck Saloon." She rolled her eyes and put her fingers to her
lips. "Do I dare even speak the woman's name in Jessica's parlor?"

Several women snickered, but in spite of Addy's own dislike
of Sassy Dillon's loud mouth and her occupation, she couldn't
help feeling a little sorry for her at the moment. After all, she
wasn't hurting these women. Addy didn't like talking about people behind their backs, and she highly resented the fact that these
women had earlier apparently been doing the same thing with
her. Ethel Brown had been spreading some kind of gossip that
had caused them to be cool toward her, apparently wary of her
background, especially when it came to men.

"I think we should picket," Jessica put in.

"It could be dangerous," Jane Rhodes added. "That's a bad
part of town, and the miners who frequent Sassy's place won't
like us trying to get rid of the women there. They're bound to

put up a fuss, maybe speak some awful profanity, make fun of us, maybe even threaten us."

"We had better ask Sam Watson to stand by in case of trouble," Susan Howard put in.

"Ha!" Ethel smirked. "We all know the sheriff wants those women there as much as the rest of the men. He's got no wife, no family, and my husband says he is seen at the Hard Luck often himself when he is not on duty."

"There are also prostitutes over at the Wildcat," Beth Howley spoke up. "And that Hurdy Gurdy across from the *Register*. Should we picket all three places?"

"At least the *Register* would support us," Hester said.

"What do you think of our idea?" Ethel asked Addy. "Do you have any objection to trying to rid our town of its painted women?"

Addy saw the look in the woman's piercing, dark eyes, as though to hint that perhaps there was something to her own past that resembled women like Sassy Dillon. "Of course not," she answered. "Prostitutes have long been banished back East. I suppose in a mining town, where there are thousands of homeless, mostly single men, such women are in demand. But their presence can only lead to crime and disease, I suppose, even to the corruption of the younger men whose youthful curiosity can lead them down the wrong path." She paused, then added, "I had the misfortune of riding here from Denver in a stagecoach I had to share with Miss Dillon."

Several of them gasped.

"You rode all the way up Clear Creek Canyon in the same coach with her?" Ethel exclaimed.

"I had no choice. She was simply one of the other passengers, and I didn't know her name or occupation. All I am saying is that she was vulgar and rude; but at the same time, since she is apparently a businesswoman in this town, perhaps we should talk to her privately first, ask her if she would be willing to leave without public embarrassment, or if she would consider just eliminating prostitution. Surely she could keep her saloon open just for drinks and such. I doubt that in a mining town it is reasonable to think we could eliminate saloons all together."

There came a few snickers, but Ethel Brown remained sober, still studying Addy intently. "Do you condone liquor, Mrs. Kane?"

Addy thought about Cole, the way he had of burying his own troubles in drink. "No. I am only saying that in a town full of drifters and hard-rock miners, saloons are a necessary evil, or a lot of the men needed for working the mines will leave. I am sure most of your husbands imbibe now and then. Men seem to think such things are important."

"Of course," Hester answered. "It's too bad. I know it would be impossible to eliminate saloons all together, but at least drinking and gambling do not spread diseases. And by staying away from saloons ourselves, we can avoid those vices. The trouble with the prostitutes is that we cannot always avoid *them*. They roam about town, are allowed to shop where we shop, eat in public restaurants. We are often forced to have to stand or sit next to one, and it is very disturbing. The fact that you, Addy, had to ride up here in the same coach with Sassy Dillon is an example." She looked at the other women. "The *Register* will support us if we march."

"Then I say let's do it," Jane Rhodes said. "Some of those crib girls have been caught stealing, which only shows that crime comes with their sinful lifestyle. It is abhorrent that Madame West's crib house is blatantly set up on Eureka Street, where all kinds of shops and businesses also are located, as though her own place was a legitimate place of business. Just a few weeks ago we read about two dance hall girls who got in a fight over some miner, right out in a public street, tumbling and scratching and screaming! Can you imagine?"

They all clucked and groaned and shook their heads. "Perhaps our public outcry will get rid of at least some of them," Ethel spoke up. "It's a start. I don't feel Sassy Dillon or any of

the others deserve any private talks or warnings. The best way
to get rid of them is to make them a public spectacle."

"Yes, something must be done," Marianne Conrad added.
"We all know that crime is on the increase. Now that the mines
are better established, with reputable owners like Grant Breckenridge and Mr. H. M. Teller, there is no necessity for the riff-raff
who first came here to look for gold. The miners now are mostly
men just here for jobs, some with families. It is time to weed
out the scoundrels and blacklegs who come to Central City simply to prowl about robbing houses and stores and threatening
decent women. We have no doubt that some men come here
simply to flee the law someplace else."

Addy's heartbeat quickened at the remark. Cole was one of
those men.

"Outlaws and homeless men find refuge in the brothels," the
woman continued. "If we rid ourselves of the whorehouses and
dance halls, and make a law against prostitution in the saloons,
we will at the same time rid ourselves of thieves and the like."

"Saturday then," Jessica Sage told them, "early afternoon,
when there are more miners in town after the shift changes. They
should know that just because they're here to work in our mines,
they cannot run this town to the point of shoving prostitutes in
our faces!"

"All right. Saturday it is," Hester said. "That gives us three
days to prepare some signs. You will join us, won't you, Addy?"

Again Addy felt the pressure of having to abide by the whims
of these women. "Of course," she answered, not really sure if it
was her right to try to chase someone out of a town where she
didn't even feel at home yet herself.

The room was filled then with excited talk among all the
women, discussions of what to wear and what their signs should
read. Ethel Brown rose and walked over to sit down beside Addy
on a love seat, smiling with victory at the club's decision to
march. She turned to Addy, scanning her quickly with her dark
eyes, as though to decide whether or not she was properly
dressed. Addy suspected the woman was also trying to find a

flaw, something she could use to say against her to others, perhaps that her dress was worn and of poor quality, which it most
certainly was not; perhaps it was too fitted and showed her
curves a bit too brazenly, which it did not; or maybe she could
find some other flaw.

"Tell me, dear, how was your outing with Grant Breckenridge
yesterday?"

Addy folded her hands in her lap. "It was quite nice. I've
never seen a real gold mine before. I learned things I never
knew."

"And Grant was a gentleman, I presume?"

Addy thought it an odd question. "Of course."

Ethel nodded. "I supposed he would be. All of us would like
to see the man find another wife and not be so alone. We could
see at the meeting night before last that he was quite taken with
you. Will you see more of him?"

It's none of your business, Addy wanted to respond. Once she
was better established here, she would find it easier to tell people
like Ethel Brown exactly what she thought of their nosey atti-
tudes. "I'm not sure," she answered. "I accepted an invitation
to dine with him tonight, but it is nothing serious. I am more
concerned right now with my teaching position. I have no ro-
mantic interest in any man, nor do I care to have one." What
was that look in Ethel's eyes? It was as though the woman could
see right through her.

"Well, perhaps Grant will change your mind," Ethel told her.
"He is, after all, quite a catch for a woman alone. You don't
know *any*one else in this town?"

Addy felt her cheeks growing a little hotter. "No. Why would
you ask that?"

"On, I just felt sorry for you being so alone, that's all," Ethel
answered.

Addy did not believe her. "Thank you for your concern," she
said. "I believe I'll get myself another sandwich." She rose and
walked to a table where the refreshments had been laid out.

Ethel watched her, lips pursed. *Why would you lie about not knowing anyone else in town, Mrs. Addy Kane?* she wondered, *unless it's someone who could tell us a few things about you that would cause you to lose your job?* She would get to the bottom of this, one way or another. Already a letter was on its way to Unionville.

Grant showed Addy into Sadie's Diner, a pleasant restaurant that he complained was not nearly as elegant as some of the dining establishments there now were in Denver. "Did you get to see much of Denver when you stayed over there?" he asked, pulling out a chair for her.

"No, I was much too tired. I just wanted to clean up and rest." Addy sat down to a table spread with a white cloth and surprisingly fine china and silverware for such a rugged town.

"Well, maybe some day I can take you back there and really show you the sights. I have some businesses there also now, but I like it up here—high, exciting, still rather uncivilized. It gives a man a challenge, but I don't suppose women enjoy such challenges."

Addy removed her gloves as he walked around the table to sit across from her. "I don't mind. Actually, having a school is just one way to help civilize a town. If I can be a part of that, then I will be doing my share to help."

A waitress in a white apron approached them, offering coffee or tea. Addy ordered tea, Grant coffee, as well as water. The waitress left printed menus.

"I'm surprised you ordered water, too," Addy told Grant. "I have learned that up here, water, coffee and tea, can all be quite expensive."

Grant smiled. "Nothing is too much for you, and I don't exactly need to worry about money. The reason it's so expensive is that all our drinking water has to be hauled up here from Denver. Clear Creek is too polluted from sewage and from the runoff from mining operations. Its name doesn't exactly suit the condition of the water. Of course, where you and I come from, no one worries about having water. Everything is different out here, so dry and barren."

"I am amazed at the determination and perseverance of men bent on getting rich, putting up with so many inconveniences," Addy told him.

Grant laughed lightly. "Like I said, some men enjoy the challenge." He studied Addy appreciatively, already having trouble sleeping at night for the want of her. She looked lovely this evening in a pale orchid dress with a matching cape and a small, feathered hat. He had enjoyed showing her around town. "Is it true some of the women are going to picket the Hard Luck saloon and some of the other hurdy-gurdy establishments?" Secretly he hoped it wasn't. He'd had some good times with some of those girls, whom he paid well to keep their mouths shut.

Addy felt embarrassed. "I'm afraid it is. I will be participating myself. I didn't have much choice in the matter, but I don't feel it's quite right, considering I am such a new citizen of the town myself."

"It's hard to say no to women like Hester Collingswood and Ethel Brown, isn't it?" Grant said with a grin.

"It certainly is."

"Well, you had all better be prepared for some pretty crude remarks from those women, and from some of the miners who don't want to see them go. You'd better have the sheriff handy."

"We intend to." Addy scanned the menu, still unable to feel comfortable with Grant in spite of his gentlemanly manner.

"I recommend the steak," he told her. "They have wonderful steaks here. They get them from—" He stopped short and looked past her toward the doorway. "Well, I believe I've just found the man I've been looking for."

Addy's back was to the door. She turned to see who he was talking about, and a man wearing a badge stood at the door with another man whose tall frame and the six-gun he wore on his hip made heads turn. Addy could feel the blood draining from her face. It was Cole Parker.

* * *

"Marshal Watson," Grant said, rising.

Addy looked away, heart pounding. Had Cole been found out? Was he under arrest? What would he think of her being here with Grant? But what *difference* did it make? It was he who had said they had to end their relationship once and for all. It was Cole who had followed her here against her wishes, and now he was supposed to be gone. Gone! Why did he keep doing this to her? If he had left when he was supposed to . . .

"Hello, Mr. Breckenridge. You told me you'd be here this evening, and you said if I found this man I should bring him to you."

"Yes! Yes!" Grant told the marshal.

Addy turned to see Grant putting out his hand. She breathed a sigh of relief that Cole was apparently not under arrest. But why was Grant looking for him? Did he know something about herself and Cole? She looked up at Cole, who glanced her way for a moment as he shook Grant's hand. The look in his eyes told her all she needed to know . . . hurt, a little anger and disappointment, a plea that she not give him away.

"I'm Grant Breckenridge," Grant was telling Cole. "May I ask your name?"

Cole withdrew his hand, glancing at Addy again, then meeting Grant's eyes squarely. "Cole Parker." He offered nothing more.

"I'll leave you alone now," the marshal told them. "He's all yours, Mr. Breckenridge." The man tipped his hat to Addy and left, and Grant offered Cole a chair at their table.

"You don't mind if I talk business for just a moment, do you, Addy?" he asked.

Addy felt warm all over, wishing there were a way to explain to Cole why she was here with Grant, wishing he had left like he'd promised. *Damn you,* she wanted to scream at Cole. *Why didn't you leave? Why do you keep doing this to me?* This was it. She was not going to let his presence ruffle her, nor would she allow it to reawaken all the hurt, the desire, the indecision.

Cole hesitated before taking a chair. "I don't understand," he told Grant. "You're apparently here for dinner with a lady, and you don't know me from Adam."

"Please sit down and I'll order you a drink, Mr. Parker. This will just take a minute. You aren't going to disturb my evening, I assure you. After all, I'm the one who asked Marshal Watson to find you for me." He nodded to Addy. "This is Mrs. Addy Kane, a widow from Illinois come here to teach in Central. I am just showing her around town, thought I'd offer her a good meal in one of our finer restaurants."

Cole nodded to Addy. "Nice to meet you," he told her.

Addy forced herself to keep from showing any sign of recognition. "And you, Mr. Parker," she replied. She felt a sudden urge to cry, and she looked away again, drinking some of the tea the waitress had brought while Cole and Grant were being introduced. She breathed deeply for self control.

"May I ask where you're from, Mr. Parker?" Grant asked.

Cole frowned. "I suppose, but I'm not prone to answering questions from men I don't even know, especially when they look me up without explaining why."

Grant grinned, but Addy noticed a little flash of irritation in his dark eyes. "I can see you're a very private person," he responded. "And very discerning. I like that. I read about your encounter with George Williams in the Hard Luck Saloon a few days ago. You apparently out-drew the man like lightning. That's what caught my eye. I asked Marshal Watson if he knew who it was, and he said you'd given no one your name but that he'd know you on sight and would bring you to meet me when he saw you again. So . . . here you are. What can I get you to drink?"

Addy felt sick at the knowledge Cole had been spending time at the Hard Luck Saloon. Had he been with Sassy Dillon? Would he be there in two days when she marched with the other women? She would feel like a fool.

"Nothing to drink," Cole said. "I wouldn't want to spoil your evening with the lady here."

Addy sipped more tea, catching the sarcasm in his remark. He was upset that she was with Grant, and he had no right to be, not after all the hurt he had caused her.

"How about just telling me *why* you were looking for me," Cole said. "Why do you care that I out-drew some guy in a saloon?"

"Because George Williams has a reputation for being the best. Is your aim as good as your draw?"

Addy felt Cole look at her again, knew what he was thinking. *Why don't you ask this lady here how good I am?* "I was a sharpshooter in the war," he answered, turning back to Grant. "And if you have a man hold out a glass of beer and drop it, I can draw and shatter the glass before it hits the ground."

"Really? That's remarkable!" Grant said. "In fact, I'd like to see a demonstration. How about tomorrow afternoon? Out in front of the Hard Luck?"

Cole sighed with irritation. "I don't like drawing that kind of attention. That thing the other night was something I couldn't back out of. And why does it even matter? Get to the point, Mr. Breckenridge."

Grant's eyebrows arched in a note of respect, and Addy suspected most men did not stand right up to the man or refuse to abide his wishes as Cole had just done. "The point is, Mr. Parker, I need a really good man to guard my gold shipments that go down to Denver, as well as the payroll for my miners that comes here from banks in Denver every two weeks. There have been raids and robberies along Clear Creek Canyon, and I've already lost one payroll. The pay is four dollars a day, which is more than the highest-paid miner, and in addition to that, free room and board at Sam's Hollow. It's not the best boarding house in town, but most are a lot worse."

Cole thought quietly for a moment, and Addy felt her heart hanging in the balance. Part of her wanted him to say yes, because it was an honest job that might help him back on the right track, but wisdom told her she should pray that he turn Grant down. She could not help thinking how ironic it was that Grant was asking Cole Parker to guard his gold. If only he knew the truth!

"I don't know," Cole answered. "I didn't plan on staying around at all. I'm just sort of drifting. I lost everything in the war, and I'm not sure where I want to land."

"Confederate?"

Cole rose. "Does it make any difference?"

"Not really." Grant also stood up then. "Tell you what. If you want the job, you be out in front of this restaurant tomorrow morning at nine o'clock. I'll take you up to the mines and show you around. Next gold shipment goes down in five days. Is it a deal?"

Cole frowned. "You don't know anything about me."

"I know you're good with that gun."

"How do you know *I* won't run off with your gold or your payroll?" Cole glanced at Addy again.

"I don't. I need a good man and I'll just have to take my chances. There will be other men along, too. Your job will be to ride ahead of the gold wagons, smell out trouble. When I hear about a new man in town who's skilled at something special, I look into it. That way I have only the best working for me. I don't go to the trouble of searching a man's background because up here most drifters are running from their past and trying to start new. Is that the case with you?"

"Could be. It's a good offer, Mr. Breckenridge. I'll think about it and be here at nine tomorrow morning to let you know."

Addy felt almost sick. What was she to do if Cole stayed and worked for Grant Breckenridge? She was bound to run into him, to have to look into those blue eyes that sent her into a whirl of indecision. She hated him. Yes, she did! If he decided to stay after all, she would see more of Grant Breckenridge just for spite!

"Fine," Grant was saying. He shook Cole's hand again. "Nine tomorrow then. Have your horse saddled and ready."

Cole nodded, glancing at Addy once more. "Nice meeting you, ma'am. You enjoy your evening."

Again she saw anger in those eyes. She supposed he thought less of her now after all, seeing another man so soon after their parting. Maybe he thought she was seeing Grant only because he had money. She realized she still didn't really know Cole Parker and what he truly thought about anything. Oh how she wished she had not been so weak in his arms, so dependent on him coming West. It would have been better for her if he had died from that bullet wound after all. "Thank you," she said softly.

Cole put his hat back on and walked out. Grant sat back down. "Sorry for the interruption, but I've been looking for that man," he told Addy. "He probably has a past he'd rather not tell me about, but that's all right. Central is full of men like that. There *is* an air of honesty about him." He drank some coffee. "So, what have you decided? Will it be a steak?"

Addy put a hand to her stomach. "I'm not terribly hungry," she answered. "In fact, I don't feel too well. I'll just have a roll, if they're fresh."

"Oh, and I so wanted to treat you to a really fine meal. I hope my bringing a stranger to the table who's apparently a drifter and a gunman didn't cause this."

Addy felt like laughing at the remark. *I've slept with that gunman,* she felt like shouting. *You've just hired an outlaw to guard your gold, Grant Breckenridge.* So be it. This was a chance for Cole to prove himself, and if he took that chance, she couldn't blame him—as long as he stayed away from her.

"Mr. Parker had nothing to do with it," she answered. "It's just that I'm still adjusting to this new life."

Grant reached out and grasped her hand. "And I'll help you. Don't be alarmed by drifters like Cole Parker. The circle of people you'll be associated with, you won't often have to be around people like that. And I must say, you do look beautiful tonight, Addy."

She wanted to feel something, anything. "Thank you," she finally answered.

Outside Cole stopped to light a thin cigar, feeling sick inside at seeing Addy with a man who was obviously one of Central's richest. The bastard! Grant Breckenridge was after the prettiest woman in town, and he couldn't blame him, nor could he blame Addy for turning her eyes to someone who could promise security. But there was something about Breckenridge that rubbed him the wrong way, something in those dark eyes that only another man would recognize. The man was a pompous ass who probably enjoyed flaunting his wealth at women, and by-God he'd better never hurt Addy Kane! It tore at his guts seeing Addy with another man, but he had no right doing anything about it. She was probably angry that he hadn't left town.

Maybe he still would. Breckenridge's offer was a damn good one, but was it worth having to see Addy with the man? Then again, what if he hurt her somehow? Maybe he *should* stay around. What better way to keep an eye on Addy's welfare and how Breckenridge treated her than to take this job?

"What a damn mess," he grumbled. "I need a drink." He headed for Sassy's place.

Eighteen

"What do you know about Grant Breckenridge?" Cole took a deep drag on his cigarette and poured himself another shot of whiskey. Sassy Dillon drank down what was left of her glass of beer.

"Grant? Why in hell you asking, honey?"

Cole met her eyes. Sassy was a foul-mouthed, brassy whore, but one thing he liked about her was that she was honest and open and didn't try to pretend she was something that she was not. Although she had practically begged him to come back to her bed, he had only slept with her that one night. He had hung around since only because he couldn't quite bring himself to leave Central—or Addy Kane—in spite of his promises to her.

"The man sought me out earlier this evening, offered me a job guarding his gold shipments and payroll along Clear Creek Canyon on trips to and from Denver. Seems a little strange to me that he'd hire a complete stranger who's good with a gun to guard his money. For all he knows, I could be an outlaw myself."

Sassy grinned in good humor. *"Are* you an outlaw? You running from the law, Cole Parker?"

Cole grinned in return. "No, ma'am. I was a choir boy back East."

Sassy belted out a healthy laugh. She leaned forward then, flaunting her breasts at him from across the table. "Come let me enjoy that beautiful body of yours again, and I'll tell you all you want to know about Grant Breckenridge."

Cole took one last drag and exhaled smoke as he pressed out

the stub of his cigarette in an ashtray. "Not yet, lady. I've go
too much on my mind."

"Yeah?" Her eyebrows arched as she gave him a knowing
look. "Like maybe that pretty young schoolteacher?"

Cole had not said one word to the woman about Addy, bu
Sassy had pestered him about her ever since that first night she'
seen the look of recognition in his eyes when she'd mentioned
riding up here with Addy in a stagecoach. "You don't give up
do you?"

"Never," Sassy replied with a light laugh. "I know men, Col
Parker, and something is eating at you real bad. My guess is it
a woman, and the woman is Mrs. Addy Kane. I don't know th
connection, but there is one."

Cole sighed, looking around to be sure no one was hearing
their conversation. The Hard Luck was full tonight, the air float
ing with smoke from cigars and cigarettes, men talking loudly
playing cards, laughing. "It's a long story," he answered, "an
I don't want even one whispered hint spilled that I might know
her at all."

Sassy caught the warning look in his eyes. She nodded. "
think I get the picture." She looked up and signaled for her pian
player to finish his break and get back to playing. The youn
man, sporting a huge mustache, nodded and set an empty bee
glass on top of the piano. He began plunking out a lively tune
and two other women who worked for Sassy moved from tabl
to table, asking men to buy them drinks and offering to giv
them pleasant favors in return. Sassy moved her chair closer t
Cole, realizing he didn't want their conversation heard. "You'r
worried certain people might discover you know Mrs. Kane. Sh
could risk losing her new teaching job, I'll bet. I know how thos
who run this town think, Cole, especially the wives of the wealth
ier men. They expect Mrs. Addy Kane to be spotlessly clean.
She ran her fingers lightly over the back of his hand. "But sh
isn't, is she?"

Cole pulled his hand away. "I didn't say that. She's a goo
woman."

Sassy's eyes lit up with new knowledge. "And you, by God, are in love with her, aren't you!" She smiled with victory at finally getting a little piece of the truth.

Cole did not smile as he leaned closer. "Watch your mouth, Sassy. I can't say I do or don't, and I said before, I don't want one connection made between us. That damn teaching job means everything to her, and I don't intend to mess it up for her. As far as *how* I know her, that's my business."

"You might have to tell me a little too much about *yourself,* huh?"

Cole grinned. "I might. Why don't you just answer my original question?"

"About Grant Breckenridge?"

He nodded.

Sassy shrugged. "He's a bastard of sorts—rich, arrogant, likes women. He pretends to be a gentleman, is on the town council, the school board, all that bullshit. He runs four mines up in the hills, owns a good share of one of them, the Jamesway. It's unclear how he got it. He's a manager for Chadwick Mining. Another Chadwick employee, Ed Foley, supposedly tried to claim the Jamesway for himself, and Grant reported it, got him fired. Foley tells it another way, says Grant double-crossed him, which wouldn't surprise me at all. Foley says Grant originally backed him, then reported him to make himself look better to the company."

"You figure Breckenridge to be the type to do something like that?"

Sassy chuckled bitterly. "No doubt in my mind. Grant can be a real bastard when it comes to business. No one seems to know the exact truth about the mess. Grant is good at coming out smelling like a rose, no matter what kind of underhanded thing he's been up to. He can be very charming when it's necessary." She drank down a shot of whiskey. "The whole deal left some real bad feelings between the two of them, mostly on Foley's part. Foley's son was working with him at the time, and both of them had to go to work at another mine. A dynamiting accident

there killed Foley's son, and he blames the boy's death on Grant
Breckenridge—says his son would still be alive if they hadn't
had to go to work someplace else. He got to drinking heavily,
let the whole business fester inside till he's become a little bit
crazy with a need for revenge, but he's never actually made any
moves toward Grant."

Cole frowned. "Sounds like you know Breckenridge pretty
good."

Sassy grinned knowingly. "I know he also has businesses
back in Chicago where he's from, a few in Denver, too. The
reason I know so much about him is because he's been in my
bed more than once. Not a bad body for a man his age, but he's
a hypocrite since he pretends to be in favor of rousting the
whores out of Central. I don't think his rich friends on the hill
who look down their noses at us realize just how often Grant
Breckenridge sneaks down to the crib houses or comes to see
me. He's real careful about it, and I know better than to say
anything if I want to keep my saloon going."

"That powerful, is he?"

Sassy nodded. "As far as him asking you to work for him,
I'm not surprised. He probably heard how good you are with a
gun. He isn't worried whether you're an outlaw or not, figures
if he pays you good enough, you'll work an honest job and not
be stupid enough to cross him. Up here a man takes what he
can get in the way of help. He just has to trust his own good
judgment. A lot of men come here for a lot of reasons, and
Breckenridge knows if he asked you to tell him everything about
your past, you'd probably lie through your teeth anyway. His
only concern is that you're good enough with that gun to look
out for his gold shipments." She reached over and squeezed his
thigh. "You gonna' take the job, honey? I'd sure like to see you
stay around."

Cole rubbed at his eyes. "She was with him."

"What?" Sassy leaned closer. "That schoolteacher? She was
with Breckenridge when you talked to him?"

"They were dining out. The man is interested in her, and

wouldn't blame her for being interested in return, considering his wealth. I'm just worried he's a sonofabitch who'll hurt her."

"She the type that goes after money?"

Cole poured himself another shot of whiskey. "No. But like any woman in her position, she wants security, respect."

"And she can't get that if she's with you?"

Cole gave her another warning look. "I'm not going to explain all that. Just tell me what you think of Breckenridge seeing her."

Sassy folded her arms. "All right. I think he *is* a sonofabitch. He's simply after a pretty, vulnerable young woman who he'd love to get into his bed. I know the man. Now maybe he wants the whole works this time—marriage and all. It's possible. I guess you have to trust her to have enough brains to figure the man out, enough intelligence not to let things go too far. You have supposedly promised to stay out of her life, so I guess that's what you should do."

Cole drank down the whiskey. "Maybe. That doesn't mean I can't still watch out for her in my own way." He rose. "Thanks. And be quiet about this, will you?"

Sassy looked up at him. "You know I will. You gonna' take the job?"

Cole thought a moment. A little voice told him to leave town like he'd promised, but a stronger feeling overcame his better sense. Seeing Addy out socially with another man tore at his guts like fire. "Yeah," he answered. "I'm taking the job."

He turned and left, and Sassy shook her head, chuckling to herself. "Well, well, well," she murmured. "Cole Parker and Mrs. Addy Kane." She had long ago stopped being surprised at what she discovered about people.

Addy heard another explosion deep in the hills, and she looked up at the maze of mines and the hundreds of buildings that were spread out around them. It was almost nine o'clock. Cole would be meeting with Grant soon, if he intended to take the job offer. She was glad he'd been offered something that would mean he wouldn't have to work deep in the mines, but worried about the problem it could mean for both of them if he chose to stay.

She turned and kept walking, her heart pounding at the steep climb. She wondered when she would ever adjust to the high altitude and thin air here, but at least it looked as though it was going to be a pleasant day. She hardly needed the shawl she was wearing, which was surprising, since it had gotten quite cold last night. She wondered just how bad things would be come winter. She'd heard plenty of stories about how harsh the season could be in the mountains. She could not imagine how anyone got up and down Clear Creek Canyon in winter, and she supposed that no matter what happened, once winter arrived she'd have no choice but to stay here until spring. Would she have to spend the whole winter trying to avoid Cole?

She kept walking toward Hester's house, where the women were to gather and spend the day making signs for their march. She had decided to walk the several blocks to get there, even though it was quite a climb. She needed the air to clear her head, and she needed the exercise to help her wake up more. She had tossed and turned all night thinking about Cole, had not fallen asleep until the early morning hours and now felt achy and worn.

This was all Cole's fault. She didn't need the man to continue following after her, nor did she need him to think he had any say in what other men she saw. It made her angry to consider that Cole Parker might think she would be swayed by Grant's money and position, and it angered her even more that Cole might feel he had a say in who she chose to see socially. How was she ever going to forget him and get settled into her new surroundings and go on with her life if he continued to show up at every turn?

The worst part was, every time she set eyes on the man she still felt a rush of desire that made her wonder if she was any different from the painted women against whom she would be marching in two days. Grant didn't do that to her. Her own husband had not brought out so much desire.

She walked faster, furious. If Cole Parker insisted on interfering with her emotions this way, then she would just be even stronger and more determined. He had played with her heart too often, stolen her most intimate feelings, invaded her most private places, then left her confused and alone. Perhaps it had all been simply to satisfy his male ego. The handsome bastard could have any woman he wanted, and he knew it! She reminded herself of what he was when she met him—an outlaw. Maybe he had plans of continuing that life after all, maybe to steal some of Grant's gold. He was a worthless drifter who drank too much, and no matter how valid his reasons for turning to that desperate life, she must face those facts. She was never going to get involved with him intimately again, and she would make him realize that by seeing as much of Grant Breckenridge as she wanted, even if she didn't like the man very much.

"No more, Cole parker," she muttered, glancing up to see she was not far from Hester's house now. "No more."

Still, here he was, in Central, considering working for the very man she would be seeing socially! She just wished she knew for sure what was going through his mind. Did he think she might fall into Grant's bed as easily as she had fallen into bed with him? Did he hate her? Love her?

And here he'd been hanging out at the Hard Luck Saloon! Sassy Dillon's place. Had he slept with the woman? Maybe he'd told her about their affair, laughed with the woman about it. If he had, Sassy wouldn't hesitate telling everyone she knew. Women like that didn't care about discretion or honor. They surely didn't understand that a woman could want a man, need to be with a man out of pure, aching loneliness, to be held, to feel like a woman again. Women like Sassy understood only sinful, wanton lust. If Sassy Dillon knew about her and Cole, the woman would probably shout out something about it when she saw her marching with the other women against prostitutes.

If that happened, her dream of making a life for herself here would be ruined, and it would be Cole Parker's fault!

She noticed two women approaching on foot from another direction, and she walked over to greet Ethel Brown and Marianne Conrad, both of whom lived close enough to Hester Collingswood that they did not need a carriage to bring them there. She took a deep breath and put on a smile, dreading having to socialize with Ethel Brown again. Already she could see that scrutinizing look in the woman's eyes as she came closer, huffing and puffing from forcing her hefty body to climb the one block it took to get here.

"I shouldn't have let you talk me into walking this, Marianne," she heard the woman telling Mrs. Howley.

"Oh, but the walk is good for you," Marianne answered. She greeted Addy with a smile as they all met at the gate to Hester's house, where several carriages sat tied. "Apparently just about everybody is here already," Marianne added. "I hope that reporter for the *Register* was able to bring us some poster paper like he promised. We must get busy with our signs."

Addy thought how she would rather be preparing herself for her teaching job. She managed a pleasant greeting for Ethel, who only sniffed a "Good morning." She looked Addy up and down. "My husband tells me he saw you out with Grant Breckenridge again last night," she said.

Addy was not sure how she meant the remark. Was the woman insinuating she was some kind of gold-digger after the richest single man in town? "Yes. Mr. Breckenridge offered to buy me dinner and show me around town a little more."

"Oh, how exciting for you," Marianne put in.

"Yes," Ethel added with a hint of sarcasm. "You do look a little tired this morning, Mrs. Kane. How late were you out?"

Addy bristled. "I was home quite early. I just had one of those nights when I couldn't sleep because of so much on my mind. I will be so happy to begin teaching."

They stepped up onto Hester's porch. "Is something worrying you?" Ethel asked.

Addy met her eyes squarely. She hated the way the woman had of making her feel like some kind of criminal, when she had done nothing wrong . . . except tell no one about Cole Parker. "No," she answered firmly. "It's just very disconcerting for a woman alone to pick up and leave her past behind and come to a place where she knows no one, to teach for the first time and have to face people who don't think a woman should *be* teaching. Right now I'd like to help you and the others with your campaign, so we had better go inside and get started."

Marianne turned and knocked at the door, and Addy kept her eyes on Ethel Brown, who nodded.

"Yes, we have much to do today," Ethel said. "I hope this march will help us rid Central of its soiled women." She wondered if she should go ahead and tell Grant Breckenridge about how Alfred Rhodes was sure he'd heard this woman secretly meet a man in the dark after her reception. Who was that man? What was Mrs. Addy Kane hiding?

Addy turned and went inside, and Ethel followed. *I'll know soon enough,* she thought. *Soon enough.*

"I thought we'd ride up to the Jackpot," Grant told Cole. He moved off the boardwalk where he'd been waiting for Cole and mounted a sleek roan mare. He wore a suit that Cole thought was a little extravagant for riding up to the mines, but he supposed men like Breckenridge felt they always had to dress in a way that showed their importance.

Show everyone you're a big-time mine owner, he thought. He could not believe such things would impress someone as intelligent and level-headed as Addy, but then maybe there were things about her he didn't understand after all. Surely she wouldn't fall into the arms of another man as easily as she had fallen into his. He liked to think they had shared things neither of them could expect to ever share with anyone else. Maybe they didn't belong together, but there was something special between them that couldn't be changed.

"Did you enjoy your evening with Mrs. Kane last night?" he asked aloud.

Grant grinned. "Very much."

What the hell does that mean? Cole growled to himself.

"Beautiful woman, isn't she?" They headed out of town side by side.

"She certainly is."

"And a widow." Grant cast him a sidelong glance, his dark eyes glittering with what Cole considered flat-out evil. "You know what they say about widows." He chuckled. "After a while they get to needing a man again."

Cole checked an urge to hit the man. "Maybe."

Grant puffed on a cigar he'd been smoking while he waited for Cole. "Mrs. Kane is not going to be an easy one. She's pretty reserved, says she's not in the mood for having to consider seeing anyone. She's more interested in throwing herself into her work for now, but I'll work on it. Hell, I might even ask her to marry me some day if she lets me keep seeing her and things work out. I've been alone myself for a long time now, although my son James will be coming here to live in a few weeks. How about you? Ever been married?"

Cole felt the old pain, but it was soothed by learning that at least Grant apparently had not managed to impress Addy too deeply yet. Still, the man certainly had an edge—wealth, charm, good looks. He wondered if he should have a talk with Addy, tell her what he really knew about the man. He suspected that even if he was married, Grant Breckenridge was the kind of man who would continue to have his share of other women.

"My wife died in childbirth several years ago," he answered. "The baby died too," he lied. He couldn't bear to tell the man the truth. He relived it enough in his dreams, and that night of horror was not something he shared readily with anyone. But Addy . . . it had been so easy to tell Addy.

"Sorry about that. No one serious since then?"

Yeah. I've slept with the woman you ate dinner with last night, you bastard. "No. There was the war, then having to decide what to do with myself afterward. I'm not exactly the settling kind right now. I don't have much to offer a woman."

Grant looked over at him, keeping the cigar in his teeth. "Well, you're handsome enough to have any woman you want. I'll bet the whores in town have been crawling all over you."

"I've had some offers," Cole answered.

Grant laughed. "You'd better get your share while you can. The cherished, pure women's society of Central is planning a march in the streets in a couple of days, campaigning to get rid of Central's soiled doves. If they get enough support, we men on the City Council will have to outlaw prostitution, which won't make the miners very happy."

Nor you, Cole thought. "Seems to me like it would be pretty difficult to accomplish, with hundreds of single men working up in those mines. They could cause a riot."

Grant nodded and halted his horse. "Mrs. Kane will be in on the march. Do me a favor. Since you seem to like to hang out at the Hard Luck, try to be around that day, keep a watch on Mrs. Kane. Those miners can get pretty nasty when they want, especially if they're drinking; and the whores can be pretty mean and foul-mouthed, too, especially Sassy Dillon." He turned away and kicked his horse into motion again. "Or at least that's what I'm told. I don't generally associate with women like that. But there's one thing I do know. If we outlaw prostitution, those women will find some way around it. They'll sneak up to the mine shacks or something. The town council won't really care, as long as they quit operating openly in the streets."

They rode away from town and headed up a steep roadway. "I'll keep an eye on things," Cole told the man.

"The *Register* has been printing articles against prostitution. They'll probably let the whole town know about the march, so it could turn into a real circus. We men on the City Council don't intend to be there. Since we all own businesses in town that serve the miners, and some of us *own* the mines, we don't want the miners to think we want to outlaw prostitution. We can claim we had to do so in order to answer the demands of the majority of those in town who are trying to civilize this place. The miners with families will understand. Their own wives might join in on the march."

"That could cause even more trouble, between husbands and wives," Cole said. "Some of the married miners will probably support the single ones who feel it's their right to have prostitutes close by."

Grant laughed. "Ought to be quite a show. This is an exciting place to live, isn't it?"

Cole looked at the surrounding mountains peppered with mines. At one time these mountains were covered with pine trees and aspen. There had been nothing here once but beauty, wildlife. "It is that," he answered. "I'll say one thing. A man can get attached to these mountains, the high country." *And the women brave enough to come here.* Maybe he should just leave, go farther west, ride free . . . away from love, away from the responsibility of a job. It would be easy to fall back into his outlaw ways out here—wide open country with no law in most places. He could raid and rob his way through the southwest and go live like a king in Mexico—and leave Addy to her teaching, her rich suitor, her nice, normal, civilized, secure life.

"I love it myself," Grant was saying. "Coming up here to gold country, seeing what can be had with a pick and a shovel, makes a man a little heady. Haven't you considered looking for gold?"

"I've considered it." Cole took a thin cigar from a shirt pocket, thinking how warm it was this morning after such a cold night. "Decided the only men who make money on gold are the ones like you who can buy up other peoples' claims and can afford to mine the gold properly. Besides, it looks to me like the ground around here has been pretty well covered. These mountains look like a beehive, there are so many holes in them."

Grant broke into loud laughter. "You're a smart man. By the way, I want you to demonstrate to me up at the mine that thing you say you can do with a beer mug. We'll use a drinking cup. I want to see if you're really as good as you say."

Cole put the cigar in his mouth and wrapped the reins around the pommel of his saddle while he lit it, letting Shadow amble on without guidance. "I don't like shooting for show," he answered.

"Hell, man, there's always a shooting contest at my miner's picnic. I need to see how good you are so I can bet on you. It's one thing to draw fast, but still another to hit your target. We have both pistol and rifle target contests."

"If I show you how good I am in front of all the miners, then *they'll* know how good I am. Then all bets will be on me and there won't be any odds for you to win with. In fact, I'd be willing to bet no other men would bother entering the contest."

Grant laughed even harder. "You're an arrogant sonofabitch about it, aren't you?"

"No more arrogant than you are about your wealth."

Grant shook his head. "All right, I'll take your word for it. I'd just better not lose any money on you at the picnic."

Cole kept the cigar between his teeth. "You won't lose," he answered. "Are we allowed to bring guests to this picnic?"

"You mean a woman?"

"I sure don't mean another man."

Grant looked over at him, smiling. "Of course. A lot of the miners are married men, and they'll have wives and kids with them. Bring whomever you want, as long a she isn't some hurdy-gurdy girl who's going to cause a stir among the wives."

Cole shrugged. "What other kind of women aren't already taken? I suppose you'll be bringing Mrs. Kane."

A look of warning came into Grant's eyes. "If she accepts. Don't tell me *you* were thinking of it. We have strict rules for our sole female schoolteacher, Cole. She shouldn't be seen with homeless strangers. I don't mean that as an insult, but, after all, we don't know anything about you. That doesn't matter for what *I* want you to do, but when it comes to seeing someone like Mrs. Kane socially, that's another matter."

Cole smiled with a hint of bitterness. Knowing what he knew about Breckenridge, it ate at his guts to have to sit and listen to the man make himself out to be the town saint. "I was only stating a fact about what you'd be doing. Believe me, I have no interest in someone as prim and proper as Mrs. Kane. I prefer my women with a little paint and a lot of breast."

Again Grant burst into laughter. "You do whatever you want as far as women. All I ask is that you guard my gold and supplies, and don't embarrass me at the shooting contests."

"You just bet plenty of money on me. If I win it for you, I want just one dance with that pretty lady you had at supper last night. Do you think she'd oblige? If it's with your approval, no one would think anything of it."

Grant looked at him, eyebrows arched. He halted his horse. "All right. One dance, *if* you win the shooting contests. Just don't get any ideas, Parker. You're a handsome young man, but women like Addy Kane need more than good looks. Besides, she's mine. I intend to make sure of that."

Cole caught the intense warning look in the man's dark eyes. *Just don't try forcing her into something she doesn't want,* he thought. "I get the picture," he answered. "I just thought a dance with a pretty woman like that would give me more incentive to hit my target."

Grant nodded, scanning him with a look that told Cole all he needed to know. Grant Breckenridge had his claws out for Addy, and he intended to have her any way he could, and not necessarily as a wife. He considered her a conquest. Cole had never thought of her that way, and if he could help it, he was not going to let her fall prey to this bastard.

"Come on," Grant said then. "Enough talk of women. Let me show you a real vein of gold. I have a little cabin up there with an office in it. I'll explain how we handle our shipments, when they take place, what you should watch for. We're having more and more trouble with thieves and outlaws along Clear Creek."

He rode on ahead, and Cole just grinned. "Maybe your trouble has just begun," he muttered.

Nineteen

Addy felt like a hypocrite, and she wanted to blame Cole for making her feel this way. Here she was joining a march with other women against prostitution, yet she had slept with a man who was not her husband. Of course she would never sleep with a man for money, but how right was it to sleep with a man out of wedlock, whatever the reason? And she was just as much to blame. She could have said no, but when Cole Parker touched her . . .

"Here is your signboard, dear." Hester Collingswood handed her a sign to carry.

NO PROSTITUTION IN CENTRAL!, it read. Addy looked around at other signs.

BRING RESPECT TO CENTRAL!

PROSTITUTION BREEDS CRIME!

LAW AND ORDER FOR CENTRAL!

PROSTITUTION IS AN EMBARRASSMENT TO CENTRAL!

NO MORE "HURDY GURDY" ON EUREKA STREET!

LEWD WOMEN ARE A TOOL OF THE DEVIL! There were more, with at least twenty-five women gathered in protest, all dressed primly, collars close around their necks, plain hats worn over plain hairstyles. Addy knew many of these women usually dressed in much fancier dresses and hats, with piles of curls on their heads, bodices cut much lower for dances or other entertaining events. It was natural for a woman to want to look her prettiest, whether for her husband or to attract other men, or sometimes to make other women jealous. She had found herself wanting to look her own best when meeting all these new people, but today they must all look the part of prim and proper and moral women. Again she felt the hypocrisy of it. They felt it was wrong for the prostitutes and dance hall girls to paint their faces and curl their hair and wear colorful dresses designed to tempt a man, but it was all right for a "proper lady" to flaunt her own beauty to catch a man.

Ethel Brown led the march, raising her sign high and facing the other women, who had gathered high on Eureka Street. They would march down through town, go up Spring Street, around and back down Main Street to Eureka again, stopping in front of the Hard Luck to sing hymns. Although Addy agreed prostitution was a flagrant sin and could not understand how any woman could abide by such a life, she did not feel right about being there. As an independent woman herself, a part of her felt that however a woman chose to make a living, in some cases just to survive, it was her choice; but she suspected that the friendship and support of these women important to her own survival and important to her keeping her teaching job depended on her participation in their meetings and social events, and in particular this march.

"Ladies!" Ethel Brown announced, "Be prepared to be laughed at by the miners and prostitutes. You will hear lewd talk from the mouths of the prostitutes, probably profanity from the men. You must ignore their remarks. Don't let them stop you, and don't let them make you tremble. Be strong, ladies, and know that what we are doing is right with God!"

A few cheers went up, but Addy could see doubt and fear in the eyes of many. Ethel stepped off. "Follow me, ladies!" She began singing the *Battle Hymn of the Republic*. Everyone joined in the hymn, and Addy could see that already the streets were being lined with gawkers, most just ordinary citizens, businessmen, other women with their children, all cheering them on. But as they approached the central business district, where most of the saloons and dance halls were located, the crowd began to change, their looks and words meaner. Soon there were no women among the onlookers except those with painted lips and low-cut dresses and dangling earrings.

"Hey, honey, you're pretty enough to come join us!" one shouted. "You'd make a hell of a lot more money than doing whatever you do now!" She laughed loudly, and Addy could not keep her cheeks from growing red. She looked straight ahead, pretending not to hear. A reporter from the *Register* moved among them now, taking notes. Another stood with camera ready one block below, so that as the marchers came toward him along the steeply descending street, they were above him at an angle where he could get a picture of almost the entire group. Addy saw the puff of smoke from his flash powder and wondered how a widow woman of little significance from a small town in Illinois could have ended up marching against prostitution in a wild mining town in the Rockies of Colorado, let alone the adventures she had had getting here— not to mention a sinful fling with an outlaw!

The marchers surged ahead, through streets lined with jeering miners and whores, many making dirty jokes, most laughing at them and holding up whiskey bottles, prostitutes hanging on the arms of men. They approached the Hard Luck, and Addy cast a sidelong glance at the swinging doors that led into the den of sin. There stood Cole, silently watching her! Just outside the door stood Sassy Dillon, her outrageously bleached hair swept up into a cascade of curls that graced her slightly plump neck, a neck adorned with diamonds. She wore a feathered pink dress that revealed a great deal of cleavage, and a wildly feathered hat to match.

The woman pointed at her. "Hey, schoolteacher, how do you like the city of Central so far?" She shrieked in that irritating laugh Addy remembered from the coach ride through Clear Creek Canyon then turned to Cole and said something to him. Addy quickly looked away, feeling like a fool, wondering what Cole must think of her being a part of this. Was he laughing at her, too? What if he had told Sassy about what they had done! Surely Cole wouldn't be cruel enough to tell the woman about

their affair. He had promised. He'd said he had too much respect
for her to tell anyone. Was it all a lie? Had he used her like he
would use a woman like Sassy? Was he just trying to prove that
all women were the same?

She wanted to run, get away from all of this, but she stood
her ground, marched on. They moved through more jeering
crowds, back to a safer part of town where regular citizens
again supported them, clapping, urging them on, some joining
them. The parade wound back toward Eureka Street, and Addy's
heart pounded at the realization they were going to return to
the Hard Luck and plant themselves there for hymns. Ethel
Brown intended to single out Sassy Dillon and order her out
of town. She realized the entire event could get ugly. Ethel
Brown was a determined woman who was not afraid to say her
piece, but Addy suspected she was no match for Sassy Dillon,
whose name certainly fit her mouth. Gradually they returned
to the center of Central's den of sins, their own numbers now
increased, several men among them who had decided to come
along to protect the "brave women" who were only doing what
they felt God meant for them to do.

But men were men, and Addy felt trouble coming. Ethel came
to a halt in front of the Hard Luck, where Sassy stood on the
front steps in all her feathered glory. Five other painted women
stood on either side of her, hands on their hips, painted faces
sneering at them. None of them was especially pretty, and one
of them was downright ugly, but Addy supposed if a lonely miner
had gone long enough without a woman . . .

She moved her gaze past Sassy to the swinging doors. Cole
still stood there. He slowly moved out as Ethel Brown announced to Sassy that the majority of the citizens of Central had
decided the city must be rid of women of sin like herself who
ran gambling and drinking halls and who also practiced prostitution. She went on to say that having women in Central who
sold themselves to men for money was a digrace, that Central
could never rank among one of the finest cities in Colorado as

long as it continued to operate as a wild mining town with no morals and no laws that controlled prostitution.

"Go march before the City Council!" Sassy sneered. "Let them decide the laws, and let our sheriff enforce them! You won't get far, fat lady! Half the men on the City Council like to drink and gamble here, and that's not all they like about my place!"

Sassy's gritty cackle filled the air, and the women with her joined in the laughter, as did a hundred or so miners who encircled the protestors.

"How dare you insult the fine men who run Central!" Ethel returned. "Men like my own husband, and Stuart Collingswood, our schoolteachers, Lee Brown, H. M. Teller, Grant Breckenridge . . . none of them would stoop so low as to enter your den of sin!"

Sassy looked at Addy. "Wouldn't they?" She looked back at Ethel, and Addy wondered if Sassy was trying to tell her something about Grant. "You'd be surprised who sneaks into my room some nights, lady!"

More laughter filled the air, and Ethel Brown reddened with anger and frustration. Some of the miners moved a little closer, making suggestive remarks. Suddenly a man grabbed Addy's arm. His breath reeked of whiskey as he jerked her close. "Hey, little lady, you're prettier than any woman in this whole town! Word is you're a widow woman to boot! Why don't you come on inside and have a drink with me? You might find out it's more fun than teachin' school!"

Men nearby laughed as Addy squirmed to get out of the man's grip. Suddenly someone came between them, a strong arm shoving the drunken miner away. "Leave the lady alone."

Addy blinked back tears as she stepped back, realizing it was Cole who had come to her aid.

"Hell, Cole, she's the prettiest one. Let's have some fun with these women."

"They have a right to do what they're doing," Cole answered. "Leave them alone and they'll be gone soon."

"It ain't your business what I do," the miner answered. He

took a swing at Cole, who held him off easily, then raised his own fist and slammed it into the man's jaw.

Immediately the fight was on. Two more men jumped on Cole, knocking Addy to the ground when they shoved Cole into her. In that brief moment, it seemed the entire street erupted into a brawl. Women were screaming and running, some of the protestors hitting men with their signs. Addy crawled out from under Cole, and he got to his feet and landed big fists into the two men who had attacked him. As Addy stumbled around in the melee, she noticed Sassy Dillon was rolling in the dirt with Ethel Brown! Both women were scratching and clawing. Ethel's hat was gone, her hair a tumble, a sleeve of her dress ripped. She grabbed at Sassy and pulled at her dress, accidentally pulling one shoulder down and causing one of Sassy's huge breasts to fall out of the low-cut bodice!

Men laughed and cheered, and Sassy seemed unaffected by the fact that half the town was seeing her bare breast. She reared up and shoved Ethel Brown hard, causing the woman to fall into a watering trough, then went after Susan Howard, who ran away. Before Addy could see what else happened, someone strong grabbed her around the waist, picked her up and ran with her. She screamed and kicked.

"Shut up! It's just me!" Cole told her. He whisked her away from the crowd and into an alley behind some boxes where no one could see them. "Are you crazy, marching into this den of wild men protesting prostitution? You should have known it would lead to trouble!"

Addy looked up at his bleeding face. He stood there panting, his shirt torn, his thick, dark hair hanging around his face in disarray. Again he had come to her rescue, and again she was struck by his handsomeness. "I had little choice," she answered, her own breath coming in excited gasps. "They expected me to join them."

"You don't belong with that bunch of stuck-up bitches!"

Addy stiffened. "Some of them have been very good to me.

need friends, Cole! I'm trying to start a new life here, remember? My job depends on what those women think of me."

His dark eyes moved over her. "And what would they think if they knew about me? That's what you're thinking."

Addy looked away. "Thank you for coming to my aid. I'd better get back out there." She could still hear screams and the sounds of fighting in the street.

"Stay away from there for a few minutes, till things quiet down. And while you're at it, stay away from Grant Breckenridge."

Addy looked up at him. "How dare you tell me who I can and cannot see!"

"There are a lot of things you don't know about him. Sassy Dillon knows him well!"

"Does she? So what? The man has been single for years. She knows *you* well, too, no doubt!" She could not help the tears that came to her eyes.

Cole braced his hands on either side of her, pinning her against the side wall of the Hard Luck. "That bother you?"

Addy dropped her gaze. "No."

Cole grasped her chin, forced her to look up at him. "Your eyes tell me different." He leaned down and met her mouth in a savage kiss, while in the background Addy could hear continued screaming and punching. She thought how Cole Parker fit right in with the wild scrambling going on in the street, had actually started it . . . over her. The thought of him enjoying a roll in bed with Sassy Dillon brought on an unwelcome jealousy that caused her to return his kiss almost as savagely as he stole one from her. Hadn't she pleased him more than that woman could? She liked to think she had, and she hated herself for caring.

Cole released her, then wiped blood from the corner of her mouth with his fingers before wiping the same blood from a cut on his upper lip with the back of his hand. "Sorry."

Addy pulled away, telling herself she should be angry. "About the blood? Or about the kiss?" When she looked up at him he was grinning.

"Just the blood. Then again, why should I apologize? Would you rather I let that man drag you into the saloon?"

Addy sighed in frustration, rubbing at her eyes a moment. "No, of course not. Thank you for stopping him, but . . ." She threw up her hands in frustration. "Cole, why did you kiss me just now? Isn't it supposed to be over? Truly over? Why are you even still in Central? What in God's name do you want of me?"

He ran a hand through his thick hair, realizing he had lost his hat back in the street. "I don't know for sure. I only know I can't forget you, that I miss you when we're not together. I can't bring myself to just leave and let whatever happens to you happen, especially when you're seeing someone like Grant Breckenridge."

"Grant is a bit pious, but he's kind to me. He is certainly not the kind of man a woman immediately turns away."

"But I am?"

Their eyes held for a moment, both of them wondering what might have been. "No. Not if you were the man you apparently were before the war."

He stepped closer. "That man is still inside here somewhere," he said, putting a fist to his chest. "I just need time to find him again. Give me that time, Addy."

She folded her arms in front of her defensively, afraid to let him hold her again. "While you carouse in the Hard Luck and sleep with women like Sassy Dillon?"

"I'm not sleeping with her. I'm working at the Hard Luck now behind the bar, as well as watching for trouble. If some drunk starts something, I boot him out. Sassy can be a good friend at times, but I'm not in her room every night. I live at Jack Sturgin's boarding house. In a couple of days I start working for Grant Breckenridge, guarding his gold shipments, remember? I'll be moving to Sam's Hollow."

"Yes. Isn't it ironic? You, of all people, guarding another man's gold. Please tell me you aren't considering running off with some of that gold, never to return."

He shook his head. "Those days are over, and I'll prove it to you. I don't have much use for Grant Breckenridge, but I have plenty of use for the money he's going to pay me. I'm going to save it and work part-time for Sassy until I have enough to get into some kind of business of my own, until I'm able to make a decent life for a decent woman . . . like you."

Addy watched his eyes. "Is that some kind of proposal?"

Cole looked away, but not before Addy caught the lingering doubt and fear in his gaze. "I guess you could call it that."

"Are you saying you love me, Cole Parker?"

He hesitated, then met her eyes. "I guess."

"You *guess?*"

He sighed. "I'm *afraid* to love, Addy. That's all it is. Please just go easy on this thing with Breckenridge and give me some time to get straightened around. I know the man can offer a woman a hundred times more than I'll ever be able to, but that doesn't mean much if you can't trust a man to be true to you, or if he's got a mean streak in him. Breckenridge can be a bastard when it comes to business dealings, and as far as I'm concerned, that means he can be a bastard in other ways. Take things slow, Addy. Give me some time. If I can get some money saved, gain some respectability, we could gradually begin seeing each other—keep it all respectable and above board. People don't need to know we already know each other. I wouldn't do anything to endanger your teaching job."

Addy walked a few feet away before facing him again. "Have you stopped drinking?"

He brushed some dirt from his shirtsleeve. "Mostly."

"Mostly? How about completely?"

"Addy, all men drink a little. I can control my drinking, if I'm happy, and thinking about maybe being with you makes me happier than I've been since the war. I only drink to forget, to sleep extra hard so I don't have those nightmares. If I can start a new life . . ." His gaze moved over her in a way that made Addy shiver. "Maybe a new family, the dreams won't be so bad. I'm getting better, Addy, since meeting you."

Addy stepped closer, hardly aware that her hat sat crooked on her head and part of her hair tumbled down the side of her face. The hem of her gray dress was torn. "I might just only be a part of the healing, Cole. And you forget that I have my own healing to do. Neither of us is sure we're doing the right thing. We can't make decisions yet, Cole. Only a few days ago we thought the best thing was to get out of each other's lives, and that isn't the first time we came to that conclusion."

He grasped her arms. "And here we are, still involved. Neither of us can quite let go. That has to mean something."

She could not look away from him. If only he were not so handsome. If only he were not so strong and dependable and able. If only she didn't already know how he could make her feel in the night, the way he had of satisfying a woman's every physical need. "Maybe it does." She sighed deeply. "You have the time you want, Cole. I am in no particular rush one way or another, certainly in no rush to build a relationship with Grant Breckenridge. Right now he's just a friend with whom it is proper to be seen socially. He's never . . ." She felt her cheeks reddening as she looked down. "Kissed me or anything. There is no romance, I assure you."

"Not that he wouldn't like it to be that way. Watch out for him, Addy. Sassy says he's a womanizer. You're just a prize to him. He doesn't see you as a wonderful woman he can share his thoughts and needs with. You're the new schoolteacher, and the prettiest woman ever to come to Central, and he means to have you for himself. You're his latest prey."

"You don't know that for sure."

His hold on her tightened. "I know he's almost old enough to be your father, and I know he could never make you feel the way I can make you feel in the night, Addy Kane."

She pushed at his arms. "Don't do this. You always do this— keep me from being able to think straight. Please let me go."

"In a minute. Look up here, Addy."

She raised her eyes, saw him lean closer. Again his lips met her own, searching, parting her mouth, his tongue exploring suggestively. She felt fire ripping through her bloodstream, every need awakening deep inside. She groaned with pleasure at the kiss, then chastised herself for her continued weakness in this man's arms. She tore away from the kiss. "Please don't, Cole!"

He let go of her, and Addy ran back toward the street, wiping at her mouth to be sure there wasn't more blood on it. She found Sheriff Watson there with a few town businessmen trying to bring order to the situation. A few men lay sprawled unconscious or badly beaten in the street, and most of the women protestors were crying, many of them with torn, dirty dresses, hats missing or askew. Ethel Brown was in a rage, her dress torn, her face dirty, her hair a tumble. She was screeching at the sheriff about the abomination of women like Sassy Dillon, who not only whored with men but who actually attacked other people, fighting in the street with no shame, allowing her nakedness to be exposed to half the town without a care. She demanded that the sheriff arrest Sassy.

Addy quietly moved into the crowd. Sassy stood on the steps to her saloon, surrounded by her girls, who were all a mess from fighting, and by a crowd of men who supported her. Sassy herself was scratched and bleeding, her dress nearly in shreds. She held up one side over her breast to cover it, but she did not look defeated. She glared defiantly at Ethel and the sheriff, a hard, mean look in her blue eyes.

"There's no need to arrest me, Sheriff," she told the man firmly. "I'm telling you now that I'll stop selling myself and my girls, but I'll by-God not stop doing business here in Central! I'll still run my saloon, sell whiskey, let my patrons play cards and dance with my girls. I have a right to that! If you try to outlaw saloons altogether like these women want, you might as well close up your mines, because these men won't put up with it! They'll go work in the mines in some other town where they can still get their whiskey and relax with a game of poker."

The crowd of men behind her shouted in support, raising fists. "You close down the saloons, and you'll see the biggest strike of miners there ever was!" one of them shouted.

Another cheer of agreement went up.

"Addy, dear, look at you!"

An arm came around Addy's waist at the words, and she turned to look up at Grant Breckenridge.

"I got hung up at one of the mines or I'd have been here sooner. I meant to come and watch out for you."

He seemed so sincere. Did this man really come to visit Sassy regularly? Maybe Cole was just making it up to keep her from seeing him. Even so, that meant Cole had been talking to Sassy about her. And if Grant really did see Sassy sometimes, maybe Sassy would tell him about her and Cole. A man like Grant could make big trouble for Cole if he knew the truth . . . and he could have her run out of Central.

"There was quite a brawl," she answered.

"I can see that. Are you all right?"

Addy noticed Cole walking back onto the boardwalk in front of the saloon. His eyes scanned the crowd, and he noticed Grant and Addy.

"I'm fine," Addy answered, still feeling the fire of Cole's kiss.

"I've never been so humiliated in my life!" Ethel was scream-ing, her face blazing red, tears streaming down her face. "You can't let this woman get away with such barbarism, Sheriff! She must be arrested!"

"Now, now, Mrs. Brown, if I arrest Sassy I have to arrest half the town. You can't expect to march through this town protesting things the miners love dearly without also expecting trouble. Now Sassy has said she'll stop the prostitution, and that'll be a good start for outlawing the same at the Hurdy Gurdy and the cribs and other saloons where we suspect women sell them-selves. You can't say your march didn't do some good, and you can't say Sassy hasn't cooperated."

Ethel Brown drew in her breath, and she reminded Addy of an enraged bull. She turned to face Sassy. "You had better keep your word, Miss Dillon! We will make sure the sheriff keeps an eye on your place, and if we find out you're still selling bodies here, I will personally make sure you are run out of Central."

"Yeah?" Sassy sauntered down the steps and walked closer. "I look forward to you trying, you fat, pompous bitch."

Ethel gasped, and for a moment Addy thought she might faint. At the same time more gasps and a round of "Oh's" moved through the crowd of protestors. Sassy just smiled, then turned and walked back up the steps.

"Come on, boys. Drinks on the house!"

A roar of cheers went up as men followed the woman inside, and Sassy moved her arms around two of them, her back to the crowd. Addy's eyes widened at the realization that to put her arms around the men meant she would have to let go of her dress and let it fall open again. The woman disappeared through the swinging doors to her saloon. Cole started in with the rest of the men when Grant called out to him.

"Cole Parker!"

Cole turned. "Mr. Breckenridge."

"Call me Grant. I came to town to look after Addy here, but I also came looking for you. I have a gold shipment going out day after tomorrow. Can you be up at the Jackpot by seven A.M.?"

Cole glanced at Addy, and she could see the warning in his eyes. He looked back at Grant. "I'll be there. Anything in particular I should watch for on the way down to Denver?"

"Yes." Grant put an already-lit cigar to his mouth and puffed it a moment, while the rest of the crowd in the street began to disburse. Sheriff Watson led a still-complaining Ethel Brown toward his office. "There is one man in this town who hates me for reasons that are no one's business. What happened is his fault, not mine, let alone the fact that he blames me for his son's death, which was an accident. I won't go into details now. The fact remains that this man has vowed to get his revenge. I think he's all hot air and no action, but you should be aware of the situation. His name is Ed Foley. Maybe you've heard something about him, seen him in the Hard Luck."

"Can't say as I have." Cole decided not to mention he'd heard the story. He thought it best Grant didn't know Sassy had been telling things about him.

"Well, it's best to be alert in any case. Foley knows explosives, and he's a bitter man, mourning his son, needing someone to blame. He has relatives in Kansas, and I'm hoping he'll go back there. He probably will, in time. Just keep your eyes open and your gun ready."

Addy felt a pain in the pit of her stomach. Cole could be hurt, or killed. She looked up at him. "Be careful, Mr. Parker."

Cole read her concern, and he wanted to hold her. "Always am." He looked back at Grant and nodded. "See you day after tomorrow." He turned and walked into the Hard Luck, and Grant looked down at Addy.

"You seemed awfully concerned for hardly knowing that man, Addy."

"Well, the fact remains you hired him to watch your gold and he is apparently risking his life for that. I would be concerned about anyone who would do such a thing. You should be grateful he's willing."

"Oh, I'm grateful, all right. He's being very well paid." He put an arm to her waist. "I have a buggy nearby. Come with me and I'll take you back to the boardinghouse. You must want to clean up and change clothes."

"Yes." Addy followed him to the buggy. "Are you sure Ed Foley isn't dangerous?"

"It's not your concern, my dear. Don't worry about it."

Addy had to wonder what he wasn't telling her. She realized Grant Breckenridge was the type of man who felt his business life was not a woman's concern, and there was a coldness to his voice at the remark that made her think of what Cole had been trying to tell her about him. She climbed into the buggy, her emotions torn again by Cole Parker's heated kiss. She glanced back at the Hard Luck as Grant drove off, but Cole had already gone inside. She struggled against renewed jealousy over Sassy Dillon, and her mind raced with the things Cole had told her. He had asked her to wait for him, had all but said he loved her. That put a whole new light on everything.

Twenty

"Are you really going to stop the prostitution?" Cole lit a cigarette as he waited for Sassy's reply.

"I suppose, if it's the only way to keep the rest of my business," Sassy answered bitterly.

The two of them sat together at the bar, Sassy wearing a battered suit jacket one of the men had given her to cover herself. The saloon was packed with men, all laughing and joking about how they had "won," making remarks about the "stiff old bags" who had come to town to try to oust the whores.

"Give me whores, or give me death!" one man shouted.

The room roared with laughter.

"Sounds to me like you have plenty of support for staying in business," Cole said with a grin. He met Sassy's eyes and saw a strange sadness there. The woman seldom showed any kind of emotion. "Hell, Sassy, these men aren't going to abide by any laws against prostitution."

Sassy shook her head, reaching up and taking a loose comb from her hair. Her face was still dirty and her makeup smeared. "It isn't that." She sighed deeply. "I could fight it, but then I might risk losing everything, and I can't let that happen. I might only be thirty, but I feel a lot older sometimes, and this business is all I know. If I didn't have my saloon, I don't know what I'd do. It's just that the prostitution brought in a lot of extra money, and I need that money for reasons nobody knows."

Cole took a deep drag on the cigarette. "How did you get into all of this anyway?"

Sassy looked around the room, then smiled at Harvey Dean, a regular customer. He came up to her and slapped her on the back. "You did good out there, Sassy," he told her with a toothless grin. "You showed them stuck-up ole' biddies what for!" The man turned to Cole. "I seen you whisk that perty schoolteacher off to the alley," he added. "I'll bet you showed that bitch a thing or two! Maybe you even got a poke at her, huh?"

Cole quelled an urge to knock the man across the room. "She isn't like the rest of them," he answered. "She's a very nice lady, so leave her out of your insults, Harvey."

The man seemed to wither a little at the remark. He knew Cole Parker's skills with both gun and fists, and he didn't care to get on his wrong side. "Sorry, Cole. I just figured—"

"You figured wrong."

Harvey frowned. "Hell, Cole, you should ought ta' have been out there in the street fightin' for Sassy's rights. Seemed to me like you was stickin' up for them female marchers."

"I wasn't sticking up for them. I was trying to avoid trouble because it would only make Sassy look worse. As it is, we ended up in a mess anyway."

"Oh, that was bound to happen," Sassy said, patting Cole's chest. "Actually I made things worse when I attacked that fat, pompous Ethel Brown. She's given me trouble before, and I just couldn't stop myself from lighting into her. It was a hell of a fight, wasn't it? I showed everybody what an uncivilized, uncontrollable thing that woman can be—brought her down to my level, didn't I?" She laughed, but Cole caught an odd pain in her eyes he'd never noticed before. Harvey laughed with her before stumbling away to ask for another drink. Sassy turned to Cole. "What *did* you do in that alley, love?"

Cole smiled sadly. "Just had a little talk with Mrs. Kane."

"About what? You've never told me the whole story, Cole Parker."

Cole shook his head. "How about you answering my question first—about how you got into all of this?"

Sassy shrugged. "I was raised by a mother who drank too

much and a gambling father who won enough money to open a saloon of his own back in Wisconsin. I never knew any other life. My pa loved women and had a lot of them. My mother died from too much alcohol when I was only twelve, and on my thirteenth birthday my pa urged me to try some whiskey, which I did." She looked away, studying a shot glass she held in her hand. "Enough not to feel the pain when my father had one of his friends take me to a room upstairs and make a woman out of me. Somewhere deep inside I knew it wasn't right, but pa had a way of making me believe that it was. I didn't even like it. I just got used to it." She drank down the whiskey. "I was pretty then. The money was good and it just went on and on. As I got older I learned to enjoy it, got to understand men pretty good, decided that if this was all there was to life I might as well at least get some pleasure out of it." She met his eyes. "Ones built like you, they bring me a good time."

She grinned, but Cole could see that part of her would have liked a better life.

"It's all I've known," she continued, "and it's way too late now to change any of it."

Cole took the cigarette from his mouth. "Oh, I don't know. Someone told me once that it's never too late to change." He thought about Addy, ached for her.

"Well, in some cases it *is* too late. Come here." She took hold of Cole's hand and pulled him toward the stairs, nodding and smiling at more men, accepting their support. "Goin' upstairs to change, boys," she announced. "I'll be right back." She leaned close to Cole. "Come up with me. I've got something to tell you."

Cole followed her up, amid hoots and hollers. He realized he needed to wash and change as well, but he decided to wait until later. He followed Sassy into her room, as crumpled a mess as he remembered it had been the first time he'd seen it. "What's up?" he asked.

Sassy asked him to unzip her dress, and he obliged. She stripped down in front of him with no apparent bashfulness or hesitation, then walked over to wash her face at a wash stand. She toweled off her makeup and turned to look at him. "Don't look too great without all the paint, do I?"

Cole saw the signs of a hard life. She still had a decent shape to her but was getting plump in all the wrong places. Her face was slightly bloated from too much alcohol, but he could see she had once had a natural beauty about her, a beauty destroyed by neglect and drinking. "Still looks pretty good to me," he answered, moving his eyes over her nakedness, knowing she needed to hear a compliment.

Sassy laughed and sauntered closer. "Good enough for a roll in bed? You do know how to make a woman feel good, Cole Parker."

Cole leaned down and kissed her cheek, then bent lower, kissing her neck, the whites of her breasts. "Very tempting, lady. But I told a certain person I wasn't sleeping with you. I feel obligated to keep that promise."

"I knew it." Sassy turned and moved past him to pull open a drawer, taking out a clean chemise and pulling it on. "You're in love with the schoolteacher. Why in hell don't you marry her and get it over with?" Then she sighed and added, "Lucky woman."

"Lots of reasons that are between her and me. And I sure as hell don't want someone like Grant Breckenridge knowing anything about it, understand? Not a word. A man like that gets jealous. He could find a way to have me killed or run out of town, and he could ruin Addy's teaching job. I'll handle Breckenridge my own way. I'll handle the whole situation my own way, so do me a favor and keep quiet."

Sassy grinned as she began lacing up a girdle. "I'm not stupid, Cole, and I like you. I wouldn't say anything. Did you tell her to stay away from that bastard?"

"I told her." ' He walked over and pressed out his cigarette in an ashtray. "You said you had something to tell me."

"I do." She sat down on the edge of her bed, now dressed in

a lacy camisole, her girdle pushing her breasts up higher than normal. "Sit down, Cole."

He came and sat beside her. "Hurry it up. You aren't making things any easier on me."

Sassy chuckled. "I don't hold a candle to Mrs. Addy Kane. Think I don't know that? You've made love to her, haven't you?"

"I told you I wasn't talking about me and Addy." He started to rise, but Sassy grasped his arm.

"I'm sorry. No more questions. There really is something I want to tell you, Cole."

Cole settled back down, moving one knee up onto the mattress and facing her. "Let's have it."

Sassy faced him in return. "I have no idea why I'm telling you this. Maybe it's because you told me about your little girl, how you lost her in that fire and all . . . the look I saw in your eyes when you told me . . . the love . . . the pain. You understand what it's like to love a little daughter."

Cole felt the sickening pain all over again. "What's that got to do with this?"

Sassy hesitated, swallowed. "*I* have a daughter, Cole. What do you think of that?"

Cole felt a tug at his heartstrings at the thought of Patty. "A daughter? How old? When did this happen?"

Sassy rose to find a dress to put on. "Oh, I got careless. It just happened, that's all. She's six years old. I was working in Denver then, until they, too, decided to get rid of their 'ladies of ill repute.' At any rate, I couldn't bring myself to try to get rid of the baby. Fact is, I wanted her. I laid low until I had her, all the while knowing I'd have to give her up for adoption. I couldn't raise an innocent little girl to know what her mother was." She took a dress from a trunk and held it to her breast, a wistful look coming into her tear-filled eyes. "I got to hold her for just a little while. Pretty as a picture, she was, my precious Lissy. Elizabeth, I named her, before they took her away from me."

She sighed, laying the dress on the trunk. "I managed to make an arrangement where I'd know who adopted her, so I could just go and look at her now and then. She's the reason I go to Denver once a month, to visit. Her adoptive parents let me come inside. I pretend I'm an old friend. They're wonderful people, letting me do that. I have opened a special bank account there in Denver in Elizabeth's name. Her parents don't have much, and I help support her. That's our agreement. Her adoptive father isn't well, and I worry what will happen to Lissy if he dies. The mother has no way of taking care of herself, and they have two other children. The time could come when I have to completely support her, so I have to keep this business going, Cole. Now you understand why I'll do whatever I have to do to make as much money as I can."

Cole was surprised and touched. "It must be hard, seeing her and not being able to let her know who you are."

Sassy grunted with disgust at herself. "It would be more painful to let her know and see the hate in her eyes." She sighed deeply. "No, it's better this way." She turned and looked at him, quickly wiping at the tears on her cheeks. "You want to see her? She's absolutely beautiful, and she's the only good thing I've ever done in my life."

Cole rose and walked to a window. It would hurt, setting eyes on a beautiful little girl the same age Patty had been when she died. But he knew Sassy wanted to show her off. "Sure."

Sassy began pulling on her dress. "You said a few minutes ago when you first came in that Breckenridge wants you to guard a gold shipment to Denver. I'll take the stage down tomorrow and wait at the Denver Inn. Once you see the shipment safely through, meet me there and I'll take you to where Lissy lives so you can see her."

"All right. I'll be there." Cole turned to look at her, and Sassy stepped closer.

"You're a good man, Cole Parker, a good friend. It's too bad Addy Kane doesn't see the goodness in you."

Cole smiled sadly. "She does. But she also saw the worst side of me when we first met. I haven't been a very good boy the last few years, Sassy. The war . . . my daughter . . . a lot of things led me to the point where I didn't give a damn, and all I could feel was hate and revenge. You guessed right when we first met. You said you suspected maybe I was running from the law or something. Well, I am, in a way. Actually they think I'm dead back in Illinois and Missouri, and that's partly thanks to Addy. She saved my neck more than once, and I saved hers. That's where our odd friendship began. But we're both so full of hurt and confusion over what's happened to us the past few years that we aren't sure we know our own minds, or hearts. We're not so sure we're good for each other, and I'm not so sure I want to care that much about anyone again."

Sassy put her hands on her hips. "My advice is to take the chance. You're both fighting the inevitable."

He came closer, touching her shoulder. "Could be. We need time to figure it out, and I need you not to tell a soul. The only reason I've told you this much is because you shared the secret about your daughter with me. No one in Central knows, do they?"

She shook her head. "No. I just—I had to explain to somebody why I do what I do. Since it's what I know best and it's too late to change my life, I figure I might as well get the most out of it that I can—for Lissy. I don't want one other person to know, because I don't want to take the chance that she'll find out the truth. It could destroy her. She would be ashamed, maybe think she's worthless because her mother was."

Her eyes teared again, and Cole patted her cheek. "You're not worthless, Sassy. You put on a good front for others, but you're all soft inside. I can see that."

She sniffed and turned around. "Button me up and get out of here, damn you. You get me all excited with that handsome face and those eyes and that body of yours. Your Mrs. Kane will come around, all right. What woman could keep saying no to something like you? But then, maybe she *hasn't* said no."

Cole grinned. "Oh, no you don't. You'll get no more out of me, woman."

He fussed with the fastenings, complaining about women wearing too many laces and stays and buttons.

"Makes it more exciting getting us out of our clothes," Sassy answered.

Cole thought about Addy, wanted her that way again. "I'll see you in Denver," he told her when he finished. He gave her a pat on the rump and left.

Sassy sighed. "You're a hell of a man," she repeated. "Addy Kane had better wake up and see what she's missing. Maybe I'll have a talk with her."

"We're building you a little house all your own," Grant told Addy. He had dropped her off to wash and change and was now taking her to Hester's house, where the women from the march were to meet and soothe each other's fears and hurt feelings.

"You really needn't go to the trouble and expense," Addy protested.

"It's all part of the deal. The male teachers make more than you because they have families and such, but we still help them financially with their homes. In your case, we've decided to foot the whole bill. We can afford it, so don't worry about it. It will be a small, one-story house, very acceptable for a lady like yourself. And we plan to build it on East High Street, not far from where we intend to build a school. It's going to be a fine school, I promise—all brick, two stories, several classrooms. It might be a couple of years before we manage it, but it will happen. In the meantime, your house won't be far from the Lawrence Building where you'll be teaching. A shed will be built out back and a fence put up for the horse you'll be using to pull your carriage to school. We'll be sure plenty of feed is always available. You *are* able to care for a horse and hitch a buggy aren't you?"

"Of course. I've been doing things like that for myself for years," Addy answered, a little irritated at the suggestion she was a helpless female.

"Fine."

Addy held on to her hat against a stiff wind that was bringing a chill to the air. "I'd rather have a place of my own, Grant. I don't like having everything done for me. Let me pay for it. I have enough money saved to put down on a loan."

"You save that for other things. This is a part of being a teacher here. Take advantage of it. We start in a couple of days, and I want you to come and see the plans, tell me if there is anything you want changed." He frowned. "By the way, are you sure you're all right? You seem so distant since the big ruckus in the street today."

"I'm fine." Addy could not quit thinking about Cole. "I really do wish you would let me build my own place. I am accustomed to being more independent."

"Just think of it as part of your job and be glad for it. Here we are, now." Grant pulled in front of Hester's house, and Hester came out to greet her. Addy set aside her irritation at the continued control these people were trying to place over her private life and climbed down, seeing that Hester was obviously quite upset. The two women embraced.

"Oh, what a shocking day!" Hester exclaimed. "Ethel is inside, her husband trying to console her. She was able to go home first and clean herself up, but her face is scratched and bruised. Lord knows what the newspaper will make of this—Ethel Brown brawling in the street with the likes of Sassy Dillon, but Ethel couldn't help it. Sassy attacked her."

Addy suppressed a grin at the memory of the sight. She had no good feelings for the nosey Ethel, who had probably gotten what she deserved for sticking that nose into yet another person's private life, no matter how wrong Sassy was to do what she did. It was up to God to judge, not people like Ethel Brown.

"I'll be back later to drive you home," Grant told her, tipping his hat to her.

Addy wondered how she was going to tell him she would rather not see so much of him . . . if in fact she should. For one thing, she truly did believe she must give this man a chance; for another, to suddenly shun him might draw suspicious questions. Hester's next remark made her realize how right she was.

"Thank God for that man who stepped in on your behalf," the woman said as she led her through the door. She turned to Grant. "I saw you talking to him after the fight," she told him. "A tall, dark man, quite handsome. He wore a gun. Did you know that he rescued Addy from a drunken miner who was insulting her and wanted to drag her off?"

Grant frowned, folding his arms. "Why, no, Addy, why didn't you say something when we were standing there talking? I would have thanked the man."

Addy forced a look of innocence. "I don't know. I guess I just was so upset by the whole thing, my better sense left me. Mr. Parker stepped in, like Hester said, and saved me from tremendous embarrassment, perhaps even physical harm."

All three stepped into Hester's parlor.

"And took you out of the way as though he was personally concerned," Ethel Brown spoke up, almost accusingly. "One would think the man already knew you from somewhere."

Addy faced the woman, her mind racing with possible answers. "Yes, he did know me," she said boldly. "I had already met Mr. Parker when Grant here talked to him one evening about working for him. That's the reason Mr. Parker got me out of there. He knew I was a personal acquaintance of Grant Breckenridge."

Ethel Brown looked properly chagrined. "I see. Well, in that case, I suppose it was all right."

Addy breathed a sigh of relief.

"Actually, I personally asked Mr. Parker to keep an eye on Addy during the march," Grant added.

Addy was relieved at the remark. It lent further credence to her own explanation.

"I'll go right back to town and thank Cole," Grant added. "He's the man that was written about in the paper, you know— the one who out-drew George Williams. He's big, strong, good with a gun. I've hired him to guard my gold shipments."

"Oh, my," Hester exclaimed. "Well, we should all thank him as a group somehow, don't you think? He actually stepped in on our behalf."

Addy decided not to mention that Cole Parker actually worked part time for Sassy Dillon. Apparently Grant had decided the same, and she was grateful for that much.

"I'll do the thanking for you," Grant told them. "You ladies go ahead and regroup now, console each other. You should be proud. You did a brave thing today, and I'm sure you left a mark in history. One man told me rumor is Sassy is already talking about quitting prostitution at her place. She announced it in public, and I think if she has any sense she'll stick to it. Once she leads the way, others will follow. You women have braved a new front in Central, helped make our city even more civilized."

Ethel straightened, heaving her big breasts in a proud sigh. "Thank you, Mr. Breckenridge. I just hope the newspaper doesn't make something out of this that was not intended. I have suffered enough embarrassment already."

Grant gave her a smile and bowed slightly. "I will go and get your husband and we'll both have a talk with the newspaper office. We'll make sure you suffer no further embarrassment. It's Sassy Dillon who will suffer the brunt of ridicule, as well she should. She'll end up with so much pressure on her, she'll have to go through with her promise to eliminate the practice of prostitution."

"Oh, it's such an ugly subject," Susan Howard moaned.

Nearly all the women were there, talking in clutches, some still crying. Grant graciously promised to call together a council meeting as soon as possible and push the measure outlawing prostitution, now that they had made some headway. "The miners won't like it, but perhaps this will at least force the prostitution to more remote locations and make downtown more peaceful and respectable," he told them. Then he turned and left, telling Addy he would return in awhile to take her home.

"Oh, you have such a treasure there, Addy," Hester told her. "Mr. Breckenridge is such a gentleman."

Addy turned away, her thoughts only of Cole and his warning to stay away from Grant. It seemed impossible that Grant would sneak around with women like Sassy Dillon and put on such a front in public against prostitution. Part of her wanted Cole to be wrong, but deep down she feared he was right.

"That big man who whisked you away didn't hurt you, did he?" Hester asked.

"What?" Addy turned. "Mr. Parker?"

"Yes." Hester searched her eyes, remembering the story Ethel Brown had told her about Addy possibly meeting some man the night of the reception for her. *Was* there someone in town she knew and wasn't telling anyone about?

"No, he was quite the gentleman," Addy answered, still feeling the fire of Cole's kiss. "He was only watching out for me because of Grant," she lied. "And I'd rather not talk about any of it. This has been a very upsetting day for everyone, but hopefully we made some progress. Tomorrow I'd like to come visiting to talk about something else. Grant tells me the school board is going to build me a house. Perhaps you can help me pick out colors, order some furniture."

"Oh, yes, that would be quite nice!" Hester patted her arm. "School starts in only six weeks, the miners' picnic in a month. We do have some fine things to look forward to, don't we? For all we know, there may even be a wedding to go to!" She giggled like a child, and Addy only smiled and nodded. Everyone was taking it for granted there was a romance going on between her and Grant. But Cole wanted her to wait for him. What would these women think of their lady schoolteacher marrying someone like Cole Parker? At least he had done something today to draw their attention and respect. That was a start.

Twenty-one

Cole rode Shadow to the front of the Denver Inn to see Sassy sitting on a veranda. She waved with delight. "You came!"

"I said I would. Got here last night. Stayed at another hotel."

"We can walk it from here. I'll go get my handbag."

Cole watched her go inside, shaking his head at how she was dressed—a very simple brown dress with white trim, her hair drawn into a bun, a small white hat on her head. When she visited her daughter she obviously hid the real Sassy.

He dismounted, feeling a quick pain in his chest, thinking how wonderful it would be if it was his Patty he was visiting. He tied Shadow, looked down the rise where the rooming house sat to scan the very new city of Denver, a sprawling city amazingly large. He'd been through here once on his original trip to Central, but his thoughts had been so full of Addy that he had hardly noticed.

He patted Shadow's rump, still amazed at how fast these gold towns grew. Already a small feud was flaring between Denver and Central over which town should become the capitol once Colorado became a state, even though that was not likely to happen in the immediate future. According to articles he'd read in the *Register,* there was a race going on for size, number of people, which town was becoming the most civilized and advanced. Both cities talked of more hotels, opera houses, parks, schools, beauty, wealth, law and order. Denver already had a couple of buildings three stories high, one of them a large hotel finer than anything in Central. He grinned inwardly at the thought of how the builders of these towns scurried to turn their settlements into cities like those they had left back East.

"Did you have any trouble?" Sassy was coming down the steps in a quick walk.

"No, but then Grant Breckenridge has a lot of men riding guard on his gold. Quite a little army. I really don't see much that Ed Foley could do. There's only the one road down and few places to pass on it. Even if Foley managed to get the best of us, he couldn't exactly make a fast getaway, and he'd need a lot of men to overcome the guard Grant has on his gold. What more can you tell me about Foley, anyway?"

"Ask ten people and you'll get ten answers. The most I've ever gotten out of Grant is what I already told you. My guess is Grant took advantage of Foley somehow. He's probably paid off the right people to keep it quiet. The high society of Central doesn't talk about it. They think Grant Breckenridge is a fine man. You just be careful. Ed Foley just might still figure out a way to get back at Grant."

"Well, this first trip down was a safe one, so let's not talk about it any more. Let's have a look at your little girl. How far is it?"

"Just a couple of blocks. That's why I stay at the Denver Inn. I've already seen her once, playing out in the back yard. I put three hundred dollars in her bank account yesterday," Sassy added proudly.

Cole put an arm around her shoulders. "You're a good mother."

Sassy's eyes teared. "I wish I could be. Thank you for coming, Cole. It's not always easy doing this alone, especially when I have to leave again."

Cole walked with her to a frame house that had a white picket fence around it. "I pose as a friend of Mrs. Donnavan's who comes to visit once in awhile. That way Lissy knows me, too, and isn't afraid of me," Sassy explained.

"What if she should come to find you when she's grown up?"

Sassy smiled sadly. "Well, I've told the Donnavans I want

er sent off to college when she's old enough. That means it will
be a good fifteen years before she's free and independent enough
to try to come visiting. By then I'll be a pretty old gal, in some
other kind of business, something legitimate. Or maybe I'll be
living someplace else so she can't talk to others in town and
find out the truth. Even so, she never needs to know I'm really
her mother."

She led him to the front door of the neat-looking house. Lace
curtains hung at the door window. Sassy knocked, and a moment
later a very prim-looking woman with kind blue eyes opened
the door. She smiled when she saw Sassy. "Hello, Sassy."

"I told you I'd be back once more today. This is a friend of
mine, Cole Parker."

"Hello, Mr. Parker," the woman said, nodding to Cole. "I'm
Mary Donnavan."

Cole tipped his hat to her. "I'm glad to meet you, ma'am.
I've heard a lot about you, all good. Thanks for letting Sassy—"
He spotted a curly-headed little girl standing behind the woman.
Her hair was blond, her eyes blue, like Patty's. An ache filled
his chest. "Well, you know," he finished.

"Hi, Miss Dillon," the little girl said with a sweet smile that
showed deep dimples in her plump cheeks.

"Hello, Elizabeth. This is my friend, Mr. Parker."

Cole pulled a peppermint stick from his pocket. He'd bought
it that morning in a grocery store. "How about a piece of candy,
Lissy?"

The child's eyes lit up. "Thank you, Mr. Parker!" She took
the candy, and Cole studied her plump, dimpled hand. He ached
to pull her close and hold her, almost wished he hadn't come.
It had taken years to get over the need to hold Patty, comfort
her. If only she hadn't died so horribly. If only he could have
rescued her.

Mrs. Donnavan invited them into her parlor, and Cole fought
against old memories. He was surprised that Mrs. Donnavan
was so gracious to Sassy, inviting her into her home when she

knew what Sassy really was. Sassy couldn't have picked a more Christian, more loving woman to mother her little girl.

"My other two children are at a friend's house today," she explained. "I'm sorry you weren't able to meet them, Mr Parker."

The women visited, and Lissy played with a doll, bringing it over to show to Cole. She was a vivacious child, not the least bit bashful, and Cole grinned at the realization that her personality was just like Sassy's.

Mrs. Donnavan served tea as Cole explained he was new to Central and worked as a guard for gold shipments.

"That sounds exciting!" the woman returned. "That's all that gets talked about here in Denver. Gold, gold, gold. My husband is an assayer. He hasn't been well lately, but he did make it to work today."

"How is he—really?" Sassy asked.

Mrs. Donnovan glanced at Lissy, then back at Sassy. "Not well at all. I'm worried."

Sassy reached out and patted her hand. "You just relax and know that I'll always help any way I can, especially financially."

Mrs. Donnovan breathed deeply, her eyes misty. "Thank you Sassy. You're a good woman. God sees that."

Sassy looked at her lap. "Well, I'm not so sure of that, but if I can do one good thing . . ." She glanced at Lissy. "Lissy come here and sit by me. I'd like to see your doll, too."

The child moved beside Sassy, happily holding up the doll "Her name is Peggy," she said, Cole's piece of peppermint still stuck in her mouth.

Sassy studied the doll, eyes, nose and mouth painted onto its rag face, yarn for hair. "She's very pretty." She reached into her handbag. "I brought you something, Lissy. Maybe your doll could wear it." She pulled out a little pearl pin, and Lissy drew in her breath in surprise and joy.

"It's pretty!" She fingered the pin. "Put it on Peggy for me."

Sassy obeyed, and Lissy giggled with delight, then hugged the doll close. Cole remembered how his own daughter had

ved a ragdoll. The doll had been found lying beside her,
rned, after the fire. A lump rose in his throat and he stood up.
, uh, I think I'll step outside for a few minutes, have a smoke,
you ladies don't mind."

"Of course, Mr. Parker," Mrs. Donnovan replied.

Cole walked to the front door.

"He lost a little girl of his own in the war," he heard Sassy
ling Mrs. Donnovan.

He walked outside and leaned against a wall, swallowing back
urge he hadn't felt in a long time, an emotion he had long
o buried and replaced with hate and revenge. It was the urge
cry. "Damn it!" he fumed, breathing deeply and wiping at his
es with the sleeve of his jacket. He took a thin cigar from an
side pocket and struck a match to light it, puffing on it for a
oment to overcome the sudden painful feelings that had over-
elmed him at seeing Lissy. He took off his hat and literally
ook his head to get rid of the screams he could still hear.

Maybe, just maybe, if he had another little girl to hold, to
ar her laughter, see her smile, maybe he could get over all of
s. With Addy . . . she'd make a good mother. Would she wait
him, or would she fall for Grant Breckenridge's charm and
cide he had a lot more to offer? He wished he had made up
mind to love her and marry her before this. Maybe he'd
ited too long. Then again, maybe he didn't deserve somebody
e Addy, or deserve another family.

He finished his smoke, went back inside and shared lunch
th Mrs. Donnovan, Elizabeth and Sassy. He could feel Sassy's
in, and he wondered which was worse—having a child die,
having her alive but not being able to be with her. Elizabeth
is a lovely child anyone could love, all innocence, pretty and
art. He could feel Sassy's pride.

Finally it was time to go. Elizabeth gave Sassy a hug and a
s, and Sassy squeezed her close. She turned, and Elizabeth
ched out for Cole. "Give me a hug bye," she said with her
npled smile.

Cole hesitated. If only she knew what this was doing to him.

He decided he'd tell Sassy he couldn't come back again. I couldn't stand this. He reached out, took Lissy into his arm struggled against a torrent of emotions. "Bye, Lissy." He kiss her cheek and handed her back to Sassy. "I've got to get out here." He turned and left, and minutes later Sassy came outsi and walked up beside him.

"I'm sorry. That was hard for you. I shouldn't have ask you to come."

"It's all right." Cole sighed deeply. "I know now what I ne to do. It's either change my life completely and have anoth family, or just let it all go to hell, maybe go on farther west a join the no-goods I hear hang out along something called t Outlaw Trail—horse thieves, cattle rustlers, bank robbers." I snickered in disgust. "Just my type."

Sassy folded her arms. "So, you're finally telling me y were an outlaw?"

Cole met her eyes. "Now you know why Addy can't jun right into marrying the likes of me. It was my own gang of m who abducted her back in Illinois after a bank robbery. I help her out. That's how we met, but she knows the worst about n It's all a big mess, and now, her with Breckenridge, me worki for him, both of us trying to keep anyone from realizing we ev know each other . . ." He shook his head. "I don't know. May I should just do what I should have done in the first place a get out of her life."

"And leave her to Breckenridge?" Sassy's eyebrows arch in surprise. "You rescued her once. I'd say you'd better do again. You stay around. She'll figure out for herself who's b for her. Something will work out, Cole."

"I wish I could be so sure." He smiled sympathetically. "B my problems don't matter right now. Seeing Lissy must be rea hard on you."

She touched his arm. "At least I know she's alive and w and loved. Your problem is much worse. I just . . . well, I ho I can always help take care of her."

"She's a beautiful child, Sassy. You can be proud."

"I am." She put on a look of confidence and toughness. "I
 pretty good, didn't I?"

Cole nodded. "You did good." He walked her back to the
nver Inn, and she turned and grasped his hands.

"I have little hope of changing my life now, Cole, but you
 Don't give up trying."

"I don't know." He turned away with a sigh and mounted up
 Shadow. "What time does the stage back to Central leave?"

"Eight o'clock tomorrow morning. You know where the sta-
n is?"

"I'll find it. I'll ride back up along with the coach."

"Good. See you in the morning." Cole rode off, and Sassy
ned to look at the Donnavan house again, her eyes tearing.
y sweet baby," she muttered. "May God always look after
, and may He keep me able to do the same."

Addy walked around the front of her house, studying it care-
ly, amazed at how fast homes and other buildings sprouted
Central. Once the decision was made, builders had her little
ne finished in three weeks. The only thing left to do was put
 shutters and window planters and to paint. She had decided
white with blue trim and the painters were coming tomorrow.
ere was still some furniture to be delivered from Denver, but
 had a brass bed and a bureau and even a wardrobe for her
thes. There was a wood-burning cook stove and an icebox in
 kitchen, along with a table and chairs given to her by Hester,
o had also given her a lovely cherrywood plant stand and a
d satin loveseat trimmed with cherrywood. Susan Howard
e her a picture of a vase of flowers, which had been in a
pment of new items for her husband's dry goods store. It hung
 an otherwise bare wall in the main room, which served as
ing room, parlor, whatever it was needed for, since the house
 only the three rooms.

She walked back inside, across a braided rug on the hardwood
or of the main room. There was a small brick fireplace on

one wall, and for the present the room held only the loves
and plant stand. She breathed deeply of the smell of fresh lum
and paint, and she felt she owed a great deal to the citizens
Central. School would start in about three weeks, not long af
the miner's picnic next week. Finally she would be able to tea
Everything would be perfect now if only she knew what to
about Cole and Grant.

She'd heard nothing from Cole these past three weeks si
the march in the streets, and she was relieved to know he'd
least had no problems guarding Grant's gold shipments, not ev
from Ed Foley. She wished she knew the whole truth about Fol
suspected Grant was not the innocent he claimed to be. S
knew Grant Breckenridge was a prize catch, but sometimes
would get a look in his eyes that gave her the shivers; she co
not get out of her mind Cole's remarks to her the day of
march that Grant was a womanizer, that she was nothing m
to him than a trinket he wanted to own.

She sat down in the loveseat. She also could not forget
fact that Cole had all but said he loved her. Cole Parker lo
her. He wanted her to wait for him. How could she *not* wait
him, even if she wasn't sure of her own feelings? Cole had s
fered much. He deserved a new life, and she didn't want to
anything to discourage his efforts in finding it. She could
imagine anything more wonderful than having him in her b
every night, knowing the sweet feeling of safety and comfor
his arms. She didn't feel that way with Grant, but any won
with common sense would tell her Grant was the better pi
rich, powerful, prominent. He lived in a fine stone mansion h
above Central . . . but none of that really mattered to her.
couldn't love with the intensity of Cole Parker, couldn't han
himself with fists and guns like Cole could. She hadn't sav
his life, been saved by him in return, traveled with him . . . sl
with him. He hadn't been in the war, suffered like Cole h
Cole understood her own suffering. Grant didn't. Grant ca
only about Grant.

Still, how often had Cole disappointed her? He never seen

to be able to make up his mind, and he'd probably change it again. If he did . . .

Someone knocked at her back door. She frowned in puzzlement, wondering why they didn't come to the front. She walked into the kitchen and around the table and chairs. "Who is it?"

"It's me—Sassy," came the reply quietly.

Addy's eyes widened in surprise. She opened the door slightly to see Sassy Dillon standing there wearing a hooded cape that hid her face, dressed very plainly so as not to draw attention.

"Nobody saw me. I made sure of it. I want to talk to you, Mrs. Kane."

Addy let her inside. "What on earth are you doing here?"

Sassy left the hood up. "I wouldn't want someone to look through a window and see you visiting with the town's most notorious whore."

Addy reddened. "Sassy, I wasn't so sure I was doing the right thing that day. I'm sorry you and your business got hurt."

"Are you?" Sassy sat down in one of the wooden chairs. "Don't worry about it. I know you must be pretty nice or Cole wouldn't be so infatuated with you."

Addy felt another pang of jealousy as she pulled out one of the other chairs. "He had no right telling you anything about me."

"Cole and I have become good friends. He knows things about me nobody else knows, and it's the same on my side. You can trust me. I won't say a word, not even to Grant Breckenridge."

Addy's cheeks grew even rosier, this time with anger. "You can't mean—"

"I can. I came to tell you it's true. Grant likes women, no matter if they're whores, married, single, too young, what have you. Don't let yourself get too close to him or be charmed by his lies, Mrs. Kane. He's a bastard, plain and simple. I know Cole cares for you, and he's on the verge of realizing he needs and wants another family, wants to learn to love again. The man won't flat-out say it, but I know he's crazy about you, so I came to ask you to please wait for him like he asked."

"Why do you care?" Addy asked with a frown.

"Because I care about Cole. He's a good man who went astray. He's scared to death to love again, but I don't think he can fight his feelings for you much longer. He's serious about saving his money up so he can invest in something, start a business, support a family. That's the only reason he's working for Grant."

Addy folded her hands in her lap. "Cole has made promises before and broken them. He keeps me torn in half, telling me to forget him, riding out of my life, then back again. I'm afraid to believe any more of his promises."

"Well, you can believe him this time. Because of how he feels about you, I just felt like it was my duty to come and warn you myself about Grant and tell you Cole is sincere. You should wait for him."

Addy rose, jealousy still getting the better of her. "He's slept with you, hasn't he?"

Sassy chuckled. "Only once, way back when we first met, but there's no doubt in my mind who he'd rather have in his bed. Maybe you've already been there."

Addy folded her arms, her cheeks feeling hot. "Of course he hasn't!"

Sassy laughed her raucous laugh. "Honey, don't lie to me. I can see it in your eyes. Besides, no more handsome man ever walked the earth, and in bed . . ." She sighed deeply. "He sure knows how to make a woman feel good, doesn't he?"

"Stop it!" Addy felt like crying. "Please go!"

Sassy stood up. "Sure. I only came because I know Cole cares about you, and because he cares, *I* care—enough to warn you about Grant Breckenridge. I'm a lot of things, Mrs. Kane, but I'm no liar. And don't be blaming Cole for being with me. A man is a man, and at the time he was sure there was no future with you. But he can't get you out of his mind, and now he's risking his life just for the pay so he can settle. I came here for your own good, honey." She looked around the room. "Nice little place Central's elite built for you. You could marry Grant and be quite the rich lady, run in high circles." She leaned closer. "But you're a teacher, well-schooled, a smart lady. Smart enough to know a man like Grant is no good. There's only one person he gives a damn about, and that's his son. But women?" She shook her head. "Never just one. Has he told you about Ed Foley? You can bet that whatever caused that man to hate Grant so much, it's Grant's fault. Now Cole, he might have done some bad things in his life, but he's no liar, and he'd never cheat on a wife or a friend."

"Perhaps not. But he's robbed banks and killed men."

"Grant Breckenridge has also robbed and killed, for pure greed. He just happens to know how to get away with it legally. Cole's reasons were different and understandable, but if Cole Parker is an outlaw, so is Grant Breckenridge. Grant is just a rich, smooth-talking sonofabitch who knows how to get away with it. He doesn't use guns and fists. He uses money and the law. He tricks people with legal papers and he pays people off to lie for him."

"Even you?"

Sassy stiffened, then grinned. "Sure. And why shouldn't I take his money? I need it—for more reasons than you could ever know."

"How do I know you won't tell Grant what you know about me and Cole? It could destroy both of us. Cole never should have told you any of it. I'm furious with him for doing so!"

Sassy chuckled. "I know who's worth protecting and who isn't, honey. Cole's been a good friend. I'd never betray him, which means I'd never betray you, either." She walked to the door. "You're a lucky woman, Mrs. Kane. You're young and beautiful, educated, living in a brand new house you don't even have to pay for, loved by one hell of a man, wanted by another man, one of one of the richest men in Central. I guess you have some decisions to make, don't you?"

Addy's eyes teared. "I've gotten myself into a mess. Grant Breckenridge is not a man to be crossed, I fear, and Cole works for him. If Cole and I dare to show an interest in each other, I'm afraid Grant could find a way to hurt him. Who knows?"

Sassy shrugged. "Well, if Cole can make himself respectable enough, there won't be a lot Grant can do about you calling on him. Besides, Cole Parker isn't a man to go up against, either. He's survived this far. He'll do okay. You wait and see."

Their eyes held, and Addy could see the woman truly cared. "I don't understand women like you."

"Of course you don't. If you'd been raised like me, it would be different. All people have reasons for the things they do. That's life. And all people have their good and bad qualities. If you knew me better, you'd see there's some good in me. As for you, pretty lady, proper as you are, I have a feeling that when you're with Cole Parker, you're very *im*proper." She chuckled. "So in some ways we're not so different, are we? See what I mean about good and bad? It's all a matter of perspective." She gave a perturbed Addy a wink and sauntered out the back door. Addy rolled her eyes and closed the door, again both loving and hating Cole Parker for the continued confusion she had to live with.

"I'll forget *both* of them," she told herself, "Grant *and* Cole. I'll just teach and attend women's clubs and turn into an old widowed woman." Yes, that was best. She would gradually and tactfully discourage Grant, and she would find a way to tell Cole it was simply too late to try to keep things going. What else could she do without hurting Cole or risking offending Grant and still hurting Cole?

She sighed in frustration, as she walked into the bedroom and sat down on the bed—a bed that looked big and empty. "Maybe that's the way it will have to stay," she murmured.

Twenty-two

Cole entered the Wildcat Saloon, eyeing the crowd carefully. He knew enough about the saloon life to realize different establishments generally had their own regular clientele, who sometimes became rather possessive of their turf. He had come to know many of the patrons of the Hard Luck, who the troublemakers were, who the regulars were, which men were poor poker players and which ones were good, who drank too much. He even knew details about some of their families. But he wasn't familiar with the crowd in the Wildcat.

The trips to Denver had gone without incident, but the drivers of the wagons full of processed ore and the other guards who rode along often expressed their concern over Ed Foley and what he might do for revenge against Grant Breckenridge. Cole wanted to see the man for himself, get an idea what he was up against, and Ed Foley was known to hang out in the Wildcat.

He walked up to the bar, feeling the stares of several men. He expected that. Any stranger who entered was someone to watch at first, but a lot of these men probably knew him because of the news he'd made over the showdown he'd had with George Williams. Some probably also knew he worked for Grant Breckenridge. What they didn't know was that he had little use for Grant himself, but the pay was good, and he was already building up a nice bank account he could use toward building a new life for himself and Addy.

Had Breckenridge managed to win her heart? Among articles in the *Register* about plans for a fancy hotel and opera house in

Central, maybe even a railroad from Central to Denver, as well as a new school building proposal, there had also been stories about the female school teacher, Mrs. Addy Kane, attending this or that social event with Mr. Grant Breckenridge as her escort. It was always mentioned that the illustrious Breckenridge was a key city planner, involved in the many wonderful building projects in the making.

There had also been an article about the new house on High Street, built for the new teacher. Cole had ridden by that house, small but quite pretty, white, the lacy lattice work painted blue. It fit Addy. Maybe she would be so contented there that she wouldn't want to consider any more changes in her life. So far he had kept his promise to stay straight, work hard, save his money, stay away from too much drinking. Would she keep her promise to wait for him?

He ordered a shot of whiskey, now allowing himself only two shots a day. He lit a cigar while he waited, looking around the room to spot young Benny Reed serving drinks to several poker players at one of the tables. The Wildcat no longer had fancy women working there. It was strictly a place for men to drink and gamble, but there were plenty of pictures of naked women hanging on the walls. One huge painting over the bar boasted a plump, full-breasted woman sprawled on a lounge with a bouquet of flowers between her legs. She reminded him of Sassy.

His drink was served, and Benny walked up to him with a grin. "Hello, Mr. Parker. I ain't seen you in a while."

"Been busy."

Benny glanced at another table as though worried, then looked back up at Cole. "I know. I hear you're workin' for Grant Breckenridge helpin' guard his gold."

Cole slugged down the whiskey. "Pay's good."

Benny set a tray on the bar. "I expect it is, but maybe you shouldn't be in here."

Cole rested an elbow on the bar. "Why? Is Ed Foley here? And watch how you react. I don't want him to know I asked."

Benny looked toward a front corner of the room, where a

piano sat. "Hey, Jerry, play us some music! It's gettin' too quiet in here!"

A balding man sitting near the piano waved back and finished a beer, then got up and sat down to the piano and began plunking out a feisty tune. Benny looked back at Cole. "That will help keep people from hearin'."

Cole nodded. "You're a smart boy."

Benny grinned. He liked impressing men like Cole Parker. "Ed Foley is sitting over near the piano himself. He's wearing the fancy black suit, a little man wearing spectacles. He's in here most every night getting drunk. Once he's drunk, he always talks about how he's gonna get even with Grant Breckenridge for stealin' his claim and killin' his son."

"I've heard it a couple of ways." Cole pulled deeply on his cigar before continuing. "Grant's men say Foley never had a claim to begin with. Something about Grant grubstaking the man but he never found anything that was worth much."

Benny shook his head. "That's not how Foley tells it. Him and his son, Ed Junior, they both worked for Chadwick Mining Company and were in charge of orderin' minin' equipment and such when new mines were staked. They came out here just like Breckenridge as employees, only Breckenridge had a lot higher position in the company. Once they got out here, they decided they wanted to do some prospectin' of their own. Foley says they found a good vein and asked Breckenridge if he'd get the minin' company to back them in some equipment to better get the gold out. Breckenridge agreed, but behind Foley's back, he got the claims agent to attach Chadwick Mining Company's name to the claim. He said as how Foley was an employee come here to explore for the company and not for himself, he couldn't claim his find in just his name."

Cole turned and ordered drinks for both of them, while the piano player pounded out more lively tunes and the crowd of men in the room got a little louder. "How can Breckenridge say that, when he owns most of the mine himself?"

Benny shook his head, his stringy blond hair hanging in his

face. "That's partly why Foley hates him so much. He made out like a champion for cheatin' Foley out of what was his."

"How's that?" Cole downed the second shot of whiskey, deciding he'd stop there. He'd made a promise to Addy.

Benny leaned on the bar, facing him. "Well, Foley, he was screamin' mad when he found out Chadwick Minin' Company's name was on his claim. I guess he raised all kinds of hell, but Breckenridge told him the only way to solve it was to take Chadwick to court, and the only legal jurisdiction for that was back in Chicago. Foley knew he probably didn't stand a chance, just him up against a big company like that, and he didn't have the money to pay for the legal costs, so he pulled out, quit Chadwick and went to work for another minin' company, him and his son both. There was an accident involvin' dynamite, and his son got killed. Foley blames it on Breckenridge, says if he'd not been forced to quit and go to work for somebody else, his son would never have been in that other mine and got killed. I'll tell you, he hates Grant Breckenridge with a passion. Ain't nobody can reason with him about it."

Cole thought about his own little girl, how much he'd hated Howard Benedict. Breckenridge wasn't quite so responsible for Foley's son's death, but the fact remained he was indirectly the cause for the boy being in the wrong place at the wrong time. "I can understand how he feels," he told Benny. "Don't think I don't realize that Breckenridge is a sonofabitch. I'm only working for him because he pays damn good, and right now I need the money." He took another drag on his cigar. "So, how did Breckenridge end up owning a mine of his own?"

Benny shrugged. "Company bonus, they say. Foley's claim wasn't exactly a bonanza, but enough to make a man pretty rich. Apparently Breckenridge handed the company some bullshit story about the whole thing—probably told them how he'd managed to keep an errant employee from movin' in on claims that should belong to the company. Who knows? For some reason, they think Breckenridge is a great and wonderful man, a valuable employee. They apparently gave him about three-quarter ownership of the Jamesway, the very same mine Foley had once claimed for himself. That put the icing on the cake as far as Foley is concerned. He don't waste any words tellin' folks about all of it and what he thinks of Breckenridge, but Breckenridge is charming and a smooth talker. Most folks of any significance in this town don't pay no attention to Foley. They refuse to believe the kind of man Breckenridge really is. They only see him as a handsome widower, a man who has money, dresses fine and donates a lot of money to town projects, works hard at buildin' churches, schools, that kind of thing. He knows exactly how to charm the pants off women and bullshit the men."

Cole felt a stab of fierce jealousy at the remark. The thought of Breckenridge getting Addy into his bed tore at his guts in literal physical pain. He nodded to Benny. "Thanks for the information. I just wanted to get a look at Foley, get an idea who the enemy is, although I can't blame him. I don't intend to work for Breckenridge a long time, just until I have enough money saved to do something of my own. I'd probably better get out of here. I'll get a good look at Foley when I go."

"Well, I wish you luck, Mr. Parker. You'd better be careful. I've got no doubt Foley will figure out a way to get back at Breckenridge before this thing is over. It's been goin' on for about six months now, ever since Foley's kid got killed. He originally came out about two years ago, and it was about a year ago that the first big blow-up came over who really owned Foley's claim. Anyway, watch your back."

"Grant's men have already told me that."

"Well, just so you know, the man standing behind Foley over there, the big one in the blue shirt, that's his best friend, Clancy Ives. The two beside him wearing guns, they're hired gunmen. Foley recently hired them to show his strength. Wants Breckenridge to hear about them, maybe shake in his shoes a little. Everybody is making bets on how Foley will get his revenge. Most think he'll blow up the Jamesway, or figure out a way to steal one of Breckenridge's gold shipments. He—"

"Hey, Cole Parker!" Cole's name was shouted from the table

where Foley sat, and two men wearing guns scooted back their chairs and rose.

"Shit!" Benny stepped back from Cole, and a few other people scattered, including the bartender.

Cole threw his cigar into a spittoon and turned to face the table. It was a chilly day, and he wore a wool jacket. He pushed it behind his gun. "Somebody want to talk to me?"

"I do," the same gruff voice replied. It came from a man in a red flannel shirt. He was big and burly, bearded, his brown eyes glittering with anger, and he wore a gun. He stood beside a smaller man with a weasel face and eyeglasses.

Foley, Cole thought.

"What's a Breckenridge man doin' in the Wildcat? Breckenridge men don't come in here," the gunman in the red shirt told him. "They know better!"

"I'm just visiting Benny here. I haven't been in Central that long, don't know many people, met Benny when I first arrived, over at the Hard Luck." He glanced at the man in the blue shirt behind Foley. That would be Clancy Ives. He wanted to remember their faces.

"I don't care what your excuse is. Mr. Foley here figures you came here to have a look at him, see who you're up against. I work for Foley, and we know *you* work for Breckenridge guarding his gold shipments. No man works for Breckenridge without knowing about Ed."

The man wearing glasses rose, facing Cole defiantly. Cole wondered how brave he would be without men with guns backing him. The second gunman stood on the other side of Foley.

"I'm Ed Foley," Foley told Cole, his chin held high, "and I'm telling you that Grant Breckenridge is no good. You ought to find yourself another line of work, mister."

Cole kept his eyes on Foley, but his concentration was really on the two men on either side of him. "It's just a job to me. I'm sorry for whatever falling out you've had with the man."

"Then let's have a talk." Foley's eyes moved over him appreciatively. "I've heard about you. You're good with that gun. A

man like you could be useful to me in finding a way to pay
Breckenridge his dues."

The thought was tempting to Cole, considering he'd like
Grant Breckenridge away from Addy. Still, he'd promised Addy
to stay out of trouble. "You'll have to find somebody else, and
they'll have to go up against me. I didn't come here to make
trouble, Foley. I'm leaving now, so just go back to your card
playing and I won't bother you." He took a step sideways.

"I say you're a damn wolf paid by Breckenridge to eat up
anybody who gets in his path," Foley growled. "Breckenridge
is a bastard, a lying sonofabitch who'll fuck any woman in
town, whore or decent, and who'll cheat any man out of everything he owns if he can! Anybody who works for him is
no better!"

Cole checked his temper, fully realizing Foley dearly wanted
him to draw his gun, thinking his own men could shoot him
down legally and get rid of him. "Save it, Foley. I said I wanted
no trouble. I came to Central looking for work, and I found it.
That's all there is to it. Your beef with Breckenridge is none of
my concern."

Foley put his hands on his hips. "My beef with Breckenridge
is the concern of *any* man who works for him, especially when
he comes here to have a look at me. You're up to something,
mister."

"You're all drunk," Cole warned. "Don't do something stupid."

"Two against one?" Foley looked at his two gunmen. "I don't
call that stupid, and there isn't a man in this bar who won't tell
the sheriff you drew first. We stick together in the Wildcat." The
man grinned. "Get rid of him, boys."

The gunmen hesitated as more people scattered, even Ives.
Cole could see the doubt and fear in their eyes. "If you both
want to live, then you'd best stand real still while I get out of
here," he warned them. He turned, heard a click.

"Jesus!" somebody shouted.

It all happened in a split second. Men everywhere ducked to

the floor. Cole whirled the instant he heard the cocking of a gun, and his own pistol was drawn and fired before the first man could get off his shot, fired again at the second man before he could get his gun all the way out of his holster. Both men jerked backward from the force of Cole's bullets, one slamming into a wall, the other falling against a stair railing and breaking it. The first man slid down the wall, leaving a bloody streak.

Foley lost his grin as he stood staring at Cole, dumbfounded. "You bastard!" he growled. His eyes blazed with drunken revenge.

Ives came to stand near him again, putting a hand on Foley's shoulder. "Breckenridge sure knows who to hire, doesn't he?" he said, looking dejected.

"You tell Grant Breckenridge his days are numbered!" Foley shouted at Cole, paying no attention to Clancy's remark. "I can always find more gunmen!"

"Let it go, Foley. You can't bring back the dead. I know that for a fact myself. Killing Breckenridge won't change anything that's happened."

"Oh, but it *will!* But then I never said I'd kill him. I only said I'd get my revenge. How I do it is something for the man to sit and wonder and worry about. You and anyone else who works for him can also worry!"

Cole slid his six-gun back into its holster, glancing at the two men he'd shot. "You'll have to hire better men than those two," he commented. He sighed deeply. "Give it up, Foley," he repeated. "You'll only end up dead or in prison yourself."

He turned and walked to the doorway, but just before he pushed at one of the swinging doors, Benny shouted, "Cole! Look out!"

Cole swung around with his gun drawn. Before he realized what Benny was yelling about, he heard a gunshot. He felt a hot sting seer across the right side of his head, felt himself fall through the swinging doors as he lost consciousness.

* * *

Cole opened his eyes and looked around the room, plain
ainted walls, the smells of medicine. There were two other beds
eside his, one empty, one occupied by a man who lay sleeping.
was a very small room, and Cole wasn't sure just where he
as. He sat up, then felt a fierce pain rip through his head. He
ut a hand to his forehead and realized gauze was wrapped
round his skull.

He struggled to think, remember. He looked down at himself,
as still fully dressed except for his boots and gunbelt, which
ung on a chair nearby. The sight made him remember another
me, lying in bed, his gunbelt nearby . . . back in Unionville.
e'd escaped . . .

He rubbed at his eyes, another memory returning. He'd gone
the Wildcat, shot it out with two men who were friends of Ed
oley. He hadn't meant to cause that kind of trouble. He'd only
anted to get a look at Foley. He sat there on the edge of the
ed, trying to figure out what had gone wrong. Both of Foley's
en had been down. He remembered a blow to the head, fall-
g . . . Had someone snuck up behind him and hit him with
mething?

"Thanks, Doc."

Cole recognized Sassy's voice, looked up when she walked
to the room wearing a blue dress that was rather demure for
er, although the oval cutout in front displayed a fetching amount
f flesh. She looked relieved when she saw him sitting up.

"He's awake, Doc!"

A man entered, and Cole recognized the town doctor,
reighton Jonesboro. The man smiled. "Well, I figured you'd
ake up pretty quick. My guess is you sustained only a light
ncussion. Let's have a look."

Cole frowned in confusion as the man knelt in front of him
study his eyes and take his pulse.

"What the hell happened?"

"You don't remember?" the doctor asked.

"I remember shooting it out with a couple of men, then leav-
g. Something hit me in the head."

"That something was a bullet," Sassy told him. "You're dam
lucky to be alive, Cole. One of the men you shot stirred aroun
and took a pot-shot at you as you left. A few minutes later h
died. Both men are dead."

"Good. There's nothing I hate more than a back-shooter."

The doctor rose. "I think you'll be just fine in a few days—i
time for the big miners' picnic. Just stay away from Ed Fole
and his friends. For now, you'd best stay right here for a fe
hours more. Would you like some coffee?"

Cole winced as another pain stabbed at the right side of h
head. "Yeah. Sure."

The doctor left, and Cole nodded toward his jacket. "Tobacc
and papers in there. Can you roll me a cigarette?" he aske
Sassy.

"Sure, honey." The woman walked over and rummage
through his pockets. "I heard the whole story from a ver
excited Benny Reed. Thanks to Benny you're not in an
trouble. He told the sheriff how you tried to *avoid* a confron
tation, but those men drew on you first. Then one of the
shot at you from behind as you were leaving. I must say, Gra
Breckenridge isn't worth risking your life over like that."

Cole rubbed at the back of his neck. "I agree. Benny told n
Foley's side of the story—about the same as what you told m
Breckenridge is a sonofabitch, no doubt about it; but it isn't hi
I'm risking my life for. It's—" He looked over at the man wh
lay sleeping, not wanting to be heard. "You know who it is.
need the money Breckenridge pays so maybe I can marry h
in a few months."

Sassy licked the cigarette paper and sealed the smoke. "I ju
hope she appreciates what you're doing." She handed him t
cigarette, then walked over to a wood stove where stick match
sat in a can. She lit one and came over and lit Cole's cigaret
for him. "I got real worried when Benny said they brought yc
over here unconscious, shot in the head. You know how stori
travel through this town. Half the folks here probably alrea

ink you're dead or dying. You'll end up the subject of another
ewspaper article."

Cole took a deep drag on the cigarette. "Yeah, well, I don't
are much for the publicity. I don't need it."

Sassy chuckled. "You're the kind of man who draws attention,
ole Parker. I—" She heard voices outside then, recognized
rant's. "Sounds like your boss has come to pay his respects."

Breckenridge stepped through the door, and Cole felt his heart
ound harder at the sight of Addy with him. He knew immedi-
ely she had only found an excuse to come along because she
eded to see for herself he was all right. She would have no
ay of explaining if she came to see him alone.

"Well, you *are* all right! You had me worried, Parker," Breck-
ridge said with a grin. He glanced at Sassy. "Hello, Miss
illon."

Cole wanted to laugh at the man's play-acting, pretending he
rdly knew Sassy. Sassy nodded in return. "Mr. Breckenridge."
he moved her eyes to Addy, and the two women glared at each
her. Cole knew why, but he was glad to know Breckenridge
dn't catch on. He apparently thought Addy was upset to be in
e same room as a prostitute.

"I'm sorry, Miss Dillon, but I'm afraid you'll have to leave,"
rant told Sassy. "It's difficult for Mrs. Kane here to be asso-
ated with—well, you know."

Cole had to look away to keep from laughing. He damn well
new what Sassy would really like to say to Grant, but she man-
ed to keep her composure.

"Certainly." she turned and deliberately bent down to kiss
ole's cheek. "I'm glad you're okay, honey. Free drinks and a
eal on me when you leave here." She patted his cheek and
rned to face Addy. "We're just friends, you know. Cole works
r me part time. I'm sure you don't know Mr. Parker very well,
it then he did save your hide a couple of weeks ago, didn't he?
e's a good man."

Addy was obviously struggling against tears. "I . . . I'm sure
 is."

A lot better than some men I know, Sassy wanted to add. She glanced at Grant, who gave her a warning look before she le the room.

"Well, I'm glad you're all right, Cole," Grant told him. " heard all kinds of rumors—dead, dying, parylized, shot in th back." He chuckled. "You're becoming quite a celebrity."

Cole scooted back onto the bed and sat up against the hea rail. "I'd rather not be."

The doctor brought him a mug of coffee and set it on a tabl beside him, then left again.

"I was on my way to pick up Mrs. Kane for dinner when heard about the shootings, so I brought her along to see yo since you're the one who got her away from that drunken min a couple of weeks ago. It's getting so I owe you more and mor Cole. You're doing a fine job. I'll bet you went over to the Wil cat just to get a look at Ed Foley, didn't you?"

Cole took a swallow of coffee. "I did. But I did not mean get into anything like what happened." His dark eyes drilled int Breckenridge. "Is the story I heard true? The reason Foley d spises you?"

Grant lost his smile. "Not at all. Foley came out here as a employee for Chadwick Mining, just like me, then tried to ste a claim from them. I caught him at it and he lost his job. That all there is to it. As far as what happened to his son—well, th was an accident. How could I have controlled such a thing? I' sorry for him. I have a son of my own, you know."

Cole set the coffee aside, glancing at Addy again. She quick wiped a tear from her cheek so Grant would not notice. "Yo said something about him coming here to live," he said.

Grant nodded, a proud look in his eyes. "His name is Jame and he's twenty-one. He's in Chicago—studying to be a lawye Smart kid," he bragged. "Started college at sixteen. I can't wa to show him off when he gets here."

"That so?" Cole took another drag on his cigarette, able understand even better Ed Foley's bitterness. Grant Brecken ridge still had a son.

"You've never said exactly when he's coming," Addy told Grant.

He moved an arm around her waist, and Cole had to look away. "Well, dear, I just found out myself recently in his latest letter. I meant to tell you all about it at dinner. He's coming just a few days after the picnic. I can't wait for him to meet you."

Addy knew how it all sounded to Cole. Grant made it look as though it was all settled. They were a couple. She was to meet his son, as though they should consider the possibility of all being a family. "I'll be glad to meet him, too," she answered. She looked at Cole, who finally met her eyes again. She tried to tell him with those eyes that this meant nothing. *I said I would wait for you, Cole.* If only they could talk. She was so happy to see he was all right, not dead like she'd heard. She wanted to hold him. "How do you feel, Mr. Parker?" she asked.

Cole shrugged. "A little sick to my stomach, got a headache. The doc says it's just a mild concussion. I'll live." He looked at Grant. "Long enough to have that dance with Mrs. Kane at the miners' picnic," he added. "Don't forget you promised."

Grant laughed. "I haven't forgotten." He kept his arm around Addy. "I forgot to tell you, Addy. I told Cole that if I win money on him at the shooting contest, he could have a dance with you. I hope you don't mind. I don't mean to offend."

Addy watched Cole, wanting to smile then. "I don't mind."

"Just be careful of your heart, Cole," Grant warned. "You'll be dancing with the prettiest woman in Central, but you remember who she belongs to."

Addy cast Grant a look of irritation, wanting to lash out at him for taking so much for granted. Her cheeks felt hot at the fact he'd said such a thing in front of Cole, who probably thought she'd gone back on her promise. She gave Cole a pleading look, hoping he understood those were Grant's words, not hers. She saw the hurt in Cole's face. He closed his eyes and rubbed at his head then.

"I'll remember," he answered Grant. He wanted to rail the man about Ed Foley. He didn't believe Grant's side of the story for one minute, but he also didn't want to lose his job. Working for Grant Breckenridge meant good money, and it meant a chance to find excuses to be close to Addy. He just hoped the look she gave him meant what he thought it meant. He was tempted to jump up and pull her away from the man, right down onto the bed with him . . . to tell the world he was more and more sure he was in love with Addy Kane, and pretty damned sure she loved him, too. How he was going to get her away from Grant and marry her without both of them getting in a lot of trouble, he wasn't sure. Grant Breckenridge was not a man to be crossed, and he couldn't just shoot the man, although he'd dearly love to do just that. He looked up at Grant again. "Thanks for coming to see me." He touched the bandage on his head. "I guess now I'll have two scars on this head."

Grant smiled. "I suppose. How'd you get the one on your forehead? The war?"

Cole glanced at Addy. "Yeah. The war."

"Well, you're a good man, Parker. Be sure you enter that shooting contest at the picnic. I intend to bet a great deal of money on you."

Cole nodded. "I'll do that." He looked at Addy. "You sure you don't mind that dance?"

Addy felt a rush of desire, and she could almost taste his kiss. It would not be easy just to dance. "I'm sure." She blinked back more tears and took a deep breath, putting on a smile for Grant. "We'll be late for the Collingswoods. I'm sure Hester's cook has a meal waiting."

"Oh, yes!" Grant reached out to shake Cole's hand. "Quite a shootout, I'm told. That should show Foley a thing or two—not to mess with the men I hire. I hire only the best!"

Cole shook his hand, but he had a stronger urge to land a fist into the man's face. "I try. I don't know how I got so careless as to turn my back like that. I thought both men were down."

"Well, consider it a lesson. You're good with a gun, Cole, but maybe you have a little bit to learn about men who shoot back at you."

Cole glanced at Addy before replying. If the man knew the truth, he'd be in prison in no time at all. "Sure," he answered. "I should have learned that in the war."

Grant put an arm around Addy again and whisked her to the door. "Get some rest, Cole. I want you well for the picnic!" He rushed Addy away, and Cole sat staring at the door.

"I'll be well, all right," he muttered. "Well enough to dance with Addy Kane."

Twenty-three

Grant looked up from his desk when the door to his study opened.

"You have a visitor," his housekeeper told him. "I was outside sweeping the porch when Mrs. Brown drove up in a buggy and asked to see you. Would you like me to bring her in here?"

Grant frowned curiously. He had no use for Ethel Brown, other than to stay on her good side, since she had a lot of influence in Central. He was instantly a little worried. Had she found out about his occasional visits to Sassy Dillon? He trusted Sassy not to tell anyone publicly, no matter what happened to her business. She had been paid well to keep her mouth shut, and he had discreetly lain low during all the hullabaloo over prostitution. "Yes, you can bring her in."

He quickly pressed out a cigar and walked to a mirror over the fireplace, smoothing back the sides of his hair and taking a last-minute look at himself. Ethel Brown was easily charmed. He tugged at a paisley satin vest, took a gold watch from a pocket of that vest to check the time. Two P.M. He walked to his desk and took a suit jacket from the back of the chair, pulling it on as he heard the rustle of skirts and petticoats in the hallway. His housekeeper showed Ethel into his study, and Ethel did not give her so much as a thank you as she put her nose in the air and swept into the room, her full figure nearly filling the doorway.

"Well, Mrs. Brown, what a pleasant surprise!" Grant lied. "What can I do for you today?"

The woman had a look of unnerving arrogance in her puffy eyes as she gave him a grim smile. "It is not so much what you can do for me, Mr. Breckenridge, but rather what I might be able to do for you." She turned and closed the door, then walked closer to his desk. "I will talk quietly so that your housekeeper doesn't hear."

Grant noticed she held a brown envelope in her hand, and his eyebrows knitted in confusion. "What on earth are you being so secretive about?" Maybe she had heard something about him and the prostitutes after all. "Please sit down, Mrs. Brown. Can I have my housekeeper get you anything? Tea perhaps?"

"Oh, that's quite all right. I don't need anything." Ethel sat down in a velvet chair, glancing around the room, feeling very important today. Not only was she a welcome guest in this important man's home, but he had allowed her directly into his study—Grant Breckenridge's study. It smelled of cigars and leather, and books lined the walls. Little did she know Grant had put them there only to make an impression. He had read very few of them, but in her mind he was a wonderful man, a lonely widower whom she didn't want to see hurt. He had to know the truth. Surely she was doing the right thing, telling him what she had learned about Addy Kane.

Ethel held out the envelope. "I am here because of this, Mr. Breckenridge." She laid the envelope on his desk. "And to bring you news that might be quite upsetting. You may even think it is none of my business, but I feel it is my Christian duty to tell you what I have learned . . . about Mrs. Addy Kane."

Grant felt a note of alarm. Addy? He picked up the envelope, read the return address. "Sheriff Nicholas Page, Unionville, Illinois." He started to remove the letter inside.

"Let me explain before you read the letter, Mr. Breckenridge."

Grant laid the letter aside and sat down in a leather chair behind his desk. "Go ahead."

Ethel took a deep breath, sitting straight and proud. "You

know that in the beginning I had some doubts about our Mrs. Kane."

Grant nodded. "I have found her to be a fine woman, Mrs. Brown. She is discreet, educated, mannerly, beautiful—"

"That is the trouble with men," Ethel interrupted. "When a woman is beautiful, they don't want to know anything bad about her. They see only the good, and I am sure Mrs. Kane has many good points. But you should know . . ." She leaned closer. "Several weeks ago, the night of her reception at Lawrence Hall, after she went home, John Withers, who also lived at Miss Ada's then, heard her come in, then go out again. Minutes later he heard voices outside in the dark. He could not hear their exact words, but it was a man and a woman. When Mrs. Kane came back inside, she seemed upset. He was sure he heard her crying. I am not saying she did anything wrong. I am only saying that this is proof that Mrs. Kane lied when she said she knew absolutely no one in town when she first came here. There apparently *was* someone she knew, and it was a man. My immediate questions were who is this man, and what is their relationship? Is he still in town? Why wouldn't she want anyone to know she knew him? Is he someone who would mar her reputation and keep her from teaching? I decided we had not investigated this woman's background enough before hiring her, so I wrote to the sheriff in her hometown to find out more about her, and his reply was shocking. There is something about her past that she never told us, and I hate to think of the possible reason why. Whether or not it has anything to do with her meeting someone the night of the reception—"

"Wait a minute! Slow down," Grant interrupted. "Give me a minute to grasp all of this." He rubbed at his chin thoughtfully. Addy had met some man after the reception, out in the dark behind the boarding house? Who? Why? Was he still around? After all the times he had called on her, taken her to dinner, social events and such, she had remained distant and cool toward him. *Was* there another man in her life he didn't know about?

The thought made him furious. He wanted Addy Kane more

than he had ever wanted another woman. He had even considered marrying her, not because he loved her, but just to be sure no one else got his hands on her. He sighed, leaning forward and resting his elbows on his desk. "All right. Tell me what's in this letter."

He noted the excitement and pleasure in Mrs. Brown's eyes, although he knew she was trying to remain very serious and pretend concern. Her pudgy face was flushed with eagerness.

"Back in Unionville Mrs. Kane was caught up in a bank robbery only a couple of weeks before she left to come to Central. She was abducted by the robbers. The whole gang rode off with her, and she was missing for five days. *Five days!* The sheriff formed a posse right away, but they lost the trail."

Grant, shocked himself, leaned back in the chair again. Addy? Abducted by a gang of outlaws? Why on earth hadn't she told anyone?

"One of the outlaws, a Nick Coleman, was shot and captured during the robbery, but then he escaped, stole a horse to do it. A few days later Mrs. Kane showed up in town, apparently un-harmed, but her dress was bloody and torn. She claimed the one called Nick Coleman was shot and killed. The robbers buried him, put her on the stolen horse and sent her back to town be-cause they feared she would slow them down. They headed into Indian Territory to hide out. Two of them, a Ted Sloan and Cal Arden, were later killed in a bank robbery in Missouri. Their leader in the Unionville robbery, Jack Slater, has never been seen since that robbery. The money they stole at Unionville was never recovered. Mrs. Kane claimed she was not . . . raped. But how can we believe that? A gang of outlaws like that . . . a beau-tiful young woman. I suspect she just never told the truth. No woman wants the general public to know about such a thing."

Grant watched her a moment, thinking what a nosey, arrogant bitch she was. Her reasons for finding out what she could about Addy were not honorable. She was just plain jealous of Addy's beauty. But the fact remained there was something very impor-tant about herself which Addy hadn't told anyone. "She was probably afraid to tell us for fear she wouldn't get the teaching job."

"Of course," Ethel nodded. "I know that what happened was not her fault, but the fact remains she could have been horribly soiled by those men. It is also possible she was a part of the whole thing, that the abduction was staged. Maybe she got some of the money."

"Addy wouldn't be a part of something like that."

"How do we know?"

"She's too educated and refined. What's Sheriff Page's opinion?"

"He feels Addy had nothing to do with it, that she was an innocent victim. He claims her reputation is quite honorable, although she was rather an outcast in town because of her Confederate connections."

"She told us that."

"But she left out some very important information that we should have been aware of. As far as her knowing some man here, I asked when I wrote if Mrs. Kane might have any male companion that he knows of. The sheriff replied that as far as anyone in Unionville knows, she had no connections or relationship with any man when she left."

Grant felt some relief at the words, but who on earth could she have been talking to that night after the reception? And what really had happened during her abduction? If the man who had helped her had been killed, why did the outlaws suddenly turn around and let her go free? "Who was the outlaw who ended up getting shot trying to help her?"

Ethel felt proud to know so much, impressed with her investigative talents. "Nick Coleman. The sheriff didn't describe him."

Grant stood up, walking to a window and looking downhill toward where he knew Addy's house sat. "Maybe that one they never found or heard about again took a shine to her and followed her out here. What's his name? Jack Slater? Maybe that's who she argued with."

"Wouldn't she tell Sheriff Watson?"

"Not if Slater threatened her life." He looked back at Mrs. Brown. "She's always behaved as though she was afraid of something, very quiet and reserved, can't seem to really enjoy herself. Maybe there *is* another man in her life, but maybe not in the way you thought. Maybe the whole thing is linked together somehow. Either way, I see nothing that would demand we stop her from teaching. I do appreciate your interest in the matter and the fact that you did a little investigating on your own. I may look into it more myself before I say anything to Mrs. Kane, and I would appreciate it if you said nothing to the other women, unless you already have."

Ethel shook her head. "I felt you should be the first to know," she answered piously. "I'll say nothing, if that is your wish, but I feel she should be confronted with this. I want to watch her eyes when she tells us she was not soiled by those men. We'll be able to tell if she's lying."

"If it did happen, it wouldn't be her fault." Grant felt a surge of desire at the thought of a naked Addy writhing under him, protesting as he took her, then giving in, coming to enjoy it. Had it been that way with the outlaws?

"I am aware it's not her fault, but there would always be doubt in the minds of others. It would become the talk of the town and would have to be explained to the children, which would be very awkward."

"I'll ask her about it," Grant replied, "but not until after the picnic. I want her to enjoy herself there. Besides, I want to wire that sheriff in Unionville first and see if I can get a description of the outlaws, maybe figure out who might be bothering her."

"Well, you can try," Ethel answered, "but so many new men show up in Central every week, I don't see how you could make a connection. Half the town are transients."

"I'll figure something out, question her myself after the picnic. You keep quiet about it until I tell you what we should do."

"Certainly." Ethel wondered just how she was going to do that. She was already bursting at the seams to tell Hester. Maybe that would be all right. Hester could keep a secret. If she promised not to tell another soul— "I hope you don't think me nosey or feel that I have overstepped my bounds, Mr. Breckenridge. It is obvious to everyone that you are quite fond of Mrs. Kane. We wouldn't want you hurt by perhaps marrying her and then finding out things about her that might change your mind about her."

"Oh, I understand," he answered, *you nosey old biddy.* Ethel Brown loved nothing more than gossip, putting other people down so that she felt perfect and pious. He doubted she would be able to keep this to herself for long. He would have to wire Sheriff Page right away and get descriptions of the outlaws. He'd send someone down to Denver tomorrow to do just that. "Thank you for your concern, Mrs. Brown. I'll keep the letter here."

"As you wish." Ethel rose and picked up her handbag and parasol. "It's a lovely day today, a bit chilly, but sunny. I hope the weather holds out for the picnic. It won't be long after that before winter begins to make itself known." She walked to the door. "The sooner you decide, the better. School starts in just over two weeks. Oh! How soon is your son coming here?"

"About the same time."

"That will be nice for you, and good for Central. A new young lawyer in town. Our Sharon will be going off to finishing school next year. With Lee being in real estate, we have lived in many locations, but Lee and I like Central best. I'm sure your son will like it here, too. Of course, you have the best reason of all to stay here—a gold mine!" She looked Grant over, and he could see the admiration in her eyes. If he had any desire for Ethel Brown at all, he had no doubt he could woo her into his bed and she would be flattered. He almost laughed out loud. If she learned the same thing about some other married woman, she would have the news spread over Central so fast the poor "adulteress" would be quickly ridden out of town in tar and feathers.

"Yes, I've been a lucky man," he answered. "Thank you, Mrs. Brown."

She nodded, obviously elated over what she had discovered. "You're welcome, Mr. Breckenridge."

Ethel turned and left, and Grant went to a window to watch her go down the steps to her waiting carriage. He turned and glanced at the letter on his desk. "What is it you aren't telling me, Addy Kane? And why?" Maybe he'd get his answer from Sheriff Page.

A pistol was fired, and several men, women and children took off in a one-legged race that left onlookers screaming with laughter. Many fell, others argued, all scrambled to reach the finish line first to each receive a two-dollar goldpiece as their prize. Addy watched from a platform in front of the *Register* office on Eureka Street, sitting beside Grant and other town dignitaries who were sharing the platform for the best view.

She laughed with the others. It felt good to laugh, but deep inside she could not stop thinking about the fact that later she was to have a dance with Cole. It would not be easy to let him touch her and not be able to embrace him. She had been so sure she should not get involved with Cole again, in spite of her promises, until she thought he might have been killed. It was then she realized how much she loved him.

There was still the problem of how to gradually get away from Grant. She would have to be very careful not to anger him. And, after all, he had been very gracious and generous to her.

She had not spotted Cole yet, and wondered if he would think she had dressed just for him. She wore one of her best dresses, orchid and white taffeta. The dress had outsized cap sleeves filled with white lace ruffles, and the bodice was cut just right to show she had a full bosom without actually revealing too much flesh. White lace graced the edging of the bodice, and also fell in a panel down the front of her dress. A fur-lined cape of matching orchid taffeta graced her shoulders to protect them against the cool afternoon, and she wore white, elbow-length gloves. An ivory cameo was tied at her neck with orchid ribbon, and the same ribbon in a mass of bows mixed with white lace decorated the crown of her hat. Her hair was swept up at the sides and twisted into a thick braid on top of her head, over which the hat was pinned.

Old Elizabeth Howley had made the dress and hat for her. She had lived up to her reputation among the other women as the best seamstress in town, and Addy had already decided to have the woman make more clothes for her. It was much cheaper than ordering the latest fashions from New York. Such items had to be shipped through Omaha and Denver and on up to Central, which was costly and took weeks, sometimes longer.

Although every woman of importance had dressed as elegantly, if not even more outlandishly, she wondered if she had overdressed, not because of the picnic occasion, but because she feared both Grant and Cole would think she had wanted to look her best for them. She had only dressed up because Hester and the others had told her that's what all the women did at this occasion, even though most of the day consisted of casual events. Still, she could see the pleasure in Grant's eyes when he had picked her up, and he'd been strutting like a rooster all day, keeping her on his arm constantly. She felt even more at a loss to know how to get away from him, and this evening she would need to deal with Cole, who had asked her to wait for him.

Two young men in their teens won the one-legged sack race and let out wild whoops when they received their gold pieces. Next came the bed races, all sorts of beds, both real and simple boxed contraptions with mattresses in the middle and wheels attached, perched at the top of Eureka just above the sites that had already been picked out for a new Methodist Church and an opera house. Although the bed races were sponsored by the various town saloons and some of the beds were ridden by gawdily-dressed ladies of "ill repute", many of whom had already given up their profession in order to stay in Central, the races were allowed because this was a day for fun and laughter for forgetting things like the women's march and the battle that followed.

Again a shot was fired, and people cheered and laughed as men began pushing the beds down the hill, the painted women sitting on them screaming instructions and shrieking with their own laughter. Addy spotted Sassy Dillon, who wore bright red today, a gaudy taffeta and organdy piece that sparkled with rhinestones and sequins. Her grating voice cut through the surrounding noise as she yelled, "Go left! No, right! Hurry it up, boys!" Her hardy laughter filled the air, and as her bed flew by the stand, Addy noticed Cole walking amid the crowd on the other side of the street. Her heart leaped with desire at the sight of him. He had dressed pretty fine himself today, wearing what looked like a new black suit, a white ruffled shirt and black string tie, and a new black hat.

For her? Was he anticipating their dance as she was? Dreading it? Wanting it? Wanting more? She did not even notice the rest of the bed race as it continued downhill into Lawrence Street. She did not see that it was won by the Wildcat. Next came a parade, and Addy lost track of Cole. An unlikely band made up of drums, fiddles, bugles, a flute and one tuba marched past, playing a patriotic tune. A few people dressed like clowns followed, then wagons decorated with ribbons and wildflowers, some with banners that read "Central for Capitol," "Vote for Statehood" and various other themes. After the parade, H. M. Teller stood up behind her and 3announced through a megaphone that it was time for the pie-eating contest on Main Street, after which there would be a shooting contest.

"That's what I'm waiting for," Grant told her. "Cole Parker is going to put some money in my pocket today." He ushered her off the platform, and with others they walked around to Main Street to watch the pie eating. Addy had herself baked one of the pies, and she had helped Hester and Ethel and other women plan some of these events. Children sat lined on either side of a long table, each with a pie in front of them and with their hands tied behind their backs. Parents stood behind them, urging them on when a man announced they should begin eating. Little faces dove into messy pies, and the race was on.

"I'm going over to the target area to place some bets with some of the other men," Grant told her, giving her arm a squeeze.

His familiarity with her in front of the others irritated her, as though he wanted to be sure they all realized she belonged to him. "The other women can join us there. It's up Nevada Street and over to the left by the Golden Lady mine tailings. Will you be all right alone?"

"Of course. Why would you ask that?"

"Just making sure. You stick close to Hester and the other women."

He left her, and Addy watched him walk away. Why had he told her to stick close to the other women? Was it because there were so many miners on the loose today, men bent on having a good time, many of them already full of whiskey? That was probably his reasoning, but something had been different the last couple of days, the way he looked at her with new questions in his eyes, sometimes a look of distrust. He often looked around carefully today, as though he were looking for someone. Who?

After several minutes a plump young girl of perhaps ten won the pie-eating contest, raising her purple face with a smile. Her mother helped wash her face while Hester presented her with a free pie for her family and a cameo necklace. The crowd then moved excitedly on up the street toward the tailings of the Golden Lady. The crowd grew much bigger, joined by many men, all of them pressing and shoving to get to the shooting contest and make their bets. Of all the talk she'd heard today, Addy had realized that the shooting contest was the most important event. There would be others, contests of strength and skill among miners, but the shooting match seemed to mean the most, and Addy could already hear Cole Parker's name being mentioned among many.

"Ain't nobody faster or with better aim," someone behind her said. "I seen him take George Williams that night at the Hard Luck. A man couldn't blink faster than that. They say he shot them men in the Wildcat before they even got their guns out of their holsters."

Memories flooded through Addy's mind and heart, the bank robbery, Cole's shootout at the cabin to save her, their first heated liaison in Abilene, the way he had ridden out of nowhere to save her from death or capture by the Indians. It seemed whenever he had a need, he was there. It would be easier to forget, to be unable to forgive him for his outlaw ways, if she didn't know the truth about his past, little Patty, the nightmares that haunted him.

The crowd turned into groups of men rushing to make bets, while others lined up to shoot, taking practice aims at targets in the distance, bottles and cans on rocks and posts. Whoever missed the fewest times would win five hundred dollars, the money put up by mine owners. Other men could make whatever bets they wanted. Cole Parker drew the lowest odds. Grant found Addy and whisked her through the mob of men to another platform that had been built specifically for Central's chosen elite.

"Too bad you're not a betting woman," he told her. "You could make some money today."

Addy sat down in a wooden chair. "If I wasn't afraid the ladies of Central would fire me, I *would* bet—on Cole Parker."

Grant laughed. "It would be a wise bet." He pointed out to the field of targets. "Some of those cans are several hundred yards away. First there will be rifle shooting for distance, then pistol shooting and a quick-draw contest."

Addy watched things being set up. The men lined up, and mass confusion reigned below them as men frantically waved money in the air shouting the names of their favorites. It took several minutes for things to calm down, and men crowded around the shooters, most behind Cole. One of the women behind her commented, "That's the man who rescued Mrs. Kane from the drunken miner the day of the march."

"He's quite handsome," another said.

"Still pretty much a stranger in town," Dresden Howard spoke up. "He sure does know how to use a gun, though."

"Yes, he *is* still rather an unknown," Ethel Brown said. The woman sat on the other side of Grant. "And yet he hurried right to Mrs. Kane's aid," she added, "as though he knew her."

Addy glanced at the woman, noticing that Grant was also

looking at her. It almost seemed as though they shared some kind of secret, and it gave her an uneasy feeling. "I assure you I do not know the man, other than the fact that he works for Grant," she told Ethel.

She turned her attention to the contest about to begin, little knowing that Grant was beginning to suspect something himself. He said nothing, but he watched Cole Parker, wondering if Addy had been too quick to defend the man and too quick to accent the fact that she did not know him. He realized that every time she had been with him in Cole's presence, she had seemed very distant and uneasy. He didn't want to think there could be any connection there. He liked Cole. He wouldn't want to have to run him out of town.

The contest began, and one by one, men dropped out as they missed their targets. Cole Parker never missed once, and it was difficult for Addy to keep from jumping up and cheering for him. She knew how much that five hundred dollars would mean to him . . . yet her heart tightened at the realization he was probably doing this for her, to add to his nest egg so they could be married some day.

Finally the rifle contest came down to Cole and one other man. The targets were set farther away and were only the size of small medicine bottles. The last contestant missed his mark. It was up to Cole. He positioned his rifle, nestling it into his shoulder. Addy was surprised he could still do so well after his head injury, but he seemed undaunted—or perhaps just damned determined. The scar across the right side of his head was still fresh but uncovered. It reminded her how close he'd come to getting killed.

He aimed carefully, squeezed the trigger. The little bottle disappeared. Addy rejoiced inwardly. Men cheered and hats flew into the air. Next would be shooting with pistols. Addy had no doubt how it would turn out. Again other men went down in defeat. People began to whisper and mumble. Who was Cole Parker? Story was he had always been good with a rifle, had hunted all his life, so he said. But to be that good with a pis-

tol—he apparently had a natural talent for it. When he took the
final shot, the crowd roared, and men began collecting their bets.
They surrounded Cole. Grant joined them, yelling he'd take bets
on whether or not Cole could draw and shoot and shatter a beer
mug once it was dropped before it hit the ground.

Men quickly held up their money, many betting against Cole
and Grant. They didn't believe such a thing could be done. Grant
promised Cole a percentage of his winnings, and Cole glanced
up at the platform. Addy could feel his eyes on her for a moment
before he finally agreed to the challenge.

More bets were made. A volunteer was chosen to hold out
the beer mug, and people cleared away from behind Cole, who
stepped back, his six-gun in its holster. The air hung with tension
and excitement, and the crowd quieted to a surprising level.

"I'll count to three," the man with the beer mug told Cole.
"Just remember to hit the mug and not me."

Chuckles rippled through the crowd.

"I don't think you have to worry about that after what we've
seen today, Jerry," one man shouted.

More laughter.

Cole pushed his suit coat behind his holster and concentrated.
"Go ahead," he told Jerry. "Let's get this over with."

Jerry nodded. He waited a moment, then counted. "One . . .
two . . ." The moment he said three he let go, and in that same
moment Cole Parker's gun was drawn and fired. The beer mug
shattered just before it hit the ground.

The crowd went wild, men slapping Cole on the back, some
collecting money from others. Some left to continue on with
contests between miners, while Grant gathered a fistful of
money. He counted it out, three hundred dollars. He gave Cole
a hundred. "Good job, my man," he said, slapping Cole on the
back.

Cole looked up at Addy again, and she could not help feelings
of pride and desire. She would congratulate him later . . . when
they danced.

Twenty-four

The evening air was filled with the smell of beef roasting over half barrels filled with smoldering wood embers, and with the sound of music. Central's City Council was determined that their annual picnic would be nothing short of first class, and a small orchestra had been brought up from Denver. There would be no amateur fiddlers here, only the best; ten musicians ground out waltzes and occasionally a peppier tune on violins and a bass fiddle. A huge platform had been built right in the middle of Main Street where people could dance, but around the corner on Eureka and down on Lawrence Street the saloons were open, and those who had been drinking and partying all day were in no mood for waltzes. There could be heard the raucous piano playing and screeching laughter of those too drunk to appreciate the finer music. Amateur fiddlers, banjo players and piano players pounded out ripping tunes that fit the mood of hard-working miners ready to let loose and forget about the dangers they encountered every day in order to line the pockets of Central's elite with gold.

There Cole continued to accept the wild congratulations of those who had seen him shoot earlier in the day, many of whom had won money on him. Cole tried to refrain from too much drinking, although his first instinct was to down enough whiskey to pass out and forget about that dance with Addy that was promised to him. A little voice told him to stay away from Addy Kane tonight. She'd been with Grant Breckenridge all day, and they looked quite the happy couple. He had never seen Addy look more beautiful, and he couldn't help wondering if she'd done herself up like that for him, or for Grant.

Stay away from it, he warned himself. *Grant Breckenridge can give her the world on a golden platter.* Trouble was, he was also likely to hurt her, cheat on her. Grant would never love her the way Cole could. Was she getting more interested in Grant, or just biding her time, waiting for him like she'd promised? He'd won a lot of money today, and his nest egg was growing fast, but he couldn't help still believing maybe it was too late for him to go back to the life he'd once known.

He downed a shot of whiskey. The Hard Luck was packed with celebrating miners preparing to go out and stuff themselves on roast beef that was now being sliced and laid out on platters on long tables set up in the streets. He turned and watched the fun for a few minutes. Although Sassy and her girls had kept their promise not to continue the prostitution, tonight they were wild and wicked. Sassy herself danced on a table, lifting her skirts to the whistles and cheers of men. Some of the other girls were being passed around like hot potatoes, laughing and screaming at the kisses and fondling.

It was a madhouse, but Cole could not bring himself to get involved in the wild celebrating. He was too full of indecision and turmoil, too full of thoughts of Addy Kane. If he was going to have that dance, he figured he'd better get himself over to where the milder citizens of the town were waltzing and chatting. The problem was, how could he *really* talk to Addy there? It would be impossible, and he had to know what she was really feeling, if she still intended to wait for him. He was sick to death of the uncertainty of their relationship, tired of being torn between.

He loved her, damn it! That was what it boiled down to, no matter how much he fought it. He was in love with Addy Kane, and he was going to tell her, flat out ask her to marry him. If he went over there and danced with her, they could secretly make arrangements to meet alone somewhere, although he knew deep in his belly that if he got her alone he'd want to do more than

talk. He'd gone too long without Addy in his bed. He wanted
her in that bed every night, but that couldn't happen until they
made up their minds they belonged together. For the sake of her
job they would have to take this slow, and that meant the sooner
he got started, the sooner she could be his wife.

A drunken miner offered him another shot of whiskey, but
he refused. He walked out and headed around the corner and up
Main Street.

Addy whirled gracefully around the platform with Grant, to
the soft music of violins. It was a beautiful night, surprisingly
warm and calm for the season. In the distance she could hear
the celebrating of Central's wilder side. Cole was surely there,
probably getting drunk, maybe rousting about with some whore.
He still hadn't come for that dance and he probably did not
intend to. She wanted, needed to talk to him, needed to know if
he still wanted her to wait for him.

She forced herself to pay attention to Grant and not keep
looking down the street to see if Cole was coming. She shouldn't
seem anxious to have a dance with a gunman, but now she
wanted that dance badly. She felt a secret pride and a rush of
desire at the performance Cole had put on today. Everyone talked
about it, and not a few women had commented on Cole's handsome face and physique. Addy had carefully avoided mentioning
him at all, had tried to give her full attention to Grant; but it was
getting harder and harder to pretend that Cole Parker was nothing more than an acquaintance, that he meant nothing to her.

Her mind was made up. If Cole still wanted her to wait for
him, if he wanted to marry her, they would find a way to make
it happen. She couldn't fight these feelings any longer.

"I was afraid there might be trouble today from Ed Foley,"
Grant said as the dance finished.

"Thank goodness there *was* no trouble," Addy answered. *For
Cole's sake,* she thought.

Grant led her off the platform and down two steps to a table where beef was being laid out on silver platters. Hired help sliced the meat and served it up on china plates. This particular table was set with fine dishes and silverware, and couples lined up for a feast. Susan and Dresden Howard stood behind Grant and Addy, and Grant turned to talk to Dresden while they waited in line.

"Have you heard any talk in the store about Ed Foley?" he asked. "I'm surprised he wasn't around today making trouble."

Dresden stuck his thumbs in the small pockets of his satin vest. "Word is he went to Denver with a few of his cohorts. I guess they're going to look for work there."

Grant frowned. "That sounds too good to be true."

Dresden shrugged. "Well, that's the way I heard it."

Grant turned and picked up a plate, holding it out for a slice of beef. "He's up to something," he commented to Addy.

"In Denver? What harm could he possibly bring, being that far away?"

"I don't know, but he'll be back, mark my word. Maybe he still thinks he can do something legally, the fool." He picked up a slice of fresh-baked bread. "Aren't you going to eat?"

"I'm not hungry," Addy answered, taking no food. How could she eat when she was so torn inside over Cole?

"Mr. Parker!" she heard Hester exclaim. Addy's heart took a leap at the words, and she glanced past Grant to see Cole approaching.

"Ah, the man who made me much richer today," Grant said, following her gaze. "Come share some food with us, Cole."

Addy noticed several of the women stare at Cole behind their husband's backs. Even Ethel Brown gave him an appreciative once-over. The handsome, able Cole Parker was building quite a reputation, and it warmed Addy's heart to see him being accepted by these people, some of whom had already mentioned they thought he'd make a good lawman for Central. She suppressed a smile at the irony of it.

"Came for that dance, did you?" Grant told him.

Cole stepped closer, glancing at Addy. She saw by his eyes

that he liked the way she looked tonight, and she in turn thought how wonderfully handsome he looked in the black suit he wore. She had never seen him dressed like this.

"Well, a promise is a promise," Cole answered Grant.

Grant chuckled. "I didn't figure you'd pass up the chance to do a few turns with the prettiest lady in Central. We're taking a little break here to eat. Fill up your plate, Cole. We have tables all set up with chairs and even candelabras for fine dining right out here in the street." He waited for Cole to get a plate of food, and they walked over to sit down.

"You're not eating?" Cole asked Addy.

"I'm not really hungry," she answered. Their gaze held for a moment, and she could see Cole understood her loss of appetite. The night suddenly seemed strangely unreal, and everything seemed to be moving too slowly. Others gathered at the table, praising Cole for his shooting skills, asking how he had come to be so good with guns. "Started hunting with a rifle when I was only ten," she heard him say. She kept her eyes averted, not wanting Grant to see her gaze at Cole longingly. ". . . the war . . ."

"Which side?" someone asked.

There was a moment of hesitation. "Gray," he answered.

"Oh, dear," Hester muttered.

"Well, the West is filled with men from both sides," Lee Brown put in. "The war is behind us now, and whatever side a man fought for, he can't be blamed for it now. Let's not get into talking about that God-awful time. Let's talk about the future, *Central's* future!"

Everyone agreed, and someone asked Cole if he would ever consider becoming a deputy under Sheriff Watson.

"I'm not sure yet what I want to do, other than continue to work for Mr. Breckenridge here," Cole answered wisely. "I'm still a little restless and unsettled."

He didn't mention losing his family.

"Yes, don't be so anxious to take away one of my best men," Grant told the others.

People laughed, and the small orchestra of violins began another waltz. Addy felt removed from reality as Grant said something about it being time for Cole to have his dance. She felt Cole's presence, felt him take her arm. "May I?" he asked.

Addy looked up into his handsome face. "Certainly." She rose and stepped up onto the platform, and Cole put a hand to her waist and took hold of her right hand with his left one. "I'm not real good at this," he told her.

Their gaze held. "You'll do fine."

Cole began turning her to the music, and a few other couples joined them. Addy could feel Grant watching them. She struggled at casual conversation, telling him she'd heard Ed Foley had gone to Denver. Cole said he'd heard the same and was glad to see him go. All the while they talked, each could read the questions in the other's eyes, and both began to feel desperate to figure out a way to talk alone. They hadn't had the chance since the day he'd stolen a kiss in the alley and asked her to wait for him.

Addy finally took an opportunity to say something without others hearing. "My house," she said. "Later tonight. Back door."

Cole felt a rush of desire. She wasn't inviting him just for a talk. He wanted to grab her close right there, taste her mouth. "I'll be there."

"I smell whiskey. No more drinking between now and then."

Cole grinned. "Promise."

The dance ended, and Cole bowed politely. "Thank you, Mrs. Kane." He took her arm and led her back to Grant. "And thank you for allowing me the dance."

"I keep my promises," Grant answered. He shook hands with Cole, but an odd suspicion was beginning to form in his mind. He couldn't quite forget the remarks by some of the women after the incident during the march that Cole seemed to know Addy. Tonight, watching them dance together, the way they had looked at each other . . . Addy again seemed strangely quiet and reserved. It struck him she was always that way when Cole was around.

Cole left them, and Addy took Grant's arm, smiling for him. "I'm getting really tired. It's been a long day," she told him "Could you drive me home now?"

He patted her hand. "Of course." He called out to his driver, who sat waiting up the street with a carriage, and he decided he couldn't put it off any longer. He had to ask Addy Kane about the abduction, find out the truth.

Grant helped Addy out of the carriage in front of her house, then walked with her up onto the front porch, where a lantern hung to keep the area lit at night. "Addy, I have to talk to you about something. May I come inside for a few minutes?"

Addy glanced at the driver. "I don't know—"

"Old Henry won't say anything, and I mean nothing disrespectful. I just want our conversation to be private."

Addy opened her handbag and fished out her key. "I suppose it's all right." What on earth did he want? She couldn't tell if he was angry about something, or if perhaps he simply wanted a chance to do something she'd rather he didn't try. Or maybe he was getting even more serious, was going to ask her to marry him. What on earth would she tell him?

They walked into the small main room, and Grant closed the front door while Addy lit another oil lamp. She turned to face him, leaving on her hat and gloves, afraid to let things get too casual. "What is it, Grant?" She wished she could better read his eyes.

"I am afraid I have been made aware of something that needs explaining. I don't mean to embarrass you, but . . . well, Mrs. Brown did some further investigating into your background in Unionville."

Addy felt a prickle of alarm, and her heartbeat quickened. Instantly she thought of Cole. She had to protect him, keep her story straight. "I am not surprised that Ethel Brown tried to dig up something terrible about me. She has never liked me, and I have no idea why."

Grant snickered. "Look, in the mirror. You're beautiful, popular, educated. Men want you." His gaze moved over her with a look Addy had never seen before. It frightened her. "Women like Ethel Brown are jealous of that." He sighed. "That doesn't matter at the moment. What matters is what she found out."

"About the bank robbery?" Addy decided to head him off. If she was open about it right away, it might help him believe she wasn't hiding anything. His eyebrows arched in surprise.

"Yes. Why didn't you tell us?"

"I wasn't sure how it would be accepted. Besides, I wanted to just forget about it. Nothing terrible happened to me, as I am sure you and anyone else who knows must be wondering. I did get knocked around a bit, out of pure meanness, but I was never . . . abused in any other way." She felt her cheeks growing hot. "I was only taken as a hostage because having me with them gave them something to threaten the law with. Once they got to their hiding place, a small cabin in the deep woods of western Kentucky, they merely asked me to cook for them." She took a deep breath to stay calm. "Later they . . . began drinking. They of course began thinking about . . . other things they could do with me. But one of them, a man named Nick Coleman, had been shot by one of his own gang members during the robbery and left behind in town. Somehow he escaped and managed to make it to the cabin just in time. Although wounded himself, he barged in just in time and stopped the leader of the gang, Jack Slater, from . . . taking advantage of me. There was a shootout, and although Slater was wounded he managed to shoot Nick Coleman dead. He had the other two men with him bury Mr. Coleman, and I tended Slater's wounds."

She finally began removing her gloves, telling herself she must appear confident and casual. He had to believe her story, and at least it was true she had not been raped. If Grant and the others thought that, they might take away her teaching job. Ugly rumors would be spread. "After the shooting incident and Slater being wounded, the excitement was gone. They left me alone after that. They were afraid Coleman had been followed by the law, since he was already wounded and had arrived on a stolen horse. They needed to get themselves into Indian Territory, where it's easy for outlaws to hide, I'm told. They decided that having me along would only slow them down. Besides that, they hoped that if they let me go, sent me back to town with the stolen horse, maybe the law would give up the chase. So that's what they did. They took me as far as they could without being caught themselves, then rode out for Indian Territory. I found my way back to Unionville, shaken and bruised but not . . . not raped." She faced Grant boldly. "I have no way of proving any of it. You will simply have to take my word. Certainly none of it was my fault, but if you and the council choose not to believe me—"

Cole put up his hand. "Now, now, don't jump to conclusions. What most disturbs me is that one of those outlaws might have followed you here."

A ripple of shock rushed through Addy, which she struggled not to show. "What! Why on earth would you think that?" Cole! She had to protect Cole! Grant was studying her intently, a hint of anger returning to his eyes. Addy scrambled to think straight, telling herself to stay calm.

"Because John Withers told Ethel Brown that you met some man out behind Miss Ada's the night of your reception, after you got home. He thought he heard some kind of argument, said you seemed upset. Did you lie about not knowing anyone here in Central? Is there some man in your life I don't know about, or is some man perhaps threatening you? Harassing you? Sheriff Page wrote that two of the men, a Ted Sloan and Cal something, were both killed in a later bank robbery, but the third man, Jack Slater, was never seen or heard from after Unionville. Maybe he followed you out here. If you're having troubles because of him, I can take care of it."

Addy turned away, her mind awhirl. Cal and Ted were dead! They could never tell anyone the truth—that it was Jack Slater who'd been killed by Cole, not the other way around! She felt like celebrating and was anxious to tell Cole. But for the moment, she had some explaining to do.

"I've never run into Jack Slater," she answered Grant. "That night after the reception, it was just some drunk," she lied. "I went outside because it was a beautiful night. You can see down on the city from Miss Ada's. The moon was full, and I could see the outline of the mountains. All that is quite new to me, you know. And after the reception, meeting so many new people, I had a lot to think about." She faced him again. "Some drunken miner was just wandering around, seemingly lost. He spotted me and began making rude remarks. I told him to please leave, but he argued, tried to kiss me, that sort of thing. I managed to get away from him and run back inside. I was quite upset."

Grant frowned. "Why didn't you tell anyone?"

Addy hated lying. One lie usually led to another and another and eventually to disaster. "I was afraid to. I was brand new to town, and all the people I had met were Central's most important people. I didn't want to begin my stay here by making trouble. And it wouldn't have mattered anyway, because it was dark and he wore a hat low over his eyes. I could never in a million years identify the man. It was just a quick encounter in the dark and I got away, so I just left it alone. I knew he was just drunk and would probably not even remember it the next day. And you know how itinerant Central's population is. He might not even be around any more."

Grant studied her a moment longer, then nodded. "He didn't hurt you?"

"No."

Grant sighed, stepping closer. "And it's true about the abduction? You weren't manhandled sexually?"

Addy felt embarrassed, but she was glad not to have to lie about something. "It's true. Do you really think that if all three of those men had . . . had done such a thing, I could have recovered so quickly and come west? It was a long, arduous and dangerous journey. If I had suffered something so horrible, I couldn't have packed my bags within the week and headed for a place where I knew no one, had no friends. I would have felt like—like I belonged among Sassy Dillon and her women. I couldn't have considered teaching, even though none of it would have been my fault."

Grant grasped her shoulders. "Well, I'm relieved. I will assure Mrs. Brown of the same. We'll have to bring it before the board, but you needn't be there. I will explain the entire situation, including the incident with the drunk man outside Miss Ada's. It will all be cleared up, and in a couple of weeks you'll be teaching school. You'll show men like John Withers and Alfred Rhodes that you're as good as they are."

Addy smiled for him. "Thank you, Grant."

His eyes dropped to her bosom, then trailed up her neck to meet her own gaze again. "I had no doubts all along, but I needed to be sure before . . ." He pulled her close in a grip that frightened her a little. "Before I told you I'd like you to be my wife someday. I know you're in no rush for such things now. I'll give you time. But you're the most beautiful woman I've ever met, and the most intelligent. I want you, Addy. I can give a woman a life of elegance. You wouldn't even need to teach, but I know that's what you want to do, so I wouldn't mind, as long as you were home with me at night." He rubbed a hand over her back and leaned closer, but Addy pulled away.

"I'm sorry, Grant. I am flattered by your offer, but it's just like you said. I'm not ready to think seriously right now, and I—perhaps I've let our friendship go too far. Perhaps I have misled you." He had not said a word about loving her, just that he wanted her. She realized that Grant Breckenridge was also caught up in lies, if it was true he'd been to see Sassy Dillon several times, let alone whether or not he had swindled Ed Foley out of a mine. There was an arrogance and an obvious greed about the man that she knew would always stand in the way of her caring about him as a husband. She could kick herself for letting their friendship go this far. The man had power in this town, and now he had power over her. He could tell the school board whatever he wished, and she sensed he was already using his power to get what he wanted . . . Addy Kane in his bed, whether she liked it or not.

"Misled me?" he asked. "Surely you know where all of this has been headed."

"I wasn't sure. It started out with you helping me meet all the right people, and things just . . . I don't know . . . just kept going. You've been so kind and attentive, and I was lonely and knew no one." She swallowed. "I'm not saying there couldn't be more. I'm just saying that there have been so many changes in my life lately that it's difficult for me to think about anything as serious as marriage."

Grant nodded. "All right. I can understand that." He came closer again, gripped her arms. "I said I'd wait, but don't make me wait too long. You're beginning to haunt my dreams, Addy Kane." He jerked her close and planted his lips on her mouth. Addy stood in rigid surprise, thinking how cold and thin his lips were compared to Cole's full, warm kisses. "Maybe that will help you start thinking my way," he told her after releasing her from the kiss. "You just remember—what Grant Breckenridge wants, Grant Breckenridge gets, sooner or later." He patted her cheek. "Anybody bothers you again, you tell me and I'll take care of it." He glanced down at her breasts again, and Addy suddenly felt naked, and angry. What made him think he had a right to grab her close and kiss her like that or make such forceful remarks? Suddenly she couldn't wait to be held in Cole Parker's embrace.

"I'll remember that," she answered.

Grant smiled, rubbing her arms a moment before turning to leave. "Keep your doors locked. Maybe we'll have dinner tomorrow night. I'd like to tell you more about my son, since you'll be meeting him soon."

He walked out, and Addy hurried over and locked the front door, breathing a sigh of relief and turning to lean her back against the door. She had let all this get out of hand. If only she hadn't already signed a teaching contract. If only she didn't feel so obligated to abide by that contract and so beholden to all the people who had backed her, paid her expenses, built her this house. She and Cole could just leave Central and start over someplace new, but she had so many responsibilities to answer to here. If Grant would just leave her alone, she could put up with the rest while she waited for Cole. Things just kept getting more complicated all the time.

She walked away from the door and into her bedroom, where she angrily removed her hat and threw it into a chair. The house was warm enough that she didn't have to build a fire, so she walked back into the empty main room and paced, arguing the pros and cons of both Grant and Cole, and of staying in Central to teach.

That was all it was supposed to be in the beginning—just a journey out of the past and into a new life, a chance to finally teach. If only things could have remained that simple. If only Cole Parker hadn't ridden into her life.

Someone tapped on the back door then, and a tight feeling came into her chest. She had just gotten rid of one man, turned down a marriage proposal from one of the richest men in Central. Now there was another man here to see her, another man who wanted to settle with her. He drank too much, had lived as an outlaw, was worth only what he had been able to earn by using guns. For the moment he had nothing to give her, and yet he was the man she ached for, the only man she wanted in her bed at night.

"You're insane, Addy Kane," she grumbled as she walked into the kitchen. Against her better judgment she opened the door, and there he stood, still dressed in that striking black suit. "Cole."

He swept her up into his arms and kicked the door shut.

Twenty-five

"Don't let go," Addy wept. "I've been so confused and lonely."

Cole held her tight against his broad chest. "It's been the same for me," he answered in a near whisper. "I love you, Addy. Damn it, I love you. I can't fight these feelings any longer."

Their lips met in a hot, hungry kiss, Addy held so tightly in his arms that she was lifted, her feet not even touching the floor. She relished the feel of his strong arms around her, the wonderful sense of safety and protection it gave her.

He moved his lips to her eyes and her hair. She nuzzled his neck, enjoying the familiar scent of him. "It was so hard coming to visit you and not being able to hold you. I thought we'd get there and find you dead! I've tried to deny my own feelings for you, Cole, but it's impossible."

Cole breathed a sigh of relief. He'd been so afraid she would do the reasonable thing and give her heart to the man who could give her anything she wanted, the man who could make her a queen of society. But here she was, in his arms. For the first time in years he knew with certainty he could love again, wanted a family again.

Addy in turn knew she could never experience these feelings with Grant Breckenridge. He could never make her feel so alive, so in love, so full of near-painful passion. She'd nearly lost Cole, and the experience had awakened her to the reality of her needs and feelings. Dangerous as he could be, a man tortured by a past that left him unpredictable at times, she still had to have Cole Parker for herself.

"I need you, Addy," he groaned, bending down and licking at her cheek, her throat.

Torturous desire surged through her blood. "Then take what you need," she sighed.

He threw his hat on the table and picked her up in his arms. Addy nestled into his shoulder as he carried her into the bedroom, easy to find in the tiny house. He laid her on the brass bed, and both realized how this had always been so easy and natural for them. That had to mean something. It only seemed right that a woman should feel a little lust for the man she loved and wanted to marry, only in Cole's case it was more than a little lust. Something about him turned her into a woman of unbridled passion.

She groaned at the delicious feel of Cole's hand fondling her breasts, moving to her throat to unbutton the top of her bodice. They had only the light of the lantern that was lit in the outer room, but it was just enough to lend a magic to the moment, just enough darkness that they didn't have to look each other in the eyes in bold light and face reality. Neither of them wanted to do that, to think of the consequences this night could bring them, to figure out how they could truly be together, what she should do about her teaching position, how he was going to find a truly settled job.

None of that mattered. Only this mattered . . . Cole's hand slipping over the cutout of her dress that showed just enough flesh to entice a man . . . more buttons being undone . . . her dress coming open, Cole's lips at her throat, the whites of her breasts. Oh, how she had ached for this, Cole's hand reaching inside her camisole, pushing out a full breast, taking her firm nipple into his mouth and tasting it hungrily. She grasped his hair and pushed against him, wanting him to take more of her. In one quick moment he was able to bring her to this kind of wanton passion, and she could not bring herself to be ashamed of it.

Cole moaned with painful need, relishing again the taste and feel of her. So beautiful this woman was, this Addy Kane who looked so much like Bethanne, who had come into his life through the incredible circumstance of a bank robbery twelve hundred miles away, in another world, in a painful past he was determined to leave behind forever.

He unlaced her camisole and pushed it open, caressed her full, firm breasts, wanting to devour her, to be inside of her and show her for once and for all to whom she belonged. He met her mouth again, cupping a breast in his hand, enjoying its incredible softness, teasing her nipple with his thumb.

Addy felt wild with need, again surprised at her own boldness. "I want to feel you against me, Cole, like back in Abilene." How long ago had that been? Sometimes it seemed like years, yet it had only been a little over two months. Their liaison in the shed at the stage station had been quick and necessary, more of a good-bye. But in Abilene they had lain completely naked, spent the night together, and there had been something special about it that could not be forgotten or ignored. She wanted that something special again, wanted to lie naked against Cole Parker's own virile body.

She sat up and let Cole pull her dress off her shoulders, then remove her camisole and toss it to the floor. It felt wonderful to let his dark eyes drink in the sight of her bare breasts. He caressed them lovingly. Another kiss, burning hot. She flung her arms around his neck and pulled him back down, both of them smiling, almost crying while they kissed. He pulled away from her long enough to remove his suit jacket, his string tie. Addy sat back up and unbuttoned his shirt, and he pulled it out of his pants and threw it aside. "Don't you go away," he told her teasingly.

He got up and removed his gunbelt, and as much as she originally thought she hated guns and his outlaw ways, she realized that those things had also attracted her to this desperado. But now it was simply Cole Parker she loved and wanted. She waited as he sat down on the bed and removed his boots, removed his pants, his longjohns. He undressed with furious speed, and as each layer came off, more and more of his splendid body was revealed, until he stood before her with bare, muscular shoulders, the dark hairs on his chest leading down to his slender waist and slim hips, his muscular thighs. She looked into his dark eyes, and Cole moved back onto the bed.

Addy lay back and let him finish undressing her . . . shoes, stockings, dress, petticoats, drawers. Finally she lay there naked and unafraid . . . unashamed. He leaned down, and she closed her eyes as his full lips caressed her belly, then moved back up, to linger at her breasts. She moaned with pleasure as he tasted them with sweet passion while his fingers gently fondled secret places, drawing her fully under his spell until she had to quell an urge to cry out with utter delight.

She told herself she had to be quiet. They still must keep this a secret, but now more than ever she wanted it to be forever, to be his wife and not have to worry about being discovered. Surely they would find a way. Then she could no longer think. She grasped his hair, moaned his name, and quickly a pulsating climax ripped through her loins, making her literally groan with the need of a man inside of her, knowing no man could fulfill that need better than Cole Parker could.

Quickly his lips found her throat, her mouth. He buried himself inside of her in one quick, hard thrust that made her gasp. He moved in furious rhythm then, rocking her body, overpowering her in every way until she felt limp from desire and ecstasy. He raised up to his knees, looked down at her like the conqueror that he was, grasped her hips and groaned as his life spilled into her with unexpected quickness. He closed his eyes and held himself there for a quiet moment, then breathed deeply to relax.

"I'm sorry," he told her, "but I needed you so badly." He leaned down there, resting his elbows on either side of her. "We'll do it again. We'll do this all night." He met her mouth again before she could even reply, and Addy returned his kiss with hungry fervor. Already she could feel his hot shaft growing harder again. He was a wild, passionate man, and this part of him was as big and wild as the rest of him. She could think of

nothing more wonderful than spending the night with Cole
Parker in her bed.

The night moved in dreamlike joy, and Addy had never been
more aware of her womanliness, nor of her own needs and
passions. This time it was more than just lust and loneliness.
This time there seemed to be more meaning to their lovemaking. It was truly more an act of love than it had been before,
two people needing to share more than bodies, needing more
than just one night of relief from loneliness and confusion.
This was a sharing of spirit, of hearts, and it had to be right.
How could it not be when a man brought out such desire and
happiness in a woman?

Dawn was beginning to light the room a little more. Was this
the third or fourth time they had made love? They had slept only
a little while, and now she had let him roll her on top of him.
She rode him like the magnificent stallion that he was, grasping
his powerful arms for support, feeling no doubts that whatever
pleased this man, it was right. She had never dreamed she would
be able to do some of the bold things Cole inspired within her.
Part of it was a desire to be wild and please him as any prostitute
would, but unlike Sassy and her kind, there was only one man
with whom she could ever do these things. She could never let
another man touch her, knew now she could not be married to
Grant Breckenridge, could not begin to imagine doing such
things with Grant. She was not sure she would want to live if
anything happened to Cole.

He grasped her hips and helped her move, their lovemaking
lasting a pleasurably long time since that first, quick act that
they had both needed so desperately. Now they could take their
time, and they could not get enough of each other. Cole rolled
her onto her back again, surged inside of her with sweet rhythm
and in circular movements that made her feel crazy with need.
Cole Parker was as good in bed as he was with a gun. Finally
he moved in quick thrusts that made her cry out his name, before

his life again spilled into her. He groaned with his own pleasure, then wilted beside her, their bodies slick with perspiration and neither of them caring.

Addy settled into his shoulder. "I don't want you to go."

"We have no choice for now."

"I know." She lay there enjoying the quiet moment, then decided she had no choice but to tell him about her earlier conversation with Grant. She raised up on one elbow and looked down at him. "I have to tell you, Grant found out about my abduction."

The love and happiness in Cole's eyes turned to alarm. "What!"

Addy sighed, laying back down and toying with the hairs on his chest. "That nosey Ethel Brown. She doesn't like me. Apparently the night you came to me after my reception, the schoolteacher, John Withers, who then lived at Miss Ada's, saw me go out, heard me arguing with a man. He told Ethel. She decided I knew some man here in town, and she thought she should check out my background even more. She sent a letter to the sheriff at Unionville, then showed the reply to Grant, and he questioned me about it. They thought perhaps I'd been . . . raped. In the eyes of someone like Ethel, I would have been too soiled to teach little children, even though it wouldn't have been my fault."

She could feel his tension building. "Did Grant believe your story?"

"I told him the same story I told the sheriff back at Unionville, and he thinks the one called Nick Coleman is dead. He seemed to believe me when I told him I wasn't raped. I explained that the reason I told no one was because I was afraid it would affect their opinion of me, and because I had been through so much on my trip west that I just didn't have the heart or the energy to bring it up. I didn't want to have to explain."

Cole caressed her hair. "How did you explain about arguing with some man in the middle of the night?"

"I just told him I'd gone out to relax and think and be alone when some drunken miner stumbled out of the darkness and made advances."

Cole grinned. "Well, a drunk *did* stumble out of the darkness and try to make advances."

Addy laughed lightly. "You weren't drunk, and you didn't stumble."

They kissed one another, then Cole stroked her hair as he spoke. "I'm glad your abduction is out in the open. Explanations have been given and this should be the end of it. Now you can concentrate on your teaching in a couple of weeks, and while you're doing that, I'll be working hard at getting settled, saving my money, earning some respect. A lot of people in this town like me. I think I could do well, maybe as a gunsmith. What do you think of that?"

Addy kissed his cheek. "I think it's a good idea. It's wonderful to hear you have made some decisions. This all just might work, Cole. One good thing came out of Ethel Brown's nosiness. In Sheriff Page's reply, he said Ted Sloan and Cal Arden had been killed in another bank robbery in Missouri. There is no one left now to tell the law you aren't dead."

Cole moved to rest his elbows on either side of her. He leaned down and kissed her eyes. "Then maybe we really can be free." His eyes grew misty. "I love you, Addy Kane. I saw a little girl not long ago, about Patty's age when she—" He closed his eyes for a moment. "It made me want a family again. If we do this right, we can be together for good. I'll get myself established as a hard-working business owner, start inviting you out, let the public see us together as though we only met since coming here. You can begin seeing less of Grant, let him down easy. We *can* make it work, eventually get married. I don't care if you want to keep teaching . . ." He kissed her lightly. "Except that you'll have to take time off to have our babies."

Addy studied his dark, handsome eyes. Yes, he really meant it this time, but there was still the problem of how to make Grant understand she was not interested in marrying him. "It won't be easy getting away from Grant. He told me last night that he wanted to marry me."

Alarm and anger came into Cole's eyes. "What did you tell him?"

"I said I couldn't make that kind of decision now, that I was sorry, but I consider us simply friends. He didn't like my answer, and there was a look in his eyes that frightened me a little. Grant Breckenridge doesn't like to be crossed or turned down." She decided not to tell him about the forced kiss. "We will have to be careful. I don't want him angry with you, and the last thing we want is for him to suspect we already knew each other."

Cole frowned with concern. "I'll have to get started on my own business, then quit my job with him, put some distance between us. While I'm doing that, you begin turning down his invitations. School will start soon. You can use that as an excuse; you're too busy and too tired; you want to concentrate on your teaching for a while." He sighed and lay down beside her again. "Or we could both leave Central, go to Denver or go even farther west and start over together."

"I thought about that, but a lot of people here have a big investment in me. I feel I owe them by doing what I came here to do. Besides that, I would have no good explanation for why I would suddenly want to depart after telling them how happy I am to have been hired, to be able to teach. Why would I leave, with no job prospects, no money to settle on my own? Grant would be very suspicious. He could even have me followed. If you also suddenly quit his employ and left, and he found us together someplace else, he'd do more investigating, I'm sure of it. You could still end up in trouble. I think staying here and taking it slow is much safer than both of us suddenly leaving Central."

"You're probably right." Cole pulled her closer. "But if we're going to take it slow, then we're going to have to find ways to be alone together like this."

She reached up and traced her fingers over his dark brows. "I love you, Cole. I don't think I told you yet."

He grinned. "Oh, I think you did a pretty damn good job of showing it."

"Did I? Am I as good as those fancy ladies in town?"

"Much better." He turned and met her mouth in a warm, delicious kiss. "I'd better leave pretty quick before your neighbors wake up. One of them might see me sneaking out your back door." In the next moment he gently pushed inside of her, both of them knowing they had to do this one more time before he would have to go. This time they made love quietly, gently, relishing every touch, every kiss, every deep thrust, glorying in the relief of having made a decision, a commitment, a promise. Their union held a beauty and fulfillment it had not held before.

"Stay there while I wash and dress," Cole said with a deep sigh when he finished. He walked over to the washstand, and Addy pulled the covers over herself, wanting to cry at the thought of his having to leave.

"It will be so wonderful when we can do this and then get up together and I can cook your breakfast, when we can be together every night."

Cole picked up a bar of soap and poured water from a pitcher into a wash bowl. "Yeah." He was worried. It made him uneasy to think of Grant Breckenridge investigating Addy's abduction, asking questions, getting names. He hoped the man wouldn't begin piecing things together—Nick Coleman, Cole Parker . . . a stranger comes to town at the same time as Addy, and he's good with guns. Had the sheriff back in Illinois described any of the men? What if he got a description of Nick Coleman, tall dark, quick with guns, a scar across his forehead at the hairline? It was the damn scar that would give it away. All he could do was hope Grant wouldn't look into it any further. He decided not to tell Addy his fears. The night had been too perfect, and he didn't want to spoil it.

He began dressing, and Addy rose and walked behind the curtain to wash, setting aside Cole's used water and putting a clean bowl on the stand. "Don't leave before I'm through," she told him.

"I won't."

She hated this, couldn't wait until they could be together this way forever. She quickly washed and then pulled on a robe. She brushed the tangles from her hair, decided to wait to dress after Cole was gone. She came out from behind the curtain to find him fully dressed, sitting on the bed and smoking. His dark eyes moved over her, and already both knew they would rather make love again.

"Come here," he told her.

Addy walked closer. He untied the robe, pulled it open, kissed the little valleys between her thighs and that secret place that belonged to Cole Parker now. No man had ever been so intimate with her. "You smell good." He kissed her belly. Addy leaned over and offered her breasts, and he sucked on them gently, massaged them lovingly. Their mouths met in a wet, delicious kiss, and Cole moved his hands over her nakedness. He pulled her onto his lap, kissing her hungrily again. He left her mouth and kissed her throat. "I'd better go before we end up in bed all over again," he told her. "We—"

Someone knocked at her front door then, and Addy straightened in surprise. She jumped up and closed and tied her robe. "Who on earth—"

"Shut the bedroom door and go answer it," Cole told her. "But first to go the kitchen and get my hat and throw it in here. I left it on the table last night." Their eyes held in alarm.

Addy turned and ran into the kitchen, picking up his hat and tossing it into the bedroom. Cole closed the door while Addy walked to the front door to ask who was there.

"It's me, Hester," came the reply. "Something has happened I thought you should know about. We aren't sure whether to celebrate or be sorry."

Addy frowned in wonder. "I'm not dressed, Hester. I was just taking a sink bath."

"It's just me, dear. I'll only be a minute. I'm sorry to disturb you this way, but the entire town is in a tizzy."

Addy glanced back at her bedroom door. Everything seemed

in order. She just hoped she didn't look too flushed herself. At least she had already washed. She opened the door, and Hester stepped inside, seeming embarrassed at seeing Addy so "undone."

"I'm so sorry, dear, but an awful thing has happened. Last night, what with all the celebrating and drinking, a few men got into some kind of row over at the Hard Luck saloon and they ended up shooting at each other. One bullet went astray and hit Sassy Dillon. They say she's dying!"

Addy drew in her breath, glancing at the bedroom door. "Sassy?" She thought about the day Sassy had come to her to tell her she should make up her mind to be Cole's woman. She had only been trying to help, was apparently a good friend to Cole. "Who shot her?"

"No one knows for sure, and one of the men in the shootout is dead, the other dying. It could have been either one of them. Some folks say that if that gunman who works for her, Cole Parker, that man Grant allowed you one dance with last night, had been there, maybe it wouldn't have happened. He wasn't there, and no one is sure where he went, or where he is now. He isn't at the rooming house where he lives. They're looking all over for him, because apparently Sassy Dillon is asking to see him before she dies."

"Oh, my. I wonder where Mr. Parker could be."

"I don't know, but I'm sure they'll find him. In the meantime, we women are having a gathering at my house in two hours to discuss this. Sassy was well liked by all the miners, of course. Funerals for such women are often quite large in towns like this. We want to decide whether or not we should buy flowers out of Denver to be thrown on her grave. She was, of course, a most shameful woman, but if she dies, she will become one of Central's most colorful figures. By putting flowers at her grave we can show that we were not hateful or trying to hurt Sassy Dillon as a person. We simply wanted the practice of prostitution to end." Hester patted Addy's arm. "You get dressed and come up to the house, dear."

"I will."

"Did you have a good time last night? You and Grant make such a handsome couple, you know."

Addy glanced at the bedroom door again. "I had a very good time last night." Poor Cole. He was close to Sassy. He must be going crazy with the need to get to her . . . and suffering guilt over her death. *Could* he have stopped it? After what happened to Patty, thinking he should have been able to help her, this would be very hard on him.

She thanked Hester, who finally left. She closed the door, and Cole opened the bedroom door and stepped out. "You heard?" she asked. He came closer, and Addy could see tears in his eyes. "Cole, you are not to blame for anyone's death, not even Patty's. I hope you don't blame *me* for this . . . for keeping you here last night."

He shook his head. "How could I blame you for that? That's the most happiness I've know for a long time, but we have a lot of waiting to do if we're ever going to be able to be together for good." He pulled her into his arms, and Addy felt his grief. "She was a good woman, Addy. There were things about her you didn't know, and there were reasons why she ended up living like she did. She never really had a choice."

"But why—"

"I'll explain later." He leaned down and kissed her gently.

"I'm so sorry, Cole. What will you tell them about where you've been?"

He sighed, wiping quickly at his eyes. "I don't know. Maybe that I was tired and turned in at the rooming house before anybody else was through partying and left early this morning to go walking alone. I didn't bring Shadow up here because I didn't want anyone to see my horse tied anywhere nearby. They've probably already checked the stables to see if he was there." He sighed, kissing the top of her head. "I'll take the long way around getting back down to town, make sure nobody sees me in this area."

Their eyes met, and both felt an uneasiness that made them

anxious. Could this really work after all? Was it all just a dream? "We can do this, Addy," he said, determination in his eyes. "You have to believe that. I'm sorry I have to leave, and doubly sorry I have to leave to go to a woman like Sassy, but she's been a good friend."

"I know. She came here once to talk to me, told me I should be with you."

Cole frowned. "She did that? And you let her in?"

Addy nodded, and tears formed in her eyes. "Tell her thank you for me—for caring, for keeping our secret."

Cole kissed her once more. "I hate leaving you, but I can't help blaming myself for this. I've got to get to her."

"I know."

He turned away, and Addy watched him walk to the kitchen, open the back door slowly. He looked back at her once more, and her heart hurt at the anguish in his eyes. He left, and Addy walked into the bedroom and stared at the bed, feeling an ache in her heart, and an odd premonition that the happiness they had shared last night might never be found again. She lay down on the bed, could still smell his manly scent on a pillow, in the covers, in the room . . . on her body. She curled up, wrapped the covers around her, wishing it was Cole's arms instead.

Twenty-six

Cole waited for the doctor to test Sassy's heartbeat once more. She lay in her own room, her eyes closed, her breathing labored, each breath mingled with moans of pain. His heart fell when he saw the look in Dr. Jonesboro's eyes. The man shook his head and walked up to Cole, taking his arm and leading him outside the door. At the bottom of the stairs the main room of the saloon was packed with men waiting to see if Sassy Dillon would live or die.

"I give her very little time," the doctor told Cole. "A few hours at the most. The bullet entered the abdomen, probably tore through the colon in so many places it would be impossible to fix such a thing. She'll die of infection, and there's nothing I can do about it. I can't even find the damn bullet. Some fancy doctor in a big hospital back East might be able to help her, but I can't." He sighed. "I don't have the equipment or the expertise to fix such a thing. She's in a lot of pain, and she's been asking for you."

Cole nodded. "I heard. I went out for an early walk, and when I came back half the miners in Central started shouting at me to get to the Hard Luck."

"Well, I've done all I can do for now. Go on in and see her before it's too late."

Cole looked into the room again, removed his hat and went inside. He bent over Sassy, grasping the head rail with one hand and taking one of her hands in the other. "Sassy? It's me, Cole."

She opened her eyes, gripped his hand tightly when pain

ripped through her belly again. "Cole," she said weakly. "I was afraid . . . you wouldn't get here in time. Where were you . . . last night?"

"I'm sorry, Sassy." His eyes misted. "I feel like this is my fault."

"No," she groaned. "Not your fault. The way I live . . . it was bound to happen I should die . . . a violent death. I don't . . . blame you. I can only blame myself. I only asked . . . where you were because I hope . . . you were with that schoolteacher . . . where you belong."

Cole grinned through tears. "Don't you tell a soul."

Sassy managed a wry smile of her own. "You devil. All night?"

Cole nodded. "All night."

"She gonna marry you?"

"She is."

She gripped his hand tighter again. "Lucky woman." She breathed deeply against pain before continuing. "Now I know I'm doing the right thing. I . . . have to tell you something."

"What is it?"

She swallowed against tears. "First, my Elizabeth . . . promise me you won't . . . leave the area. Promise me you'll see that . . . she's taken care of . . . if something happens to her father."

Cole thought about the little girl's dimpled smile and sweet personality, and how he'd feel if his Patty were threatened with being orphaned or deprived. "I promise, Sassy." What would Addy think of his helping support a prostitute's child?

"I'm going to . . . make it easier . . . for you to stay and settle here . . . take care of my Lissy . . . marry that schoolteacher. I'm going to make you . . . a proper, respected businessman."

Cole frowned. "What do you mean?"

"You get the doctor . . . back in here . . . and a lawyer— somebody intelligent whose word is respected."

"Sassy—"

"Witnesses. I need witnesses . . . honest men. Do it quickly . . . before I'm too weak to get this done."

Cole leaned down and kissed her forehead. "Whatever you say." He left, summoning Doctor Jonesboro and Howard Dresden, who had happened by out of curiosity. Both men came into Sassy's room, Dresden hesitantly, not too happy about half the town seeing him summoned into the notorious bedroom of Sassy Dillon. "What's this all about?" he asked with irritation.

"I don't know myself," Cole answered. "Sassy's got something to say and she apparently wants witnesses. You willing?"

Dresden shrugged his thin shoulders. "I suppose." He adjusted his eyeglasses and looked around the room curiously, frowning at the gaudy wallpaper and clothes strewn everywhere. He walked around the other side of the bed with the doctor while Cole leaned over Sassy again, taking her hand. "I've got your witnesses, Sassy. What is it you want to say?"

She studied his eyes, turned her gaze to Dresden Howard and Doctor Jonesboro. "You tell Jim Lechner . . . over at the Federal Bank . . . that Cole Parker has full control of my account there . . . that he's now the owner of the Hard Luck saloon. I'm . . . giving it to him."

Both men's eyebrows arched in surprise, but neither man was as surprised as Cole.

"Sassy, I don't deserve—"

"Yes, you do. You've been . . . a good friend . . . and you've had a hard time since the war. It's time for you . . . to settle." She looked at Dresden Howard and the doctor. "You make sure . . . people know it's just because . . . Cole worked for me and was a good friend. I have a . . . a sister back East who needs . . . financial support," she lied. "Cole promised . . . to take care of her. I want you to know that's why I'm doing this. I trust Mr. Parker here to run my business . . . and to keep his promise to support my sister. That's the only reason for this. There is nothing more to our relationship . . . than friendship. He hasn't been sleeping with me . . . or living here . . . nothing like that. You make sure people know that. He's a man to be . . . respected. He might want to some day . . . marry a respectable lady in Central . . . so I want no rumors going around. I'm sure he'll . . . run this place respectable-like . . . no prostitution or that kind of thing. Do you men understand?"

Dresden nodded. "Yes, ma'am. The doc and I will tell Jim over at the bank." He looked over at Cole and smiled wryly. "Congratulations, Mr. Parker. I'm sure Sassy does a lucrative business here, even without the prostitution. Once you get situated, maybe you ought to join our town council meetings. Looks like you're here to stay."

Cole thought the man rude for already talking about council meetings when a woman lay dying in front of him. "Sure. I'll think about it."

Dresden looked at the doctor. "I'll go talk to Jim Lechner. You'd better stay here."

Jonesboro agreed, and Dresden left the room. As soon as he hit the bottom of the stairs Cole could hear the man trying to answer a furious barrage of questions from the men waiting there. The doctor checked Sassy once more and again shook his head.

"Leave us . . . alone . . . another minute," Sassy told him. She waited for the doctor to leave, then looked back at Cole. "I wanted . . . to set them straight about us . . . so you'll be more respected. This place brings in a lot of money. Mr. Lechner . . . can help you learn to keep the books and all. Everything is in my desk . . . in a room in back of the bar. You'll do okay . . . gain some respect in town as one of its businessmen."

Cole felt overwhelmed with gratitude. "Sassy, I don't deserve this. It isn't right."

"Yes it is. You're the only one who knows about my Lissy . . . the only one I trust to take care of her and keep . . . putting money in her name. The account is at the Denver National Bank . . . in Lissy's name and Mrs. Donnovan's. I know you'll do the right thing . . . no matter how bad you've been in the past, Cole Parker. I know because I saw the look in your eyes . . . when you talked with Lissy. You already love her . . . because you know what it's like . . . having a little girl to love. That means everything to me. I know you'll keep it a secret . . . who

Lissy's mother was. But you can tell that schoolteacher. She'll understand. You being a respected citizen of Central . . . that will make it easier for you to start seeing Mrs. Kane socially. You keep her away . . . from Grant Breckenridge." She managed another grin. "I'll bet after last night . . . he's the farthest thing from her mind. I could tell when I went to talk to her once . . . that she's crazy about you. I hope you don't mind that I visited her. I wanted to warn her about Grant, make sure . . . she does the right thing."

Her hand gripped his tighter again, and she gritted her teeth before letting out a wrenching groan. Cole hung on, feeling sick at how white she was. Her face was bathed in perspiration, and there were deep purple circles under her eyes.

"Sassy, I don't know what to say . . . how to thank you."

She breathed in quick pants for a moment before replying. "You'll thank me by taking care of Lissy . . . and by staying away from liquor . . . forgetting the past and making a new life with that teacher. The only other thing I want is a nice funeral . . . a good casket. I know I'm dying . . . and there's no way around it. You make the undertaker build me a good tight one . . . and line it with red satin. Will you do that?"

"Of course I will." He blinked back tears. "I'll miss the hell out of you, Sassy. I haven't even known you that long, but you have a way of making a person feel like they've always known you. You're a better person than anyone knows, and God will welcome you with open arms."

"You really think so?"

He smiled through tears. "I do."

"It's nice . . . to think so." She closed her eyes. "I'll ask Him to make sure my Lissy . . . is happy all her life. And I'll put in a good word for you . . ."

The last words were slurred and barely whispered. Cole felt her grip weaken, and he called for the doctor. Jonesboro came inside and examined her again, pulled open her eyelids to check her pupils. "She's going even faster than I expected."

Cole quickly wiped at his eyes. "I'll stay here with her until it's over."

Grant watched from his offices as the funeral procession passed by. Sassy had died two days ago, and he could feel nothing but relief. He had always worried that the brassy bitch would some day blurt out to the whole town that Grant Breckenridge had visited her often. He sure wouldn't want Addy to know that. Trouble was, Addy was still playing hard to get, in spite of his respected position and his money. He couldn't figure the woman out. She had become a challenge that he intended to win. And the thought of her in his bed . . .

The parade below was nothing short of spectacular. For the last two days Sassy had lain in a solidly-built pine casket lined with red satin, her head on a white pillow, so he was told. He had not gone to see. She had been on display in the main room of the Hard Luck were men had come through by the hundreds to view the body, some of them crying over her death. Grant shook his head at the thought of anyone actually having feelings for the likes of Sassy Dillon. Now her closed casket was being transported to the graveyard high above Central. It passed under his windows now, on a decorated wagon being pulled by four shiny black horses.

Cole Parker rode beside the wagon, and Grant felt a little resentment at the news that Cole had inherited the Hard Luck. He had already come to tell Grant he would no longer be working for him because of his new responsibilities. He had seemed rather humble about his new-found wealth. It seemed to Grant that the man should be jumping up and down with joy, and he couldn't help wondering why Sassy would have done such a thing. He figured the man must be well endowed in the right places. That was the only thing that would mean anything to a woman like Sassy.

He shook his head at the sight of hundreds of men following behind the casket, heads hanging, most cleaned up and wearing

suits and hats. They had a long walk ahead of them, winding
around Central up to the graveyard. A reporter for the *Register*
was among them, stopping occasionally to write something
down. This would make the whole front page of the local paper
Grant was sure. How ironic that just a few weeks ago the news
paper itself had joined Central's "proper" ladies in their ques
to force Sassy to give up prostitution. Sassy Dillon had the mos
notorious reputation of anyone in Central and the surrounding
gold towns. Now she was being eulogized as one of Central'
most colorful and perhaps misunderstood figures, a woman who
would be sorely missed.

"Not by me," he muttered, turning away from the sight. Hi
thoughts went back to Addy. The woman had been even mor
reserved the last couple of days, had turned down an invitation
to dinner that night. He didn't like being turned down. Eve
since the other night when he asked her to marry him, sh
seemed less receptive than ever. What had he done wrong? H
had so much to offer a woman.

He sat down at his desk, unable to shake the feeling that ther
was another man in her life. He wanted to believe her story about
her midnight visitor the night after the reception, but he couldn'
help having his doubts. Something still wasn't quite right. H
had apparently satisfied Ethel Brown's questions, had even spo
ken with the entire school board. All agreed Addy was a respect
able young woman who had done nothing wrong, and that th
whole matter of her abduction should be dropped. But some
thing still nagged at Grant, that odd nervousness about Addy
that little hint of lying in her eyes. Was he just imagining it? H
simply could not figure out why a young, eligible woman lik
her would not want to pursue a relationship with a wealthy wid
owed man who could give her the life of a queen. The onl
reason he could think of was that some other man owned he
heart, but who the hell could steal her away from a Grant Breck
enridge?

He hit his fist on his desk. Damn! He wanted her, had though
at first that maybe he could get her into his bed without eve

marrying her, but the bitch was untouchable. She had even acted like she didn't want to kiss him. He got up and paced restlessly, went to the window again. The funeral procession was still passing. He shook his head and turned, and just then the door to his office opened. One of his couriers to Denver walked in, looking tired and needing a shave.

"I have the wire from Illinois you've been waiting for," he told Grant. "You told me to watch for it this past week at the main telegraph office so you could get the message quicker."

Grant walked up and took the envelope. The man who had brought it remained curious as to why Grant had sent him to Denver with a sealed message only the telegrapher there was to see, rather than the telegrapher in Central. He'd been given instructions that he should hand the sealed envelope to the telegrapher, who in turn was to simply send the message without revealing its contents to anyone present. The reply was to be given back in another sealed envelope. Grant's man had been tempted to take a peek at the message, but since the envelope instructions had come from Grant Breckenridge, he decided he'd better abide by them and not risk losing his job. Besides, it probably just involved some kind of business deal.

"Thanks, Joe," Grant told him. "Go on up to the Jamesway and see how they're coming with the next shipment to Denver. I've lost Cole Parker as a guard. You'll have to ride in his place this time."

"What happened to Cole?"

"You haven't heard? Sassy Dillon gave him the Hard Luck Saloon."

Joe looked surprised. He removed his hat. "I'll be damned. I just heard about Sassy getting shot when I got here. Quite a funeral procession, isn't it?"

"Quite," Grant replied absently, walking back to his desk. "If you want to join them, go ahead. Just get up to the mine as soon as it's over."

"Sure, Mr. Breckenridge. I hope whatever is in that wire, it's what you've been looking for."

Grant rubbed at his mustache. "I'm not really sure *what* I'm
looking for."

Joe shrugged and left, and Grant stood staring at the envelope
a moment before ripping it open. He'd been careful that no one
in Central knew about this, not even Ethel Brown. He intended
to marry Addy Kane, and there could be information here he
wouldn't want the rest of the town to know.

Regarding inquiry of men who abducted Mrs. Addy Kane, he
read. *Gang of men led by Jack Slater, confederate outlaws, bank
robbers, killers.* He read on through descriptions of Slater and
his men, then came to one that made his blood tingle. *The man
wounded who escaped to help Mrs. Kane was Nicholas Parker
Coleman, from Kentucky—tall, dark, good looking. Scar across
forehead at hairline, believed to be from war wound. Sharpshooter in war. Good with firearms. Was wanted in Illinois and
Missouri for bank robbery and murder.*

Grant's eyes widened in shock and anger. A scar across his
forehead at the hairline! Tall, dark, handsome, good with guns!
Nicholas Parker Coleman. Cole Parker fit the description perfectly! And seeing the name, the new name, if that's what it was,
made sense. And he had arrived in Central roughly the same
time as Addy had!

He rose, went back to the window. Cole was already high up
on Eureka, out of sight. He read the letter again. Nick Coleman
had apparently helped rescue Addy Kane but had supposedly
been killed doing it. That was what Addy had told everyone.
Had she lied for him because he'd helped her? What the hell had
really happened? Had he followed her here? Maybe even traveled with her most of the way? Was Cole the man she had argued
with the night of the reception?

The more he thought about it, the more sense it all made.
Addy always seemed so nervous and reserved when Cole was
around. Was he somehow threatening her? Was she protecting
him from the law? Why? Was she in love with him? He read the
telegram a third time, and there was no doubt in his mind that
Nick Coleman had not been killed after all. He was alive and

well, and he was in the city of Central in Colorado, about to take his position as a new businessman in town, popular with everyone because of his skill with guns. Addy Kane damn well knew him, was protecting him, had lied to Sheriff Page about him and probably kept him from a hanging!

"You have some explaining to do, Mrs. Addy Kane," he growled. He folded the wire angrily and put it into his pocket.

James Breckenridge disembarked from the stagecoach and took a look around Denver, surprised to find a western town that was so big and bustling. His father had written telling him how fast these gold towns could grow, but he was still impressed by what he saw. He asked the stagecoach driver when they would leave for Central. "Right away in the mornin', son," the man answered. "What you gonna do up there?"

"I'm a lawyer," James answered with a proud smile. "Going to set up practice there. My father already lives there. He's Grant Breckenridge, a manager for Chadwick Mining Company, and he has a seventy-five percent share in one of their mines. He says Central is a big town. Is it really?"

The driver threw down his bags. "Yup. They're even talkin' about makin' Central the capitol of Colorado when we become a state. There's kind of a feud goin' on between Central and Denver because of that. We'll see what happens. At any rate, there's a lot of people up there from Black Hawk to Central, enough to keep somebody like you busy, I expect."

James felt excited. The mountains were beautiful, and he was going to go up there and join his father. He hadn't seen the man in a long time, but back in Chicago, after his mother died, they had been close. He had no doubt his father could be a ruthless businessman, but he'd been a good parent. Now he'd help him set up a practice in Central, a town about which he'd heard a lot of exciting things on the way here. He picked up his bags and looked up the street, figuring he'd have to go and find a hotel for the night. He didn't notice a man was watching him, but as he started up the street the man called out.

"Hey, kid!"

James turned.

"You James Breckenridge?"

The handsome young man smiled. "Yes, sir."

The man came closer, a stocky man wearing a suit that didn't fit him well, as though he'd dressed to impress him but was not really accustomed to wearing suits. "I thought I heard you say you was Grant's son," the man told him. "I'm Clancy Ives. I've been watching and waiting for you."

James set down his bags. "You have? Why?"

"Well, because your pa asked us to. I'm here with Ed Foley. You remember Ed, don't you?"

James's smile faded. "Yes, but . . . well, wasn't there some kind of trouble between him and my father?"

Clancy waved him off. "Oh, that's in the past, son. Ed came here as a favor to your pa, said he'd bring you up to Central himself. We've got a horse for you and everything, so you don't have to wait for the stage. Besides, the trip up by stage is pretty dangerous. It's a narrow, winding canyon road and there have been accidents. Your pa was a little worried about you taking the stage. You're safer on a horse."

James grinned again. "Well, good! I'm glad my pa and Ed are getting along all right again. They were good friends from clear back in Chicago, although I never knew Ed that well myself. When do we leave?"

Clancy stooped down and picked up one of his bags. "Heck, we can leave today, son. Ed's at a boarding house not far from here. We've been taking turns watching for you, knew you were due to arrive any time. If we leave soon, we can make it to a little boarding house at the mouth of the canyon, stay there the night, then go on up the next day—get there a lot sooner than the stage would."

"Well, I appreciate it. I only have these two big carpetbags

I have a lot of law books coming yet, but they'll be shipped separately."

"Fine, then, we don't have much to take with us. Just follow me, boy. You're a little late, aren't you? We expected you a few days ago."

"I had some problems getting away, one final exam to take, a stagecoach that was two days late—Indian trouble, I guess. You probably know how it is trying to get out here."

"Oh, yes. It can be pretty difficult." *Things are going to get a lot more difficult, kid,* Clancy thought. *Just wait till Ed Foley gets his hands on Grant Breckenridge's son.* He felt a little sorry for the boy, but he didn't feel sorry for Grant, and the payoff would be worth it. He just wished he could see the look on Grant Breckenridge's face when he found out that Ed Foley had his boy.

James picked up his other bag and followed Clancy. From his father's letters, he'd been sure that the misunderstanding over the mine ownership had put his father and Ed on some pretty bad terms, but apparently they had patched things up somehow. Maybe Ed was working for Chadwick Mining again. It was wrong of him to try to steal that mine from the company, but maybe it was all just a big misunderstanding that had finally got straightened out. Either way, he was going to Central, and soon there would be a sign hanging outside an office that read, JAMES BRECKENRIDGE, ATTORNEY AT LAW.

Twenty-seven

Addy opened the front door to a knock, and found Grant standing there with a strange look in his eyes that frightened her. "We have to talk," he told her flatly.

Addy swallowed, angry with herself for getting into a relationship with a man so powerful that he thought he could control everyone around him. "I told you the other night that I'm not ready—"

"Not about that," he interrupted. "Get your cape and gloves and come out to my carriage. It wouldn't look right, me coming in here to visit alone." His eyes raked over her almost scathingly. "Although I'm not so sure I should be concerned about your reputation, other than the fact that I want you to be my wife. I'm driving the carriage myself so we can be alone once we get out of town. Right now I'm leaving this between just you and me."

Addy stiffened, afraid of the glitter of near hatred in his eyes. "The way you're looking at me, I'm not sure I want to go anywhere with you."

"Oh?" He leaned closer, looking down at her with threat in his dark eyes. "You'll come, if you want to save Nick Coleman's ass!"

Her eyes widened, and she could feel the blood draining from her face. He knew! But did he know *all* of it? The remark had struck her with such surprise that it was impossible to hide her shock, which only gave her away. Immediately her defenses rose, a defense of Cole, not herself. "There are a lot of things you don't understand."

"That's obvious, including the fact that the woman I want to marry has been sleeping with an outlaw!"

"I've been doing no such thing!" Addy felt removed from reality, felt as though everything around her was crumbling. In one quick moment the dream she and Cole had shared three nights ago had turned into a nightmare.

"We'll see about that," Grant answered. "Either way, there is a wanted man in Central who probably deserves to be hanged! Get your cape!" With these words he turned and walked out. Addy dreaded a confrontation with someone like Grant. He held all the cards, and there was a ruthless look in his eyes. A lump rose in her throat, and her eyes teared as she scrambled to think straight. The most important thing was to protect Cole, and she couldn't do that without trying to reason with Grant. She had no choice but to go with him. If she refused, it would only make him angrier.

She could barely feel her own legs as she half stumbled to her bedroom to get her cape. She wore only a plain day dress, and her hair was braided and twisted on top of her head. She had done no primping today, but right now she couldn't care less about how she looked. She tied her cape with shaking hands, stuck a fur hat on her head. It was quite chilly today, and she'd been thinking it would be cold and windy up high where the graveyard was.

From the front porch she'd been able to see the procession in the city below, knew Cole would be right at the front of it. The fact that Sassy Dillon had given him her saloon was all the talk among the women's circle, along with gossip over why she would do such a thing. Most saw nothing wrong with it. After all, Cole Parker had been a single man. In spite of her bad reputation with her personal life, Sassy Dillon was known to be quite the shrewd businesswoman. If she thought Cole Parker was capable of taking over the Hard Luck, then he must be an intelligent, dependable man, a man who would now join the circle of downtown businessmen. Besides that, most of the women thought him quite handsome, albeit mysterious. All were fascinated by his skill with guns and his rather quiet demeanor, and they had been impressed by his loyalty to Grant Breckenridge, all saying how it was too bad Grant would lose him.

Addy hadn't even had a chance to talk to Cole yet about what she'd heard, but in spite of some jealousy over Sassy's feelings for him, she'd been glad to hear the Hard Luck would be his. It would give him a chance to get established in Central, make good money, perhaps become accepted enough to begin seeing her publicly.

Now this. She fought a need to weep openly. Cole! His whole world would come to an end, and with it her own. How had Grant figured it all out? Who else knew? What could she do to protect Cole? She took a few deep breaths and picked up her handbag, pulling on a pair of light gloves as she went out the door. She walked to the carriage and climbed up on the seat beside Grant, who said nothing as he snapped the reins and urged the two black horses pulling it to head uphill. He headed right toward a cross street where the funeral procession had passed by, so that they caught the tail end of it.

"Quite a spectacle," he commented. "There wouldn't be a bigger turnout if it was the president in the coffin up there. Instead it's the town's most notorious slut! Now she's apparently given over her saloon to her favorite stud. How does *that* make you feel?"

Oh, how she hated him! "I have no particular feelings about it. The woman had a right to do whatever she wished with her property, and if Cole Parker—"

"Nick Coleman! Call him by his right name. We both know that's who he is, and he won't live long enough to be running any tavern."

He guided the carriage around a winding back road that took them to the graveyard, parking in full view as the hearse made its appearance, Cole riding beside it. He didn't notice at first, but finally he looked in their direction, saw them together. What was he thinking, her and Grant Breckenridge there at the grave . . . together. He must think it awfully strange, let alone probably upset to see her with Grant. *Run, Cole!* she wanted to shout. *Run!*

Grant chuckled as Cole stared at them. "Just as I thought. Wouldn't this be a fine time to make the announcement as to who Cole really is? Most of the population of Central is here."

"Please don't," Addy answered quietly. "Please let's talk first."

Grant looked at her, but she refused to meet his eyes, knowing what she would see there. He turned the horse and drove over a hill, far enough away from the gravesite that no one could hear them. He stopped, pushed on the brake, tied the reins around a hook on the buggy. He turned in the seat, facing her.

"I decided to dig a little deeper than Ethel Brown did, thinking I was doing it for your protection. I asked for a description of the men who attacked you, found out one of them was Nicholas Parker Coleman, a remnant from the war turned outlaw, a desperado, wanted, a man who'd have been hanged if captured. The description of him tore at my guts, Addy! Tall, dark, good with guns, and a scar across his forehead at the hairline." He grasped her arms painfully and forced her to turn and face him. "I want the truth! Either that man is following you to make trouble for you, maybe threatening you to keep quiet about him still being alive; or you have *feelings* for him! You lied to Sheriff Page about his being dead, lied about not knowing anyone up here, pretended all this time not to know Cole Parker. I want the truth. Did he rape you and then threaten you? Or maybe you were together long enough after your capture that it wasn't rape at all!"

Addy jerked away, wanting to hit him. "He's a good man," she said, a few tears beginning to spill out of her eyes. "His wife died in childbirth, his little girl and grandparents were murdered by Union sympathizers. His little girl was *burned* to death when the raiders set fire to Cole's house! It was a terrible thing for him! She was only five years old, and he could hear her *scream-*

ing for her daddy, but he couldn't get to her. Something like that can do things to a man, change him, fill him with hate and revenge. He went after the men he thought were responsible, fell into a pit of self-pity and alcohol and outlaw ways until he hardly knew how to get out of it. I tried to help him see the error of his ways, urged him to change his life."

She turned away and wiped at her eyes with her gloved hands. "He saved my life and my virtue, Grant, risked his life in a shootout to keep the other men from hurting me. I saved his in return by taking a bullet out of him. We became friends." She faced him. *"Friends!* Nothing more." She prayed he believed her. "Because of things I told him, he decided maybe he would try to start over. He followed me here because I told him if he came to a place like Central he could have a new life. On the way here he saved my life twice more, from Indians. Why *shouldn't* I try to help and protect a man like that? I *owe* him! Please, *please* let him stay here and leave him alone. If no one else knows about this, then please keep it to yourself, tear up whatever papers you have. Let the man start over. Let him be happy. I *beg* of you!"

Grant took hold of her chin, pressing it between his strong fingers threateningly. "I am not a stupid man, Addy. I saw how you looked at each other a couple of times when you danced. He's a handsome man, and the two of you were apparently alone together quite a bit. He has an aura of danger about him, and sometimes that attracts women. I don't believe for one minute that what you had was just a friendship. I think you fell in love with him, and him with you. Maybe you even *slept* together!"

"We didn't—"

"No more lies, Addy!" He squeezed her jaw tighter. "I feel like beating the hell out of you. I'm not a man to do such a thing, but when it comes to sluts and whores, I have no qualms about using my fists. However, in your case I have another proposition."

He leaned closer and kissed her violently, hurting her lips.

Addy turned away and wept, rubbing at her mouth. "My God, what is it you want of me?" she groaned.

He grasped her arms again. "I want you to come to your senses. I'll grant you some leeway here, you being a widow, lonely and confused. You didn't know what you were doing. But I want you to wake up and see where you belong, with *me!* I want you, in my bed, on my arm, the wife of Grant Breckenridge. If you're so bent on protecting Cole Parker, then *marry* me. Do that, and I won't say a word. If it's true you haven't slept with the man, then it shouldn't matter. He shouldn't care. He's trying to better his life, and you're trying to better yours."

Addy felt sick at the thought of being Grant's wife, having to sleep with him. Even if she was his wife, going to bed with him would make her feel more like a whore than sleeping with Cole without being married. At least she'd loved Cole. They had shared more than just a lust for each other. They had shared souls, spirits, hearts. How could she ever know a moment's happiness married to Grant; yet how could she bear watching Cole Parker hang from a noose, or perhaps having to head out on the run again, to have to turn back to the life of a wanted outlaw, forever alone?

Maybe, just maybe, even if she married Grant, Cole would continue to try to change his ways. After all, he was the owner of a profitable place of business now, beginning to be accepted. "Why would you want to marry someone who doesn't love you?" she asked in a subdued voice.

"Because I can *make* you love me. You'll have everything you want, clothes, jewelry, respect, a lovely home. We'll travel. I'll even let you keep teaching, if that's what you want. My son will be here soon. You'll like him when you meet him. He's a good boy, smart, likeable. He'll like you just fine." He put a hand to her back, rubbing at her dress under the cape. "You'll realize you did the right thing. A woman like you is worth more than a Cole Parker . . . certainly more than a Nick Coleman. He'll get over it in time, and that will be the end of it. After all, the two of you could not have built much of a relationship yet since you can't even be seen together. If you did sleep with him, it was probably because you were confused and lonely. Tell him that you feel it isn't wise to let it go any further. Tell him you have accepted a proposal of marriage from me. He already knows we've been seeing each other."

Grant let go of her. "It makes me sick to think of the times the three of us spoke and you two pretended not to know each other. Now I understand why he stood up for you the day of the march. Some of the women said it seemed like he knew you, and I was too enamored with you myself to see the truth. Once we're married I don't want you anywhere near him. It will be *over,* and that will be the end of it. He doesn't need to know that I am aware of the truth. I'll let him go right on living however he chooses, and Addy Kane will be my wife. We'll have a grand wedding. The whole town will turn out for it!"

He breathed deeply to calm himself. "I don't like being turned down, Addy. Now you *can't* turn me down, unless you want to fall into disgrace and on top of that watch Nick Coleman hang. You make the choice."

There were no words of love. He wanted her, like a prize. It was obvious to Addy that Grant considered this a challenge, like a fistfight with Cole Parker. He had dealt the lethal blow, won the battle, was poised to take the spoils. She was nothing more to him than a trophy, and she had no doubt that because of what he knew, he would not be a kind and patient man. He would take her like a whore, maybe even hurt her whenever she made him angry . . . or if he suspected she had even said hello to Cole Parker.

Still, what other answer was there? She couldn't even fully explain to Cole. She would have to lie and say she had "chosen" Grant after all. If he knew the truth, his temper would get the better of him and he would go storming after Grant, probably shoot the man rather than let him abuse her. He'd give himself away to the whole town. He'd risked his life for her several times. He'd do it again, face a hanging before he'd let her marry someone she didn't love. It would not be easy lying to him, making him believe she was doing this because she wanted to.

"Fine," she said coolly. "I'll marry you."

Grant shook his head and laughed. "So, you care that much about him, do you? Well, once you're my wife, you'll realize you did the right thing. I'll make you forget him soon enough. I know what's right for you, Addy, and it isn't a Confederate outlaw who drinks too much and isn't about to settle down for long. He'd end up breaking your heart anyway. In fact, I can easily run him out of business. He'll leave Central eventually, and that will be the end of it."

She hated his cool attitude, his ruthless arrogance. The man knew nothing of true love, at least not with a woman. The only thing he really seemed to care about was his son. Other than that, whatever Grant Breckenridge wanted, he went after it and got it. Now he'd found a way to have her.

"It will be a grand wedding," he told her. "The biggest event Central has seen yet." He untied the reins, slapped them against the horses' rumps. "I'll take you home now. You think about it. You're doing what's best for yourself, and what's best for Cole Parker, as you seem to prefer to call him. You say he saved your life a few times. Now you're saving his."

Addy felt ill. "How do I know you won't still turn Cole in after we're married?"

Grant sat straight and cocky. "Because, my dear, I may be a lot of things you don't like, but one thing I am is a man of my word. I don't break promises. Besides, I would then have to explain your part in the picture, and I wouldn't want to bring that kind of shame on Mrs. Grant Breckenridge. My wife should be a woman of honor and virtue. Marrying me is your very best assurance that Cole will not be found out. I will write Sheriff Page and tell him that no one in Central fits the description of any of the men he told me about. I had said I feared one of them had followed you here. He will go on thinking Nick Coleman is dead, and that will be the end of it. Unionville, Illinois, is a

long way from our wonderful little mountain town. Nick Coleman will be long forgotten."

Addy looked around at distant mountain ranges, studied the
gold pilings that dotted the surrounding hillsides. She had loved
this town when she first got here, had loved the idea of being
able to teach. Now her dreams and plans were shattered. She
couldn't really blame Cole for it. She had fallen into his arms
as willingly as a sliding down an ice-covered hill. She had let
this happen. She could have refused Cole from the very beginning, discouraged him more vigorously, demanded he leave Central. But no matter how much she had protested, she had not
really wanted him to go, and he knew it. She had allowed herself
to love an outlaw, and now she would suffer for it.

The wind picked up, cutting at her face, and she wrapped her
cape closer, thinking how this winter was going to be much
colder in her heart than it would be outside.

Addy sat rocking in a chair Susan Howard had given her to
set by her fireplace. A fire crackled there now, all the light she
wanted. She couldn't sleep for thinking of her dilemma. Her
head ached, as did her heart, and her mind spun with the various
ways she might have of explaining to Cole that she didn't want
to marry him after all. She had to make him believe her, and
she hated breaking his heart that way. She only wished she would
not also break his spirit, so that he turned back to his old ways
after all.

She huddled in a heavy cotton robe, fur slippers on her feet.
Outside the wind blew, rattling the windows, and the rocker
squeaked each time she rocked back. Never had she felt so utterly alone, not even in the times before when she would make
up her mind not to see Cole again. She stared at the crackling
fire, feeling too empty even to cry, and the flames so entranced
her that she did not realize at first that someone had tapped at
her back door. The second time he tapped louder, and her heart
seemed to skip a beat. Cole? She put a hand to her chest. She

wasn't ready for this! She slowly rose, her knees feeling weak. She clutched her robe and walked into the kitchen. "Who is it?" she called out.

"Me," came the only reply. She knew the voice.

"Dear God," she whispered. She opened the door, and before she could even begin explaining anything, Cole swept her into his arms and kicked the door closed.

"We can finally be together, Addy," he told her, kissing her hair. He picked her up and carried her into the bedroom, setting her on the bed and sitting down beside her. "Did you hear about the Hard Luck being mine?"

She met his eyes, saw his grief over Sassy. "Yes. I'm sorry about Sassy, but I'm glad about her giving you the saloon. I do hope you'll keep it a respectable place."

He leaned closer and kissed her cheek. "I intend to start seeing the town's only female schoolteacher. Of course I'll keep it respectable. I have to be respected myself if I'm going to start visiting you, marry you." He got up. "There is something you should know about Sassy, Addy, part of the reason she gave me the saloon."

I can't marry you, Cole. "What's that?"

He faced her. "She has a daughter, a little girl about Patty's age. She lives in Denver with adoptive parents."

Addy was surprised and curious. "A little girl? Sassy?"

Cole nodded. "Unplanned, of course. She couldn't even be sure who the father was, but she didn't have the heart to try to get rid of the baby. She wanted to be responsible for one good thing in her life, so she had the baby and let some nuns give her up for adoption. The parents know who her real mother is. They even let Sassy come visiting as just a friend once in a while, so she could see her little girl. Her name is Elizabeth."

He came closer, sat beside her again. "I went with her to visit the child, and she's beautiful, Addy. She's bright, sweet, outgoing. She sat on my lap and actually put her arms around me, and that's when I knew I wanted a family again, maybe another little girl. It felt good to hold her." He sighed. "At any rate, Sassy helped support her, has a bank account set up for her in Denver. She knew what I'd been through with Patty, knew I had a soft spot for little girls, so when she knew she was dying, she made me promise to always keep that savings account going for Elizabeth. Her adoptive father isn't well and might be dying. Sassy wants to be sure Elizabeth never wants for anything. That's part of the reason she gave me the saloon, so I'd be sure to have a good income to take care of the girl."

Addy listened in astonishment, and with an aching heart. He truly had changed. He was showing his softer side, the side of the family man he'd once been. Why now? It couldn't be a worse time.

He got up and paced again. "Sassy loved that child as much as any mother loves her child, but she didn't want the girl ever to know who her real mother was—what she was. She felt it was too late for her to try to change any of it. She couldn't erase the past, so she did what she thought was best for her daughter, gave her up to respectable people who could raise her as their own. Everything she did to make money was for that little girl." He came over and knelt in front of her. "I hope you don't mind that I would put some of my profits into the bank account in Denver for Lissy. That's what they call her. She's the child of a prostitute, but that's not her fault. I just hope you understand—"

"It doesn't matter."

Cole frowned, his smile fading. Only then did he realize something was wrong. "What?"

Addy looked at her lap. "It doesn't matter. I . . . I'm not going to marry you."

The room was painfully silent for several seconds. "What the hell did you say?"

Addy swallowed, twisting her fingers in her lap. "I'm just not sure it would work after all. Your past could catch up with you any time, and you'll be a saloon owner. That's not so terrible, I know, but—"

"Hell, I'm already thinking of turning the saloon into a restaurant that would serve drinks, something like that. I don't in-

tend to run the wild kind of place Sassy ran. There won't be any
women working in there, if that's what bothers you. Or is it that
the most notorious prostitute in Central gave the place to me?
Addy, I told you there was never much between us. We were
just friends. If that bothered you, why did you sleep with me
the other night? Why were you so open and—" He grasped her
arms. "What's going on?"

She couldn't bring herself to meet his eyes, to see the agony
there. "I've decided to marry Grant."

She felt his grip tighten. "What! Damn it, Addy, what is going
on? Why would you marry that bastard! You *know* he's no good!
He could never love you like I do! He's a womanizer and a cheat.
The sonofabitch stabbed his best friend in the back!" He shook
her so that she gasped. *"Look* at me, Addy! Do you really expect
me to believe what you just told me?"

She swallowed. She had planned to be very cool about this,
very convincing. But he had surprised her by coming too soon,
before she could figure out the best way to let him know. Her
eyes filled with unwanted tears. "Yes," she answered, "because
it's true. I'm marrying Grant Breckenridge. I've wrestled with
this too long. I decided . . . our relationship has been too tem-
pestuous, and you have been too undependable. Your past could
affect our children's lives. You might go back to drinking. So
many things could go wrong."

Cole watched tears slip down her cheeks. "I don't believe
one word you're telling me. You're a rotten liar, Addy! Something has happened you aren't telling me. We love each other.
The woman I left the other night was the happiest, most passionate woman I've ever held in my arms, and I've never loved
anybody more, not even Bethanne! This thing with Grant is some
kind of goddamn sacrifice, and I want to know why!"

She shook her head. "No. It's what I want."

He studied her eyes, then leaned closer, pressing his mouth
against hers in a desperate kiss. She couldn't be telling the
truth. She wouldn't do that to him, would she? Not Addy. Not
the woman he'd made love to all night long such a short time

ago. She resisted at first, but he would not release her, and finally she weakened, whimpering as she threw her arms around his neck and returned his kiss with a kind of desperation that alarmed him. He could taste her tears as he stood up, keeping her in his arms. She broke down then, sobbing against his chest.

"Don't cry, Addy. Just tell me the truth."

"I . . . I slept with him," she sobbed. "I'm pregnant . . . and it's his."

His grip tightened. "I told you a long time ago that I knew you were a decent woman. I never once lost my respect for you, Addy Kane, and I don't believe for one minute you slept with that man. Try again."

She cried harder. "Dear God, Cole, let it go! Just let it go!" she said, trying to pull away. She gasped when he pushed her back almost violently, keeping a firm hold on her arms.

"The truth, Addy! It's *me,* isn't it! You're *protecting* me! He knows, doesn't he? He knows who I am, knows about us, and he's blackmailing you into marrying him! *How,* Addy? How did he find out?"

She looked at him pleadingly. "Don't do something foolish, Cole! I'd rather lose you this way than watch you hang!"

He shoved her down on the bed and stood back, the same wild fire in his eyes she'd seen the day he robbed the bank in Unionville. "And *I'd* rather die than see you married to Grant Breckenridge! If that's what it takes, I'll do it."

"No!" She stood up and grabbed his arm. "You can get away. We can leave together——"

"And make you a fugitive for the rest of your life? No, ma'am. You don't deserve that. You came here for peace, to teach school, to have a new life. I won't let all that be ruined because of me. I figured I'd make something respectable out of Sassy's place, figured maybe God would let me start over so I could help take care of her little girl, figured He brought you into my life for a good reason. I guess I figured wrong. I'll get what I've got coming, and as long as that's the case, I'm taking Grant Breckenridge out with me. I'll kill him before he has a chance to tell the whole town about us for spite and ruin your reputation. That's what he'll do if you don't marry him, and I won't let that happen!"

"Cole, please—"

"How did he find out?"

Addy sniffed and turned away. "He wrote Sheriff Page, asked for a description of the men. He thought maybe I hadn't told the truth about one of them following me here. He said he'd never say a word . . . if I married him. So far he's the only one who knows. He said he'd tear up the sheriff's wire. Oh, Cole, I'm losing you for good this time. I don't want to lose you." She wept harder, then trembled with utter grief when his hand touched her shoulder.

"I'm sorry, Addy, for messing up your life like I have. I should have stayed away that first time I rode off, but I just couldn't. I kept hoping—"

He took his hand away, and Addy heard his footsteps as he walked slowly toward the front door. "Cole, wait!"

"I've got somebody to see." He opened the door.

"Cole!" Addy ran to the door to try to stop him, only to realize he stood there staring at someone.

"I can drop you before you pull the trigger." Cole said.

Addy's heart pounded when she realized Grant was standing on her porch with a rifle in his hand.

"Get back inside!" he told Cole.

Cole glanced at Addy, then back to Grant. "Only for Addy's sake. I don't want to bring her scandal by having a shootout on her front porch."

"Smart man." Grant used the rifle to wave him inside.

Addy stepped back as both men came in and Grant kicked shut the door. "I've been looking for you," he said to Cole. "You weren't at the Hard Luck, and you weren't at the boarding house where you stay. It didn't take long to figure out where you'd probably be. God only knows how many times you've been here in the night, me totally oblivious to what was going on."

"If you want any respect left for the woman you plan to call your wife, you'd better not pull that trigger in here," Cole warned. "How would you explain it?"

"I didn't come here out of jealousy, and I didn't come here to kill you." Grant slowly lowered the rifle, and by the light of the fireplace Addy noticed a wild look of anguish in his eyes. He closed them and rubbed at them, and he seemed oddly subdued, like a beaten man. What had brought on this change? "I came here to ask for your help," he told Cole. "Everything is changed."

Cole eyed him warily, his hand ready at his side. He longed to put a bullet between the man's eyes. "What are you talking about?"

To Addy's astonishment, Grant blinked back tears. "Ed Foley. He's got my son."

Twenty-eight

"Your son?" Cole glanced at Addy. She stood shivering, her face tear-stained. She grasped the collar of her robe and pulled it closer around her neck, and Cole could see she was as confused as he was about this strange turn of events.

"I don't know just how it happened," Grant told them, his voice strained, "but Ed Foley has kidnapped my son."

Addy thought Grant suddenly looked much older than he had before. He must be telling the truth. Something had affected him deeply.

"What did you mean about asking for my help?" Cole asked, glancing at the rifle still in Grant's hand. "Right now I'd like nothing more than to kill you. Fact is, knowing you as I do, I can fully understand Ed Foley's hatred. You really *did* cheat him out of that mine, didn't you? And now you're blackmailing Addy into marrying you, you bastard! Do you think I'd let that happen? That I'd let her marry you just to save my own neck? I'd rather *hang,* if that's what it takes!"

Grant's breathing was labored from fear and anger. "I *told* you, everything is changed!" He laid the rifle across the arms of the rocker. An eerie light filled the room from the fire in the fireplace, and Addy breathed a sigh of relief that Grant had set aside his weapon.

"I couldn't get him to believe me, Grant," she said in a shaky voice. "He figured it out."

"It doesn't matter," Grant replied, keeping his gaze steady on Cole. "None of it matters now. The one person I'd give my life for, the only person in this world I truly give a damn about, is in the hands of a man who hates me and who blames me for his own son's death. Now he's threatening to kill *my* son, and he'll do it. I need help, and I can't think of anyone else who has the skills needed to get my son back alive. I'm asking you to help, Cole."

Addy listened in surprise, wanting to believe this could be the answer to her prayers, but hating the thought that Grant's son might have to suffer for it.

"Why don't you go to the sheriff?" Cole asked.

Grant reached inside his jacket and pulled out a folded piece of paper. "Because he'd botch it. He'd form a posse and go charging in and Foley would put a bullet in my son's head. Nobody knows about this, not even any of my own men. When I got back to my office this afternoon I found this lying on my desk. No one knows who put it there."

Cole took the paper and unfolded it to read.

"I decided not to tell anyone because news spreads too fast in this town," Grant continued, "and I want to be careful how I handle this. I have no way of knowing who is a spy and who isn't. Whatever plans I make, word could get back to Ed Foley and ruin any attempts at saving my son."

Cole read the letter aloud. "Escorted your son, James, from Denver personally. He's waiting for his father to come and get him at a little cabin in Chase Gulch. You know the place. We did some exploring there once for Chadwick Mining. If you want to see your son alive again, you bring me fifty thousand dollars. You owe me a lot more than that, but with fifty thousand I can start my own mining company. I have that coming. You don't bring the money within forty-eight hours, the boy dies. It's your fault I lost my own son, Grant Breckenridge. You're lucky I don't take an eye for an eye. And you'd better come alone with the money and never tell a soul. Your son will be waiting with a noose around his neck. If I see one other man with you, he'll hang. Revenge is sweet. Ed Foley."

Addy moved closer to Cole as he folded the letter and handed it back. "Why should I help you after what you've just tried to do to me and Addy?"

Grant took the paper, agony in his eyes. "Because James Breckenridge is a fine young man who doesn't deserve this, and because if you help me, I'll forget about who you really are. I'll never say a word. You can be with Addy. I won't give you any trouble about it. Nothing is more important to me than my son. Nothing. Addy says you lost a daughter in the war. You know how it feels to lose a child."

Cole remembered the pain, was surprised at this human side to Grant Breckenridge. Apparently when it came to children, most men had the same feelings, no matter how rotten they were about other things. He walked cautiously past Grant, taking a thin cigar from his own jacket pocket. "Why don't you just go there and give him the money and get your son?" He picked up a piece of kindling and held it to the flames of the fire to light it, then used it to light his cigar while Grant replied.

"Because Ed Foley is a crazy man. He's let this fester in his soul until his only desire is to make me suffer. He wants me there because he intends to make me watch him hang my son. The money is just a ruse. He'll take it and shoot me and go his merry way. The spot he's talking about along Chase Gulch is well hidden. It would be days, maybe weeks before I was found, and by then Ed Foley would be long gone. He's crazy enough to think God is on his side and that he can get away with this!"

Cole threw the kindling into the fire and straightened. "Everyone would know it was Foley. He'd be found and hanged."

"Maybe so, but that wouldn't help me and my son much, would it? The man just wants us dead. He doesn't even care if he dies for it himself, but he'll make a grand try at using that money to start a new life someplace else."

Cole puffed on the cigar. "I can't believe an educated man like Foley would stoop so low and do something that crazy."

Grant stepped closer, a pleading look in his eyes. "Just think how *you* felt when your family was killed. You wanted revenge.

You wanted to kill! You damn well know better than most people what a man will do for revenge, including throwing away the good life he once had. You ended up a wanted man yourself, but now you have a chance to have a whole new life! I'll help you, if you help me with this! I don't trust Ed Foley. I'm telling you he intends to kill me and my boy! There is only one way to save us, and to do it, I need a man who shoots straight."

Cole looked past him at Addy questioningly.

"Do it, Cole, if not for him, then for us."

"I'll pay you well," Grant told him.

Cole studied his eyes. Part of him feared this whole thing was some plan Grant had laid out to get him killed. Maybe his son wasn't even out there in danger. Still, there was a terrible agony in Grant's eyes he'd never seen there before, a show of love and desperate fear unusual for a man like Grant Breckenridge. The night had taken a strange turn, from happy anticipation to the horror of learning Grant knew who he was and intended to use that to claim Addy as his own. Now this, a dim light of hope. If this was all true, and he could help, he and Addy could at last be free.

"What's your plan?"

Grant looked hopeful. "I'll go in, just like Foley asked me to do. I'll take a briefcase with the money in it. You follow, but stay well back when we get close. Keep to the rocks and underbrush but try to get close once I go in. If Foley takes the money and gives James over to me and we're able to get out of there with our lives, we'll leave it at that. I'll gladly give up fifty thousand dollars for my son. But if Foley makes any move against us, you shoot to kill. I have no idea how many men he might have with him, but I'm guessing it can't be more than one or two. With too many he'd risk someone talking. He's not the type of man to form a gang. Most men don't have the guts for a thing like that and couldn't be trusted not to tell the law, so I don't think Foley has many men with him. You shoot him first, because he's the one most likely to murder us both. Then you go for the others. The way you shoot, you can down them all before they know what's happening."

Cole took off his hat and ran a hand through his hair, then replaced his hat. "The fact is, believe it or not, I'd go help your son whether you make me any promises or not. I'm not the cold-blooded bastard you think I am. That's *your* area. You cut men down by deceit and cheating. You use legal means to do it, then lie about it and present yourself as a fine, upstanding citizen. You'd just better keep your promise to keep your mouth shut about me and Addy. It's your son I care about helping, not you. I still won't hesitate to come after you if you screw things up for me and Addy."

Grant's eyes lit up with hope. "I'll keep my promise. I just want my son back alive."

"I'm taking a chance going out there with you alone. This had better not be a setup, or you'll go down first."

"It's no setup. Fact is, I'm scared to death. Ed Foley blames his son's death on me, but if something happens to my own boy, that *will* be my fault, for what I did to Foley. I couldn't live with that."

Cole folded his arms, the thin cigar still between his teeth. "Well, well. Grant Breckenridge has a human side after all."

Grant raised his chin defensively. "Doesn't everyone? You were willing to get yourself hanged just to keep me from marrying Addy. Men do strange things for strange reasons, don't they?"

Their eyes met in new-found respect, but Addy could see they each held that respect grudgingly. They had not expected to be put in such a position.

"When do we leave?" Cole asked.

"Sunrise. I'll leave my office at six. I already took fifty thousand out of my account this afternoon, soon as I read the letter. The bank was getting ready for a shipment of money to a bank in Denver, so I was lucky they had that much. The bank here doesn't generally keep much more than fifty thousand on hand at any time. It's not safe in these gold towns. Stuart Collingswood over at the bank had a lot of questions. I just told him I was making a business deal tomorrow that I didn't want to talk about yet. The money is in my own safe at my office." He picked up his rifle. "You wait for me up behind Snow Peak Mine. I don't want anyone in town to see us riding out together. I have to be seen leaving alone. Do you know the road behind Snow Peak Mine? It's pretty deserted up there."

"I'll find it. I'll head straight there at sunrise."

Grant nodded. "You save my son, and I'll give you some shares in the Jamesway. Between that and the Hard Luck, you'll be a rich man. You can give Addy a good life." He turned and faced Addy. "I wanted you from the first day I laid eyes on you, Addy Kane, and I'm used to getting what I want. I guess in this case, I lose."

"You can't buy people, Grant," she answered defiantly. "And you can't force feelings where they don't exist. Do you really think we could have been happy?"

Grant glanced at Cole before replying. "I just figured you'd come to your senses, especially if there was only friendship between you and Cole. It's obvious it was a lot more than that, or I wouldn't have found him here late at night with you in your robe. Now I don't care. All I care about is James."

Addy blinked back tears. "Sometimes God answers prayer in strange ways. I've been sitting here praying for a way out of this mess, and here you are asking for Cole's help. I just hope he doesn't get hurt or killed himself."

Grant's mouth moved into a defeated smirk. "Cole Parker knows how to watch out for himself." He looked at Cole. "See you bright and early. I'm trusting you to save *my* ass, too, not just James's. It would be real easy for you to hesitate and let one of Foley's men put a bullet in me, wouldn't it?"

Cole stepped closer, his blue eyes drilling into the man. "I guess you'll just have to trust me, won't you?"

They glared at each other a moment. "I guess I will. Addy

says you're a good man. I guess I'll find out. I'll save the thank-you's until it's over and you've come through for me."

"The only thank you I want is to be left alone and be able to start seeing Addy openly."

Grant nodded, then turned and left. Cole looked at Addy. "Strange turn of events."

She walked closer and moved her arms around him. "Be careful, Cole."

He kissed her hair. "I'm always careful, except when it comes to you. I'm sorry for all the hurt and sorrow and confusion I've caused, Addy." He pulled away reluctantly. "I'd better get some rest if I'm going to get up before sunrise."

She looked up at him, touched his cheek. "I'll be praying for you."

"You just promise to help Elizabeth Donnavan if she needs it, if something happens to me. Her parents are Harold and Mary Donnovan. They live not far from the Denver Inn. Helping that little girl makes me feel like I'm doing something to make up for not being able to save Patty."

"That's the main reason you're doing this, isn't it? If you're free, you can help Sassy's little girl."

He touched her chin, leaned closer. "And be with you." He kissed her.

"I know I said you should do this, but I'm afraid for you. If Ed Foley is as crazy with revenge as Grant thinks—"

"Don't worry. I'll be all right."

She searched his eyes. "Do we dare believe we can really be together?"

He grasped her face between strong hands, leaned down to kiss her gently. "We have to. The thought of it will give me all the courage and skill I'll need to do this. I love you, Addy Kane. It feels good to say it." Reluctantly he turned and walked into the kitchen, then stopped to look back at her once more before heading out the door.

Addy put a hand to her stomach and closed her eyes. "God

be with you, Cole," she whispered, "and with James Breckenridge."

Grant rode cautiously along the remote trail behind the Snow
Peak Mine, a briefcase full of money tied to the pommel of his
saddle. It was a cold morning, and his horse's breath came out
in puffs of steam. It was dead quiet here, and he wondered if
Cole Parker had skipped out on him, what he should do if he
had. Without Cole, he and his son were both dead men.

"Keep riding." The voice came from somewhere in the surrounding rocks. Grant scanned his perimeter, but he could see
no one.

"Cole?"

"I'm here. You keep going. You're being followed. I'll take
care of him."

"They'll hear gunshots."

"Trust me. Just keep going. I'll catch up. Hurry it up before
the man trailing you hears us talking."

Grant breathed a sigh of relief that Cole had at least shown
up. He felt better already, but his whole body tingled with fear
for James. Maybe the boy was already dead. Whatever Cole did,
it might not be soon enough. He rode forward, heading along
the winding trail and down into a deep ravine.

Cole watched until Grant was out of sight. He'd had an eye
on him from a high viewpoint earlier and had noticed a man
following him out of town. He figured it was one of Ed Foley's
men, probably planning to stay behind and make sure Grant
could not beat a retreat. In Cole's book, one less man now would
give him an even bigger edge later. This fellow was going to get
his due. He waited, watched, listened. Finally he heard the sound
of a horse's hooves. He'd tied Shadow in a stand of thick trees
behind him, where he couldn't be spotted, and had waited behind
a pile of tumbled rocks, which in turn were hidden by scrubby
brush.

He smiled to himself at how this country was made for outlaws. So many places to hide—caves, crevices, rocks, brush, ravines. A man could get lost out here in minutes, or lose any-body trailing him. Finally the man following Grant appeared, following the winding trail from a steep drop below up to Cole's level. Cole waited, moved higher onto the rock formation so that when the man passed by, he was above him. He recognized him as one who'd been in the Wildcat the day of the shootout with two of Ed's men.

Cole quietly slipped a hunting knife from his boot, then sprang onto the man's back, knocking him from his horse. Both men tumbled to the ground with grunts, and Cole managed to roll the man onto his back and straddle him. He pressed the huge knife blade to his throat, nicking the skin. "How many are there?" he growled.

The man stared at him, wide-eyed. "Cole Parker!"

"Hurry it up!" Cole fumed, trying to keep his voice down. "You want to die for somebody else's revenge? It's not worth it!"

The man swallowed. "Ed promised us a lot of money, and shares in whatever mine he claims for himself once he strikes gold. We were all going to go up to Montana. They're finding new veins up there every day, seems like."

"Just tell me how many men there are up ahead with Foley. I don't have much time."

"Three," he answered, pretending to give up. "Plus Ed."

Cole grasped his shirt. "Get up," he said, moving off of him. "I'm going to tie you up and you're going to sit here until I come back for you. You're going to town to explain all of this to Sheriff Watson." He removed the man's gun from its holster and threw it aside, waving the knife at him in a signal to get moving.

Foley's man realized Cole couldn't use that famous gun of his without giving this away to Ed and the others. He gauged himself to be just as big as Parker, probably just as strong. He slowly rose then turned to walk to an aspen tree where Cole pointed. But before reaching it he suddenly swung around, raising one leg as he whirled and landing it into Cole's side, knocking him off balance. He dived for his gun, but Cole intercepted him, ramming the knife into his leg.

The man cried out, grabbing his thigh. The wound made him even angrier, and when Cole got up, he put his shoulder into Cole's thighs and tackled him to the ground again. Both men rolled and wrestled for the knife. The man grabbed Cole's right arm with both his hands as Cole tried to stab him. He was on his back, Cole on top of him again. Cole gouged at his eyes with his left hand, but the man hung on, jerking hard and forcing Cole's arm down and inward.

Cole grunted as he felt the knife blade sink into his own left side. Immediately he realized he could lose everything if he didn't win this battle. Addy! She'd be left alone after all. He could see her face, hear her calling to him. From somewhere deep in his mind he had the sense to reach over to his right side with his left hand, while the man he fought with rolled him onto his back and kept shoving the knife even deeper. He hadn't wanted to use his gun, but now he had no choice. He managed to get it free, shoved it into the man's belly and pulled the trigger. To his great relief, because the gun was already buried in the man's middle when it was fired, the shot was muffled. It only made a light bang that probably couldn't be heard for very far and could easily be mistaken for noise from the distant town.

The man's eyes bulged in surprise, and blood began to ooze from his mouth. Cole grimaced as he managed to shove him off, and as the man rolled away he continued to cling to Cole's knife hand, pulling the knife out of Cole's side as he flopped onto his back, a bloody hole in his belly. Cole, panting from the scuffle, looked down at himself, opening his jacket to see he was bleeding badly at his left side. "Damn!" he muttered. He couldn't let this stop him. If he was going to keep Addy Kane, he had to save James and Grant Breckenridge from Ed Foley. Grant was getting close by now.

He rolled to his knees, his gun still in his left hand. He managed to get to his feet, re-loaded the chamber left empty from the bullet he had put into Foley's man. He shoved the gun into its holster, and stumbled over to pick up the other man's gun. He looked over where the man lay, and it was obvious he was dead.

Pain ripped through his side, and he pressed his hand to the wound, praying he could keep his senses long enough to do what he had to do. Groaning and panting, he managed to get to Shadow and mount up. Already his pants were getting blood soaked at the waist. He kept his right hand to his side, leaning over slightly as he held the wound, futilely trying to stop the bleeding, while he took the reins in his left hand and led Shadow down the hill and out along the path Grant had taken. There was no time to lose!

Grant's heart fell when he reached the clearing where he and Ed Foley had once investigated together for gold. There was a gnarled old pine tree that stood alone, and under that pine tree was a crate. A man was standing on it with a noose around his neck. His hands were tied behind his back. The crate was positioned so that the man's feet barely touched it, giving him just enough support so that he couldn't completely choke on the noose.

"James," he whispered. Another man stood under the tree, and three more sat at a campfire nearby. Grant took a deep breath and rode closer, making himself visible, wondering what it was like to die. If Cole wasn't close behind him, that's what was going to happen to him today.

"Dad!" James called out when he saw him. Grant sensed fear and desperation in the young man's raspy voice. What a hell of a thing to have happen on his first trip to Central. God only knew what Ed Foley had told the boy about the incident over the mine, about his own son's death. Grant didn't care if what he'd told the boy made James hate him, as long as his son didn't die today.

"It's all right, James," he tried to reassure the boy.

"Well, well! If it isn't the great Grant Breckenridge, come crawling with his tail between his legs, and fifty thousand dollars in his fancy briefcase," Ed Foley said. He strutted out toward Grant, clean-shaven, wearing a neat suit and his ever-present spectacles, as though he had dressed for a business meeting. "Welcome to our little camp." He turned and looked at James. "How do you like our leading entertainment of the day?" he asked.

Grant wasn't sure where his next breath would come from. He was unarmed, and there were four men here. Two of them walked over to where James stood on the crate. "Let him down, you bastard!" he told Ed.

"Oh, I'm not so sure I need to," Foley answered with a pompous smile.

"Dad, help me," the boy croaked. It was obvious he'd been beaten first, probably hadn't had any water. Grant had never felt so helpless. Where was Cole? Was he watching? Ready? He'd stayed behind to wait for a fifth man. What if something had happened to him?

"I've kept my end of the bargain!" Grant growled. "The money is right here on my horse. Now keep your end of the deal and cut my son down!"

Ed just continued to grin with the pleasure of making Grant Breckenridge squirm. "Throw the money down. Then you get down. I'll have a look inside the briefcase."

Grant untied the briefcase and let it fall, then dismounted. His horse skittered sideways, and Grant stood facing Foley. "I kept my promise," he repeated. "Please get my son down off of there."

Foley opened the briefcase, while his third man walked closer, holding a gun on Grant.

"By God, I think it's all here, Clancy," Foley finally spoke up. "What do you think of that?"

Clancy Ives, a former Chadwick employee who had left when Ed was fired, grinned eagerly. "I think we're rich men, Ed."

"That we are." Foley rose, facing Grant. He stuck his thumb

into his vest pockets and paraded around Grant like a strutting rooster. "How does it feel, Grant, being the one who has to take all the shit? How does it feel, having to come crawling to Ed Foley instead of the other way around?" He came around to face him again, standing shorter than Grant, having to turn his head up to meet his eyes. "And how does it feel knowing your son is in danger? Knowing that in the next few seconds he'll *die!*"

Grant grasped his lapels and jerked him close. "You stinking murdering bastard!"

Clancy placed the barrel of his gun to Grant's throat. "Let go, or your adam's apple will be coming out the back of your neck."

Grant could not help desperate tears of fear. "Please, Ed. If you want me to beg, then I will. Just don't hurt James. He had no part in any of this. He's never done anything to you!"

Ed's eyes blazed with revenge. "That's true, but he is his father's son. I believe the Bible says something about the sons suffering for the sins of the father, something like that. Well, that is what's going to happen here today. Your son is going to pay for *my* son's death, and you are going to watch him swing from that noose, feet kicking as he slowly strangles to death. You are going to know what it feels like to watch your son suffer, as I watched *mine* suffer after the mining accident, before he finally was released from his pain in death."

"Ed, you said nobody would get hurt," Clancy spoke up. "Let's take the money and get out of here."

Ed looked at the man scathingly. "This was *my* plan, and I have the right to carry it out however I wish. I will never get over losing my own son, and I won't rest until someone pays for that!" He turned and marched over to where James stood on the crate. "First, we'll have a little farewell speech. Apparently Grant came alone, like I asked, since we haven't heard any gunshots from Richard behind us. We have time for a proper eulogy. When it's over, we'll bury the two bodies side by side, like father and son should be buried. It will be days, maybe weeks, before anything is discovered—maybe never. By then, men, we will be well on our way to Montana and wealth."

"You crazy sonofabitch!" Grant shouted. "You'll never get away with this! I kept my promise, so let us go!"

"Ed, I don't want to kill anybody," Clancy put in.

Ed faced him, clearly irritated. "Then you won't get a share of the money, either." He picked up the briefcase and again walked back to James, where the other two men stood. "You boys agree? Clancy can leave, but he gets no money. Are you two with me?"

"Hell yes," one replied. The other nodded.

Grant could see both men had been hired from the dregs of Central's lawless and jobless, men who would do anything for a few dollars.

Ed moved his cocky gaze to Clancy again. "How about it, Clancy? You with us or not? Don't forget what Grant here did to me—what he'd do to you if the situation arose. You said yourself he's a rich bastard who needs his nose straightened."

"You shut up about my father!" James shouted. "I'm tired of hearing your lies. Even if it's true, you don't kill a man and his son in cold blood for something like that!"

Grant's heart was torn at the sight of the boy, his clothes torn, his eyes bloodshot. Apparently Ed had waited for him in Denver, pretended they were still friends, offered to take him up to Central himself. How devastated James must have been when he realized the truth. Grant's only hope was that they would stall long enough to give Cole time to get here, or maybe Clancy would do something about this.

Ed glanced back at his other two men, then met Clancy's eyes again. "Of course, my friend, you know the real truth here is that I can't just let you go if you want out of this. I can't leave anyone behind who might tell someone what happened here today."

Their eyes held knowingly, and Clancy swallowed. "I've come this far with you, Ed. I guess I might as well go all the way," he said, dashing Grant's hopes that the man might try to help.

Ed smiled victoriously, then turned defiantly to Grant. "I'll give you two minutes to say what you want to your son before he dies," he said. He folded his arms and waited, and Grant stepped closer, barely able to speak for his grief.

"I'm sorry, James. I was so proud and excited about your coming to Central. I had an office all set up for you." He stopped and choked back a sob, wiping at his eyes with his jacket. "I'm so damn sorry about all of this. I never thought one misunderstanding could lead to this."

"Misunderstanding?" Ed walked past him and stood beside the crate. "It was more than a misunderstanding, Grant Breckenridge. It was deliberate theft, and because of it, my son is dead. I see the horror in your eyes, Grant, the devastation, the heartache, and it warms my heart!" Before Grant could say another word, he kicked the crate out from under James.

"No!" Grant screamed. He started toward James, but Clancy grabbed him from behind. Then from out of nowhere, Grant heard a gunshot and James's body fell to the ground, the noose still around his neck but only a short piece of rope hanging from it.

"What the hell—" Clancy said, letting go of Grant.

Another shot . . . then another. The two men who had been standing near James went down. "Cole!" Grant whispered. He threw himself over James. Two more shots cracked through the crisp, cold air. Then all was quiet.

Grant raised himself up and looked around. All four men were down, Ed Foley writhing in pain. It had all happened in a matter of seconds. He looked down at James, who was gasping for breath, and he quickly ripped the rough rope from around the boy's neck, tossing it aside. The rope had left an ugly red burn mark, but his son was alive. Grant pulled him into his arms and stayed on the ground with him a moment, holding him close. He looked up at the dangling rope, the end of it in shreds. He realized then that Cole Parker had shot through the rope as soon as Ed kicked the crate out. How many men in the whole country could shoot at a tiny target like that? Only Cole Parker could do such a thing, and he would be indebted to the man the rest of his life.

Father and son finally managed to get to their feet, arm in arm.

"Dad, I couldn't believe it when Ed told me what he was going to do." James wiped at his eyes. "If this is what it's like out here all the time . . . maybe I'd better go back to Chicago."

Grant gave him a hug. "It's not always like this, James, but things like this are why we need educated young men like you out here, helping bring law and order to cities like Central." He turned and hugged the boy again, hardly able to believe he was alive and all right. "My God, I thought I'd lost you!" He held his son tight for a few minutes before gathering his senses.

"Dad, what happened here?" James let go and looked around. "They're all dead. I think even Ed Foley is dead. Who did this?" Grant turned to look for Cole, wondering why he hadn't come out from wherever he'd lain in wait.

"His name is Cole Parker, and he's the best shot anyone has ever seen. I hired him to follow me up here. I knew he was the only one who could help, but I sure never thought he'd have to shoot through a skinny rope to save your life." He scanned the surrounding rocks. "Cole! Where the hell are you! Come on out and meet my son!"

There was no reply, and Grant began to feel uneasy. "I don't understand." He walked away from James. "Stay there and rest. I'll get you back to town as soon as I find Cole, and we'll explain all of this to Sheriff Watson." He turned and smiled at the boy, never loving him more. "You'll get a hell of a welcome, James. You just wait."

Grant walked up toward the distant rocks, calling for Cole. Finally he noticed a leg sticking out from behind a boulder. He ran up to the spot to find Cole sprawled face down over a large, flat rock, unconscious, his rifle still in his hand. A stream of blood ran out from under him, over the rock, dripping onto the ground. "My God," Grant muttered. "James!" he yelled louder. "Get up here and help me! He's hurt!" He looked back down at Cole, rolled him over and yanked off his jacket. He tore open his shirt to see what looked like an ugly knife wound in his left side. "Jesus," he muttered. He quickly wrapped his shirt around Cole's middle, using the sleeves to tie it tightly to help stop the bleeding, but he worried the man had already lost too much blood.

He realized this must have happened when Cole tried to stop the man who'd been following him. He put his own jacket back on, and by then James reached him. "That's him?"

"Yes, and we've got to get him to town before he dies. We owe him a lot, James. It looks like he was wounded farther back on the trail. He told me someone was following me and he was going to take care of it. I can't believe he managed to shoot you down from that noose. He saved our lives. Now we've got to try to save his. Get his horse."

James, still badly shaken and hurting himself, staggered over to Cole's horse and brought it to Grant. Grant took down the canteen and told James to take a quick drink. The young man gulped some water and handed the canteen back to Grant who poured some water over Cole's face.

"Come on, Cole. Wake up. We'll help you mount up. You're too big and heavy for us to get you on that horse ourselves." He leaned down, slapping Cole's face as he began to wake up.

"Addy," he mumbled.

Grant felt a stab of jealousy, but it didn't matter now. The man deserved to be with the woman he loved. "You get yourself on that horse and you'll be with her soon enough," he said.

Cole opened his eyes, stared blankly at Grant for a moment, then looked past him at James. "Your . . . son?"

"My son. You saved his life, Cole, and for that you're a free man." He stood up and took hold of Cole's hand. "Come on."

It took every effort for Cole to get to his feet. He put his arm around Grant's shoulders for support, then grabbed hold of the pommel of Shadow's saddle. "I . . . can't . . ." he muttered.

"The hell you can't!" Grant took hold of his arm. "Do you want to leave Addy Kane to me?"

Cole turned his head to meet Grant's eyes. "You sonofabitch!"

Grant grinned. "I am, aren't I? So you'd better get on that horse and get to town and live, Cole Parker. You don't want Addy Kane left all alone in Central, do you? She's waiting for you, Cole. Don't disappoint her."

Cole breathed deeply, still hating Grant Breckenridge but knowing a new respect for him. "Your boy's . . . okay?"

Grant nodded. "He's okay."

Cole turned and managed to get one foot in a stirrup. Grant and James helped push him up onto the mount, and Grant took the reins and led the horse down to where his own mount stood. "Go get one of those other horses for yourself," Grant told James. "We'll bring men back later to see about picking up these other bodies and getting your things."

James nodded. "Dad, who's Addy Kane?"

Grant smiled sadly. "One hell of a woman," he answered.

Cole clung to his horse's mane, telling himself to hang on. Addy. Yeah, Grant was right. She was one hell of a woman, and she was waiting for him. What a bitch it would be for him to go and die on her now.

Twenty-nine

The headlines of the *Register* were huge. JAMES BRECKEN-
RIDGE KIDNAPPED! HANGED! In smaller letters underneath,
SAVED BY COLE PARKER!

Cole was the talk of Central, and a hero. Addy did not doubt
he would have a huge funeral if he died . . . a man who was
supposed to already be dead. She could only pray that would
not become a reality.

She sat watching him now, still not quite over the shock of
how he'd looked when she first came to see him. Grant was
keeping him in a bedroom at his home, had hired a woman
to watch and wait on him whenever Addy could not be there
to do it.

She was grateful to Grant for bringing Cole here, where she
could visit him without anyone wondering why. People thought
she was coming here to visit with Grant, that she was merely
concerned about Cole because of the wonderful thing he'd done
for Grant and his son.

All anyone in town could talk about was the fact that Cole
had saved James's life by shooting at a thin, swinging rope from
a seemingly impossible distance. Not only had he made an amazing shot, as well as killed all those who had tried to murder
James and Grant, but he had done it after being severely
wounded himself. Addy had heard the story herself a hundred
times, and poor James had been asked to tell it more often than
that. He, too, was a celebrity, and the young man had built Cole

into such a hero that Cole couldn't be more accepted in this town than he was now.

But would he ever know about the praises that were being sung about him? Doctor Jonesboro had done all he could, cleaned the wound as best as possible, stitched it. That had been a week ago. Then the dreaded infection had set in. Addy had never seen a man in such agony. Through it all Cole had slipped in and out of consciousness, always asking for her when awake, so often that Grant had had to explain to the doctor that he and Addy had become "friends" on their trip west. He had made the doctor promise to keep the news to himself.

"Cole Parker doesn't deserve any bad gossip," Grant had told the man. "He and Addy became very close and I accept that. Cole saved her life more than once on the trail here."

It didn't matter to Addy whether or not Dr. Jonesboro understood. All that mattered was whether he was good enough to save Cole's life. She still shivered at the memory of helping the man cauterize the wound to burn out the infection. She still remembered Cole's pitiful cries of pain as he bit down hard on a piece of rawhide. Dr. Jonesboro claimed that he was doubly in danger because not only had the infection weakened him, but he simply had lost too much blood. If he could live until his body managed to replenish what he had lost, he would probably be all right. "A man his size, it takes time," he'd told her.

Yes. A big man, with a big heart. That was the real Cole Parker, not the man she'd met robbing a bank in Unionville.

Grant had kept his word, was actually being very gracious to both of them, insisting on the best care for Grant, allowing her plenty of time alone with him. She had seen a side to the man she wasn't sure existed, and she didn't doubt that the incident over his son had taught him a good lesson about what his ruthlessness and greed could cost him. But she was not surprised that he had managed to charm his way out of any responsibility for Ed Foley's behavior. Grant was simply the poor victim of a crazy man's whim. Addy didn't doubt he'd deserved to suffer that way, to know the kind of pain he'd caused Foley; but for any man to ruthlessly hang an innocent young man like James was too horrible to comprehend.

She reached over and dipped a rag in cool water and wrung it out, then placed it on Cole's forehead. The room was cool, but he looked hot, perspiration on his face. He groaned when he felt her touch, opened his eyes.

"Addy," he said in a near whisper. "You didn't go away."

She smiled through tears. "Since two days ago?"

He frowned. "That's the last time . . . I was awake?"

"I'm afraid so." She gently washed his face. "How do you feel now?"

"I don't know. Just weak. But the pain isn't so bad now."

"That's good. Doc Jonesboro said when the pain goes away it usually means the infection is gone. Now you have to lie still and let your blood build up more before you try to do anything. I'm just glad to see you awake and talking sensibly. You've been delirious most of the time." He had yelled for Patty in those moments, flailing his arms, reaching up into the air for his little girl.

Grant had seen his burned arm once, had seemed genuinely touched. "I didn't know it had been that awful," he had commented about how Cole lost his daughter. The man had a new respect for Cole, and that was good.

Cole moved slightly. "You've probably put up with too much," he said in a weak voice. "You should go home and get some rest."

"I can't rest until I know for certain you'll be all right." She set the rag aside and leaned over him, kissing his cheek. "Do you want some water?"

"Yeah." Cole watched her turn and pour water from a fancy pitcher into a glass. The pitcher reminded him of where he was. He had a vague memory of someone telling him he was at Grant Breckenridge's home. He looked around the room, fancy wallpaper, velvet curtains . . . he looked at Addy. She was a natural in a place like this, but she didn't want Grant Breckenridge or his fancy house. She wanted Cole Parker. She leaned over him again, holding out the water and slipping a hand under his head, helped him raise up slightly so he could drink.

He swallowed some water, realizing his constant thirst was from loss of blood. He was not going to let this wound get the better of him, spoil all that he'd aimed for these last few weeks. "Did Grant . . . keep his promise?" he asked, unable to clearly remember all that had happened or been said since the incident over Grant's son. He had only little flashes of memories . . . holding his rifle steady in spite of pain and weakness, pulling the trigger, Grant's son falling from the tree where he'd been hanged . . . Grant making him get on a horse, telling him something about living for Addy . . . voices . . . someone crying . . . terrible pain . . .

"Yes," Addy answered, setting the glass aside. She took his hand. "He's been wonderful. He's a very grateful man, and so, of course, is James. He still can't get over what you managed to do in spite of being wounded. Neither can the whole town. You're a hero, Cole, an absolute hero. You've been in the *Register,* and people have come here asking about you. We can start seeing each other now, just like we planned. We can be together, Cole." She squeezed his hand. "But you have to *live.* Don't die on me now. We've been through too much together to get to this point. It's been a long journey for us both, but now it's over."

It all seemed too good to be true. Grant happened to come in then to check on Cole. Cole kept hold of Addy's hand as the man came closer, and when he was able to focus clearly on Grant's face, he was surprised at the look there, one of genuine concern. The man smiled.

"Well, you're awake! And this time you look as though you have your wits about you. You've been pretty incoherent, Cole."

"I'll get . . . out from under your feet soon as I can. Thanks for . . . putting me up here."

Grant sobered. "A small enough attempt at thanking you. I'd never be able to do a good enough job of that the rest of my life. I want you to know I'm giving you twenty-five percent of my shares in the Jamesway, and any help I can be business-wise, just let me know."

Cole shifted in bed, winced with pain. "I don't want anything except Addy. I just want you to keep your promise . . . to leave her to me . . . and to never let on who I really am."

Grant frowned. "I told you that would be part of the bargain. I have to say, Cole, that at the time I was only saying it to save my son, but now I say it out of a genuine respect for you and Addy. It took guts to come there and do the job after being wounded like you were."

"They're all dead?"

Grant nodded.

"And I'm not . . . in trouble with the law?"

"Hell no! All the proof the sheriff needed that you did right was to listen to James tell him what Ed Foley did to him. He's got the burn marks on his neck to prove Foley tried to hang him, and he saved the piece of rope to show people where it had been torn in half by your bullet. The damn piece of rope is actually on display in town, and so were the bodies of Foley and his men before they were actually buried. It was like a circus out there, people standing around gawking at the bodies, stories floating around about you."

To Cole's surprise the man's eyes suddenly teared. "When you saved my son, Cole, it was like saving my own life. There is no price a man can put on a thing like that, but I intend to give you a damn good reward, and any help you need getting settled once you're out of bed, I'll give it. I'll never be able to thank you enough, and when you've had a chance to get to know James better, you'll know you did the right thing. He's one thing I've done right in this life, a son to be proud of. He's not the bastard his father is."

Cole could not help a wry grin. "He'll learn."

Grant broke into a smile. "You saying you agree I'm a bastard?"

"Completely."

They studied each other, both feeling a mutual respect neither thought could be possible. "You'll never fully trust me, will you, Cole?"

"No," Cole answered.

Grant laughed. "I can't blame you there." He glanced at Addy. "But I mean every word of it. I'll be eternally grateful, and I'll help the both of you any way you need it." He looked back at Cole, leaning closer. "When I saw my son hanging by that rope, I wanted to die. You gave him back to me. When he fell into my arms, all my wealth and success became suddenly nothing. I was holding the only thing genuinely good about my life, the only thing that truly mattered. It opened my eyes to a lot of things. I'll say it once, and I want you to believe me when I say it comes from the heart—and this bastard does have a heart somewhere down under all the hard businessman he is on the outside—just a plain thank you, Cole. Thank you from the bottom of my heart."

Their eyes held. "I accept," Cole finally said.

Grant reached down and took his right hand and shook it. "To the winner goes the spoils. I hope you and Addy have a good life together." He blinked quickly and turned away, leaving the room.

Cole looked at Addy. "Can you . . . believe that?"

"I think it's wonderful." Addy kept hold of his hand. "And we *will* have a good life together, Cole. I just hope you can finally give up that gun and not have to live by it any more."

He squeezed her hand with the small bit of strength he had. "No more guns. I'm through with all that, Addy. I want a wife again, a family. I want some peace. The war ended two years ago, but it continued to . . . rage in my heart. That war is over too, now. You helped end it."

She felt a lump swell in her throat, and she leaned down to kiss his hand. "I knew the day we parted when you took me back to Unionville that I loved you, Cole. I tried to deny it, even after Abilene . . . but it was always there."

"It was . . . the same for me. I was just afraid . . . to care about anybody again. But I couldn't . . . forget you."

His voice drifted, his eyes closed. Addy leaned down and kissed his cheek again. "I love you, Cole Parker." Her eyes teared. "We made it. Just get better soon."

Spring 1868 . . .

If there was one thing Central was known for, it was for making a grand event out of the simplest happening. Since the beautiful young schoolteacher, Addy Kane, was marrying the very honored Cole Parker, the ladies of society had agreed it should be a spectacular wedding, with even important people from Denver invited. Gossip among the women, Addy knew from suggestive questions, had been the fact that she had turned down Grant Breckenridge for a man of far less wealth; but it amused Addy to see them tittering and whispering among themselves about the reasons why she would do such a thing. She had no doubt they all considered Cole not only a hero, but a damn handsome one at that. Grant himself had helped quell any rumors that he might have any hard feelings. He had made sure everyone believed he and Addy had never been more than casual friends. There had never been a romance between them, and after all, Cole had saved his and his son's lives. How could he have hard feelings against a man like that?

It was Grant who had worked with the women's circle to plan a lavish wedding for Addy and Cole, footing the bill himself. Addy thought it ironic that after all she and Cole had been through, hiding their relationship, trying to stay apart, then trying to figure out how they could be together, that now they should be marrying in such a flamboyant manner. Elizabeth Howley had made her an absolutely extravagant wedding dress of ivory satin shipped up from Denver. The gown was completely covered with an overlay of hand-made lace of astounding beauty and intricacy. A coronet of crystal-beaded flowers leading to a hem-length veil adorned her deep auburn hair, which was piled on top of her head in a cascade of curls.

She stood in an upstairs bedroom of Hester's house and looked at herself in a mirror while Hester and Ethel Brown fussed and pulled and arranged things, excitedly looking her over to be sure everything looked right. Was this really happening? Even the weather had cooperated. There was still snow on the surrounding mountains, but in town things had dried out. The sun shone brightly, and it was warm, all necessary for today's ceremony, which would take place outdoors because most of the town wanted to watch. Hester and others had made quite a public event out of it, which Cole was not crazy about, but they seemed to have no choice in the matter. After a long, cold, eventless winter, people were ready for a reason to celebrate. The ceremony would take place on Eureka street at the site of a planned Methodist Church, and the couple would then get into a fancy carriage provided by Grant and pulled by two white horses. The carriage would take them down Eureka to Main, down Main street and around and down Spring Street to Lawrence, then back up to a spot on Main where cake and punch would be served and where people could come and express their congratulations to the happy couple.

Already Addy knew it would be difficult to have to put up with all of that, waiting for the only thing she and Cole really wanted . . . to be in each other's arms at night. It had taken several weeks for him to fully recover, and over the winter he had brought his strength and weight back to normal. During that time they saw each other socially, gently breaking the news to Central's elite that Mrs. Addy Kane was interested in Cole Parker romantically. To be sure not one ugly rumor was ever spread, Cole had not come visiting her in the night. They had decided to wait until they were married, but a month ago the waiting had become impossible. They loved each other too much, needed each other too much. They had allowed themselves one glorious, passionate night together, and never had their union been more fulfilling, knowing that soon, at last, they would be married and wouldn't need to hide their love any longer.

After a long day of ceremony and celebrating, the carriage

driver would take them to a new house Cole had had built for them in the hills above town. It was not yet completely finished, but enough for them to spend tonight there as husband and wife and celebrate their new home.

"So beautiful!" Ethel Brown exclaimed. The woman had taken a surprising change in attitude toward her. Addy supposed it was because she was not marrying the richest man in town after all, or because she was satisfied that there was nothing dark and unknown about her past . . . or perhaps it was simply because Grant Breckenridge approved of this, so that made it all right.

"Ravishing is a better word," Hester added. "I think you're ready, dear."

Both women were gussied up in their own finest, Ethel Brown wearing a feathered hat so extravagant that Addy thought it bordered on something a prostitute would wear. She would not, of course, tell Ethel that, for she seemed to think she had never looked more lovely. The thought of her looking like a prostitute was preposterously funny, and Addy stemmed an urge to laugh. The thought brought to mind Sassy Dillon. She would have loved an occasion like this, and would have liked to know she and Cole were marrying. It was too bad she couldn't be here, but she lived on in a strikingly pretty little girl with dimpled cheeks.

Two weeks ago Addy had taken time off from teaching and had gone to Denver, with the excuse she wanted to do some shopping for her new home and for her wedding; but she had used the trip to find the Donnavans, explaining she had known Sassy and that she was marrying Cole Parker. The gracious Mrs. Donnavan had let her inside, and she had immediately been touched when she met Lissy, who was every bit like her real mother in her outgoing personality and vivaciousness, and she was a child of exquisite beauty, with bouncing blond curls and a smile that would melt anyone's heart. It was no wonder she had won over Cole, a man with a soft spot for little girls. At least now he seemed to have overcome his grief and loneliness over Patty. He had told her the nightmares were finally gone, and he had not had a drink of liquor all winter. He was a changed man, and he insisted it was her love that had changed him. But Addy believed the change was due to his own strength, the good man deep inside that was the true Nick Coleman. The only thing he couldn't do was use his real name. Nick Coleman was supposed to be dead, and truly he was.

Hester and Ethel helped her down the stairs, Ethel picking up the train of her dress and veil so they did not get soiled. She climbed into the waiting carriage, feeling like a princess. The driver turned and handed her a lovely bouquet of spring wildflowers, the only kind of flowers available in a remote mountain town. Flowers shipped up from Denver usually were wilted by the time they arrived. The stems of the wildflowers were wrapped in cloth so she would not soil her ivory satin gloves. The carriage was off, and Addy could still hear Hester and Ethel chattering like excited magpies as they climbed into their own carriages, their husbands already waiting for them.

From then on the day became dreamlike. Addy was flabbergasted at the crowd that lined the streets in town. The carriage drew close to the church site, and right behind her were Hester and Ethel, quickly walking up to help her get down. The driver pulled the carriage out of the way, and now Addy could see Cole waiting for her. Never had he looked more handsome, wearing pin-stripe pants, a gray satin, double-breasted vest set off by a bow tie and a black frock coat. Her heart pounded with anticipation and joy. At last!

A piano had been set outside, and Susan Howard began playing the wedding march as Ethel spread out the train of Addy's dress and Hester pulled the veil over her face. James Breckenridge stepped up beside her, a very handsome young man who was already being hounded by Central's available young ladies.

"You ready, Mrs. Kane?"

Addy looked at him, wanted to hug him. He was the reason this moment had come to be. And because of his respect for Cole, he had agreed to escort Addy. Grant Breckenridge, of all people, was best man. He stood beside Cole, looking quite hand-some himself in an obviously expensive suit, his dark hair slicked back—a charmer, he was, but not charming enough for Addy Kane. Grant Breckenridge was no Cole Parker.

Hester walked over to stand near Cole, taking a bouquet of wildflowers from one of the other women nearby who had held it for her. Hester would be Addy's matron of honor.

"Let's go," James told Addy, taking her arm.

A distance of several yards had been left for her to walk to Cole, and in spite of hundreds of people watching the ceremony, Addy was aware only of Cole. She never took her eyes from his as she came closer, and he never wavered in his own gaze. She could tell he was remembering the same things she was . . . a bank robbery, an abduction, a rescue . . . a liaison in the wild western town of Abilene . . . the pain of thinking they must part . . . an Indian attack . . . another liaison . . . How many times had this man been there to rescue her? How many times had they made love and then said good-bye, only to be unable to bear being apart?

There were other memories, memories that hurt, memories that had to be left behind now as they started a new life, a new family, together. They would always carry certain secrets that no one else would know. The whole town would think that to-night would be their first coming together. Only Addy and Cole knew about the precious, tender, passionate moments they had shared, first out of need and desire, then out of a burning love that could not be quenched, a love that had been tested over and over.

Now she was beside him, pledging herself to him. Her first marriage almost seemed as if it had never happened. She had been young, and they had been together such a short time . . . and now it seemed like such a long time ago.

"For better, for worse . . . in sickness and in health . . ." *No matter the past,* Addy thought. *Looking only to the future.* Cole slipped a wedding band on her finger. More words. He lifted her veil, leaned down and kissed her lightly, flicking his tongue against her lips suggestively, reminding her that tonight they would do much more than kiss.

"I love you, Addy Parker," he said softly.

Addy Parker. She was Mrs. Cole Parker now. "And I love you so, Cole," she answered, tears in her eyes. This was real. She was his wife. He grinned, picked her up off her feet and whirled her around. The entire town broke into an uproar, and the celebrating was on, Central City style. No one knew better how to celebrate the smallest event in the grandest way than the members of these wild little mining towns. Cole kept an arm around Addy during the parade of their carriage around town, and Addy could not help blushing at the remarks made by some of the miners. Saloons were already in an uproar, the Hard Luck packed. Cole had turned the upstairs into an eatery, and it was a respectable place now.

Finally the carriage stopped in the middle of Main Street, where a platform had been erected for the bride and groom and Central's dignitaries. Gifts were stacked everywhere, and women had been hired to serve cake and punch to whoever wanted some. Addy supposed just about every woman in Central must have baked a cake for the occasion, there were so many ready and waiting to feed the hundreds of well-wishers.

Sheriff Sam Watson came over to congratulate them. "You realize, Cole, that the whole town wants you to run for sheriff when I retire in a couple of months, don't you? You'd be perfect for the job."

Cole looked at Addy, stifling an urge to laugh. If only Watson knew the truth. But that was not the reason he wouldn't take the job. "I'd have to turn them down," he answered, giving Addy a squeeze. "I'm a married man now, and I want a family. I'm through with guns, Sheriff. The closest I'll get is I intend to open a shop for selling and repairing firearms. That's one thing I know like the back of my hand, but I'm not going to live by the gun. Not any more."

"Well, the job is yours if you want it. There's no doubt in my mind who everybody would vote for." Watson congratulated them again and left.

Addy looked up at Cole. "I hope you mean that, Cole. I couldn't bear worrying about you getting shot at, you always needing to wear a gun."

He kissed her cheek. "I was a family man once, Mrs. Parker. I want that life back. I intend to be nothing more than a gunsmith and a business owner . . . a husband and a father."

Addy could hide the news no longer. "Good, because you *are* going to be a father, sooner than you think."

He sobered, studying her eyes. "What?"

"Remember that visit you paid me a month ago?"

A deeper love moved into his dark eyes. "You're carrying?"

"I'm almost sure. I've missed my time." She blushed at the words, embarrassed to have to talk about such things, even with Cole.

A rush of emotions swept through Cole. A baby! He would be a father again. It almost frightened him to think how much he would love this baby, because he would never forget how it felt to lose a child. But he wouldn't lose this one. The war was over. This time his family would know only peace. He pulled her close. "Thank you, Addy."

She put her arms around his neck, and a few whistles and cheers came from the watching crowd. Their gaze met, and he kissed her hungrily, amid whoops and hollers and raised whiskey bottles. Women began serving cake, and Cole and Addy spent the next several hours accepting gifts and good wishes.

"You think Cole would really turn down a chance to be sheriff?" Sam Watson asked Grant. "He'd be damn good, better than me, I have to admit. Not many men would give Cole Parker any trouble."

Grant nodded. "I agree. But then the man deserves a little peace in his life." He grinned. "I'll say one thing. I doubt anybody could handle robbers and outlaws better than Cole Parker. He seems to have a knack for understanding how they think."

"Folks say maybe he hunted renegade outlaw soldiers after

the war. He doesn't talk much about his past," Watson said. "Sometimes I look into those eyes and I see a desperado. What do you think?"

Grant put a hand on the sheriff's shoulder. "Watson, sometimes a man's past is better left just that—the past."

"What does that mean? You know something I don't?"

Grant grinned. "I only know that Cole Parker is now a respected citizen of the city of Central, and because of him, my son and I are alive. That's all I need to know, all *anybody* needs to know."

Watson nodded. "I understand. It's just interesting to try to imagine how he got so good with those guns."

"Well, my friend, it might be worth a lot of money to you not to look into it."

Watson grinned. "How much?"

"Name your price."

Watson laughed. "That much, huh?" He rubbed his chin. "Well, I like the man, and Mrs. Kane, too—Mrs. Parker, I should say. You don't have to pay me to stay out of the man's past. He looks pretty happy now. I'll leave it that way."

"Good decision," Grant answered, a warning look in his dark eyes. An orchestra hired from Denver began playing, and Cole and Addy danced, first with each other, then Cole with Hester and Ethel and some of the other ladies among Central's finest; Addy danced with Sheriff Watson, Dr. Jonesboro, Lee Brown, even John Withers, who had once tried to destroy her reputation. She danced with Grant, and he kissed her cheek. "That's for what might have been," he told her.

The afternoon turned to dusk, and finally the happy couple was able to get back in the carriage and go off to their new home, amid cheers and well wishes. Central would celebrate tonight, and so would Cole and Addy Parker . . . and they wouldn't need friends and whiskey and dancing to have a good time. They would need only each other.

From the Author

I hope you have enjoyed this latest addition to my long list of western and Indian novels. To learn more about other books I have written, just send a legal size, (#10) self-addressed and stamped envelope to me at 6013 North Coloma Road, Coloma, Michigan 49038. I will send you a newsletter and bookmarks. Thank you so much for your interest and support!

TODAY'S HOTTEST READS
ARE TOMORROW'S SUPERSTARS

VICTORY'S WOMAN   (4484, $4.50)
by Gretchen Genet
Andrew—the carefree soldier who sought glory on the battlefield, and returned a shattered man . . . Niall—the legandary frontiersman and a former Shawnee captive, tormented by his past . . . Roger—the troubled youth, who would rise up to claim a shocking legacy . . . and Clarice—the passionate beauty bound by one man, and hopelessly in love with another. Set against the backdrop of the American revolution, three men fight for their heritage—and one woman is destined to change all their lives forever!

FORBIDDEN   (4488, $4.99)
by Jo Beverley
While fleeing from her brothers, who are attempting to sell her into a loveless marriage, Serena Riverton accepts a carriage ride from a stranger—who is the handsomest man she has ever seen. Lord Middlethorpe, himself, is actually contemplating marriage to a dull daughter of the aristocracy, when he encounters the breathtaking Serena. She arouses him as no woman ever has. And after a night of thrilling intimacy—a forbidden liaison—Serena must choose between a lady's place and a woman's passion!

WINDS OF DESTINY   (4489, $4.99)
by Victoria Thompson
Becky Tate is a half-breed outcast—branded by her Comanche heritage. Then she meets a rugged stranger who awakens her heart to the magic and mystery of passion. Hiding a desperate past, Texas Ranger Clint Masterson has ridden into cattle country to bring peace to a divided land. But a greater battle rages inside him when he dares to desire the beautiful Becky!

WILDEST HEART   (4456, $4.99)
by Virginia Brown
Maggie Malone had come to cattle country to forge her future as a healer. Now she was faced by Devon Conrad, an outlaw wounded body and soul by his shadowy past . . . whose eyes blazed with fury even as his burning caress sent her spiraling with desire. They came together in a Texas town about to explode in sin and scandal. Danger was their destiny—and there was nothing they wouldn't dare for love!

Available wherever paperbacks are sold, or order direct from the Publisher. Send cover price plus 50¢ per copy for mailing and handling to Penguin USA, P.O. Box 999, c/o Dept. 17109, Bergenfield, NJ 07621. Residents of New York and Tennessee must include sales tax. DO NOT SEND CASH.